Never Date a Magician

Jay Palmer

All Books by Jay Palmer

The VIKINGS! Trilogy:
        DeathQuest
        The Mourning Trail
        Quest for Valhalla

The EGYPTIANS! Trilogy:
        SoulQuest
        Song of the Sphinx
        Quest for Osiris

Souls of Steam

Jeremy Wrecker, Pirate of Land and Sea

The Grotesquerie Games

The Grotesquerie Gambit

The Magic of Play

The Heart of Play

The Seneschal

Viking Son

Viking Daughter

All Books by Jay Palmer
(Continued …)

Dracula – Deathless Desire

Murder at Marleigh Manor

Never Date a Magician

Cover Artist: **Jay Palmer**

Website: **JayPalmerBooks.com**

To my greatest blessing,
Wise and lovely
Karen Truong

Jay Palmer

Chapter 1

Everyone in SeaTac International Airport stared at him; a grown man wearing a classic white Stetson fedora with a spotless matching suit, resembling Humphrey Bogart in Casablanca, spinning a brightly-colored yo-yo in each hand. He grinned as his yo-yos spun outwards and returned with obvious mastery. I wondered if he was insane yet, as I watched, two small children ran up to stare at him, chased by an aggravated mother dragging rolling suitcases. He performed an amazing yo-yo trick for the kids, spinning both over his head, caught his yo-yos in his hands, and then spoke softly to their mother. Removing the string-loops from his fingers, he presented both yo-yos to her excited children. Gleefully the kids accepted the new toys, and began attempting to perform basic returns. Their mother smiled and thanked him profusely. He gave her a curt bow, tilted his hat, and walked off smiling.

It was nice to see a generous act. However, since I didn't know them, I turned back to reading my book, an exciting mystery I'd read before. In the back of my head flitted the idea that this strange, generous man seemed more like a character in my book than someone walking through a busy airport.

Soon I became engrossed in the petitions of a main character trying to convince a suspicious police detective why he couldn't be the murderer. I'd assumed that I'd never see the strange man in the white suit and fedora again.

My plane arrived twenty minutes late. When it came, I waited impatiently while arriving passengers hurried off, most loudly complaining about missing connecting flights, and rushing off to other gates.

I loved flying first class. My company paid for my flight, but I'd used my miles to upgrade. I boarded with the first group, and was met by a middle-aged stewardess whose friendly demeanor was so over the top that I wondered how she plastered on the same smile all day. I sat in the aisle seat beside a large man who stank of cigars, busy peering through his tiny window. Before us sat a woman with a small boy. Already whining, the little boy sounded fussy. I feared that he'd cry the whole flight.

"Is that a magic pencil?" came a clear, smooth voice.

The whines of the boy stopped immediately. I recognized the man who'd given away his yo-yos sitting across the aisle from the boy. He reached out, took a long, yellow pencil from the boy's hand, and held it vertically before him.

"See these words ...?" the man said, pointing near the eraser at the shiny lettering printed on the side of the pencil.

Suddenly he waved his other hand between the boy's eyes and the pencil.

The printed letters vanished!

"Where'd they go?" the man asked the boy.

"Can we bring them back?"

The man waved his hand over the pencil again, and the shiny letters reappeared.

The little boy looked amazed, yet I knew that, while distracting with his other hand, he'd simply turned the pencil around so that the lettering faced him. He handed the pencil back to the boy.

"You'd better take good care of this," he said. "Magic pencils are rare and priceless!"

Also watching the 'magic', the cigar-smoker grunted a few chuckles. The small boy fell silent, playing with his pencil, which relieved everyone in first class. I reopened my book, yet stole a glance at the stranger.

He was thin and young, wearing an immaculate, old-styled white suit with wide lapels and a black bow tie. He had mirrored sunglasses propped on his head, which no longer supported his white hat. He had strangely-colored red hair, almost like iresine herbstii flowers, nicknamed 'chicken gizzard'. Why he'd dyed his hair that color I couldn't guess, yet I ignored him and returned to my innocent main character and stalwart detective teaming up to solve a ghastly murder.

The thin young man was clearly a magician. About an hour into our flight, the boy asked the man to do the pencil trick again. This time he made the pencil vanish by dropping it into his sleeve and made it reappear behind the boy's ear. Then he drew out of a pocket five cards, four aces and a jack, and proceeded to do sleight-of-hand tricks I couldn't begin to follow. Simply by turning the five cards around horizontally, he made the jack move from the top to the bottom of the stack, and when he spread out the cards, the jack had turned into a queen.

He pocketed all five cards, then plucked the jack

out of the little boy's t-shirt.

"You're trying to steal my jack!" the magician jokingly accused.

The little boy laughed.

Five hours later, I finished my book while our plane landed and taxied off the Hawaiian runway, onto the tarmac. Outside the too-small windows, an infinitely sunny glare highlighted an azure infinity broken only by high, white clouds. I smiled to see tall palm trees and colorful tropical plants in the distance.

Sadly, North Dakota has no tropical beaches.

I'd needed my jacket when I boarded, and expected I'd be too hot for a jacket when I disembarked. Yet I had my large purse, laptop, and carry-on bag; I kept my jacket on for lack of means to carry it.

Hawaiian warmth outside the airport always amazed me. Most expect scents of the sea to permeate, yet the coast was miles away. The air smelled clean, but not briny. Sunshine beamed down, shining in a nearly cloudless sky of perfect, intense blue.

I needed to smear myself in suntan lotion before it cooked my pale, North Dakota skin!

After retrieving my suitcases from baggage claim, I reached the taxi pick-up area. The line was long, yet taxis were pulling up at a steady rate. The magician stood before me, talking to an elderly couple.

"No, we own a vacation timeshare on the north side," the elderly woman said. "We use it every year."

"That's where the surfers compete," the old man said. "North side gets the biggest waves. I can't surf anymore, but still watch. Have you ever ...?"

"Unfortunately no," the magician said. "It looks fun; maybe I'll give it a try ... take a lesson ..."

"You won't regret it," the old man said. "Nothing

equals riding a crest of pure liquid energy!"

A uniformed man ushered the elderly couple into a taxi, which drove away, then turned to the magician.

"Destination ...?" he asked.

"Downtown Waikiki," the magician said.

"You alone?"

"Yes."

He turned to me.

"Destination ...?" he asked.

"Waikiki," I said.

The uniformed man glanced at the long line behind me.

"Would you mind sharing a cab?" the uniformed man asked us. "Very busy today."

The magician turned to me and smiled.

"Ah!" he said. "You were seated behind me." He turned back to the man. "At the lady's discretion, of course."

"Ma'am ...?" he asked.

I didn't want to share a cab with any stranger, but several annoyed parents with fussy children could overhear, so I nodded. A cab pulled up, and my bags were loaded into the trunk. Then the back door was opened and held for me. The magician walked around to sit behind the driver.

Soon we were cruising across a highway, where tropical plants abounded, but it hardly looked like Gilligan's Island. The sounds of the road and sights of waxy, flowering plants growing out of chain-link fences and around dirty steel telephone poles didn't look like any 'tropical paradise'. Yet I'd expected it; all the manicured gardens anyone could want awaited in the tourist's section.

11

"Business or pleasure ...?" the magician asked.

"Business," I replied. "Of course, Hawaii's always a pleasure. You ...?"

"Pleasure is my business," he said. "I'm doing a short-week fill-in for a friend at a local dinner theater. I'm a stage magician."

"I saw you on the plane," I said. "You kept the boy quiet."

"He was just bored," the magician said. "I'd be honored if you'd come to my show."

"Maybe I will," I said.

He held up his hand, snapped his fingers, and a red rosebud appeared.

"For you," he said.

I smiled. I hadn't seen how he'd done it, what pocket he'd fished the flower from, or how he'd transferred it to his hand, but doing things without others seeing how was every magician's mainstay. I took the rosebud on its short, de-thorned stem, and thanked him. It was real, soft, and fresh, and I inhaled its strong scent deeply. I wondered how he'd kept it from wilting on the plane. I'd seen no one selling fresh roses between the terminal and the taxi stop.

I stole a glance at the magician. He was clean-shaven, with a fair complexion, taut and youthful skin, with trim eyebrows. His bright eyes almost radiated, yet were deep set, as if hiding secrets, above high cheekbones, and Hollywood white teeth. He had a thin, toned body, looked only a few inches exceeding my height, and an erect posture which made him appear an inch or two taller. His hands were narrow, with long fingers, not unexpected for a magician. He wasn't unattractive, yet he didn't look like he'd last a day in North Dakota.

As always, crowds filled downtown Waikiki. I appreciated the bustle of tourists hurrying about the tiny, colorful merchant's tents crammed into alleys between high-end, elegant shops and restaurants. Every view was cultivated to attract shoppers, and high levels of civility were common.

We arrived at the Outrigger Tiki Luau Hotel. I reached into my purse, but the magician stopped me.

"Please, allow me," he said, and he pulled out his wallet.

"My treat," I insisted. "You gave me a rose."

I paid with a company credit card, and startled to see the magician get out when I did. He stood in the bright sunlight on the wide sidewalk while the taxi driver unloaded my suitcases from the trunk.

Curiously, I noticed that the magician didn't have a suitcase.

"Thank you for your company into town," the magician said. "I hope I see you again."

"At your show," I smiled, wishing he'd leave.

"Exactly," he said. "The Majestic Dinner Theater, within walking distance from here. Starts at seven."

With a polite bow, he walked away. I felt relieved ... until I saw him walk into the Outrigger Tiki Luau.

Frowning, I followed slowly, giving him time to depart. Oahu was a big island, with thousands of tourists arriving every day; the odds that we'd run in to each other again seemed remote ... even if we were staying at the same hotel.

I rode the escalator up and headed for the front desk. The magician was already there, and the cute girl behind the desk was just handing him his room key and a small paper bag. Suddenly he presented her with a red rosebud. She beamed, delighted, and I stood waiting for him to depart as she promised to come see his show.

Taking his key and complimentary bag in one hand, he turned around, faced me, smiled, tilted his hat, and then walked off toward the elevator, still with no luggage.

"Aloha," the girl smiled at me. "Welcome to the Outrigger Tiki Luau. I'm Noelani, and we're glad you're here."

"Checking in, please," I said, and I pulled my suitcases forward and fumbled for printouts of my reservations. I set my purse and rosebud on the desk to flip through complex confirmations.

"Oh, you got one, too!" Noelani smiled, looking at my rosebud. "Nice man. I was quite surprised."

"Yes," I said noncommittally, and handed her my papers.

Noelani scanned my papers, asked to see ID, and confirmed my reservation. Then she gave me my card key, gift bag, and asked if she could perform any other service to make my stay enjoyable.

"No, thank you," I said, gathering my things.

"Welcome to Hawaii, Ms. Penelope Polyglass," Noelani said. "Wow! I like your name."

"Thanks," I said, accustomed to that reaction.

"Did you ... see how he did it?" Noelani said, lifting and waving her rosebud.

I tightened my jaw.

"No, I didn't," I said, and I pulled my suitcases toward the elevators.

I had to scan my room key to open the elevator door. I liked this; odds of thievery seemed remote with security this tight.

I found my room, and appreciated its clean decor, which resembled most things in the tourist's district. Opening the sliding glass door, I admired my tiny, partial view of the ocean; my company's sales force didn't merit palatial settings. Yet even my narrow view of the sea was nicer than the endless plowed fields of wheat on view back home.

I stared at my empty room; I missed my kitty ... who was doubtlessly being overfed at my mother's house.

I unpacked and hung up my dresses, leaving the rest in my suitcase; I never understood those who use hotel dressers. Then I was free ... in Hawaii ... to go anywhere I pleased. I touched up my makeup, changed into a short, sleeveless, brightly-colored dress, grabbed my purse, and stole one last glance in the mirror. I'd overly pinked my cheeks for going outdoors, yet perfectly exaggerated my sweeping lashes over wide-set, mocha brown eyes under carefully-plucked eyebrows; if they hoped to be successful, salespeople always attended to their appearance. I had peachy skin, which I kept out of the sun to avoid turning tawny, with mostly the same figure that I'd had when I graduated high school, yet I avoided men who stared at me too long.

I made sure I had my key card, locked my door, and went adventuring.

The Outrigger Tiki Luau had tourist shops inside it, yet I walked past them, eager to get into Waikiki proper. Soon I was strolling crowded sidewalks in tropical sunshine, my colorful dress fading perfectly into the miasma of bright shades walking past me. Most wore tropical flower patterns, yet many men bore red and green parrots, leaping dolphins, or patterns of surfboards. Young girls wore bikini tops over wrap-around skirts, and some young boys walked shirtless; exposed flesh abounded.

Soon I was where I felt most comfortable, walking through the International Market, past windows displaying thousand dollar watches and jewelry I could only dream about. The decorations here were reserved and dignified, rather than the ostentatious displays outside the cheaper shops. I paused at an iron railing and peered down at a public show; three musicians and two hula dancers were entertaining a small crowd of tourists, with many young children who were playing on fake stone mushrooms and plastic benches set around tall statues of famous folk from Hawaii's past.

On a whim, I decided that I wanted pineapple with dinner. When I got back onto the street, I walked slowly, reading posted menus and pricing favorites. I didn't have a destination ... except for a new experience, to dine in a restaurant I'd never visited before.

A familiar voice reached my ears. As I crossed the street, I saw the magician, still in his white suit, speaking to a pair of middle-aged Asian or Polynesian women, each holding a rosebud. To my surprise, he was speaking their language. Not wanting to be noticed, I ducked my face and hurried past.

I didn't find any place special ... I got tired of looking. I chose a place that looked clean, ate sesame ahi tuna with roasted asparagus, and drank an icy pineapple daiquiri, which held more rum than I'd expected. Everything was delicious, and grew tastier as I sipped my daiquiri.

I exited at nearly sunset, then strolled between two tall hotels to the beach, where kids played in the surf while couples walked the sand. Everyone in a nearby group had tiny cameras, and were clicking madly. I grinned at them, yet the sunset was so beautiful I pulled out my camera and took several digital pics.

Early evening fading, I walked through tropical parks and visited specialty shops. Loud bands blared from nightclubs, yet I ignored the younger crowds waiting in lines. I didn't want to enter a club alone, prey to local lotharios, so I headed back to the Outrigger Tiki Luau and my safe hotel room.

I didn't want to watch TV, but it was early. I flipped through its options, and found a Hawaiian music channel. Scenes of tropical beaches and attractions scrolled like a screensaver. I opened my curtains and sliding glass door, filling my room with rich sea air. Most of my view faced the tall hotel next door, and I could easily see into their lighted rooms. Not wanting to be watched, I turned off my lights, draped a thick towel over my bright TV screen, and closed the sheer inner curtains, watching them billow in the breeze as I stared through their gauze at my narrow glimpse of the sea.

I considered going outside onto my balcony. It was dark enough; no one would see me, and my lacy nightgown revealed less than any beachcomber would see on any given day. Yet I wasn't courageous. I stayed behind my sheer, blowing curtains, before my sliding glass door, and enjoyed the sensation of moist, tropical wind wafting against my skin.

The gentle music soothed. I loved Hawaii, especially Waikiki. The weather, the sounds of the sea, and the friendliness all suited me. Half of the friendliness was from merchants wanting to sell you whatever they had, yet most tourists were delightfully happy, relaxed, and looking for novel ways to have fun. I'd been to the other islands, which were more relaxing ... if you were with someone. When traveling alone, I preferred Oahu.

Eventually I turned down the TV volume until I could barely hear the music, stood by my balcony door, let the sheer curtain flap against my nightgown, listened to crashing waves, and breathed in the cool, clean ocean scent. When I finally crawled into bed, I realized that I'd been smiling all evening, and I truly appreciated my pineapple daiquiri.

Chapter 2

My morning wakeup call didn't annoy; I'd been half awake, delighted by the rhythmic crashes of waves on sand. The sea was the heartbeat of the island, its pulse strong and steady. After a quick shower, I feasted on one of the two blueberry muffins in my welcome bag, then dressed for work, took my display, and began a desperate search for coffee.

Trapped in my trade show, the next six hours dragged. I showed strangers colorful promotions, flashed displays across my screen, described our product in the memorized words I'd spoken a hundred times, and got tired of talking to lonely men more interested in my slim figure than my company's software. I declined four invitations to dinner, and when 4:00 PM freed me, I was relieved to pack my things. Still, five days of talking to bored convention goers, mostly businessmen, for six hours a day, seemed a small price to pay for a week long Hawaiian vacation.

I pulled my heavy case and computer back to the Outrigger Tiki Luau to deposit my gear, shower, and change. I put on my new floral swimsuit, as I had hours of daylight left, slipped on my thick robe, grabbed a towel, and took nothing but my room key.

Many played or relaxed on the beach. Everyone watched a catamaran as it sailed slowly closer, avoiding the swimmers. It looked like it was about to beach itself, so I quickly chose a spot, buried my room key in the sand, and set my towel and robe over it. Then I hurried into the water, hoping people were too busy watching the ship land to notice me. I had a figure that turned heads, but I was also shy, and didn't like to be stared at. Besides, these beaches were crowded with bikinis, many on younger girls, whose swimsuits could've been replaced with thin strips of Christmas ribbon; I didn't stand out.

The water was startlingly cool, but only compared to the heat of day. A few thick, billowy clouds had moved in, yet sunlight shone brightly around them. I splashed in, hurrying past the churning waves, to where I could drop down to my neck, hiding my figure. When a wave struck, I'd jump to spare my head a dunking, but I didn't always succeed.

I wasn't a great swimmer, however I'd dipped in the ocean at least once every trip. How could I explain that I'd visited Hawaii and hadn't touched the sea? The cool water felt good, and the waves striking Waikiki were small and gentle.

I didn't go out deep enough to reach coral, which I knew lurked just off-shore. Coral was high and sharp; others had been picked up by waves and thrown onto it, vacations ruined by shredded skin and hospitals.

The novelty of ocean waves pushing me around, washing over my skin, slowly dimmed. I gritted my teeth and headed for the beach. I emerged, arms crossed over my breasts; wet bathing suits were more clingy than dry. Several pairs of eyes locked on me as I slogged up the wet sand onto dry, but I quickly shook out my thick robe, wrapped it protectively about me, hung my towel over one shoulder, and dug my card key from the sand. Then I headed for the pool area, where a low outdoor shower allowed me to wash the sand off my feet before I took the elevator back to my room. There I showered and dressed for another solo dinner adventure in Waikiki. However, this time I indulged my whims to actually walk into several stores where I could afford nothing, and then I ate at a popular chain where I knew the seafood was good.

I stayed out late that evening. Eventually I felt uncomfortably cool. I returned to my room; Hawaii felt perfect during the day, but some nightly ocean breezes made for mandatory jacket weather. This time I clicked through all the free channels on my TV, yet none I wanted to watch. I returned to the Hawaiian music station, turned off my lights, and sat alone ... watching festive, tropical images flash on my screen.

I wished that I had someone to share my vacation. My last relationship had ended a year before, and no one I'd met since seemed mildly interesting ... or they were already married. I refused to give in to 'all the good ones are taken', but I also rejected the 'good men are made, not found'. I wasn't in college anymore. Men my age should be adults. My last date had spent most of the night describing his favorite video game.

I reached for the hotel phone and used the automated teller to set my wakeup call. I hung up bothered; I know machines are cheaper, but I'd rather speak to a live voice when on vacation.

In the light from the TV, something bright caught my eye. On the table beside the hotel phone rested a paper I hadn't noticed before. At first I thought it was an advertisement because of its colorful printing, but then I realized it was a small envelope.

The Majestic Dinner Theater ...

A cold shiver ran up my spine. I opened the envelope. Inside was a complimentary ticket.

The magician had been in my room ...!

Terror welled in me ... yet slowly I calmed. No one could've been in my room ... except the maid. Even if he was staying in this hotel, he couldn't have gotten onto this floor ... unless his room was also on this floor. My door auto-locked ... and I always double-checked. How could he ...?

My purse! I'd set my purse on the bedside table when I'd first arrived. He must've slipped the free ticket into my purse's pocket ... and it fell out beside the phone. He was a magician; he could do things like that.

I examined the ticket; *tomorrow night's show.*

If he'd expected me to find it, why hadn't he given me one for tonight's show ... or last night's ...?

I glanced at my open sliding glass door, wondering if I was being watched in the light of my TV. My sheer curtains were closed, and I could see nothing of the rooms in the hotel across from me, unless their curtains were open and lights on. I assumed that I was equally hidden. Yet I rose, closed and locked my sliding glass door, drew the heavy curtains, and still felt uneasy. I changed into my nightgown as quickly as I could, jumped into bed, and pulled up the thin hotel covers.

Chapter 3

All day, while attempting to sell software, I couldn't stop thinking about my free ticket. My balcony door had been latched when I'd gotten back after dinner. I could've failed to lock it securely, which seemed unlikely, and all he would've had to have learned was my room number. When I wasn't there, he could've climbed from another level, along the hanging balconies, eight floors above the ground, and gotten inside my room. Then he left his free ticket, locked my sliding glass door behind him, and walked out of my room's door into the hallway, allowing my door to auto-lock behind him ... all without being seen or breaking his neck ...

Ridiculous ...!

Every invasion scenario seemed unlikely. The sheer number of coincidences it would've taken were staggering ...

"Hello!" said a familiar voice.

I looked up from my display and startled. The magician stood before me, in the conference center, wearing his white Stetson fedora, but now with a dark Hawaiian shirt showing a crimson sunset over a sandy

23

beach ... looking nothing like Humphrey Bogart.

"You ...!" I gasped. "How did you ... get in here?"

He shrugged and pointed to the white sticky badge, with his name printed on it, slapped onto his shirt.

"You ... buy software ...?" I asked.

"Certainly not," he laughed. "I have friends that do ... I came with them. So, this is what draws computer professionals to Hawaii ...?"

I stared at him, uncertain what to do. Potential customers were walking past, and I couldn't act unprofessionally.

"How did you do it ...?" I demanded in a soft, hissing whisper.

"Do ...?" he asked. "Oh, my tricks ...! Most are professional secrets, and the rest are just practice. Is there a specific trick you're interested in?"

"Did you use your fame to pressure someone?" I asked.

"I don't approve when people abuse fame," he said.

"Did you bribe a maid ...?" I asked.

"Bribe ...?" he asked. "Even if I had that kind of money, I wouldn't spend it on ... what makes you think I bribed a maid ...?"

"I found a ticket in my room," I said. "Beside my bed. A free pass to dinner and your show ..."

"Excellent!" he said. "I hope you enjoy it!"

"How did your ticket get into my room ...?" I demanded.

He looked confused.

"You ... don't know ... where the ticket came from?" he asked, pretending innocence. "That's ... wow!

24

How could it have gotten there?"

"That's what I'd like to know ...!" I hissed between teeth to keep from being overheard.

"Ummmm...., this is weird," he said. "I understand your assumption, but I didn't put it there. How could I?"

To all outward appearances, his plea seemed truthful, yet I knew better than to trust a magician.

"Look, I don't know who you ...," I began.

"Oh, I'm sorry, I thought I had ...!" he said. "I'm Emmerich the ... well, I'm really Emerson Eastgate. My stage name is Emmerich."

"I don't want to know ...!" I hissed. "Look, I work here. I can't make a scene ... but if you're a stalker ...!"

"Stalker ...?" he scowled, looking offended. "Penelope, please ...!"

"How do you know my name?" I demanded.

"Lucky guess," he said, and when I glared at him: "It's on your name badge ...?"

I glanced down; *I'd forgotten.*

"Listen, Penelope," he said. "I do stage magic for people who pay to be entertained. I also do children's birthdays, and holiday parties. I make people happy. I don't force myself on anyone ... or stalk ... and I'm just as baffled as you are by your unexplained ticket. I got a gift bag ... there were no tickets in mine. I'd love to have you come to a performance ... but, to be honest, I've said that to everyone. How a ticket got in your bedroom ...? I don't know ... but I hope you don't waste it. I ... well, I put on a great show."

"Thank you, Mr. Eastgate," I said, being noncommittal. "If you'll forgive me, I'm supposed to be talking to customers ..."

"Oh, of course," he said, and he tilted his hat. "Hope I see you there."

I watched him walk away nonchalantly, as if he hadn't a care in the world. He nodded to those manning the booth next to mine, then went to look at an exhibit two booths away, where a demonstration was in progress.

I was almost shaking ... although if from fear or relief I couldn't tell.

Closing hour approached ... then finally arrived. Most of the customers had already left, and many workers, including me, started breaking down early.

"Penelope!" called a voice that made me jump. I whipped around, ready to confront Emmerich, but it was Mr. Jenklie, the local event manager. "Oh, my! Did I startle you?"

"No, I'm fine," I said, struggling to recover my breath.

"First, how's it going?" Mr. Jenklie asked.

"A few bites, mostly nibbles," I said.

"Well, that's to be expected," Mr. Jenklie said. "Most sales happen ..."

"... On the last day," I finished his sentence.

"Obviously not your first event," Mr. Jenklie said. "There's a group of vendors, up to eleven, with room for one more, going out tonight ... just for fun. I thought you might want to join us."

"Sounds wonderful," I said, eager to keep from being alone.

"Excellent!" Mr. Jenklie said. "We're going for dinner and a show."

I froze.

"What show ...?" I asked.

"A magic act ... at the Majestic Dinner Theater," Mr. Jenklie said. "Should be a hoot. It's not far, just two

26

blocks south of here. We're meeting there at seven."

Nervously I packed up my computer and bag and returned to my hotel room. I opened my door slowly, peeked inside, and checked my closet, bathroom, balcony, and under the bed.

I wondered if I should change rooms ...?

Six o'clock ...

Shoving my work equipment into the closet, I sat just long enough to calm down. I wouldn't be alone. Other vendors would be there ... and protect me. This was just another coincidence ...

I hated coincidences!

I changed clothes, but stayed in my room until the last second. Then I had to hurry. I didn't want to be late and make a bad impression, yet I did bring the complimentary ticket. I had a fifty dollar a day food allowance, whether I ate or not; free meals were extra money in my pocket. I was just so nervous that I wasn't sure if I'd be able to eat.

In the theater lobby, I recognized several vendors, and joined them just as the doors opened. We had three tables next to each other, and I chose the one farthest from the stage. Mr. Jenklie sat at a different table, yet waved to me.

Three men sat at my table and introduced themselves. Kent Burken was a salesman for a medical information warehouse. Mark Shindee promoted a Chinese pharmaceutical manufacturer. Abu Gupta represented my competition, another company that specialized in patient tracking and treatment management software with tie-ins to every major medical database. Each greeted me politely.

"Is there a problem?" Abu asked. "You seem ... anxious ..."

"Oh, I'm just ... I don't really care for magic," I said. "I know it's not real, but ..."

"I know most of their tricks," Kent said. "I had this buddy in college ..."

"Magic is just deception," Mark said. "We should be able to figure it out, if we watch closely ... try to notice everything."

"The goal of magicians is to control attention," Abu said. "Their banter is the entertainment."

The menu consisted of five choices; I chose salmon. The food was what I expected, neither the best nor the worst, and the bottle of wine Kent bought for our table vanished into me at an alarming rate.

After our plates were taken, a tray of honeyed macadamia cookies and chocolates were set onto each table. Then one of the waiters stepped onto the stage before the curtain, and drew most diner's attention.

"Has everyone had a great meal?" he asked, followed by general applause. "Hello, I'm Don Flankston, and I'll be your host for the rest of the evening. I hope you're excited; we've flown in a special treat for you. Our entertainer is an amazing man, graduate of the Lester McVey Academy of Magic and an associate of the International Legerdemain League, a veteran of every showcase in Vegas, Hollywood, and Walt Disney Studios, with his own Showtime special, the marvelous, the astounding, that incredible master of illusion, Emmerich the Amazing!"

The overhead lights flickered as a deep *boom!* resounded, and a puff of smoke blew the curtains apart. The magician ... Emmerich ... Emerson Eastgate ... stood on the stage spreading his arms wide.

"Welcome, welcome, welcome!" he cried, smiling and gesturing dramatically. "For my first trick, I'd like to appear before you drunk ... Yes! Incredible! I love starting with a success ...!"

The crowd laughed ... phony and pretentious, and they loved it. The magician wore an outlandish suit; purple, green, and yellow covered with sparkly rhinestones reflecting the bright lights.

"You came to see amazing sights," Emerson ... Emmerich said. "Now, most of you don't believe in magic. Poor souls, I'm not going to try to change your minds, but I will make you doubt your senses. To begin ..." He pulled off his hat ... a green Stetson ... and a little bird flew out and fluttered to a tall stand to his right. "Now ... how did that get in there? Oh, well, look what she left behind ..."

From out of his hat, he drew three large white eggs, and began to juggle them.

"You're probably wondering how three large chicken eggs came out of a spotted wren," he said. "Well, I try not to pry into the social lives of my birds ... that's kinda weird, but I do take advantage of them ...."

He tossed all three eggs high, and caught them in his green Stetson. Then he pulled out a tall glass of milk, poured it into his hat, dropped a small square of butter into it, sprinkled in some salt and pepper, and added three shots of Tabasco. Lastly, he poured in a little brandy, lit it on fire, stirred it with a long spoon, lifted an ordinary dinner plate with his other hand, and flipped his hat overtop the plate. When he lifted his hat, his plate was covered with a steaming pile of freshly-cooked scrambled eggs.

"Thank you!" Emmerich shouted over the applause. "Thank you! That was amazing ... or it would've been ... I was trying for over-easy!"

As the audience laughed, and some applauded,

he tossed the whole plate over his shoulder. The scrambled eggs flew to splat the curtain behind him, and the plate broke loudly upon the floor.

"There we go! Over-easy! Another fabulous trick!"

I started to breathe easy. This was the type of magic I'd expected, stage illusions and sleight of hand. No one seemed shocked, and his amusing banter made it all seem funny. I took another sip of wine; it helped.

He brought out eight large steel rings next, then handed all of them out to the tables near the front, letting audience members examine them, to prove that they were real. Mr. Jenklie took two and passed one to someone sitting next to him, examined his, then handed both back.

"See, as I said, solid rings, no breaks, no gaps, no deception," Emmerich took back all the rings, then started to juggle them, then looped two over his head and three on each arm and began to spin them like small hula-hoops. This performance earned scattered applause.

"The trick, if there is one, is similar to marriage," Emmerich finally said, bouncing his rings off the floor, then collecting them and holding them up high. "Each partner gets a ring, knows what they can do with them, tries not to cheat, and when you do, you get caught."

He dropped all but one ring ... and each ring was solidly linked to form a long chain.

I applauded along with everyone else. Emmerich really was an excellent entertainer. Most of his tricks were corny and obvious, but then he'd throw in something no one expected. His banter was the best part of his show, and I began laughing and joining in the fun.

"Is there anyone here from California?" Emmerich asked, and hands at two tables rose. "My deepest sympathies ... I hope you get to move to someplace better soon. Now, this table over here ..." he pointed to a center table "... I think I'm sensing someone here ... someone ... a man ... and his name is ... Joe ...?"

From the reaction at the table, Emmerich was right. Joe was asked to stand and introduce himself, then given a small clipboard. It held one sheet of paper with questions whose answers had to be written in little boxes. Emmerich asked him to hold the clipboard so that he couldn't see the paper, fill out the form, and sign it.

"The first box is your favorite color, the second box is the name of your first pet, and the third box is the cost of the last item you purchased with a credit card not including tax," Emmerich said. "Now ... you do know how to write, don't you?" He turned to the others at his table. "How long have you known Joe? Did he go to school? Yes! Joe has filled out my little form! Now ... pass it around, show it to everyone, let them see ... but don't let me see ... wouldn't be much of a trick if I just read it, would it?"

Joe showed his answers to everyone at his table, then at the next table. Emmerich insisted that he hand the clipboard to someone else, and they passed it on to another table. At least fifteen people glanced at it before Emmerich had the person holding the clipboard, three tables away from Joe, stand up and introduce themself.

"My name is Mary," she said.

"What a coincidence!" Emmerich cried. "My mother's name was Mary, and she was more than a mother to me. We're from Kentucky, so she was also my aunt, second cousin, and a half-sister by marriage. Now, Mary, I'm going to give you a color, and I need you to tell me if it matches Joe's answer. All right ... my favorite color ... doesn't matter, because that's not the question. One more time; Joe's favorite color is ... olive green!"

Mary looked shocked, then nodded emphatically, and everyone applauded. Emmerich thanked her and asked her to hand the clipboard to someone at another table, which she did. This was an older man, whom Emmerich asked to stand and introduce himself.

"I'm Ron," the man said.

"Ron!" Emmerich exclaimed. "That was my dad's name! He wasn't a great dad, but don't worry; I was acquitted for lack of evidence. Ron, let me ask you ... no, I'm not going to ask you ... I'm going to tell you what Joe wrote down as the name of his first pet. It's a spot ... right here on my jacket ... I should only drink wine naked ... but that's not my answer! The name of Joe's first pet was ... Terry!"

"It says Terry!" Ron announced, and more applause followed.

Emmerich had Ron pass the clipboard all the way up to the front. Taking it, Emmerich pulled out a pen and began writing on it, then took the page off the clipboard, and held it up for all to see.

"Now, you may all remember, those who aren't drunk like me, that I asked Joe to write on here the cost of the last item he purchased ... and sign it. Well, Joe, I hate to tell you this, and I appreciate your gullibility, but never sign anything and then give it to a magician! Now, I've written on here the date and the amount you wrote, thirty-eight dollars and fifty cents, in longhand, and now ...!"

Emmerich lifted a pair of scissors, and carefully

cut a rectangle out of the paper. Then he peeled back the paper on which Joe had written. Another piece of paper lay underneath ... which was a blank check ... made out for thirty-eight dollars and fifty cents, and signed by Joe!

"A legal, valid check!" Emmerich lifted the check and showed it to everyone. "Any bank in America would cash this check ... unfortunately it's not enough for me to escape to the Bahamas! Yes, Joe, carbon copies are magic. But this check is real ... yet I know you never meant to sign it, so I'm going to fold it in half and tear it in two ... and again ... and again!"

Repeatedly Emmerich folded and tore the check in half, then sprinkled the tiny sections into his green hat, which he then dumped into a metal trash can he pulled out from underneath his table, then threw the can over his shoulder into a back corner, where it crashed loudly. He apologized to Joe and offered him a real gold coin to pay for abusing his trust. He held up a chocolate coin wrapped in gold foil and tossed it to Joe, who caught it. Then he asked Joe, if he would, to eat the chocolate; Joe opened the gold foil and took out the chocolate ... and with it came a tiny folded rectangle of paper. Upon request, Joe unfolded the paper; it was the signed check Emmerich had just torn up.

The applause was tremendous. Emmerich smiled and bowed. I laughed and clapped.

Emmerich did several other tricks, with giant cards and massive dice whose dots kept changing colors, and kept his banter flowing as freely as the alcohol. Each trick earned prodigious applause, doubtlessly helped by powerful alcoholic drinks. Finally I fully relaxed.

"Now, I've just one last trick to show you,"

Emmerich said. "Before I do, I want to thank all of you. You've been a wonderful audience, and for a magician, there's no greater magic than to delight and entertain. I really am grateful to you, and also grateful to the Majestic Dinner Theater, for allowing me to come and demonstrate my act tonight. Our host, our wait-staff, our cooks, our bartender, and of course all of you ... I think we all deserve a round of applause."

The applause was enthusiastic.

"I'm a magician, and my magic is trickery ... I wouldn't try to deceive you. That being said, my final trick requires a volunteer from the audience ... and this isn't someone I've never met before. No lie, I was lucky enough to share a cab from the airport with this beautiful young woman ... whom I'd never met before ... and she's a sweet lady, unsurprisingly suspicious of me ... most people are suspicious of magicians, with good reason, so I'd like to set the record straight and prove to her that there's no sorcery happening here. Would you please help me invite up onto my stage ... Penelope!"

Kent, Mark, and Abu seemed delighted, clapping along with everyone else. I tensed; I didn't want to go up, but everyone was watching and cheering me, and I felt too ashamed to refuse. Despite cascading trepidations, I slowly stood and walked forward ... up the tiny stair, onto the stage, and found myself face-to-face with Emmerich.

His wide smile was alarming.

"No harm, I promise," he whispered without moving his lips.

"Ladies and gentlemen, please attend; this beautiful young lady is just as real as any of you. Penelope, could you tell everyone what you do for a living that brought you to Hawaii ...?"

I felt self-conscious with every eye looking and lights blaring.

"Medical software sales," I said.

"Fascinating!" Emmerich said. "Now, you and I have met before, but we only met a few days ago. We're not related, and you're not part of my act in any way, are you?"

"No," I said.

"Do you trust me?" Emmerich asked.

"No," I said, and everyone laughed. I hadn't meant to say no, but I felt nervous with everyone watching. Emmerich laughed at my answer.

"I wouldn't trust me either," Emmerich chuckled. "Now, all I want you to do is stand here. See the 'x' on the floor? Just stand still. This won't take long, and it won't hurt a bit. Well, it shouldn't hurt ... it's never hurt before, but this is the first time I've ever tried this trick ... with a live person. Don't worry. I've got a silk curtain here, soft silk, hanging from the ceiling. I'm going to wrap this around you. You won't be able to see, which is probably for the best. I just need you to promise you'll stay here, on this spot, until I open the curtain. Will you do that?"

Hesitantly I nodded.

"Let's give Penelope a big hand, shall we?" Emmerich asked.

Everyone applauded.

"Just stand here, try not to move, and this will be over soon," Emmerich whispered to me, again using ventriloquism.

I nodded.

The curtain was faux green silk, probably rayon, hanging from wires on a runner, set on decorated stands on each side of the stage. Emmerich pulled one edge of it to one side of the stage, then took the other edge and pulled it to the other side of the stage, displaying it to the crowd. It was just a thin curtain that fell to the floor, and with a nod to me, he held out one edge and asked me to hold it tightly. I did, and Emmerich took the other edge and walked a wide circle around me. His smile was the last thing I saw ... and then everything was green silk. Yet I heard every sound; Emmerich walked around me three times while several voices sniggered.

"Now, with this yellow sash, I'm going to tie this curtain closed, not tightly, just enough so it doesn't fall open," Emmerich said, and I felt the sash press against the curtain and lightly tighten around my body, just below my elbows.

Seeing only green silk, I tried not to move.

"Now, I want all of you to look at this," Emmerich said, and the crowd gasped. "Don't say anything ... we don't want to frighten poor Penelope! Listen to it!" Something banged solidly. "Now ... please watch ... and I pray you: don't make a sound ...! This is a very delicate trick ...! Penelope, remain very still ...!"

I couldn't tell what was happening. I felt a poke, like a finger, upon my shoulder, and heard the audience gasp. Another gasp followed a poke against my left arm, my hip, the center of my back, and finally the side of my head.

"Oh, my God ...!" one woman muttered.

I wondered what they were seeing. Emmerich was right; I didn't feel a thing, certainly not any pain, although I was getting tired of standing still like a green silk burrito. I wished I hadn't drunk so much wine.

I heard a long hiss, as if two stiff fabrics were sliding against each other, and suddenly it ended. Emmerich's footsteps began circling me again. Layers of green silk lifted. The last layer fell free ... and the crowd jumped to its feet, applauding.

"Penelope, safe and sound!" Emmerich shouted over the loud clapping, and he nodded to me, took my hand, and bowed to everyone, pulling me into a fumbling bow. I felt awkward, but apparently I'd been part of his most amazing trick.

I tried to pull away, but he held on, letting the crowd applaud, and then he turned and bowed to me. He let me go at the same time, and I wanted to flee, but I awkwardly bowed to him first, then fled. The applause kept going even as I stepped off the stage and hurried back to my seat.

Even though I had no idea what had happened, my heart was pounding. Kent, Mark, and Abu looked greatly impressed, and turned their clapping hands to face me as I rejoined them.

"Thank you! Thank you! Good-night ... and may every day of your lives be magical!" Emmerich shouted, and with a puff of smoke, the main curtains closed and lights brightened above us.

The applause quickly died, yet everyone looked excited.

"You must tell us how it worked ...!" Kent said.

"That was incredible ...!" Mark exclaimed.

"I actually feared for you!" Abu said. "When that needle passed through you ...!"

"*Needle ...?*" I gasped.

No one believed I wasn't in on the trick. Yet everyone was getting up to leave, some chugging drinks to leave only empty glasses on their table. One lady was taking all the treats that hadn't been eaten, even from other tables, and wrapping them in napkins. A few put on light jackets.

"Penelope, you have to tell us ...!" Mr. Jenklie said, coming up to my table. "My heart was pounding ... I'm surprised I didn't pass out!"

"I ... can't ....!" I stammered.

"She's part of the act!" Mark said. "Not revealing the trick ...!"

"It was astounding ...!" another woman said. "I almost screamed ...!"

"We'll get it out of her," Kent said. "I could use another drink. What say we find a nearby bar ...?"

Many agreed, yet I begged off. Their reactions frightened me more than the green silk. I didn't know what had happened ... and I didn't want to be called a liar all night.

"I ... don't think I'm up for a late night," I said. "I would ... appreciate ... not having to walk back to my hotel alone."

This was readily agreed to, and over half the salesmen, and two women, escorted me back to my hotel, where they tried once more to elicit the secret they swore I had. I refused, and wished them all good-night. However, the Outrigger Tiki Luau had a swing band playing in its bar, and as I hurried to the elevator, digging my card key out of my purse, they headed to join the fun.

I carefully checked my room, and found nothing out of place, before I dared to relax. *Some vacation ...!* I tried to hold my hands still ... and my fingers slightly twitched.

I turned on the TV, double-checked to make sure that my door and the sliding glass door were locked, closed the heavy curtains that the maid must've opened, and laid down on my bed. I felt exhausted, beaten, and worn out.

This wasn't how I'd planned to spend my nights in Hawaii!

A new version of the same terrible nightly news was being reported by a blonde woman and a dark-skinned man, each slathered with more makeup than I owned. I flipped the channel to a rerun I could quote, then changed to a movie with a girl screaming. I didn't care to know what scared her, so I kept clicking, mostly to endless commercials. I found the Hawaiian music station and left it there.

My room might as well sound like I was enjoying Waikiki.

My nerves were shot. I fell asleep to the music of crashing waves and a strumming ukulele ...

Chapter 4

I awoke in the night, clicked off the TV, looked at the alarm, then dropped back onto my pillow. I hadn't set a wake-up call, but it was an hour before I had to get up. I laid back, listening to the comforting *whoosh!* of the ocean. I didn't have any more muffins, but if I got up early then I could have a real breakfast before work.

Showered and dressed, I exited the elevator to the enticing scent of coffee. Guests in the restaurant were greeted by a Hawaiian girl in a bright pink dress, resembling a flamingo, yet I didn't comment on it. She escorted me to a table near the breakfast bar, and I set my work equipment onto the floor beneath my table, then headed straight toward caffeine. Cream. Sugar. I drank deeply despite how hot it was, deposited my cup on my table, and started custom-making a waffle, breaking up a crisp slice of bacon and crumbling it into the mix before I lowered the lid. While my waffle rose, I grabbed a plate and put some orange and grapefruit slices on it, more bacon, added hash browns and toast, and more bacon. I set my breakfast on my table just as the beep sounded, and then I flipped my waffle over, and chose from a selection of colorful syrups.

Well-fed, watching waves roll upon sand through open-air windows, I finished my second coffee, then hurried to the conference center and tried to set up my equipment. The doors for the public weren't open before several vendors came over.

"Look, whatever magic he did, he didn't need my help," I told them. "I don't even know what he did."

"If they'd allowed it, I would've videoed it," one man said. "Most amazing trick I've ever seen."

"Magicians don't like being videoed; it reveals their secrets," a woman said.

"What happened ...?" I asked.

"He sewed you," a man said. "He took out a steel needle ... it must've been two feet long, and threaded it with a thick, red cord. Then he poked the needle right through you ... where you were supposed to be, and sewed the cord through you."

"That wasn't you, was it?" another man asked. "You were dropped into the basement after he wrapped the silk curtain around you, weren't you? You were replaced by a dummy, and then you were lifted back up ..."

"I wasn't dropped anywhere," I said.

"You must've felt the needle ... or the thread," the woman said.

"Obviously he didn't stab you, but it must've been near misses every time," another man said.

"I didn't feel a thing," I said ... but no one believed me.

I was the gossip of the vendors. When the day was done, I packed up, fending off the same questions I'd been denying all day. I hurried back to my hotel, determined to lose my frustrations with another cool soak in the ocean.

As I unlocked my door, I didn't feel the need to search my room or check the lock on the sliding glass door. The maid had visited; my bed was made and my heavy curtains were wide again, only the sheer white curtains hanging closed. With frustrations brimming, I pushed them aside, unlocked, and flung open my sliding glass door. Delightful breezes caressed me. It felt good; I didn't go to Hawaii enough to waste a minute of paradise.

In the bathroom, I changed into my other bathing suit, a skimpy red bikini that my girlfriends had bought me, which I'd promised to bring, but had no intention of wearing. Then I stepped out onto my balcony and, feeling emboldened, displayed myself to anyone watching. I wasn't naked, half the women on the beach wore bikinis. Yet I refused to spend the rest of my vacation cowering in my room.

Concealed inside my robe, and with my towel around my neck, under my hair, I took the elevator down, emerged beside the pool, and walked right out onto the beach. Several heads snapped in my direction, mostly men, yet I didn't care. I found a spot near some sunbathing elderly ladies, buried my card key in the sand, covered it with my robe and towel, and then strode straight toward the water.

Floating, although not so far out that I couldn't stand up if a wave crashed over me, I released my tension into the sea. I needed this, needed to forget that damned complimentary ticket. Perhaps the last person to use my room had gotten the ticket and, realizing they'd be gone before the appointed date, they left it for whoever could use it. That made sense, far more than a crazed stalker risking their neck to break into my room and deposit an expensive ticket I might not use.

Finally I flipped over, dog-paddling between waves, each of which seemed to wash away my fears as they splashed and bubbled. I had to be careful; I wasn't wearing waterproof sunscreen, and nothing ruins a vacation like burned skin. Soon I'd had enough ocean to last me; I felt relaxed, my confidence restored.

As I stepped out of the waves, a young man stared at me ... until the young woman walking beside him cuffed his arm. I didn't like being stared at, but my figure was lithe and my legs long; I could command attention when I wanted it. I hurried to grab my robe, towel, and key, and walked proudly to the pool area where I could rinse off my sandy feet before I returned to my room.

Little children were laughing as they played in the pool, swinging balloon swords of bright colors, and a little girl ran past me carrying a yellow balloon giraffe. I smiled at her; she stopped and looked at me. Then a woman, still shouting at kids playing in the pool, ran up, grabbed the child, and carried her back into the pool area. I washed until my feet were sand-free, shook the sand out my towel and robe, and turned to head for the elevator.

"*Penelope ...?*"

The magician's eyes were wide, his expression frozen. The balloon animal he'd been making slipped from his fingers; it sputtered and flew from his hands, darted about, and fell deflated beside the pool. The child he'd been making the balloon animal for laughed and ran to get it.

I closed my eyes, tried to throw on my robe, got one arm stuck, struggled to cover myself, conceal my wet red bikini ... and all the flesh it wasn't covering. Blush reddened my cheeks, and I felt like I'd flushed beet red all the way down to my other cheeks. I wanted to run, yet not look childish.

"Lovely ... to see you," the wide-eyed magician said, his tremulous voice much closer.

I was shaking ... with rage or embarrassment ... yet I steeled myself and opened my eyes.

"Mr. Eastgate ...," I nodded, tightly clenching both sides of the front of my robe closed.

He looked stunned.

"E-Emerson, p-please ...," he stammered. "I-I was hoping to see ... I mean, t-to run into you. I wanted ... to ask ... what you thought ..."

"Thought ...?" I demanded.

"About my show ...?" Emerson asked.

"Oh!" I fumbled, fluttered and distracted. "Well, ... I need to go to my room ... right now."

"Of course ...," Emerson said, seeming equally flustered. "Perhaps another time ...?"

"Perhaps ...," I mumbled, and I pushed past him, then walked to the elevator in as fast a pace as couldn't be described as escape velocity.

Hours later, showered, changed, and swearing I'd never wear that red bikini again, I double-checked my locks, then emerged from my room. I checked the hallway first, and finding it empty, rode the elevator down. Before I got out of the elevator, I checked the lobby to make sure it was magician-free, and then I walked to the front of the Golden Aloha, the restaurant in our lobby, and told the hostess that I was looking for someone. Slipping past, I checked to see if the magician was there. Fortunately he wasn't, and so I returned and asked for a table. The hostess asked if I was waiting on someone ... and seemed puzzled when I told her no.

If I hadn't been hungry, or wanted to pay extra for room service, then I'd have stayed in my room all night. Emerson's expression, as he'd seen me in my red bikini, haunted; he'd looked shocked, almost comical. I never dressed that scandalously. I couldn't believe I hadn't covered up the instant I'd climbed out of the sea.

Of course, onstage, the magician dressed crazily, too, in his outlandish purple, green, and yellow suit covered with sparkly rhinestones ...

Suddenly I froze.

The magician hadn't carried a suitcase from the airport ...!

Where'd he get that suit ...?

"Ma'am ...?" the waitress asked. "Are you all right ...?"

"Huh ...?" I glanced up.

"I asked if you'd like a drink," she said. "We have specials on strawberry-pineapple margaritas and screaming red zombies ..."

I couldn't let her distract me. *I had him ...!*

"Margarita, regular, blended," I said.

"Yes, ma'am," she said. "Food, or appetizer ...?"

I glanced at the menu.

"I haven't decided," I said.

She hurried to get my drink. I smiled wickedly. There was no way that crazy suit could've been already here, waiting for him. It fit too perfectly. It had to be custom-made, and ... what about all those props? Magicians didn't trade magical props, and no one could arrive and buy all the stuff they needed for a practiced stage act. Where did all that stuff come from? Besides, where on Hawaii could you buy huge steel rings, a live spotted wren, the special paper on his clipboard, or all the other things he'd used ...?

I had him!

If he dared cross my path again ...!

"Penelope ...?" his voice came from behind me.

I gritted my teeth, not surprised at all. Under a light jacket, he was wearing a green t-shirt covered with cartoon characters. One side were Marvel and DC heroes, the Avengers and the Justice League, and on the other side were Disney and Pixar characters, Mickey, Pinocchio, and Shrek, and both sides were charging the other, fists raised. I would've laughed but I was too angry.

"Again ...?" I sneered. "For someone who's not a stalker, you appear wherever I go ...!"

"I wanted to apologize," Emerson said. "I was making balloon animals for the kids. I never meant to embarrass ..."

"How did you know I was here ...?" I demanded.

"My show just ended," he said. "I came back for my jacket ... just happened to look in here ..."

"Another coincidence ...?" I demanded.

"Again, I'm sorry," Emerson said. "I'll leave you alone ..."

"You didn't bring a suitcase ...!" I almost shouted over the music. *"Where'd you get all that stuff ...? Where'd you get that suit, props, and these clothes ...?"*

Emerson opened his mouth to speak, but then the waitress arrived with my margarita, and he paused. She glanced at him, standing beside my table, and looked like she was going to ask, yet with a glimpse at my expression, she fled.

"You want answers ...?" Emerson asked ... and he gestured at the chair across from me. "Normally, magicians don't give away secrets, but ... I feel that I owe you."

I fumed, torn; I didn't want him to join me, yet I did want answers. When I didn't object, he slid into the seat.

"Do you really think I could pack all my props in a suitcase?" Emerson asked. "I use large ship-any-weight boxes from the post office. I mail them to the theater ... packed inside my clothes, to pad my props. I hate hauling suitcases; it's hard to advertise shows with full hands."

My mouth fell open. To hide my disillusion, I grabbed my drink and took a salty sip.

I'd thought I had him ...!

"Penelope, I'm sorry if we got off on the wrong foot," Emerson said. "I think you're a nice, obviously beautiful lady, but I'd never force my company on anyone. If you'd like, I'll walk out of here right now and you'll never see me again. However, there's one point I'd like to make and one question I'd like to ask ... if you wouldn't mind ...?"

I sighed deeply and stared at him.

"First, I'm a magician," Emerson said. "I can't explain everything. It's not a matter of trust, it's professional courtesy. When another magician shares a secret with me, I can't betray their trust ... it's just not done. Their income ... and mine ... depend on it. Secrecy is our highest discipline."

He looked at me imploringly. Slowly I nodded; *that made sense.*

"My question is always the same: what did you think of my show?" he shrugged his shoulders. "It's really three questions: Did you like it? What was your favorite part? Was there anything you think could be improved? That's all I ask; your honest opinion ..."

I took a deep breath and stared at him before

answering.

"If you hadn't scared me with that complimentary pass, I'd have loved it," I said.

"I didn't ...!" he insisted.

"How did it get there?" I asked.

"I don't ...!" he started, and then he held out his hand. "Grab my wrist ... trust me."

Warily I looked at him, and then I reached out ... and closed my hands over something bulkier than expected.

"It's a magician's jacket," he said. "Six rosebuds in tiny, hidden pockets all around both wrists. Now, look at my watch."

He stretched out his arm to expose his wristwatch. A large, flat watch ... and behind its thin clock-arms, it had a black background with white writing. It read: 'Always Say Yes'.

"A magician's watch," he said. "People on stage are usually nervous ... unsure what to do ... and this tells them what to say. It almost always works."

I stared from the watch to his frowning face. He sat back and sighed.

"I can't tell you much more," Emerson said.

"Everyone keeps asking how that trick with the green curtain worked," I said.

"That I can't tell anyone," Emerson said. "What about the trick with the clipboard? I knew the answers he wrote; that's an old vaudeville act ... every magician knows it."

"All right ...," I acquiesced.

"Remember that pen I gave to ... Joe, wasn't it?" Emerson said. "The pen was long and black with a bright, shiny tip on its back end. When people write, especially numbers, the back end of a long pen moves in the exact opposite of the tip they're writing with ... like a mirror image. With a little practice, well, years of it, you can watch and read those numbers and letters as they write ... just as if they were drawing them in the air."

He raised one finger and scribed the word 'Magic' into the empty air before me, and I could easily read his gestures.

"Amazing," I said, truly impressed.

"Did you really think I could perform miracles ...?" Emerson asked.

I shook my head and sipped my margarita.

"I'm not used to being around magicians," I confessed.

"Magicians capitalize on your unfamiliarity," Emerson said. "Now ... before I do another trick, answer my last question; was there any part of my act you think could've been done better?"

"I'm ... no expert on magic acts," I said. "It was the talk of the trade show. Every vendor wanted to know how your magic worked, and none of them believed me ... they told me about the needle ..."

"The magic is in the needle," Emerson said. "That's all I can say. Now, before I reluctantly do my last trick ...," he snapped his fingers and another rosebud appeared. He held it out to me and I took it. "I hate final performances. Before I do my disappearing act, please know I'm truly sorry if I frightened you in any way ... and I'm sorry we couldn't get to know each other better. You are ... far more beautiful than I realized when I saw you on the plane, and I'll forever be glad I had the chance to ... meet you."

With a complacent frown, Emerson rose from his chair and stepped into the aisle. With a polite nod and a tilt of his hat, he walked away, leaving me alone.

"Wait ...!" I called softly.

With loud, canned music playing, I was surprised that anyone heard me, yet he stopped.

I snapped my fingers ... and pointed at his empty chair.

Magic never worked faster than my gesture. His smile beamed, and he returned and waved for the waitress. A moment of blushing smiles later, she appeared, and he ordered a scotch on the rocks. I was hungry, but didn't want to share a meal; I ordered an appetizer of spicy **BBQ** bacon wrapped pineapple.

Two hours later, more than tipsy, we rode the elevator up and I drug him into my room. I knew better; I didn't do things like this, yet I couldn't resist ... my yearnings were too long unfulfilled. I closed and locked my door, snatched his white Stetson off his head, dropped it onto my dresser, and kissed him hard and deeply.

Emerson proved that he was Amazing. He had a lithe, swimmer's body, toned and finely-muscled. I virtually danced upon him. Awash in a haze of desire and urgency, we writhed and gasped in a unison I could only describe as magic.

I'd never live it down if my friends ever learned how successful their red bikini had been!

Chapter 5

I awoke cuddled against the magician. I snuggled, then tensed; *what had I done?*

Why had I drunk four margaritas ...?

Had he gotten me drunk ...?

Why did I invite him inside my room ... inside ... inside me?

He couldn't be a boyfriend ... or a serious relationship! Soon I'd be going back to North Dakota, while he'd be staying here ... or flying to Vegas!

Did magicians seduce innocents in every new city?

How was I going to get him out of here ...?

My vacation was ruined. I was lucky to visit someplace interesting once a year. He lived on the road. This was nothing but a vacation fling, which made me feel cheap and dirty.

No alarm! I glanced at the clock ... *I was late!*

"Oh, damn!" I jumped up. "I should've left ten minutes ago! I'm sorry ...!"

"Please ...!" he said. "No, my fault. I knew you got up early ..."

"I've got to shower, change, ...!" I said.

"Go," he said. "I'll get dressed."

I didn't like leaving him alone, but I had five minutes to shower, and even less to dress. I jumped in before the water got warm, washed off the scent of our night together, trying not to get my hair wet, then I was out, drying off. He was half dressed when I emerged in a towel and rifled through my suitcase for clothes. I hated throwing off my towel with him watching, which felt insane after the things we'd done most of the night, yet I had no choice.

"Will I see you tonight?" Emerson asked, as he searched for his Birkenstocks under the bed. "My performance ends at nine, and I can be here by nine-thirty."

"I ... I'll ... have to think ...," I said.

"I'll wait for you in the Golden Aloha, but we can go somewhere else ...," Emerson said.

"We'll see ...," I said. "I've got to go ...!"

"Penelope, I don't do this ... unless I think I've found ... something that can last," Emerson said.

Dressed, he picked up his hat, came over, and gave me a quick kiss as I was buttoning my blouse.

"I hope ... I see you again," Emerson said. "Have a great day. Sell lots."

I mumbled a 'you, too', and he walked to my door and departed. I grabbed my makeup and stuffed it into my purse, yanked my computer and work case out of the closet, and hurried toward the elevator, pausing only long enough to insure that my door was locked behind me.

A family with kids in bathing suits shared my elevator ride to the lobby.

On the street, I practically ran, having no time to

find a cab. I made it to the trade show just minutes before they opened to the public; a short line of customers watched me enter, flashing my vendor's badge. Over a dozen customers had already walked past my booth before I finished setting up my colorful, animated display.

I hadn't had coffee, and when one man in the booth beside mine offered to get coffee for his group, I begged. I reached for my purse, but he waved me off; plain coffee in the lounge was free for vendors, a fact that I hadn't known, despite being here three days. Yet I manned my booth alone, so I didn't have the luxury of walking around, seeing what was available. I asked for cream and sugar and he nodded.

Marge, the only woman working the booth on the other side of me, called me over during the first lull.

"Dear, I don't mean to be ... your hair is a mess ... in the back," Marge said.

"Oh, crap ...!" I said. I hadn't looked in a mirror all morning.

"I'll watch your booth," she said.

"Thanks!"

I hurried to the ladies' room, and was horrified to discover that I looked like I'd had a wild night. My hair stuck out in odd places, and the tiny brush in my purse proved inadequate to do as nice a job as I preferred. I had only minutes; I did the best I could, quickly added a touch more mascara and lip gloss, and then hurried back.

Coffee ...!

Marge nodded to me as I sipped deeply. Then another wave of customers stole our attention. We recited our spiels, handed out cards, brochures, and explained how our products could make their businesses more stable, efficient, and profitable.

Saturday was the busiest day of trade shows. Another woman presenter joined Marge. At lunchtime, she stepped over into my booth.

"I'm going to get lunch for us," Marge said. "There's a combo plate for $18 ... that's what we're having. Would you ...?"

"Yes, please!" I said, reaching for my purse. "Thank you!"

"For an additional cost!" Marge smiled wickedly. "I've been married for 13 years and spent every night in my room, watching Jeopardy and sit-coms. Please tell me ... you didn't watch TV last night ...?"

I hesitated and looked at her.

"I miss being single," Marge said. "Trust me; I was once as wild as a teenager can get."

I swallowed hard.

"I ... I did ... something ... I shouldn't have ..," I said.

"Oh, those are the best somethings!" Marge smiled. "Please ... let me live vicariously ...!"

"I wish I could," I whispered. "I know nothing about him ..."

Her loud, shrill giggle drew the attention of other vendors.

"Nothing ...?" she asked in a whisper. "Good looking ...?"

"Of course," I said. "He drinks scotch ... and I drank way too many margaritas!"

"Maybe I need a margarita," Marge said. "All my romance lives in trashy novels ... which I devour to have any at all!"

"I've read a few of those," I said, nodding my head. "This time yesterday I hated this guy ... never wanted to see him again ..."

"Oh, this sounds good ...!" Marge said. "Was he good ...?"

"Magical," I confessed.

She squeezed her eyes shut and shivered from her shoulders down. Then she sighed.

"Oh, I'd better go get in line before I start salivating," Marge said, breathing heavily.

She took my cash, and I watched her step out into the flow of attendees and head toward the end of our row. The crowd quickly blocked my view of her.

I called to passersby, introduced my company and our product, and began my accustomed recitation, trying to not sound like I was bored; I speak in monotone when I'm not careful, and nothing glazes over the eyes of potential customers as a voice whose tone never changes. Vendors need to be animated, almost theatrical; customers can feel our excitement.

Just like a magician playing to his audience ...

The combo plate turned out to be teriyaki chicken with a side of overcooked rice, something green that looked like a soggy salad, and a tiny fried vegetable spring roll. I snagged a bite every time a customer walked away, then swallowed before I recited my spiel again.

One old woman, who looked like she'd wrestled alligators in her youth, kept asking complex questions. She absorbed my time for almost an hour. She claimed that she was a charge nurse before she moved into management, so she knew what caregivers needed at every level. She balked when I told her my price, but complimented my design and usability, and the variety in which our data could be output, especially in reports for managers who *'wouldn't know what to do with an old-*

school thermometer even if they could read them'.

Finally she asked for a demo at her corporate headquarters in Atlanta. I assured her it was possible. She gave me her card and filled out a request form ... *in my last three trade shows not one customer had filled out a request form!* She claimed that she managed over two thousand seats ... which would mean millions to my company annually. I thanked her profusely as she left ... carrying one of every handout I had and my personal card.

During the next lull, I called my manager, and read to him her contact information.

The rest of the day passed in a breeze. My manager was ecstatic ... which meant I wouldn't endure his usual tirade about the costs of these trade shows and my travel expenses. Also, if this worked out, I should get an annual commission ... I could use a raise. But this was still preliminary; I didn't want to get my hopes high.

Yet I felt like celebrating.

After the customers were gone, as I was packing, Marge came over.

"Are you seeing him again ...?" she asked. "Big dinner plans ...?"

"He works evenings," I said, and her eyes rolled.

"Are you going to call him?" she asked.

"I didn't get his number," I said, and when she looked exasperated. "He asked me to be waiting for him ... in the hotel bar ..."

"What time?" Marge asked.

"Nine-thirty," I said.

"Will you be there?" Marge asked.

"I haven't decided," I said.

"Well, I'll be thinking about you ... wishing you the best," Marge said. "I'm in the Waikiki Palace

Regency; we get every TV station ..." she grinned wickedly, "even the good ones."

"I'm in the Outrigger Tiki Luau," I said. "My boss wouldn't splurge on a palace."

"Too bad," Marge said. "Maybe I'll have the hotel masseuse come visit me tonight ...?"

"It's possible to regret a Hawaiian vacation ...," I reminded her.

"That's the saddest thought ever," Marge said.

I headed back toward the International Market, yet never made it there. I got diverted into narrow alleys, where portable booths were set atop asphalt. Clothes, jewelry, bobble-head hula dolls, tiki totems in wood, stone, and plastic, and just about anything you could name with the word 'Hawaii' printed over a few green leaves ... usually beside a painted coconut tree. Some wrap-around dresses caught my eye. The cute dealer swore that they were made by her aging grandmother in a small village on the other side of Oahu. However, according to the tags inside the dresses, the name of her village was Taiwan.

I bought two dresses anyway.

By nine o'clock, I was in my hotel room, pacing back and forth. I was wearing one of my new dresses, a flower-hair pin, a shell necklace, and matching bracelets. I wore new sandals on my feet, and had a pile of souvenirs on my tiny table; no idea what I was going to with them once I got back home. I'd eaten a shrimp scampi dinner so long ago that I could barely remember it. Yet I wasn't hungry; my stomach churned.

Did I really want to see him again ...?

At nine-twenty seven, I raced to the elevator, and trembled all the way to the lobby. Loud music met my ears ... no canned music tonight; another swing band was playing. The dance floor was crowded, and at least two couples actually knew how to east-coast swing. I stared about, peering between the other patrons ... not seeing him.

A different hostess seated me. I ordered a lemonade. I'd just started to drink when Emerson came in.

"Sorry, got held up," Emerson said. "Glad you're here."

"We should go somewhere else," I said over the loud music. "Somewhere quieter."

"I'd love that," Emerson said.

I dropped a five dollar bill beside my barely-touched lemonade and followed him out. We walked past the bar. Marge was sitting on a tall stool, margarita in hand, smiling brightly. She gave me a big thumb's up. I frowned at her and shook my finger warningly. She broke out laughing, and I was glad that the loudness of the band hid her amusement ... and the dim colored lights hid my blush.

"Nice dress," Emerson said as we emerged onto the street.

"I ... succumbed to an unexpected shopping spree," I grinned.

"That happens," Emerson smiled. "Have you eaten?"

"Yes. Have you?"

"I always eat before a show," Emerson said. "I don't perform as well if I'm hungry."

"How many shows are left?" I asked.

"Tomorrow's my last night," Emerson said. "The theater is closed on Mondays and Tuesdays, except during the heavy tourist season. Suzzannia the Sorceress ... have you heard of her? ... will be back on Wednesday.

Her sister had a baby two days ago, and she's been on the big island taking care of her."

"I fly home on Tuesday," I said. "North Dakota."

"I've never been there," Emerson said. "I've been to Mount Rushmore, but I suppose it's not the same."

"No," I agreed, not sure what else to say.

"How often do you travel?" Emerson asked. "For your job, I mean."

"Once every month, usually," I said. "Most of my trips aren't this nice ... I mean, to somewhere this nice."

Emerson smiled, but then he sighed.

"Look, Penelope, I don't know how to say this, but I've got a million questions," Emerson said.

"There's a few things I'd like to know," I said.

Emerson veered our path to the park where I'd walked before, past a marble war memorial, and we found a lonely bench looking out over the starlit sea. We sat. I felt certain that he was as nervous as I.

"Do you like peanuts?" Emerson asked.

I burst out laughing.

"I ... don't mind them," I said. "I never buy them, but ..."

"They're my favorite on the beach," Emerson said. "Sand can't get inside their shells; you open and eat the nuts. Birds love the shells ... until the sea washes them away."

"Are we exchanging resumes?" I asked.

"I'm hoping we ... share some interests," Emerson said.

"Flash answers," I said. "Favorite movie?"

"Ouch!" he said. "I love so many. I have to watch horror and fantasy ... professional requirement ...

but I like old musicals, too. Adventures. Comedies. Favorite band ...?"

"Same ouch," I said. "Dance music, mostly pop, I'm afraid. I hear way too much country and spiritual ... not enough ballads. School ...?"

"Three years, one at Harvard," Emerson said. "I've tried for three degrees, but never lasted more than a year in any college; my job pulls me away. I enjoy learning. Favorite food ...?"

"Italian ... or seafood," I said. "You ...?"

"Japanese," Emerson said. "Actually, I love Mexican, but it's so heavy. I try to never clear a plate ... on stage, every ounce shows. Mountains or ocean ...?"

"Ocean to live, mountains whenever I can," I said. "I've never lived by an ocean, yet I love beaches. Pets ...?"

"I love animals, but I usually set them free," Emerson said. "Or I give them away. Birds and rabbits. I once had a monkey ... I used him in my act. You ...?"

"I've got a cat, Mephistopheles, but I love all ..."

"You named your cat Mephistopheles ...?" Emerson exclaimed.

I blushed, and we both chuckled.

"I'd just seen Cats," I said. "I liked his song."

"Very interesting ...!" Emerson mimicked Tim Conway's voice.

"Don't you like cats?" I asked.

"Cats are fine ... because they're cats," Emerson said. "Most people wouldn't be friends with a human who treats them like cats do."

"So, not a cat-lover," I said. "Ambitions ...?"

Emerson sighed and looked serious.

"I'd rather hear about yours," he said.

"I asked first," I countered.

"I've traveled a lot," Emerson said, leaning back and looking out at the starlit sea. "Europe, South America, and parts of Asia and Africa. I don't have goals like most people ... a huge house, servants, swimming pool ... my goals are ... find and stay with the right person. Where we live doesn't matter."

We both sighed.

"You ...?" he asked.

I shrugged.

"Not having to work," I said. "Retirement ... someplace where people are doing different things, and there's lots to do. North Dakota is great if you want the same thing every night. I went to a local restaurant before I left; it was packed ... and I knew everyone. I like having friends I've known my whole life, but ... I know every conversation within half a sentence ..."

"I know that feeling," Emerson said. "We've a lot in common. Family?"

"Mother, and two brothers who won't speak to each other," I said.

"Family can be frustrating," Emerson said.

"What's your family like ...?" I asked.

"Don't have one," Emerson said. "Foster care ... taken by the state. No idea why. Not an orphan ... as far as I know. I knew my mother ... before she moved away. She left me with her friends, and didn't say good-bye. She moved to Wisconsin, then Denver, then Idaho. I never knew where in Idaho she moved to, and I've no idea if she's still there."

I looked at him curiously. Emerson shrugged.

"Criminal history ...?" Emerson asked.

"I once shoplifted on a dare," I said. "I didn't get caught, yet I took it back and left it on their doorstep in the middle of the night. You ...?"

"Foster care's a rough life," Emerson said. "A few things, long ago ... petty stuff."

"Like what?" I asked.

"Trespassing ... living in an abandoned house," I said. "I once borrowed a bicycle ... never meant to steal it, but some boys were chasing me. I didn't return it to the place I'd taken it from ... and someone had seen. A few college parties got too wild ..."

We fell silent and stared as the bright moon glowed reflections upon the eternally dancing waves.

"One more question," Emerson said. "Can I put my arm around you?"

"Yes," I smiled.

After a long, pleasant while, we talked again. He claimed that he'd like to believe that some invisible friend was watching over him, but no one had ever looked after him but himself. He read popular books so that he could follow trends, but when left alone, he read a variety of fantasy, mythology, and non-fiction psychology books. He'd read many classics and could quote some; I tested him on this only because I love to hear a man recite Shakespeare. He could also quote Twain and Dickens. A shiver, that had nothing to do with temperature, ran down my spine.

I told him of the mystery and romance books I read; my non-fiction was mostly about sales.

"So ... you read mysteries ...?" he asked, pretending deep concern. "I guess my secrets won't stay hidden much longer."

"Do you fear smart women?" I asked.

"What would I have in common with a dumb woman?" he asked.

That night, we stayed in his hotel room. I'd insisted, and was surprised at how sparse it was. A single mailed box held almost everything he carried, and a hand-written notebook of expenses was stuffed with new receipts sticking out the top. His white suit was the only thing hanging in his closet. Men are lucky that they don't need the wardrobe women require.

That night required no wardrobe ...

Chapter 6

At 6:30 AM, fingers gently traced lines up and down my back. I became dimly aware of waves crashing on the beach, warm arms holding me ... and desire. We made love again in a miasma of magic. When finished, I rose and pulled his heavy curtains apart a few inches; Emerson's room was on the third floor and faced the ocean. Overheated from lovemaking, I reached through the sheer inner curtains and opened his sliding glass door, relishing in Hawaii's cool breeze. The roar of each wave rose louder and more distinct than in my room. I grinned through the tiny crack in the curtains, standing naked in the dawn, as early beachcombers looked for shells not far below. I felt a giddy naughtiness ... as if secret lovers from my novels were admiring my naked flesh.

Arms wrapped around my waist and a kiss graced my shoulder.

"Would you like to do ... something physical tomorrow?" he asked.

"I thought we just did ...," I said.

"I was thinking ... an outrigger canoe," Emerson said. "I can get us a reservation."

"I don't know how ...," I said.

"Nothing like that," Emerson said. "It's a group thing ... with an instructor who takes you on a tour ... but paddling is required."

"Sounds interesting," I said.

"I'm free at the same time tonight ... unless I have to sign autographs," Emerson said.

"I'll be waiting near the bar," I promised.

"I slipped a business card in your purse," Emerson said. "My personal card with contact info, not the card I give to fans."

"I have to get going," I said.

"I don't have your phone number," he reminded me.

"Good," I said. "That means you need to be nice to me ...!"

Several kisses later, in last night's clothes and with my sandals in hand, I rode the elevator up to my room. There I showered, dressed, and made my way to a quick breakfast with a most-delicious cup of coffee, then hurried to the trade show.

Marge ran up to me before I'd even started unpacking.

"You lucky girl ...!"

"And again this morning," I smiled at her.

Eyes and smile widened.

"He's cute!" Marge said. "Did you get his number ...?"

"I got his everything ... in everywhere," I answered, and she squealed in delight. "What about you? How many margaritas did you have?"

"Enough to enjoy a long conversation ... not enough to ruin a marriage," Marge said. "He was an old retired guy ... invited me to join him at the Elk's Club tonight."

"Are you going?" I asked.

"Talking to a nice man in a bar isn't cheating," Marge said. "Meeting that same man on what could only be called a date ...? I don't think I could explain that ..."

The morning passed without a nibble. Some days are like that. Sunday attendance was low; sometimes I could look in both directions and see nothing but vendors playing on phones.

Marge had her booth-mate watch my things, and we went for lunch together. She wanted explicit details; size, shape, and positions, yet I refused.

"I can't tell you more than I'd want Emerson telling his friends about me," I said. "Trust me ... we've done about half of everything in a trashy novel."

"Saving the best for later?" Marge asked. "Where's he going after you leave? Where does he live?"

"I ... don't know," I said. "It's early ... I don't even know if we have a relationship. So far, it's just a Hawaiian fling ... but I'm hoping ...!"

"When do you leave?" Marge asked.

"Tuesday ... afternoon," I said.

"Not a lot of time to set the hook," Marge said.

"We're nowhere near 'hooks'," I insisted.

"He's hot and magical," Marge said. "What are you waiting for?"

"The parts I don't know ... the sides no one shows to strangers," I said.

"Cautious lovers make lousy novels," Marge said.

"Novels end," I said. "Happily-ever-after isn't real."

"Get the romance while you can," Marge warned. "Mine can't say thank you when I bring him a beer so he doesn't miss a second of televised sports ... and he watches every game."

Late that evening, a different band was playing. Sweet jazz alternated between fast and slow. I sat waiting, imagining his show, and wondering how it was going. On time, as one of my favorite songs was playing, Emerson arrived.

"Do you like sports?" I asked.

"Only when the person I'm with wants to watch," Emerson said. "I enjoy sports, but I'm a doer more than a spectator. Anything is fun if you do it together."

"Hobbies ...?" I asked.

"Have you been sitting here dreaming up questions?" Emerson asked.

"Pretty much," I said.

A new, spritely song began.

"One question ... then dance," Emerson said.

"Where do you live?" I asked.

"Today ... here," Emerson said. "Let's go."

Emerson knew only the basics of ballroom dance, yet he was amazing at free-style. We attempted to dance a jitterbug, and free-styled to a fast song that kept changing tempo, and then a slow song began. He wrapped his arms tightly around me. I squeezed against him until the last note. I wanted to whisper something romantic ... to tell him how I felt ... yet I didn't want to scare him off ... or find out that I'd never see him again.

I took a deep breath on the way back to our table. I couldn't stay in Hawaii and I didn't want this to end. I needed a safe subject.

"Canoe ...?" I asked.

"Tomorrow at 1:30 ... just up the beach about six blocks," Emerson said. "I thought we could have lunch

70

first."

"Emerson, where is this going?" I asked. "I ... ?"

The waitress arrived and Emerson requested two lemonades and some won-ton taco appetizers.

"Penelope, we just met, and if we weren't both visiting Hawaii, then it would be too early for this conversation," Emerson said.

I nodded my head.

"I got a call today ... another job starting Friday," Emerson said. "I fly out Thursday."

"Where ...?" I asked.

"Georgia," Emerson said.

"Atlanta ...?" I asked.

"Yes," Emerson said. "Have you been there?"

"No, but I may have made a sale to a company from there," I said.

"Well, I need to be there by noon on Friday, with all my props," Emerson said. "To answer your earlier question, I was born in Kansas, raised in Mississippi. Every foster home I lived in started there. My last foster family moved to Wisconsin, but I don't know anyone in either state ... not anymore. I've lived mostly in New York City, Vegas, and Washington, DC. I travel the circuits, and like actors, there're places we know ... flop houses. We all chip in on expenses, sometimes we get a bed or couch ... or a spot on the floor ... it depends on how many are there. Good venues like this pay for hotels. I don't have a permanent home ... which isn't saying I'd object to one, but I need to travel. I'd like to visit North Dakota, but ...!"

"No magic acts in North Dakota ...?" I asked.

"None that I know of," Emerson said. "However, that's not the problem ..."

"What ...?" I asked.

"No one has invited me ...!" Emerson leaned close and whispered as if this were a secret.

I laughed.

"I have a one bedroom apartment, but I have to warn you; anyone seen walking in or out of my apartment will be the local topic of discussion for weeks," I said.

"Sounds wonderful," Emerson said.

"That includes my family," I said.

"Can't wait to meet them," Emerson said.

"I ... this isn't a promise ... or a commitment," I said. "We still need to get to know each other."

"Of course," Emerson said. "But can we dance first?"

The dance floor was crowded, and some of the dancers were drunk, stumblers, or way too excited. We danced two dances, then returned to our waiting won-ton tacos, which had three dips: teriyaki, ginger aioli, and coconut lime.

Again, we walked the sidewalks of Waikiki in the cool evening breeze. Tiki torches lit doors to popular establishments. Hawkers offered late-night deals to touristy attractions. Lots of young people walked about. Music was playing from everywhere, and we slipped into what looked like a mall of shops, which turned out to be a fancy hotel built around three floors of souvenir stores, restaurants, and boutiques.

Orange and blue birds of paradise grew out of planters, and another hula dancing demonstration was happening. We joined in the crowd, watched, and applauded. Then they invited several people in the audience to come up on stage and learn to hula. I would've refused, but Emerson took my arm and held up his hand, and soon we joined eight other tourists willing to embarrass themselves before total strangers.

I was so self-conscious that I remembered nothing of the steps afterwards, but we were better than most, and had lots of fun. I wondered how Emerson could stand working on stage with everyone watching. Then, as we started back to our seats, someone recognized him.

"You're him, aren't you?" a man with a heavy Indonesian accent asked. "The magician ... we saw your act!"

"Emmerich the Amazing," Emerson said, and he shook their hand. "I hoped you liked my show ...!"

"Mr. Emmerich, can we have a photo?" the man asked.

The hula dancers were delighted, and drug us back onto their stage. We spent ten minutes taking photos. Emerson insisted I be in some, but then he posed with several families, and with the hula dancers. I felt nervous, but allowed that this was part of dating an entertainer ... assuming that we were dating.

Emerson gave a card to each family, not the card with his phone number. He finished by making three rosebuds magically appear, and he gave one to each of the lady-hula dancers. Everyone applauded, and he bowed.

Soon we were back on the sidewalk, headed for the main street. Arm-in-arm, we slowly made our way back to our hotel.

We spent the night in my room with the lights off and the sliding glass door open ... and the things we did that night I'll never tell anyone.

Chapter 7

Blowing into my room all night, the cool ocean breeze forced us to cuddle for warmth ... and neither of us were in a hurry to leave. We indulged in the passions of budding romance, ravenous, slightly awkward, testing limits and thrilling to pleasures, touches, and intimacies. Yet, half-past nine, as the morning sun lit paradise, we took our first shower together, and explorations of each other's limits began anew.

Wrapped in towels, we left the steam. Emerson sat on the bed.

"You will get wet today," Emerson said.

"I assumed," I said, and I pulled out my floral one-piece swimsuit.

"No red bikini ...?" Emerson grinned.

"Never again ...!" I promised. "Look what happened the one time ...!"

"That's okay; I'll watch you put on ... or take off ... anything," Emerson grinned.

I tightened the towel covering me.

"I'm not performing on your stage!" I insisted.

Emerson laughed, and I sent him off to his room to dress without a sneak-peek.

Emerson took me to a small, elegant Italian restaurant. We were both under-dressed for the setting, but we wouldn't have time to change. We sat beside tall wine racks and had one of my best meals ever. I had a rich, meaty lasagna, and it was a fabulous new experience in taste.

Afterwards, we walked more than four long blocks to face our adventure.

I wore a light windbreaker and shorts over my swimsuit. Emerson wore shorts and a gaudy orange Hawaiian shirt swimming with tropical fish. We arrived at our destination, and I stared at the long, narrow outrigger canoes with no small trepidation. However, when a tiny crowd had gathered, a shirtless, muscular young Hawaiian man came out and gave us instructions on what we'd be doing, and a quick rowing lesson. The ka'ele, or hull of each ship, had two arched iako, or outrigger booms, which connected to the ama, the long, outrigger float, which looked like a stabilizer to balance us when waves hit.

We were divided into teams, each with a Ho'okele, a steerer, who would sit in the back and guide us. Our Ho'okele knew how to Hoe, or paddle, and how to Kahi, to hold the paddle still so its blade 'cuts' the same line as the canoe.

Emerson stood behind me near the Ho'okele, and the five guests before me were a family with three children. Together we grabbed our beached canoe and slid it into the frothing sea, and then performed the 'E'e, where we all jumped into the boat.

I wasn't an expert, and certainly not athletic, but I managed, and only got my sandals slightly wet. Then we were floating. As our Ho'okele commanded, we picked up our oars and started to row.

One of the kids before me splashed their oar across the froth, and sent a spray of salt water into my face. I sputtered as their mother apologized, and their father chastised them and showed them how to paddle properly ... as we'd just been instructed. I gritted my teeth, wondering if I was going to get soaked, and paddled hard just to prove I could do it. Sadly, my first attempt hurled water all over Emerson and our Ho'okele. However, both only laughed.

We were supposed to match our rowing to the pace of the calls of our Ho'okele. Most of us couldn't, not even Emerson. Then we were supposed to swap sides, on which we were paddling, in unison ... without splashing each other or missing the beat. All of us failed. I frequently dripped onto the back of the young boy before me, soaking his t-shirt, and his splashes drenched my chest. I got our Ho'okele so wet that he nicknamed me 'Rain-Maker'. I grimaced, yet Emerson thought this moniker was hilarious.

Our excursion actually proved more successful than I'd expected. Despite being amateurs, we managed considerable speed, and raced the other boat over a mile up the beach. We rested several times, and each time our Ho'okele recited a speech on the history of outrigger canoes and modern canoe races, which in many places are considered a popular sport.

Emerson had brought a sealed plastic bag in which we'd placed our phones and wallets. We took them out and snapped photos during our breaks, and finally we rowed back. We'd been rowing the waves for an hour and a half, and my arms were sore when we beached and hauled our canoe back up onto the sand.

Emerson tipped our Ho'okele generously, and we walked away wet and salty, yet delighted. Before we reached the main streets, the Hawaiian sun and breeze had dried our clothes, and we were laughing, holding hands tightly. I was glad we'd gone rowing; I wanted to do that again someday.

"*Emmerich ...!*" cried a woman's voice.

A gorgeous Hawaiian woman came running toward us. She spread her arms wide and threw herself against Emerson, large boobs first, hugging him tightly.

"*Susan ...!*" Emerson cried.

"Aunt Susan!" she corrected him. "I have a nephew!"

"Congratulations!" Emerson said, and he extricated himself from her enticements. "Susan, this is Penelope."

I stared. Susan was beautiful, clearly Hawaiian, with voluptuous boobs pushed up high, tall and thin, with thick, long black hair.

"Hello!" Susan smiled at me, nodding politely.

"Congratulations," I said, looking askance at her familiarity with Emerson.

"I told you about her," Emerson said to me. "This is Suzzannia the Sorceress, whom I came to fill in for."

"You were great!" Susan said. "We got four comments online. And I'm grateful; I got to watch my nephew birthed. I'm trying to talk Robin into having one."

"Where's Robin?" Emerson asked.

"Giving surfing lessons," Susan said. "He's working for the Hyatt now."

Susan turned to me.

"So, how did you two meet ...?" Susan asked.

"Shared a cab from the airport," Emerson said.

"That's quite a coincidence ...!" Susan said,

eyeing Emerson.

"Don't embarrass her," Emerson hissed.

"I never embarrass anyone!" Susan scolded him.

"I've seen your act," Emerson laughed at her, and he reached out and took my hand. "Penelope is special ..."

"Good," Susan said. "Emerson needs his wings clipped ..."

"Susan ...!" Emerson warned.

"He's a ... tall Menehune," Susan said to me. "Watch him closely."

"A tall what ...?" I asked.

"Hawaiian legend," Emerson sighed. "Menehunes are mischievous magical dwarfs who inhabit the hidden forests and valleys of Hawaii's islands."

"Menehunes use magic arrows to pierce the hearts of couples," Susan grinned.

"We'll be real careful," I promised, narrowing my eyes.

Susan appeared to be loud and brash, and I wasn't sure if she was an ally or a threat. Fortunately, I noticed that she wore a wedding ring, which slightly eased my mind.

"Don't you need to be going ...?" Emerson asked in a forceful tone.

Susan reached out and squeezed my free hand. Then she gave Emerson a kiss on the cheek, whispered something in his ear, and walked off into the crowd of tourists.

Emerson shook his head.

"What'd she say?" I asked.

"Nothing," Emerson said.

"Keeping secrets ...?" I asked.

"Only when they're embarrassing," Emerson said.

"Now I have to know ...," I said.

"You will," Emerson said. "Not today."

"Why not?" I asked.

Emerson turned to look at me.

"I could say that she said you were cute," Emerson said. "You've no way to know if it was a lie, and I'd be off the hook. However, I don't like to lie. Yes, there are things about me you don't know yet, but I want us to learn together, not the wrong way ... from blabbermouths. Susan's a drama queen; can't see a fire without adding gasoline."

"Will I know all your secrets?" I asked, tracing a printed fish on his Hawaiian shirt.

"I hope so ... but there's a price," Emerson said.

We kissed ... a quick, playful peck, yet with intense sincerity.

He led me into a tourist shop, which turned out to be mostly an art gallery ... obviously to change the subject. I let the matter drop. I had a past, too; numerous relationships I regretted, and I wasn't ready to reveal everything. We walked through the gallery, talked to one of the artists, and spent the afternoon playing tourist.

I tried not to think that I'd be on a plane tomorrow ... headed home. As we walked through little gift shops, I clung to Emerson's arm.

Finally we went back to our hotel to wash off the salt and dress for dinner. I'd brought both of the room keys I'd been given. I gave one to Emerson and sent him to his room to fetch clean clothes, and then come bathe with me. I was determined to give him every reason to keep our relationship going ... even after I flew home.

When he arrived, I greeted him wearing nothing but my red bikini.

Emerson took me into the shower still dressed, and removed my bikini delightfully slowly.

"What is it with you and showers ...?" I teased.

"No point in wasting soapy-naked opportunities," Emerson smiled.

An hour later, we arrived in the lobby dressed for a night on the town. After our great Italian lunch, neither of us wanted a heavy meal, so Emerson took us to a little hamburger joint only blocks from our hotel. This swinging joint was decorated from the 1950s with jukeboxes, photos from 77 Sunset Strip and Route 66, statues of Jerry Lee Louis and Marilyn Monroe, and cardboard cutouts of Bogart and Vincent Price. We split a Hawaiian burger and fries, and then went searching for an evening of adventure.

Through the course of the evening, we visited three different nightclubs, all loud and crowded with long lines, but every bouncer knew Emerson. We were quickly ushered into each place we visited. When we weren't escorted to a reserved table, we luckily found places to sit. We danced before live bands playing wide varieties of music. The first was a cover band of 80's hits, the next was loud and fast and had a light show flashing so brightly that I could hardly see the stage. The last was hip-hop, with a younger crowd, including many teenagers. We only had one drink there, danced a few songs, and then left.

It was past midnight and we were tired, yet Emerson insisted that we visit one last place ... a small tea shop. I wouldn't have even noticed it. From the street, it was just a shadowy glass doorway with a tiny sign. Inside, a long hallway led to a large, dim room with harp music playing softly from hidden speakers. We were seated at a table, and the waitress set ceramic cups before us and proceeded to fill them with steaming tea.

After the loudness of the nightclubs, I could barely hear the gentle strums of harps.

Emerson lifted his tea cup and motioned for me to do the same. We clinked cups and drank. It was a spicy tea, not too strong.

"So ... what's your preference?" Emerson asked. "Which club ...?"

"The first was the most danceable," I said. "I couldn't see anything in the second ..."

"I'm usually in the mood for the first," Emerson said. "They're all fun, but impossible to speak in. I know you have to go home tomorrow; I wanted to show you everything."

"Have you shown me everything?" I asked.

"Not yet," Emerson said. "Mostly ... but it may take some time to digest. I just wanted to make tonight ... special."

"You've got a show in Georgia," I said. "How long before we'll see each other again?"

"As soon as I can make it," Emerson said. "Penelope, I've got one thing I'd like to tell you tonight."

I almost dropped my tea cup. Emerson set his down when I did.

"It's nothing bad," Emerson said. "It's quite good, actually. But it's mundane ... about money ... never an easy topic."

"What is it?" I asked. "Broke ...? In debt ...?"

"Quite the opposite," Emerson said. "How do you think I can afford my hotel room for the rest of the week ... with only five shows? Penelope, I like my job ... I like doing shows ... but I don't need to work all the time."

"You ... you're rich?" I asked, eyes wider than I wanted them.

"Not exactly," Emerson said. "I couldn't retire. Yet I don't have ... a lack of funds ..."

"You were raised in foster care ...," I started.

"It's not an inheritance ... or bank robbery; nothing illegal," Emerson said. "I just wanted you to know ... I'm not a starving artist. I hadn't planned on meeting you ... or anyone ... or I'd be flying out with you. Yet, we will be seeing each other soon ... if I'm still invited. That's a promise."

I blew him a soft kiss and he blew one back at me. We both smiled, raised our tea cups, and clinked them again.

Love-making that night was different, more passionate, less playful. Depth and intensity I hadn't expected overflowed, and lasted longer than our usual lovemaking. We climaxed repeatedly, then held on to each other as if unwilling to let go.

Jay Palmer

Chapter 8

I laid awake for hours, listening to ocean waves and watching Emerson sleep. I didn't know when I awoke ... or merely shifted from dreams in my mind to dreams in my bed. I'd miss both the waves and Emerson. He was beautiful, at least to me, his smooth skin and soft touch. I couldn't help feeling excited; his sudden intrusion into my life opened possible futures I'd thought dead for a year; my life shared, perhaps marriage and children, never again feeling alone. These were fancies; we'd only known each other a week ... and half of that I'd spent trying to avoid him.

How could I be thinking of forever with a man I'd barely begun to know?

In only six hours, I'd be on a plane flying back to North Dakota, thousands of miles from Hawaii. He'd be alone on this tropical paradise... with hundreds of bikini-clad girls walking around every day.

Would he call me ... or move on to his next gullible tourist?

If he did move on, if I never saw him again, then would the doors he'd opened close and stay locked forever? Would I ever be able to open them again ...?

Love; we hadn't known each other long enough to suggest it. That word, spoken too early, ruined relationships. Yet how could I let him leave without telling him? We only had a few hours left!

His breath fluttered against my skin. I wanted to wake him, to ravish him while I could, but I loved watching him sleep. He worked evenings; normally I'd be on my third cup of coffee while he was still lost in dreams. I wondered how softly I could play with his body without awakening him; probably not much, so I laid quietly beside him ... imagining.

When he awoke, I pounced on him like a hungry tigress. I couldn't cum too fast or hard enough, and we made love in primal savagery. He tried to say something, but I cupped his mouth with my hand, then smothered him with something infinitely softer. I wanted him ... and needed him to feel my desires.

Panting, we collapsed sweating, covers thrown aside.

"Too ... hot ...," Emerson muttered, and he rose, stumbled to the heavy curtains, pushed them open, and flung open the sliding glass door.

"Eeeeek ...!" I eked.

I grabbed the edge of my twisted sheets, pulling them over me. The sheer curtain blew wildly ... and Emerson was standing naked before it, relishing in the cool, sunlit breeze. He turned his back to the ocean wind, letting the sheer curtain stick to his sweat-wet back. Then he saw me, covering my nakedness, and laughed.

"People can see ...!" I hissed.

Emerson closed the heavy curtains, yet left the door to my balcony open.

"Modesty ... after all that ...?" Emerson chuckled.

"That was for your eyes," I said.

86

"Do you really think people in that hotel ...," he pointed toward the curtains, "... stayed up all night, and are ignoring the beautiful view of dawn over the ocean, in the hopes of spying a brief glance from four hundred yards away ...?"

"Don't think my body's worth it ...?" I asked.

He came back over and kissed me.

"I do, but they wouldn't know," Emerson said. "I hate to say it; I'm hungry."

"Where would you like to go?" I asked.

"Wherever's closest," Emerson said.

We showered and I dressed. Emerson put on my robe. Then we walked to his room. While he dressed, I checked my make-up in the mirror outside his bathroom, and absently noticed the closet behind me. Three Hawaiian shirts hung on hangers today, one red, one floral, and one with little gray sharks, hanging beside his white suit. When Emerson had his shorts and sandals on, he came in and grabbed the latter.

"What happened to your other shirt?" I asked.

"Other ...?" Emerson asked.

"The dark one with the sunset ...?" I asked.

"When clothes get dirty I stuff them in a bag," Emerson said. "I'll be right out."

Emerson stepped into his bathroom and closed his door. I heard him sit down ... and hurried to his dresser. Quietly I slid open his drawers and found nothing in them, then closed them. He had no suitcase. Where were his dirty clothes ... let alone his clean socks and underwear? Stage magicians had to be mysterious, but in all the times I'd been in his room, I'd never seen the necessities ...

I was about to leave my heart with a man of mystery ...

I must be crazy ...!

I considered looking under his bed, but heard the toilet flush. When Emerson emerged, I was holding back his heavy curtain and looking at distant, early beach-walkers. Some woman not much older than me was already laying on a towel on the sand, alone, her nose in a book. If I hadn't met Emerson, that might be me.

I was betting my hopes upon a man about whom I had more questions than answers ...!

He dropped his Stetson onto his head and held the door for me.

We ate buffet in the Golden Aloha. An omelet chef was there, and we had custom-made omelets stuffed with our favorites ... and Emerson gulped orange juice and ate buttered toast while I sipped coffee and chewed bacon.

I chastised myself. I shouldn't have been snooping ... or I should've looked under his bed first.

If anyone could put on a convincing act, it was Emerson.

He could be a master player ... playing me.

I wasn't stupid. I'd have noticed if something was amiss.

I didn't need another failed romance.

My red bikini; *would I thank my girlfriends or curse their lewdness ...?*

"You don't have long," Emerson said. "I'll take you to the airport ..."

"No," I said. "I want our last moment to be ... private."

"Last moment ...?" Emerson asked. "We'll see each other ..."

"When ...?" I asked.

"After my show in Atlanta," Emerson said. "I'll be on a plane to North Dakota ... with you."

"With me ...?" I asked.

Emerson shook his head.

"To be with you," Emerson corrected himself. "Penelope, I ... I can't lose you. You mean ... so much to me."

"I wish we could both stay in Hawaii," I said.

"No, you don't," Emerson said. "You have a life, family, a home. I want to be a part of it. But tell me; if you had to leave it, at least, if you were on the road with me, and only came back a few times a year, would that be acceptable?"

"Exactly what are you asking ...?" I prodded.

"Nothing ... that we've known each other long enough to say," Emerson said, and he took my hand in his. "Yet ... all those words I can't say: I mean them."

I blushed, rose, kissed him, and went to get more bacon. I didn't dare keep talking ... lest I say aloud the word we hadn't known each other long enough to say.

After breakfast, we walked along the morning beach, hand-in-hand, smiling ear-to-ear. I had a million questions, but only one mattered; *the one I couldn't ask.*

I drank in the tropical sights, sounds, and smells of Hawaii. I'd miss them every minute for weeks. How would I be able to sleep without rushes of crashing surf?

How would I be able to sleep ... without Emerson ...?

Emerson showed me his watch; I obediently said 'yes', and we walked back to the hotel.

I asked Emerson to wait in the lobby. He objected, but I said 'please', and he nodded. I rode the elevator alone. If Emerson stepped anywhere near my bed I'd miss my flight.

Fifteen minutes later I was packed and ready. Purse and computer hanging from different shoulders, I wheeled my work case and suitcase to the elevator and down.

Emerson rose as I stepped out of the elevator. I pulled my cases toward him, and he frowned.

"You're crying," he said.

Emerson kissed me, and then he reached up, plucked his Stetson off his head ... and dropped it atop mine.

"Hold onto this for me," Emerson said.

Sobs burst. I hugged him tightly.

I didn't want to go ...!

"Security at the airport," Emerson reminded.

He waited while I checked out, then he pulled my work case, with my big screen and displays for the trade show, and I took my luggage ... with all my new dresses and souvenirs. On the street, Emerson hailed a cab, and one appeared almost instantly.

"What are you going to do today?" I asked.

"The Majestic Dinner Theater," Emerson said. "I've got to find a laundromat, wash, dry, then pack my boxes, and mail them to Atlanta. Maybe I'll watch Susan ... Suzzannia the Sorceress; her husband and I shill for her."

"Isn't that cheating?" I asked.

"Not all tricks are sorcery," Emerson said.

We both laughed, and then we kissed. The taxi driver grunted softly and closed his trunk loudly; he had loaded all my suitcases.

"Good-bye," I said.

"Aloha," Emerson corrected.

I got into the taxi. Emerson closed my door and blew me a kiss as the driver pulled out into traffic. I blew him one back, but then a truck blocked my view of him, and I'm not sure if he saw.

I was wearing his Stetson ...!

I took it off and looked at it, caressing it gently.

"Nice hat," said the driver. "Wish I could afford one."

"My boyfriend just gave it to me," I said.

"Must be rich," the taxi driver said. "Or ... he really likes you."

"Why ...?" I asked.

"A three hundred dollar Stetson ...?" he glanced at me in the mirror.

My mouth fell open.

"Seriously ...?" I asked.

On the way to the airport, he recited everything he knew about hats. His favorite was top-hats, but he had a bowler, a bomber cap with goggles, a ten-gallon cowboy hat, and collector sports caps of many teams, including some that had broken up decades ago.

I kept caressing Emerson's valuable Stetson.

I checked my suitcases in the airport lobby, then headed to the security line. It looked a mile long, and everyone in it seemed angry.

"What a waste!" the woman in front of me lamented, catching my eye. "I could've spent another two hours on the beach ... instead of standing in this pointless line."

"I can think of a lot of things I'd rather be doing," I agreed.

"With a man ...?" she asked, and she drew out one of those little packets of tissues and handed me one. "Fix your eyes, dear; your mascara's running."

I took the tissue and wiped my eyes.

"Tear-proof, my ass," I sniffed.

She nodded.

"I know how it feels," she said. "Where are you headed?"

I told her about North Dakota, how excited my boss was about my possible sale, and how I was looking forward to seeing my friends and family. She didn't believe of word of it, yet she nodded and told me about her late husband and how much she missed him ... now that he was gone. Before, she'd complained constantly; he couldn't wash a dish, or hold a door, or a thousand other things she'd always wanted him to do. Yet none of that mattered anymore.

For some reason, she talked about a cruise ship to Alaska; their last trip together. They'd gone shopping at every port and spent a day riding a train just for the view. She was just telling me about this beautiful Eskimo-made blanket she'd bought when we had to remove our shoes and walk through monitors ... which we both hated. On the other side, she wished me well; she was on a different airline and had to hurry or miss her flight.

I thanked her again.

"He's probably feeling just the way you are right now," she assured me, and then she walked away.

I glanced at my purse, which held my phone. I wanted to call him, but didn't want to appear desperate.

I found my terminal, checked at the desk to make sure I was at the right one, and sat down in a chair to wait.

If Emerson was coming to North Dakota then I seriously needed to clean my apartment.

If ...!

Thirty-five minutes later, my plane taxied out onto the runway, and its engines started to rev.

As we rose into the air, I stared out at Oahu, drinking in every last sight of it. The buildings grew tiny ... then they were dots, and then only ocean and clouds.

I wasn't in Hawaii anymore.

Somewhere behind me, in coach, a child started to complain. Emerson wasn't here to do his magic pencil trick. I started to cry.

My flight attendant was male. He offered me a mimosa. I asked if he could make me a blended margarita, but he didn't have the fixings. I took the mimosa ... and then another.

Tipsy in Seattle, I had to get help finding my connecting flight to Minneapolis, where I ordered more drinks.

Hours later, home in North Dakota, I stumbled my way off the small shuttle plane from Minneapolis, staggering into other passengers. The long ramp from the plane to the terminal tilted wildly, and someone asked if I needed help.

I didn't need help; *I had Emerson's hat!*

"Penelope!" cried a familiar voice, yet it sounded alarmed. Strong hands grabbed me. I looked up into a face I'd known most of my life, but it wasn't Emerson; it was Julie.

"What the hell ...?" Julie gasped, looking at me.

"It's your faulttttt ...!" I slurred. *"You and thatttt ... red bikini!"*

I don't remember getting my luggage or driving home. I knew where I was, but I couldn't see any palm trees.

"Drunk as a skunk!" Julie said into her phone. "I'm going to need help getting her up the stairs."

Lyn opened my door, Stacy right behind her.

"She came off the airplane like this," Julie said.

93

"She's drunker now than when I found her."

Next I was in my living room ... and then I was throwing up in my bathroom. All three stood in the doorway, watching, talking ...

I'd no idea what they were saying.

When I finished, I rinsed my mouth at the sink, slogged some minty mouthwash, and spat. All three of them fell silent and stared at me.

"Where's my hat ...?" I demanded.

Julie, Lyn, and Stacy stripped me and put me into my comfortable bed. To placate me, they gave me his hat.

"What's his name?" Stacy demanded. "Penelope, look at me! What's his name ...?"

"Emmerich the Amazing," I said.

Chapter 9

I grabbed my beeping phone and pushed the green blur.

"Hello?"

"Penelope ...?" asked Rosanne's voice.

"Yes ...?"

"Where are you?" she asked.

"Sleeping!" I said. "Why are you calling so early ...?"

"It's eleven o'clock," Rosanne said. "I'm going to lunch."

"Oh, crap!"

I almost stepped on Emerson's hat, which lay on the carpet by my bed. I put it safely on my dresser, then hurried to shower and dress.

I'd missed at least three meetings ...!

My head was spinning and my stomach needed coffee.

Espresso in hand, I arrived at the office four hours late.

"Penelope ...!" Rosanne said, waving me over to her desk and pointing.

On her screen was photo of Emerson.

95

"Emmerich the Amazing ...?" she asked. "You ... and he ...?"

"How ...?" I asked.

"Bismarck Express," Rosanne said, which meant the local gossip channels.

I'm going to kill Julie, Lyn, and Stacy ...!

I looked at his photo longingly.

"We shared a taxi," I said.

"I want every detail ...!" Rosanne said firmly.

Before I could open my mouth, Mr. Dawes, my boss, came out of his office.

"Penelope!" he shouted. "There's my sales-girl! We're having a meeting with Devonshire-Slate Medical on Friday!"

"Who ...?"

"The account you got us!" Mr. Dawes said.

"Oh, yes," I said. "That's great!"

"This could mean big things for us," Mr. Dawes said. "They're one of the largest medical consortiums in the South. Come ... I need to hear all about it."

In his office, I told Mr. Dawes all about the old nurse ... whose name was Mrs. Abigail Bennett, from the moment she appeared at my booth to the instant she left. Mr. Dawes took notes, made me describe her reactions in detail, her attitudes, expressions, everything I could remember. Some of my answers I just invented; my head was hurting and I kept taking sips of coffee to give me time to think. He copied down her joke about 'old-school thermometers' verbatim, insisting that 'details cement deals'.

"Management is going wild," Mr. Dawes said. "Penelope, if this works out, you'll be glad you're part of it. And just think; in three weeks you'll be in Nebraska ...!"

I groaned; the Nebraska Medical Trade Show ... in downtown Lincoln ... compared to Hawaii, it sounded abysmal.

Showered with appreciation, I departed Mr. Dawes' office, glad to get back to my desk and collapse onto my chair. Rosanne kept staring at me.

"Lunch ... Tomorrow," I promised. "I can't talk here."

Emerson's photo was still on her screen.

I spent the remainder of the afternoon reading and replying to emails. However, as soon as Rosanne got up and walked away from her desk, I googled Emmerich the Amazing.

Photos of him littered the internet. Many showed his horrible, flashy purple, green, and yellow suit covered with sparkly rhinestones. Others showed suits equally outlandish. Videos of him performing magic tricks were numerous, many obviously taken from phones in the crowd, yet I didn't watch; I'd want to turn the volume up ... and I didn't want Rosanne to hear what I was watching. I found his web page with his name in flashing letters that turned into rosebuds. This, too, I shut down, as I didn't want to read it here. Hundreds of images showed him posing with fans, some of them pretty girls ...

I closed my browser; *I couldn't cry at work!*

My phone beeped. Rosanne spun around to stare as I tried not to look nervous.

"We'll be coming over right after work," a familiar voice said.

"Thank you, *Lyn ...!*" I said, and Rosanne looked disappointed. "I'm delighted at how quickly you ride the Bismarck Express ...!"

"I didn't tell anyone!" Lyn insisted.

"Someone did ...!"

"It must've been Julie or Stacy."

"How late did you stay at my place?" I asked.

"We left shortly after you passed out," Lyn said.

"I went to sleep," I corrected her.

"I've slept that hard, too," Lyn said.

"Did you go home?" I asked.

"We went to Arnold's," Lyn said. "We ..."

"Who else was there?" I asked.

"Just Gwen, Nancy, Kathy, Joel, Brendan, ..."

"Did they overhear you ...?" I asked.

A long pause followed.

"I've gotta go," Lyn said. "We'll be at your apartment by six."

Every eye in the office followed me. I tried not to notice, but this was Bismarck; I'd eagerly listened as the gossip train disembarked secrets about my friends and coworkers. As the capital of North Dakota, we thought of ourselves as big-city people, but compared to places like LA and New York City, we were just small town yokels.

Secrets were hard to keep in small towns.

If Emerson did come here, he'd be swarmed.

If he never came, I'd be humiliated.

Bonnie stood waiting outside my apartment ... holding a cake and Mephistopheles.

"I heard," Bonnie said.

"Obviously," I shook my head, taking Mephistopheles, who seemed offended that I'd left her at mother's again.

"Spill," Bonnie ordered.

"Julie, Lyn, and Stacy are on their way," I sighed. "I only want to tell it once."

"Red bikini ...?" Bonnie asked.

"We were having sex within twelve hours of his first sight of it," I said.

Bonnie cheered the whole way up the stairs.

Julie, Lyn, and Stacy arrived armed for a siege with food, wine, and a thousand questions. I tried to object, but each of them reminded me that I'd grilled them after countless dates and one-night-stands; my pretense of having a moral high ground fell flat. I'd known Bonnie since preschool, Julie and Stacy since grade school, and Lyn since college; they held no secrets I didn't know.

Between bites of take-out sweet and sour shrimp, almond chicken, and BBQ pork, which Mephistopheles cried about until we gave him some, I told them everything. My turn-around from suspecting Emerson was a stalker to dragging him to my hotel room made them all laugh. I blushed countless times ... which only made them laugh louder.

They emptied the bottle of wine, while I drank tea; I'd need a few days before I started drinking again. Bonnie laughed the loudest.

"Don't you need to be home ...?" I asked her.

Bonnie was married and had four kids, and Stacy was on her second marriage, which was already rocky. Lyn was divorced and dating someone in the army, currently out of state, and Julie was single with two kids, and looking for a husband.

"You need me," Bonnie said.

"I'm fine," I said.

"No, you need me," Bonnie insisted. "Otherwise I have to go home."

The cake was delicious, chocolate with raspberry filling. We ate as I was pressed to describe Emerson's penis.

"No!" I repeated.

"Fine, just point," Lyn said, and she held up a salt shaker in one hand and a tall candle in the other.

"No," I said firmly.

Laughing, Julie lifted up a plastic coffee thermos - I ignored her.

Stacy read aloud Emerson's personal description on his website. Bonnie brought out her tablet, and we watched a video of him doing his magic act in Atlantic City. Lyn sighed and exclaimed over how handsome he was. Julie insisted that she had to visit Hawaii soon.

"Need a red bikini ...?" Bonnie asked her.

"I prefer white," Julie snipped in a saucy voice. "Wet, they're practically invisible!"

"About the only white you could wear ...!" Stacy sniped.

Within twenty minutes, Bonnie, Julie, Lyn, and Stacy were planning my wedding and naming all my children. I complained, but they wouldn't stop. Soon I was touring the world, onstage, as Emerson's magical, lovely assistant, in a dress so short and tight it left no questions, and then we were married and retired to our own private Caribbean island ... where our palatial estate included private bungalows for each of my dearest friends ... and hunky, muscular masseuses to rub lotion onto their tanned skins during their frequent visits.

"That's enough," I said. "I need to unpack, relax, and recover from ..."

"All the sex ...?" Bonnie interjected.

"Good-night!" I said forcefully.

All four objected.

"Before we leave, why don't you call him?" Lyn suggested.

"Yes!" Stacy agreed. "He'll never know we're

here!"

"Because you won't be here ...!" I argued.

"Prince and Princess Penelope Amazing!"
Bonnie laughed.

"Out ...!" I shouted.

My phone beeped. All four stopped and stared
at me. I glanced at my phone, then answered it on
speaker.

"Hello, *mom ...,* " I said.

"I just heard ...!" mom exclaimed.

"Hold on, mom; I'm kicking Bonnie, Julie, Lyn,
and Stacy out my door," I said, pointing. "Good-night!
Stop talking in public!"

They departed laughing, and Mephistopheles
tried to sneak out with them.

The Bismarck Express had visited my family,
and mom was calling to confirm. I gave her an
abbreviated version without details, yet mom was more
interested in my plans to see Emerson again. I told her I
didn't know when, that we both traveled a lot, and no, he
didn't do card tricks in bed.

After she hung up, I walked around. My
cluttered apartment felt terribly lonely. I wondered if
Emerson would ever see it, and if I should clean it up in
case he does ... and if I'd ever hear from him again ...
never ten inches from my phone ... which never beeped.

Jay Palmer

Chapter 10

I didn't want to get out of bed. I shut off the alarm, ignored it, and fell back asleep.

Emerson hadn't called.

I got to work barely on time, barely awake. I attended meetings, was congratulated by salesmen and managers, yet I had nothing new to report. I sat and listened as the latest programming updates were demonstrated. At lunch, Rosanne and I went for pizza, and I was forced to again relate my adventures with Emerson. I gave her a moderate account, more than I'd told my mother, but less than I'd told my friends. Rosanne was delighted, yet speculated more on the bonus I'd get if the Atlanta sale solidified.

As I sat at my desk after lunch, my phone beeped. I grabbed it, dropped it, and fumbled to see who it was.

Emerson ...!

I glanced at Rosanne; she'd turned her chair around to stare at me. I gestured for her to turn back; she smiled and shook her head.

"Hello?"

"I hope this is a good time," Emerson's voice

came over my phone. "I wanted to call yesterday but ... times didn't work out.   Robin took me out on his new boat ..."

"Who ...?"

"Suzzannia the Sorceress' husband," Emerson said. "He got a new boat; he's all excited. We went fishing and barbecued everything at his house last night. Robin had friends over; it got crazy. Susan got home after her act to find her house full. By the time I got out of there, it was 3:00 AM your time."

"Probably best you didn't call," I said.

"Well, I just wanted to let you know," Emerson said. "I'm headed to the airport; my plane leaves in three hours. I'll be staying in the Atlanta South Regency Alms. I have to be onstage at 8:00 PM tomorrow."

"Good to know," I said.

A brief pause.

"Penelope, you ... sound strange," Emerson said. "Am I still invited to Bismarck ...?"

"Of course," I said. "I'm ... at work ..."

I gave Rosanne a death-glare, yet she flashed me a smirky grin.

"Oh, of course!" Emerson said. "Timezones - I just woke up; it's early dawn here. However, I do need to get going. I assume you can't talk now ..."

"Not without others hearing," I explained.

Rosanne stuck out her tongue.

"I'll call from Atlanta; our clocks will be better aligned," Emerson said.

"Sounds perfect," I said.

Long pause.

"You're at work ... you hang up first," Emerson said.

"Don't miss your plane," I said. "Good-bye."

Rosanne stared expectantly, yet I turned to my screen and opened a customer file. Rosanne scowled.

I bit my lower lip to keep from smiling.

Emerson had called ...!

The rest of the day, the stares at the office didn't bother me.

I stopped at the grocery store on the way home, got my usuals and a roasted chicken, which should last me for days. If Emerson was coming, I needed to clean everything.

No one came over uninvited, yet I kept my phone on speaker as I cleaned house, overlapping phone calls from Bonnie, my mother, and Lyn, while scrubbing; I didn't want Emerson to think I lived like a slob. I even carried my laundry down and back while talking on speaker.

Before bed, I washed, slipped on my pajamas, and sat watching late night TV wearing Emerson's hat. I felt foolish, like I was still in high school, but my fear that he'd never call had been alleviated. My reputation was saved. Rosanne lived on the Bismarck Express, and news that Emerson had called would save me from people thinking I'd been dumped after being seduced by a minor celebrity on a brief Hawaiian fling.

I closed my eyes, and wished that I was back in Hawaii ... with Emerson.

Chapter 11

Work started with a three hour meeting attended by several executives. Having repeated my report, I sat silently listening. Mrs. Abigail Bennett turned out to be a Senior Director of Devonshire-Slate Medical, which included seventy-two facilities, ranging from small clinics to hospitals. Fifty-one private medical firms partnered with them.

Rosanne wasn't at her desk at noon, so I snuck out for lunch alone. I took a new book, another mystery, but too many facts and numbers were running through my head to concentrate.

The office fell silent. Everyone important attended the next meeting, which meant that the rest of us could surf social media with no one noticing.

I was closing down multiple windows and packing to go when a cheer came from the meeting room. Managers rushed out, all with busy mouths, discussing success.

"Change of plans," Mr. Dawes said, smiling. "Rosanne, get Penelope plane reservations for Monday and a hotel near the home office of Devonshire-Slate Medical. Get her a rental car, too. Mrs. Abigail Bennett asked for her specifically. Penelope, on Monday, you'll be leading the demonstration, and if things go well, you'll be there most of the week, maybe longer."

"Just me ...?" I asked.

"Bessy Andrews and Nathan Qui will be with you," Mr. Dawes said. "He'll take care of technical details, installing and setting everything up on their network."

"What am I going for ...?" I asked.

"Because Mrs. Abigail Bennett wants you," Mr. Dawes said. "Penelope, we need this. Come into my office."

Twenty minutes later, I walked out of Mr. Dawes office, my eyes bulging.

My yearly bonus, if this went through, would be twice my current monthly salary! In addition to my regular pay ...!

I'd get an office ...! A staff ...! Maybe a raise ...!

"You're scheduled," Rosanne said. "Bismarck to Minneapolis to Atlanta on Sunday, leaving at 9:00 AM."

"Thanks," I said, still dazed. "Hotel ...?"

"Atlanta South Regency Alms," Rosanne said.

"What ...?" I gasped.

"It's the closest nice hotel," Rosanne said. "I'm trying to find you a rental car; I'll have it before I leave."

I stared at her.

"Something wrong ...?" Rosanne asked. "Do you know that hotel ...?"

"No," I said. "But I've ... heard about it."

Another coincidence ...!

Same airport ... coincidence.

Hundreds of passengers; I noticed him in the airport ... coincidence.

Same destination ... coincidence.
Same flight ... coincidence.
Same first class seating ...
Same taxi ...
Same hotel ...
Free pass to his magic act ...
He visited my sales booth ...
Coworkers took me to his magic show ...
Balloon animals at the pool as I walk by in a scandalous red bikini ...
Meeting in the Golden Aloha ...
My referral to a medical conglomerate ... whose home office is in the same city where he's doing his magic act ...
Only days after we said good-bye in Hawaii, I'm boarding a plane to the same city he's in ...
Same hotel ...
I'd named my cat Mephistopheles ...
Too many coincidences ...!!!

I sat down at my desk. The world usually worked against me, never in my favor.

This many accidental situations couldn't be ...!

"Penelope ...?" Rosanne asked. "Are you all right ...?"

"I ... don't know," I said.

I opened a search engine. I typed 'magic act atlanta' and pressed enter.

Top listing: The Illusion Emporium.

I glanced at the map beside a photo of the outside of the theater.

The Illusion Emporium was in the bottom section of Atlanta.

The south-side.

Shivers ran up my spine. I'd had many

suspicions about Emerson ... he'd appeared everywhere I went. He'd allayed my suspicions, but ...!

No! It was madness! Emerson had told me he was going to Atlanta before I'd told him about my contact! He couldn't have known I'd get this sale ... certainly not so quickly ... or that Mrs. Abigail Bennett would ask for me! I normally didn't go on sales presentations! He couldn't have known that the Devonshire-Slate Medical home office was within driving range of The Illusion Emporium!

Too many coincidences ...!

Everything was driving us together.

I wanted us to be together!

But I didn't trust coincidences ...

"Penelope ...?" Rosanne asked again.

I forced myself to calm down. I glanced at my new book sticking out of my purse; before the end of most mysteries, I'd figured out the solution, or limited the guilty down to two or three.

This was just another mystery ...!

I could figure this out ...!

Shivers; I was being manipulated ... like a character in a book ... which meant that I wasn't the author of my own life.

"I need to go," I said to Rosanne. "Could you ... email me everything ...?"

"I already did," Rosanne said. "Except for your rental car ... which should be easy ..."

"Oh, it'll be easy," I said, certain, yet unwilling to admit it.

Rosanne gave me a puzzled look.

On my way home, Lyn called.

"Interested in doing dinner?" Lyn asked. "Julie

was going to meet me at Arnold's, but one of her kids is sneezing ... might have a cold ..."

"Sure," I said. Nothing was waiting for me at home but leftover chicken. "I'm being sent out again ..."

"Already ...?" Lyn asked. "You just got back!"

"Big sale," I said. "I leave on Sunday ..."

"How far from Arnold's are you?" Lyn asked.

"I'm almost home," I said.

"Turn around," Lyn said. "Meet you there in fifteen."

Lyn's car wasn't in the parking lot. I went inside anyway.

"Penelope ...!" Gwen shouted.

Half of the usuals were there; I'd forgotten that this was Friday night. In a few hours, there wouldn't be an empty table in the restaurant.

"Hello Gwen ... Nancy ... Joel," I said, noting the not-full beers in front of them. "Starting early ...?"

"Weekends are for celebrating," Joel said.

"Usual ...?" Becky asked me, reaching for the beer tap, a glass held at the ready.

"No ... passion-fruit lemonade," I said.

"Too many free drinks in first class ...?" Gwen asked.

"The Bismarck Express never misses a stop," I noted. "Who blabbed ...?"

Each assumed an obviously-fake expression of innocence ... even Becky as she poured my drink.

"Be that way ...," I sneered.

"Tell us about Hawaii," Nancy said.

"It's the fiftieth state of the union," I said.

"You know what we mean ...!" Gwen laughed.

I put on my own obviously-fake expression of innocence.

111

"I'm sure you know as much as I do," I lied. "He called, we talked, we've made no plans ..."

"He called you ...?" Nancy asked. "That's something."

"Did he teach you magic tricks?" Joel asked.

"Yes," I smiled. "To not answer questions ...!"

They were still badgering me when Lyn arrived. About six tables were occupied, and I recognized every face ... most I'd gone to high school with ... yet Lyn talked to Rachel and got us a table as far apart from any listeners as possible. I smiled and carried my drink to join her as complaints chorused from the bar. She wanted to talk about Bonnie, but stopped the instant that she saw the look on my face.

"Have you told Emmerich ...?" Lyn asked.

"I'm not pregnant!" I sneered. "And ... please, call him Emerson."

"What's the problem?" she asked.

"I'm having doubts," I said.

A wild idea entered my mind.

What if I didn't tell him ...? What if I just showed up ...?

"Phone him," Lyn said.

"I will," I said, not sure if I would.

"Now," Lyn insisted.

"Stage magicians work evenings," I said. "I couldn't bother him before a show."

"I wish my life was interesting," Lyn said.

"When's Ivan coming back?" I asked.

"He doesn't know," Lyn said. "No time soon."

"Who else are you dating ...?" I asked.

"No one," Lyn said. "What's wrong ...? Did Emerson call ...?"

"He called," I said. "We talked. He was in a

112

hurry ... plane to catch."

"Where ...?" Lyn asked.

"Not here," I said, and Lyn looked disappointed. "He said he wants to ... stay in touch."

"That's all ...?" Lyn asked.

"If I tell you, Stacy will hear, you can't leave out Julie, Bonnie will make you tell her ... and all of you will claim you didn't breathe a word ... but everyone will know."

"Like you never fueled the Bismarck Express ...!" Lyn scowled.

Rachel came up with a beer for Lyn and asked if we planned to eat.

We both knew their menu and ordered our favorites.

"This is different," I said after Rachel left. "I'm not sure ... if I want to see him again."

"What did he say ...?" Lyn asked. "I won't tell ...!"

"Only if you promise," I said. "Not Stacy, Julie, Bonnie, anyone ...!"

"I promise," Lyn said.

I didn't believe her for a minute ... but I had to talk to someone.

"Do you believe in coincidences?" I asked.

"Shit happens," Lyn said.

"How many coincidences would have to happen before you suspected ...?" I asked.

"About that free pass ...?" Lyn said. "Anyone could've left it ...!"

"Hypothetically," I said. "How many coincidences ...?"

"I can't give a number," Lyn said. "You're not planning on dumping Emerson because of one

113

coincidence ...?"

"What if you met a guy at a bar?" I asked. "The next night you run into him at the bowling alley? The next night at Bonnie's bridge club? The next night at the grocery store?"

"If he's single and good-looking, I'd make sure he got as lucky as me," Lyn grinned.

"What about Ivan?" I asked.

"There's no telling when Ivan's coming back ... if he comes back at all," Lyn said. "He's guarding a secret military airport somewhere ... I think it's in Iraq, but he can't tell me. Who knows where he'll be heading when he gets out ...? He's there for at least another seven months ..."

"That's a long time," I said. "Do you love him?"

"Do you love Emerson ...?" Lyn asked.

"We only had a few nights together," I said. "The word didn't come up. Yet ... I'm not sure how I'd react if it did. I'm not sure I trust Emerson."

"You swore you'd never wear that red bikini ...," Lyn reminded.

"Yet I did," I said. "Out in public ... on the beach. Isn't that ... another coincidence?"

"Coincidence ...? " Lyn laughed. "A man sees you in a skimpy bikini and wants to sleep with you ...? Every man who saw you probably had fantasies ...!"

I blushed ... *those fantasies were why I'd sworn not to wear it!*

"You have to see him again ...!" Lyn insisted.

She didn't know how right she was. After all that had happened in Hawaii, was there any chance we could stay at another 'same hotel' and not run into each other?

"What more do you need?" Lyn asked. "A cartoon arrow pointing at Emerson with a sign saying

114

'he's the one, stupid-head'? He's a magician; he might be able to pull that off. But ... I don't know ... maybe it's God's will ...?"

"What have I done to merit divine intervention?" I asked.

"You dated that football player in college," Lyn said.

"...until I caught him kissing a cheerleader," I reminded.

"I should get such a miracle!" Lyn said. "We pray for miracles ... do we run away when one happens? He's a celebrity ...!"

"He's a guy," I said. "He's not rich ... he told me so. He's a good magician ..."

"Better than an Uber driver living in his mom's basement," Lyn said. "Look, I'm not saying marry him. I'm saying don't give up on him ... not until you catch him with a cheerleader ..."

"What if I do ...?" I asked. "What if I get my hopes up ... and then ...?"

"If that's going to keep you from starting relationships, you need a dozen more cats ...!"

Our meals arrived, and with them, into Arnold's came Kathy, Brendan, and several other regulars. Without invitation, Kathy and Brendan joined us.

To put them off, rather than tell them anything, I asked what they'd heard. They agreed only if I promised to confirm or deny everything. They basically knew everything my mother knew, and a lot of imaginative, highly personal details. I denied all of them.

"No, we didn't have sex on stage, the beach, or the plane," I shook my head. "Why would you believe those things?"

"Hoped, not believed," Kathy said.

"Made a good story," Brendan said.

"No skinny-dipping, surfboards, or private beach," I said.

"I knew that," Brendan said. "Sand ruins the fun."

"People around here," Kathy sighed. "They'll believe anything."

"Vicarious sex doesn't carry risks ...," Lyn said.

"Better vicarious than no sex," Kathy said.

"The Bismarck Express' main cargo is lies," I said.

"So, what's the truth ...?" Brendan asked.

"Apparently you'll know before I do," I said.

After eating, it took me half an hour to escape ... and then only because I followed a smoker outside, talking to them, and everyone assumed that I'd be coming back. I drove home intending to get some cleaning done, but turned on my TV and sat ignoring my mess. After eating, Mephistopheles fell asleep on my bed, and I had nothing to distract me.

What was I going to do?

Hours later, the phone rang.

"How's my hat?" Emerson asked.

"Unfortunately empty," I said. "I expected to find pockets in it."

"It's not a stage hat," Emerson said. "I miss you."

"I miss you," I said. "I'm about to get ready for bed ..."

"Tease ...!" Emerson laughed.

"It's true," I said. "I'm sitting alone ... in the dark ... with a bottle of wine ... wearing only your hat ..."

"So am I!" Emerson lied. "You're still in your work clothes, aren't you?"

"That's my secret," I said.

"Keeping secrets ...?" Emerson asked.

"Maybe ...," I said.

"If I got a computer, would you video-chat?" Emerson asked.

"Not the way you'd like," I said.

"Red bikini ...?"

"Not a chance ...!"

"Less ...?"

"Not that much magic in the world."

"You'd be surprised," Emerson said.

"Really ...?" I asked. "Tell me about magic ... real magic."

"Real magic is dangerous," Emerson said. "It's a trap."

"Trap ...?" I asked.

"What happens when someone is convinced that you do real magic?" Emerson asked. "They want to know how it works, if you can teach them, and if you'll do magic for them. They want magicians to make them rich, give them super-powers, or heal their wounds and diseases. They latch onto you. You can't get away ... and if you try, it angers them."

"Is there real magic ...?" I asked.

"I'd like to think there is," Emerson said. "I'd like to see it ... but I hope it doesn't make me one of those fanatics who stalks magicians."

"Does that happen?" I asked.

"It has," Emerson said. "Usually someone with severe mental issues ..."

"I hope you're not describing me," I said.

"Any time you want to stalk me ...!" Emerson laughed.

"I may just do that," I said.

I told him about my friends and co-workers

visiting his website, watching his videos, and even about my mother and the Bismarck Express. Emerson laughed.

"Friends and family are always problematic ... until you don't have any," Emerson said.

Emerson described his day fishing with Robin, which was mostly two guys and a cooler of beer, and then the wild party.

"Were any cute girls at the party?" I asked.

"Yes, but none magical," Emerson said.

We talked a while longer, yet I could hear him yawn. He'd had a busy day and crossed many time zones; I pretended to be tired, and finally we hung up.

I hadn't told him that I was coming to Atlanta.

I had an idea, but didn't want to risk it yet.

Chapter 12

Saturdays were busy. Bonnie wanted me to go to her kids' baseball and soccer games ... mostly to keep her company. One of Julie's daughters had a dance recital in the evening, and her other daughter had a cold. Stacy's husband had to work, and she had shopping to do. Lyn worked weekends, and still wanted to party each night.

Everyone called to include me. By happy hour, I'd watched half a soccer game and most of a little league game, sitting on aluminum bleachers eating from a picnic basket. Then Bonnie dropped me off at Stacy's, where I watched her cook dinner while listening to her complain that she wasn't sure if her husband would be home to eat. We'd told her not to marry him, yet reminding her of that only made her cry, so I nodded and agreed with her endless criticisms. Stacy invited me for dinner, yet I refused; I didn't want to be their buffer.

I spent my evening alone; Lyn wanted to take me to a casino, yet I knew what would happen, and I didn't need a late binge before a business trip.

If this sale went through my income could double ...!

I kept thinking of my other plan, and watching the clock. Emerson was an hour ahead of me, probably onstage, performing his act. Would he call afterwards?

I truly hated Saturday evening television!

Late that night, my phone beeped. Mephistopheles complained as I stopped petting him long enough to pick up my phone.

"Atlanta's awfully lonely," Emerson said.

"It can't be that bad," I said, and I sighed heavily.

"What's wrong?" Emerson asked.

"Nothing," I said. "How was your show?"

"Amazing ... as always," Emerson said. "Lots of laughs. Had a heckler ... I've got a store of comebacks. The audience loved our back-and-forth. He came up after the show; he's an amateur magician and was trying to help."

I described my busy day with the girls in deep detail ... going into excruciating minutia. Then I asked what he was planning to do tomorrow.

"I ... I don't have any plans," Emerson said. "Atlanta has a world-famous zoo. I could ... go by myself."

I tried not to smile.

The time to bait my hook had come!

"I was hoping to surprise you," I said. "My company made the preliminary sale."

"Preliminary ...?" he asked. "What's ...?"

"Companies don't buy software like shoppers buy shampoo," I said. "First, we demonstrate it to their executive staff. If they like it, we set up our software on their private network, and prove it works on their systems. Then we input their data and link our front end into their existing databases. If it all works, and they like it, then they sign a contract .. . or the deal is lost."

"Sounds complicated ... like it could take weeks," Emerson said. "Any chance you'll be coming down?"

"I wish," I lied. "They talked about me, but my manager overruled ... he's going in my place."

"What ...?" Emerson exclaimed. *"But the old nurse lady asked for you ...!"*

I held my tongue during the long pause. *Dead silence.* I couldn't even hear Emerson breathing.

I'd nailed him!

"You ... are coming down," Emerson sounded defeated. "I should've assumed you'd figure it out. Any novel-reader would ... a mystery reader even sooner."

"How do you do it?" I demanded.

"I planned to tell you everything ... eventually," Emerson said. "I can't tell you over the phone. Please, give me a chance ..."

"I have a ...," I began.

"Rental car," Emerson finished. "I know."

"That's creepy," I said. "You will explain everything when I get there."

"You're the boss," Emerson said. "I wanted to tell you. It's just a matter of ... timing."

"Be inside my room when I arrive," I said.

"How can I ...?" Emerson asked.

"Just do it," I said.

"I'll be there," Emerson promised.

"Good-night."

I hung up on him.

He'd put me through the wringer; *now it was my turn!*

No more coincidences.

I owned him!

Chapter 13

Sundays are the worst travel day for lines. I stood in five lines so I could sit in two different cramped coach seats. I stood in line to get off each plane, pushed through a crowd to get my luggage, and another line to get my rental car. I programmed my phone to direct me to the Atlanta South Regency Alms. I drove in lines of traffic to get there.

Georgia is beautiful. I like North Dakota, but it's too flat. Georgia has tall green trees towering on hillsides, beautiful colors, of every shape and size. From a distance, Atlanta seems to rise out of a sea of leaves.

After I checked in, I entered my room. It looked empty. I stepped inside; it was a normal hotel room ... except for ... my bed was turned down ... and something was on my pillow.

A lottery ticket ...

I picked it up and looked at it; a scratch card. No one had scratched it.

My phone beeped.

"Congratulations!" Emerson exclaimed.

"What is it?" I asked.

"Five hundred dollars," Emerson said. "You're a

winner!"

"You were supposed to be here," I said.

"You'd never have believed me," Emerson said. "That's why I couldn't tell you right away. I wanted to ...!"

I pulled a dime from my purse, set the lottery card on my nightstand, scratched, and examined it for three matching numbers.

$500 ...!

"I won," I said accusingly.

"I know," Emerson said. "I'd like permission to tell you how I know. Can I come in?"

I walked to my door and opened it. Emerson stood there holding two dozen red roses in a glass vase.

"I apologize," Emerson said.

"Don't apologize; explain." I ordered. "What did you do ...? Buy a hundred lottery tickets and x-ray each one ...?"

"Nope," Emerson quipped. "Can I come in?"

I took the flowers. He took that as consent. I gestured to the chair, and he complied. I set the flowers by the TV and sat on the foot of my bed.

"Belief in magic changes as we age," Emerson began. "Kids live in magical worlds. As kids get older, they're taught that magic isn't real. That's a bitter pill; who wants to give up on magic? That's the job of magicians; we kill beliefs. Magicians create the illusion that all magic is sleight of hand and birds up our sleeves."

I stared at him.

"Hollywood magic is just as false," Emerson said. "Levitation, flying brooms, casting lightning bolts ... I'd do those things if I could."

"Are you saying that you can do real magic?" I

asked.

"I'm trying to not say it," Emerson said.

"What's real magic?" I asked.

"Usually, just coincidences," Emerson said.

"Show me," I said.

"Answer me first," Emerson said. "What if ... I tell you the truth ... and you don't like it?"

"Then you leave," I said. "We never cross paths again."

"Did that work in Hawaii ...?" Emerson asked.

"You're going to explain to me why it didn't," I ordered.

"Coincidences," Emerson said.

"I don't believe in ...," I started.

"You're not supposed to," Emerson said. "Our disinformation campaign is designed to keep adults from believing."

"Why ...?" I asked.

"Adults don't change beliefs easily," Emerson warned. "Transition is painful. You want the truth; I'll tell you. But I can't make you accept it."

I leaned back.

"I'm not excited about hurting you," Emerson said. "I don't mean physical pain. World views, core beliefs, and personal perspectives; changing those can be agonizing."

He was trying to frighten me.

"It's like .... a sense," Emerson said. "Taste, touch, sight ... on an island of primitive, uneducated blind people, your ability to see would seem magic. Coincidences are ... alternate time-lines. They swirl around us. True magicians see time-lines. We choose coincidences."

"So ... the tricks you do on stage ...?" I asked.

"Illusions, easily explained," Emerson said. "Most of them you could google."

"The ticket you left in my hotel room ...?" I asked.

"I mailed it to the former occupants on their last day," Emerson said. "They left it behind. Another coincidence: the maid didn't see it. I arranged that ... so it would be there when you arrived."

"How did you know which room I'd have?" I asked.

"Predicting numbers is an easy coincidence," Emerson said.

"We ran into each other ...?" I asked.

"Coincidences I chose, including your coworkers bringing you to my show," Emerson said.

"Why me ...?" I asked. "You got what you wanted in Hawaii ..."

"My goal wasn't to 'get' you," Emerson said. "Anyone who can navigate time-lines can put themselves in the path of countless desperate women ... but those kind of women aren't what I want ..."

"What do you want ...?" I asked.

"A relationship ... a long ... possibly permanent relationship."

"Why me ...?"

"I didn't choose you," Emerson said. "I chose a path where I'd meet my perfect match."

"What ...?" I almost laughed. *"Fate brought us together ...?"*

"Multiple, ever-changing time-lines preclude the existence of fate ... at least, of any single, preordained outcome," Emerson said.

"You're saying ... I'm your perfect match?" I asked.

"I trust time-paths," Emerson said.

"How can I be your perfect ... anything?" I asked.

"My perfect match ... would be my equal," Emerson said.

"I'm not a magician," I said.

"Not everyone who navigates time-lines works onstage," Emerson said.

"Are you saying ... I can ... arrange coincidences?" I asked.

"Yes," Emerson said. "I believe so."

I stared at him; *did he really mean ...?*

"Imagine if I'd walked up to you in the airport and told you this; you wouldn't have believed me," Emerson said. "Something like this ... has to be learned slowly."

"I don't like being lied to," I said.

"I've never lied to you," Emerson said. "I ... delayed telling you certain things ... for timing, so I don't dump too much on you at once."

I stared at him, uncertain what to say. Everything that had happened since we'd met was ... *impossible!*

"I'm not Samantha Stevens ... or Lord Voldemort," Emerson said. "My ... what you'd call real magic ... is subtle. Have dinner with me tonight, and I'll show you tomorrow ... you can even choose the test."

"What test?" I asked.

"Anything you can think of," Emerson said. "It has to be something possible; I can't levitate or make Abraham Lincoln arise from the dead, but if you wanted ... say ... to see a clown in full costume and make-up standing on the side of the road, I could arrange that."

"How ...?" I asked.

"Clowns exist in Atlanta," Emerson said.

"Circuses, kids' parties; one of them could be driving by and have their car break down right in front of us. Highly unlikely ... but it's possible."

"I can choose ...?" I asked.

"Anything that's unlikely, yet possible," Emerson assured me. "The more unlikely, the more difficult it will be."

I didn't want to get into a car alone with Emerson, so I insisted that we eat at the hotel restaurant inside the Atlanta South Regency Alms. Unfortunately, my two coworkers were staying in the same hotel. Mrs. Bessy Andrews was an executive, Mr. Dawes reported to her. Nathan Qui was a systems technician who specialized in installations. They saw us enter and insisted that we join them.

"I didn't do this!" Emerson whispered to me as we sat down.

He was right; I knew they'd be here. *I could've avoided this.*

Emerson's skills as a magician proved invaluable. Bessy didn't believe he was a stage magician, so he presented her with a rosebud, drew an ace of spades from behind her head, and with a few passes of his hands, changed the ace into a queen of hearts. Nathan demanded to know how he'd done it, but Emerson declined and slid the card into his pocket.

"If we teach how magic works, we're not magicians anymore," Emerson said. "You wouldn't want to put me out of work, would you?"

Nathan subsided, and Emerson asked Bessy about their prospects for a successful presentation. Conversation turned to work, which allowed Bessy to regale Emerson with the advantages of companies using our software. Nathan was less enthusiastic; his job would be to integrate our software with their 'obsolete, stone-age databases'. He described in detail how companies regrettably always invested in new software first, then upgraded hardware as needed. If companies invested in hardware first, then upgrading software would go smoother.

I chimed in as needed, allowing Bessy and Nathan free reign to voice their opinions. I could've corrected them a dozen times, as I knew the newest features best, yet my goal was to avoid them asking about my relationship with Emerson, whom I'd introduced as a 'friend who happened to be performing not far from here'.

Emerson looked attentive, which I knew he was doing for my sake; only those in the business, and maybe investors, care about medical software. He asked questions and listened intently. Yet he seemed to enjoy it; his attentiveness kept me from asking questions he didn't want to answer.

After our dinners arrived, Emerson coyly changed the subject to living in North Dakota. Bessy loved Bismarck, and swore she'd never live anywhere else. Nathan had lived in New York City and relocated after three years with my company; he didn't hate the Plains states, yet he longed to return to the 'fast lane'.

To my relief, Bessy and Nathan drank far more than Emerson or I, and when I reminded them that we had to be at our best early in the morning, suddenly both realized that they'd feel better with a good night's sleep.

Their insistence on walking us to the elevator saved me again; I wanted to sleep with Emerson ... but not until he'd proven his claims. His room was on a lower floor, and we said a cordial good-night in the elevator. Then I went to my room alone.

Chapter 14

Our business presentation went well. I presented, Bessy fielded questions, and Nathan spoke only briefly. None of their executives understood a word of his technical explanations, yet they nodded like experts.

Senior Director of Devonshire-Slate Medical, Mrs. Abigail Bennett, greeted me warmly, yet sat silent through our presentation. She nodded with the others, yet frowned so deeply that I thought she regretted bringing us here. However, her attitude brightened after our presentation, and afterwards she complimented me on our professionalism.

We left around 1:00 in the afternoon, not knowing how our chances looked. Unable to get away, I was forced to have lunch with Bessy and Nathan, where we discussed how the meeting went until I didn't care anymore.

As we rose to pay, Bessy asked if I'd be seeing Emerson again. I told her we'd be having dinner together ... she stared at me as if trying to force me to say more.

I told them good-bye at the elevator, unlocked

my room, and instantly realized that my TV was on. I stepped inside to find Emerson sitting on the foot of my bed, clicking the remote to turn the TV off.

"Gee, what a surprise," I said. "How ...?"

"No magic; locks are a breeze for magicians," Emerson said. "You don't sound happy. How did it ...?"

"You already know how the presentation went, don't you?" I asked.

"How could I ...?" Emerson began.

"That's what I'd like to know," I said.

"Time to pay the piper," Emerson said. "What do you want?"

"A piano," I said. "Let's take a drive. I want to see someone moving a piano outdoors."

Emerson looked stunned.

"That's no easy task," Emerson said. "Couldn't you ... start smaller?"

"You said 'anything' ...," I reminded.

"I'll try," Emerson said. "I'd better drive."

We drove for over two hours. The roads in Georgia seemed well-made and kept in repair, yet we crisscrossed Atlanta. Finally we turned into a narrow alley and found our path blocked by a truck.

"No room to go around," I commented, glancing at trash bins stacked beside a rustic loading dock.

"Wait for it," Emerson said.

Two workmen approached the back of the truck. One waved that we should go back and turn around, while the other opened their wide sliding door; the back of the truck was filled with furniture ... and foremost was a piano.

"Satisfied ...?" Emerson asked.

"How ...?" I stammered.

"I told you ... it'll take time to explain," Emerson

said, and he put my rental car into reverse.

"How much time?" I asked.

Emerson stopped backing up.

"How long to explain it, how long to prove it, or how long to master it?" Emerson asked. "The latter will take some time ... months or years. I hope to explain it today, as soon as we get back ... but how long it'll take for you to believe, I can't say."

"What now ...?" I asked.

"I have three hours before I have to be onstage," Emerson said. "Would you like to eat or learn?"

"Learn," I said.

We went back to my hotel room, stopping only at a store where I bought a bottle of Merlot, my favorite wine. Emerson took the wrappers off the little plastic cups and poured for two, each half-full.

"Not everyone can do this," Emerson said. "Most people are just ... too damaged, too beaten by life, to even consider the possibility. Once the child in your heart dies, that's it. What magicians do ... takes joy."

"Joy ...?" I asked.

"Think of it as ... educated innocence," Emerson said.

"Joy ... or the power to believe in the impossible?" I asked.

"Is there a difference?" Emerson asked.

"That depends on the impossibility," I said. "Going to Tolkien's Mordor is impossible, and you wouldn't feel joy to find yourself in it."

"You're halfway there," Emerson smiled.

"How ...?" I asked.

"All kinds of people read books and watch movies," Emerson said. "Only those with joy in their heart consider the possibility of actually going into a fantasy world."

"But it's impossible ...," I said.

"That's not the point," Emerson said. "The thought entered your mind. To be a magician, you need an open mind ... where emotions travel freely. Emotions let you see."

"See what ...?" I asked.

"When they become visible, then you won't need to ask," Emerson said.

Emerson set his wine on the low dresser, over which stood a tall mirror. He dipped both of his forefingers into his wine, then touched one finger just inside the top corner of each side of the mirror, leaving two large red drops of Merlot on the glass. Both dripped slightly.

"Drops run down the mirror's glass," Emerson said. "If I keep adding more, eventually they'll drip all the way down. Of course, they could stream straight down, drip to the sides of the mirror, track toward its center, or streak back and forth; it's very random. For both streaks to run to the center, and join, would be an unusual coincidence."

"Is this a trick?" I asked.

"Yes, but not by me," Emerson said. "For this trick to work will take an exceptional coincidence. You're going to make this coincidence."

"*Me ...?*" I began.

"Don't talk," Emerson said. "Don't wrinkle your forehead concentrating. Willpower isn't part of this ... that's what trips up most people. Just stare at the drops. Which way will they move? Fill your mind with that question. Don't try to think of any answer; focus on the question."

I sighed.

"If you think it's hooey, then it will be," Emerson said. "You can end this now ... by not even trying."

"I feel silly," I said.

"Will you feel silly if it works ...?" Emerson said.

"No, then ... I don't know how I'll feel."

"Are you willing to find out?"

"Yes."

"Then do."

I stared at the drops. It felt crazy, yet I believed Emerson could do it.

The drops didn't move.

Emerson dipped his forefingers into his Merlot again, and added drops to the tops of the pale red streaks. I could see the additions stream down. Both lines dripped farther ... straight down. One slowly streaked six inches, while the other rapidly dropped ten inches, then stopped. As I watched, one dripped toward the center, but only slightly.

"Which way will it drip now?" Emerson asked. "Don't answer; ask."

He added another drop to the top of each. I could see the lines of moisture, newly thickened, as both drops traveled existing paths. The longer line dripped another four inches straight down, but the shorter line arced toward the center, dripped diagonally six inches, and caught up.

It was impossible. Even if it did work, there'd be no proof I'd caused it. Wishing didn't make things happen ... or asking ... or thinking about questions. If the two lines met, while I was focusing on them, it would just be a coincidence ...

Which was exactly what I was trying to make happen ...

Emerson added another drop to each side.

What path would the drips take ...?
Would they come together ...?

The left line quickly extended straight down eight inches, but the right line, the one I was concentrating on ... slowly dripped diagonal toward the center.

No, this can't be ...!

Both drips ran straight down.

"You're losing focus," Emerson said. "If you're afraid, it won't work ..."

"I'm more afraid it will," I said.

"I don't think it can," Emerson said. "They've dripped too far. To join now would require the most unlikely coincidence. No point handicapping you. Let's try again."

Emerson dipped his fingers and dripped new drops on the mirror near the top, but only six inches apart.

"This should be easier," Emerson said. "Relax. Don't fear. Don't force. Let the coincidence happen. Slip into the circumstance. Ask. Question."

I focused on the two new drops ... they were closer together.

Subtle sensations flowed in the silence. I felt ... anxious ... unsettled ... worried ... and foolish ... all at once. As before, Emerson added drops, and both lines crept lower.

Which way ...?

"Coincidences aren't random happenstance," Emerson said. "Nothing's random. Forces affect everything; drops are altered by gravity, surface tension, dust on the mirror, streaks from the last person to clean it, and even static electricity. If you knew all those factors, then their paths would be obvious. You and I are part of the forces affecting it; our mass, our body heat, our breaths moving the air, even the faint electrical fields generated by our nervous systems. We're part of the forces affecting these drops. Yet, if we try, we can control ourselves ... and how we affect them."

More drops added. Both drips streaked lower ... and got closer.

When both drops reached the bottom of the mirror, they were only an inch apart.

"It's a start," Emerson said. "Like I said, it takes time. Yet look; both these streaks veer toward the center ... toward each other ... just what you wanted. If the mirror was longer, and their trajectories continued, they would've met. With practice, they will."

"Can you do it?" I asked.

"You add the drops," Emerson said.

I stood and looked at the streaked mirror over the dresser, then carried my Merlot into the bathroom.

"Don't trust me?" Emerson asked.

"This is a lot to ask," I said.

I dipped my forefingers into my Merlot and wet spots on the bathroom mirror about a foot apart. As Emerson stood in the doorway, watching, I added more drops to each spot. Both dripped.

Four times I added more drops ... before the dripping streaks met in the middle, joined, and flowed down to the bottom of the mirror.

I staggered back against the towel rack. Emerson grabbed my arm to steady me.

"Don't be alarmed," Emerson said. "It's just coincidence ...!"

"B-b-but ...!" I stammered.

"That's enough for tonight," Emerson said. "I need to get going anyway. You can stay here ... but I recommend that you don't practice. You'll progress better if you allow time to let your fears settle. Watch TV. Read your book. Don't dwell on what you've seen. Smart people never enjoy instant acceptance."

Emerson half-carried me to my bed, sat me upon it, and set both my book and the remote control within easy reach.

Then, as if hesitantly, Emerson kissed my cheek.

"I'm proud of you ... how you took it," Emerson said.

Emerson cavalierly kissed my hand.

With a slight smile, Emerson left.

For long minutes I stared at the closed door. Then I shifted my gaze to the wine-streaked mirror over my dresser. Slowly, tremulously, I rose and walked into the bathroom. I could still see the wet streaks, angling inwards from opposite sides and joining only two inches before it dripped to the thin metal frame on the bottom of the mirror, where it spread widely in both directions.

Coincidence ...!

So much of our lives depended on coincidences.

Controlling coincidences ... manipulated ...!

My eyes traced both lines of moisture a dozen times.

They joined every time.

Every coincidence since I'd first met Emerson flashed through my mind ...

I'd first seen him doing yo-yo tricks in an airport ...

Before he gave his yo-yos to kids ...

Before we boarded the same flight to Hawaii ...

Everything that had brought us together was a coincidence ...

Coincidence ... but not random ...!

I grabbed my Merlot and drank straight from the

bottle.

> *Emerson had said ... he wanted a long-term relationship ...*
>
> *I'd always wanted a long-term relationship ...*
> *Coincidence ...?*
> *No, most people want that ...!*

But ... that's the trick of coincidences ... you never know. You have to accept it's random chance ... or believe without proof ... because you can never be sure.

Questions mounted ... until my head hurt ... and I drank until I dared drink no more. Filling a cup with water, I drank deeply to avoid a hangover. I tried reading my book, another mystery, and then tried watching TV, but every few minutes my eyes would drift to the mirror. Eventually I couldn't see the evaporated lines of wine-drips clearly ... but their existence haunted.

Chapter 15

Mrs. Abigail Bennett catered lunch for our meetings the next day. I was polite and professional and sat and listened. Bessy led the meetings with lesser executives, and Nathan spoke when addressing hardware techs. I fielded questions about our newest features and usability. Yet I couldn't stop thinking about droplets of red wine dripping down mirrors.

Emerson was inside my hotel room when I arrived. I got settled, then he showed me three playing cards; an ace, a king, and a queen.

"These are normal cards," Emerson said. "No tricks, no marks; slight-of-hand would ruin what I'm trying to teach."

After showing me the cards, he mixed them up, and then dealt them face down on the foot of my bed.

"Now, don't pick a card," Emerson said. "Just hold your hand over each, slowly, one at a time. As you do, consider that the card your hand hovers over could be the ace. Don't forget to feel for joy."

I did as instructed but ...

"I feel nothing," I said.

"Don't talk," Emerson said. "The ace could be

141

any of them. Selecting the right one would be pure
random chance ... a coincidence. Don't feel for the ace;
that's the mistake. Feel for the coincidence. One card
will feel differently. Don't guess. Feel for the difference
in your hand."

I tried yet ... nothing.

"It's subtle," Emerson said. "Take a moment,
clear your mind, and hold your hand over each card.
Which card would be a coincidence?"

I tried to clear my mind, felt nothing, and finally
pointed at a card at random.

"Turn the card over," Emerson said.

I did. *I'd chosen the ace!*

"Excellent!" Emerson said.

"No, I didn't feel anything," I argued. "It was just
a ...,"

"Coincidence ...?" Emerson asked.

Emerson scooped up all three and tucked them
in his pocket.

"We'll do that again soon," Emerson said. "Best
not to try it now; you're still in shock."

"What ... what are we going to do?" I asked.

"Eat," Emerson said. "Life doesn't change just
because you're learning. Your world just gets bigger."

Emerson's rental car was nice, a flashy sports car,
much better than mine.

"Let me guess; they ran out of cheap, boring
cars?" I asked.

"Upgraded without having to pay extra,"
Emerson grinned.

"Coincidence or luck ...?" I asked.

"Is there a difference?" Emerson asked.

We drove to a fancy burger place playing loud
music. I ordered a cob salad and white wine. Emerson

chose a Hawaiian burger and scotch on the rocks.

"How did I choose the ace?" I asked.

"You didn't," Emerson said. "You chose the coincidence."

"It just happened to be the ace ...?" I asked.

"If it hadn't been the ace, it wouldn't have been a coincidence," Emerson said.

Our drinks arrived and I gulped my wine.

"That won't help," Emerson said. "Change is painful. Deadening pain only delays acceptance."

"I'm changing ...?" I asked.

"Whether or not you believe in coincidences," Emerson nodded.

"I don't," I said.

"Then you're halfway there," Emerson said. "Like wine-drops dripping down your mirror, affected by countless forces, there's a cause for everything. Coincidence is when those forces align."

"Can I try again?" I asked.

"Here ...?" Emerson asked, gesturing to the other diners. "Too many distractions."

Emerson asked how my day went. We both knew he was distracting me; he didn't care if my company sold their software. Yet I gave him the boring details, and then our food arrived.

"What about Suzzannia the Sorceress?" I asked. "Can she manipulate ...?"

"She's a master," Emerson said.

"Have you and she ever ...?" I asked.

"Are we both going to list our previous relationships?" Emerson asked.

"Just curious," I said.

"Magical relationships add a whole other list of problems to what everyone else suffers," Emerson said.

"Some make relationships work, but it's hard ... whole new levels of suspicions creep in ... when normal coincidences occur."

"Normal coincidences ...?" I asked.

"The kind everyone faces," Emerson said. "In a relationship with someone who can manipulate ... you know ... how do you know which coincidences your lover caused ... and which just happened?"

"Trust must be difficult," I said.

"Love is difficult," Emerson said. "Trust comes with love."

I almost dropped my wine glass; for the first time in my presence, Emerson had mentioned love ... without referring to movies or Mexican food.

We still didn't know each other well enough for that talk!

Emerson was staring at me.

"Tell me about Bismarck," he said.

Ignoring that he hadn't denied an intimate relationship with Suzzannia the Sorceress, I indulged him in past gossips of Bonnie, Julie, Stacy, and Lyn ... everything that they'd ever done worthy of the Bismarck Express. Of course, stories about them included me, our mothers, Bonnie's father, Gwen, Nancy, Joel, Kathy, and Brendan. I described each briefly, as I extolled on every embarrassment they'd ever suffered. I might as well; if Emerson ever came to Bismarck, they'd regale him with my worst moments.

We were both laughing as we walked out to the car. Yet the drive back to our hotel was troubled; I didn't know what was about to happen. *Did he ...?*

Emerson was right; I knew when any other man was trying to manipulate me. I didn't know magic. *Could I trust him ...?*

We went back to my room.

"Can I do the card trick again?" I asked.

"It's not a trick," Emerson said. "It's discovering a new sense."

"How many people have it?" I asked.

"It's not like we're wizards and everyone else is muggles," Emerson said. "Everyone is born with it, but in varying degrees, like empathy or sensitivity to heat or cold. For those with strong sensitivity, some upbringings squash it, and religions deny it, but most people simply never look for it."

"Out of sight, out of mind ...?" I asked.

"By definition, coincidences are startling," Emerson said. "Most seek to expose them, yet fail; people search for the cause of the effect, not the cause of the coincidence."

"Like, if I and my mother happen to be shopping in the same store, we look for the reasons why we're both there at the same time, not the subtle sensations that caused our reasons to shop," I said.

"Exactly," Emerson said, and he tossed me his three cards.

I tried repeatedly to reproduce my success, and failed four times.

"You're trying to guess," Emerson said. "Focus on your question, not the answer. Seek to feel the coincidence ... inside you."

I did ... and chose the ace three times in a row.

"I've got a show to do," Emerson said. "I have to leave in an hour."

"I know," I said.

"Can I ask you a question?" Emerson asked.

"Sure," I said.

"Where's my hat?"

"In Bismarck."

"Am I still invited?"

"Maybe."

"Not very definite," he said.

"Decisions take time," I said.

"I've given you a lot to think about," he acknowledged.

"Is God real?" I asked.

"What ...?" he gasped, eyes widening.

"If you can do this ...?" I suggested.

"If there's a God, he ... or she ... would be the ultimate manipulator, and he or she hasn't chosen to let me know," Emerson said. "Coincidences aren't magic. It's more like ... being able to clearly see things far away, or hear frequencies most can't."

"To most people, this would be magic," I said.

"I haven't told you everything yet," Emerson said. "I will, but ... timing. Until you're an expert at sensing coincidences, you're not ready for the next step."

"What's the next step?" I asked.

"Choosing coincidences," Emerson said, and he cut off my next question. "No, I can't explain farther. Walk before you run. But don't keep trying all night. Give yourself long breaks."

"I will," I promised.

Emerson rose from my bed and stood expectantly.

"I ... I want a kiss, but I'm ...," I stammered.

"Afraid ...?" Emerson asked. "I've opened you to a wider world. Complexity can be alarming."

I didn't know what to say. Emerson came over, bent down, and we kissed. He stared long into my eyes, then glanced at the three cards on my bed.

"I'll be here tomorrow when you get off work,"

Emerson promised.

"No ... not here," I said. "I'll call you ... when I get back."

Emerson nodded and started out the door.

"Break a leg," I called after him.

Chapter 16

We didn't have any meetings all day. Mrs. Abigail Bennett took Bessy out for a private lunch, and Nathan was trapped in their network room all day, installing our software on servers and linking databases, with two of their top programmers assisting him. I found a nearby tavern and ate lunch alone, thinking about Emerson.

He wasn't a stalker. He was ... extraordinary, yet I feared getting too far ahead of myself. His magic, which I'd practiced half the night with too few breaks, was astounding, like taking off dark, dirty glasses and discovering that you've been living in a beautiful, mysterious garden.

His magic was real ... which didn't make him my perfect partner ... no matter what his Fates wanted.

I had to take things slowly, discover this new world before I jumped into it.

For the twelfth time, I took his three cards out of my pocket, examined them closely, and put them safely away. *Taverns weren't a place to practice magic.*

Bessy and I were able to leave early, yet we talked in the hotel restaurant for almost an hour.

Everything was positive, which bothered Bessie; real sales never went well. Someone at every company opposes new purchases, and the fact that we hadn't heard their arguments only meant that we couldn't refute them.

Bessie asked about Emerson. I told her that we weren't an item yet ... but I'd kill him if I found him sleeping with someone else.

I'm pretty sure that I was telling the truth.

I unlocked my hotel room door around the same time I usually got there ... and struggled with the decision I had to make.

Five minutes after I phoned, Emerson knocked on my door.

"Who's there?" I asked.

"You know," Emerson said.

"Come in ... and close the door."

Emerson stepped inside. I smiled at him, stretched across my bed ... wearing nothing but my red bikini.

True magic showed in his expression ...!

We almost rolled off the bed twice. My covers ended up on the floor. We reveled in our rejoining.

If only the sounds of crashing waves filled sea-perfumed air ...!

Three hours later, we had to leave. Emerson had called the theater; fortunately they had an empty seat available. I met him in the lobby, dressed elegantly. I'd selected my trusty low-cut little black dress, red heels, and a single strand of pearls with my hair gently wrapped in a chignon at the nape of my neck.

We didn't have long. We stopped at a fast food place that looked like a giant red chicken and ate hurriedly. Then we drove straight to the theater.

I followed Emerson backstage. He unlocked a tiny storage room where all his props lay. I closed the door, and he changed into his flashy stage suit ... with me watching. I grinned, but he scolded me; he had a lot to prepare. Over half an hour, Emerson carried all his props and carefully arranged them on the stage, exactly where he'd need them. He set up his tall tripods and made sure his green silk curtain slid open easily. I watched from a distance, staying out of his way.

On the other side of the room, opposite the stage, a bartender was setting up his station. A manager came to talk to Emerson, to confirm curtain-time, and give Emerson a short list of names and the places where they'd be sitting. Emerson took notes, worked quickly and meticulously, carefully laying out every prop and double-checking his pockets, his sleeves, and his green hat. He finished only minutes before his performance was scheduled to begin. His last act was to have the bartender microwave his cold plate of scrambled eggs.

I was sent out through a series of narrow halls, and emerged into a crowded lobby, where a different bartender was selling libations.

A young woman came in and rang a small gong.

"Ladies and gentlemen, the spirits have informed me that the host of our evening, Emmerich the Amazing, has just crossed over from the mystical realm," the woman spoke in a comically spooky voice. "The master awaits your presence ... let the portals be opened!"

Two sets of large, twin doors, made of polished walnut, never moved. Instead, the wide, decorated, paneled wall between the doors split in half and opened up; a secret door. Several gasped and a few twittered delight, and then everyone started forward.

Tickets were asked for at the entrance, parties

identified, and each was directed to their assigned seat. This wasn't a dinner theater; sixty old fashioned red chairs stretched in long rows, as if this were an antique movie house. Most headed straight for their seats, but more than a few stopped at the bar in the back.

I was seated near the back, on the end; not a great seat, but obviously Emerson hadn't planned on me being here. That comforted me; *I'd surprised him with my request.*

Finally, the lady who'd rung the gong appeared in front.

"The spirits are pleased!" the woman shouted. "The master awaits ... and your journey is about to begin! Welcome to The Illusion Emporium! We are delighted to have your company, and we ardently pray that most of you will still be here when our evening ends. Our master tonight is a graduate of the Lester McVey Academy of Magic and an associate of the International Legerdemain League, a veteran of every showcase in Vegas, Hollywood, and Walt Disney Studios, with his own Showtime special, the marvelous, the astounding, the incredible master of illusion, Emmerich the Amazing!"

The crowd applauded loudly. I joined in. The woman's dramatic voice had set the mood. I'd noticed that she'd been reading Emmerich's resume from a card in her hand, which she'd been trying to hide. Then the lights suddenly dimmed and soft, eerie music swelled.

With a flash of light and a puff of smoke, Emmerich appeared between the opening curtains sporting his purple, green, and yellow suit covered with sparkly rhinestones. Two spotlights centered on him, and the crowd applauded louder.

"Welcome, welcome, welcome!" Emmerich

cried, smiling and gesturing as I'd seen him do in Hawaii. "What a night! The moon is full, the fog ghostly, and spirits are available from Harry in the back! Wave to everyone, Harry!"

Heads swiveled around to see the bartender waving at them. I smiled; Emmerich knew his banter and was already controlling the crowd.

"For my first trick I'd like to appear before you drunk ... Yes! Incredible! I love starting with a success ... although I think Harry was more successful than I!"

The crowd laughed. I smiled; *I'd seen this performance before.*

I set my drink in the little cup holder on the arm of my chair so I could applaud louder.

"I know you came to see some amazing sights," Emmerich said. "Now, most of you don't believe in magic. Poor souls, I'm not going to try to change your minds, but I will try to make you doubt your senses. To begin ..." He pulled off his green hat and his little bird flew out and fluttered to a stand to his right. "Now ... how did that get in there? Oh, well, look what she left behind ...!"

He did his first trick exactly the same, adding the three eggs, milk, butter, salt and pepper, and Tabasco into his hat. Then he poured in the brandy, lit it on fire, stirred it with a long spoon, lifted an ordinary dinner plate with his other hand, and flipped his hat overtop the plate. When he lifted his hat, his plate held his steaming pile of freshly-reheated scrambled eggs.

"Thank you!" Emmerich shouted over the applause. "Thank you! That was amazing ... or it would've been ... I was trying for over-easy!"

He tossed the plate over his shoulder. The scrambled eggs flew to splat the curtains behind him and the plate broke loudly upon the floor; I wondered how many plates he'd broken.

"There we go! Over-easy! Another fabulous trick!"

He repeated his show exactly, he and I the only ones there who knew what was about to happen. Emmerich brought out his eight steel rings, performed his amazing routine, and ended by linking them.

However, when he began his signed-check trick, his banter changed.

"Is there anyone here from Florida?" Emmerich asked, and hands rose. "Oh, you lucky people! I used to live there. Disney, Universal, and Sea World ... on a too hot, overgrown, insect-ridden, crocodile-covered swamp invading an unsupported sandbar constantly pulverized by hurricanes; I really miss it!"

The person he chose to fill out his form was Angelica, who was from Boston, slightly drunk, and blushed profusely while giggling like a schoolgirl. She was barely able to hold his clipboard still and write on it; someone beside her helped.

"Yes, please hold that clipboard for Angelica." Emmerich said. "She's obviously experiencing an earthquake not affecting the rest of us."

The crowd laughed and Angelica blushed deeper.

"My name is Frank," said the man she passed the clipboard to.

"What a coincidence!" Emmerich cried. "I once tried to be frank ... almost died from honesty. Maybe you could speak frankly to Angelica? She's very pretty ...! No? Well, why don't you read what she wrote down as her favorite color. Not yet! Wouldn't be much of a trick if I guessed it after you tell everyone. Now, I'm going to need a second ... got to commune with several spirits ... I hope they're not illiterate ... What? Really? Oh, I can't believe it! Help me out here, Frank! Tell me Angelica didn't write down the color ... blue ...?"

"Her favorite color is blue," Frank said.

Everyone applauded and Emmerich bowed. He really was a different person on stage. I clapped loudly, trying to help, yet now that I knew how he did it, the magic felt lessened. Still, everyone seemed to enjoy the banter more than the magic.

Emmerich thanked Frank and asked him to hand the clipboard to someone in another row. Several reached for it, but an older woman plucked it from his hand.

"I'm Carla Easton," the woman replied.

"Thank you, Carla, for helping us out!" Emmerich said. "Now, where are you from?"

"Memphis," Carla said.

"Memphis!" Emmerich exclaimed. "I knew a Carla from Memphis! She was my college study partner! She had the most incredible pair of ... well, she was quite shapely, too much, if you get my meaning. She graduated and I didn't. Carla, you didn't tease boys you went to school with, did you?"

"I went to an all-girls school," Carla said.

"So did I!" Emmerich exclaimed. "Well, until they kicked me out for ... that's not important. Now, let's put that all-girl's schooling to good use. Somewhere on that clipboard Angelica wrote down the name of her first pet. I'm going to guess it ... and you tell me if I'm right. Okay? Here we go ... give me a second ... I hate calling upon the spirit world and getting put on hold ... the name of Angelica's first pet was ... Scotty!"

"It's Scotty!" Carla announced.

155

Applause followed and many were laughing.

Emmerich had Carla pass the clipboard all the way up to him. He pulled out a pen and began writing on it, then took the page off the clipboard, held it high, and continued his spiel. After he cut out and peeled off the blank check, Angelica screamed with laughter, then begged him not to cash it.

"Not cash it?" Emmerich pretended to be horrified. "This is how I make money! You didn't think they paid me to be here, did you? I'm sorry, Angelica, but carbon copies do count as magic! This check is real, valid in any bank ... yet I know you never meant to sign it, so I'm going to fold it in half and tear it in two ... and again ... and again!"

Emerson sprinkled the torn sections into his green hat, which he then dumped into the same metal trash can he'd carefully placed underneath his table, then threw the can into a back corner, where it crashed loudly. He apologized to Angelica and offered her a real gold coin to pay for abusing her trust. However, when Angelica realized that it was a chocolate coin wrapped in gold foil, she opened it and immediately bit into it.

"Wait! Wait!" Emmerich shouted. "Don't swallow! My biggest trick is in your mouth!"

Laughter exploded, and to their continued amusement, Angelica had to pull out of her mouth the tiny folded rectangle of paper. When she unfolded it and found her signed check inside, she almost fell over, and two men on both sides had to grab and keep her from flopping down onto the floor. She held up the check, showing it to everyone.

"Thank you, Angelica!" Emmerich shouted. "I really appreciate it ... although I try to get to know a woman better before I let her put my biggest trick in her mouth."

The crowd roared, and several almost fell out of their chairs, and then everyone applauded long and hard.

The rest of the act was an exact repeat. I laughed and clapped my hands along with everyone.

Emmerich did the other tricks I'd seen with giant cards and massive dice. Each trick earned tremendous applause, yet it was his banter that everyone loved.

"Now, I've just one last trick to show you tonight," Emmerich said. "Before I do that, I want to thank all of you. You've been a wonderful audience, and for a magician, there's no greater magic than to delight and entertain. I really am grateful to you, and also thankful to The Illusion Emporium for allowing me to come and demonstrate my act to you tonight. Our lovely hostess, Miss Elessa Emerald Enchantress, Harry our bartender, and of course, all of you ... I think we all deserve a round of applause."

The applause was enthusiastic, and I leaned forward; *this was what I wanted to see!*

"You know I'm a magician, and my magic is all trickery ... I wouldn't try to deceive you here ... my final trick requires a volunteer from the audience. Who would like to come up and help me?"

Several hands rose.

"Let's see ... you're all good choices ... and the spirits tell me ... you!"

A pretty girl near the front squealed. Those near her laughed and everyone applauded.

"Let's bring her up here, shall we?" Emmerich asked.

Under pressure from the audience and her friends, the woman was coerced to step up onto the stage. Emmerich grabbed her hand to pull her up; she swayed as if too drunk to be on stage.

"Now, what's your name?" Emmerich asked.

"Teresa," she said. "Teresa Cummings."

"Everyone, let's hear it for Teresa!" Emmerich said, and applause followed.

"Ladies and gentlemen, please attend; this beautiful young lady is just as real as any of you. Teresa, could you tell everyone what you do for a living that brought you to the fabulous Illusion Emporium ...?"

Teresa blushed and looked at those seated in her row.

"I'm visiting my sister," Teresa said.

"Is your sister in the audience?" Emmerich asked.

Teresa pointed, and a redhead sitting by her empty chair tried to hide under her hands.

"What's your sister's name?" Emmerich asked.

"Tammy," Teresa said.

"Tammy ...!" Emerson exclaimed. "I have a sister named Tammy ... and she'll be out of Fulson Prison in two weeks!"

Laughing hysterically, Tammy scooched down to hide, but the man next to her pulled her up.

"Is this your whole family?" Emerson asked.

Teresa laughed at them, almost fell over, and began pointing.

"That's Tammy's husband, Mark, and my brother Jake, and his wife Anne," Teresa said. "These are my cousins, Andy and Chloe."

"Well, Tammy, Mark, Jake, Anne, Andy, and Chloe, would you like to see Teresa help me with my final, amazing last trick?" Emmerich asked.

"Make her vanish!" Jake shouted.

"No, vanishing is far too easy!" Emmerich said. "We must do something special! Now, Teresa, do you trust me?"

"Yes," Teresa said.

"Silly girl!" Emmerich laughed. "I mean, we can change that! I mean, that's ... perfect! Now, all I want you to do is stand here. No, you have to stand all by yourself. See this 'x' on the floor? Stand on it and be very still. This won't take long and it won't hurt a bit ... well, it shouldn't hurt a bit ... it's never hurt before, but this is the first time I've ever tried this trick on a live human being ... you are human, aren't you? Don't worry; the brochure said it wouldn't hurt. Now, I've got a silk curtain here, soft silk, hanging from the ceiling. I'm going to wrap this around you, so you won't be able to see, which is probably for the best. Trust me, no one will be able to see you, either. I just need you to promise you'll stay here, standing on this spot, until I open the curtain. Will you do that?"

Blushing, Teresa nodded.

"Let's give Teresa a big hand, shall we?" Emmerich asked.

Everyone applauded.

Emmerich pulled one edge of the thin green curtain to one side of the stage, then took the other edge and pulled it to the other side of the stage, displaying it exactly as he'd done when I'd been on stage. Then he had her hold onto one edge of the curtain, and he took the other edge and walked a wide circle around her, wrapping her in the same faux green silk.

"With this yellow sash, I'm going to tie this curtain closed, not tightly, just enough so it doesn't fall open," Emmerich said, and he tied it around her waist.

"Now, I want all of you to look at this,"

Emmerich said, and he lifted up a long, sharp steel needle, as thick as a finger and over a foot in length. The crowd gasped. "Don't say anything ... we don't want to frighten poor Teresa! Listen to it!" He banged the hard, solid needle against his podium. "Now ... watch ... and please don't make a sound ...! This is a very delicate trick ...! Teresa, remain very still ...!"

He moved his podium aside so we could all see Teresa's outline wrapped in green silk. Then he lifted up one end of a red silken cord, threaded his giant needle, held a finger to his lips, and motioned for quiet. The crowd silenced.

Emmerich pointed his needle at Teresa's trapped form ... and pushed it through her shoulder. I almost screamed; *he'd done this to me!* The crowd gasped, astounded.

Emmerich proceeded to pull the needle through, drawing it out her back with the red cord following. Then he stabbed her again and again, through her stomach, hip, and finally the side of her head, each time dragging the red cord, sewing it through her.

I couldn't believe my eyes; *Emmerich was doing real magic on stage!*

Emmerich set down the needle, grabbed the red cord, and slowly pulled. It slid through her, through the four stitches, and out the side of her head. The crowd reacted as horrified as I.

The red cord pulled free. Emmerich grabbed the green silk curtain, unwrapped his victim, and there stood Teresa, looking confused, inebriated, and more than a little nervous.

The crowd jumped to its feet. The applause was tremendous.

"Teresa, safe and sound!" Emmerich shouted

over the loud clapping, and he nodded to her, took her hand, and she anxiously bowed to the audience.

Finally Emmerich assisted Teresa down to join her family.

"Thank you! Thank you! Good-night ... and may every day of your lives be magical!" Emmerich shouted, and with a puff of smoke, the stage curtains closed.

The applause quickly died, yet every smiling face looked excited.

In the front row, everyone was questioning Teresa. I smiled, knowing what she was feeling.

I waited until everyone had picked up their jackets, purses, and finished their drinks, then rose and slowly filed out. I pretended to join them, last in line, but when they'd all exited, I turned and walked back to the empty stage. I stepped up onto it, pushed through the curtains, and in the back, I found Emerson cleaning up his eggs and broken plate, picking up all his props, and packing them into boxes. His wren chirped at me from its small cage. I stared at Emerson.

"You did that to me?" I demanded. *"How ...?"*

Emerson smiled, but shook his head.

"Penelope, we talked about this," Emerson said.

"Show me this one trick and I'll never ask again," I said.

Emerson paused and stared at me.

"You promise ...?" he asked.

I crossed my heart with a finger.

Emerson reached into a box and lifted out his big steel needle. He rapped it against the box; it was real. Then he set it back in his box and pulled out an identical needle. Yet this one collapsed between his fingers until it was only four inches long.

"Spring-loaded," Emerson said. "I switch when I move my podium aside. Under the stage lights, it looks like the real one. I hold one in each hand. They collapse when you squeeze their sides. The red cord slides through pockets in the curtain."

My shoulders drooped.

"You thought I was doing real magic ...?"

Emerson laughed.

"I wouldn't put it past you," I said.

"The only real magic is choosing the best subjects from the crowd," Emerson said. "Pretty girls are best; they distract the audience most. Slightly drunk helps, too drunk is a disaster."

"I'm sorry," I said.

"Don't be," Emerson said.

"I didn't trust you," I said.

"Never trust a magician ... onstage," Emerson quipped. "Not even me."

Chapter 17

The next morning, I entered the lobby to find Bessy and Nathan waiting.

"Nathan, go ahead," Bessy said to him. "We'll find you in the meeting room."

Nathan nodded, and left with only a wary glance. As he was walking out, Bessy stared at me.

"I knocked on your door last night," Bessy said.

"Oh ...?" I asked.

"You weren't there," Bessy said.

"I didn't get home until late," I said.

"I saw when you got home," Bessy said. "I was going down for the continental breakfast ... about thirty minutes ago."

I stared and said nothing.

"Your magician friend ...?" Bessy asked.

I nodded.

"I'm not trying to intrude," Bessy said. "However, when we're at Devonshire-Slate ..."

"All my attention will be on insuring our sale," I promised.

"That's all I need to know," Bessy said. "Off the record, I'm glad you got together."

"It was a lucky ... coincidence," I tried not to grin or frown.

In two back-to-back meetings, I was called upon to demonstrate the latest features of our product. I did so with ease, and answered questions about creating new accounts, entering and cross-linking notes, logging hours, and creating new categories for assigning medical equipment and practices. When they asked for features we didn't have, or expansions of features I'd demonstrated, I took notes and promised to get feedback from our developers right away. Whatever they asked for, Bessy assured them it was already under development ... even when I knew it wasn't.

After our second meeting, Bessy went to a meeting I wasn't invited to. I sat alone in a conference room and phoned Rosanne, who only wanted to know if I was still phoning Emmerich. I told her we'd talked, then had her organize an online meeting between Mr. Dawes and I. Yet I heard her talking to him and she said to call him right away.

I'd almost clicked 'Connect' when my computer rang, and a video conference window opened on my screen.

"Mr. Dawes," I answered.

"How's it going?" he asked.

"Well, I'd say," I said.

I described the meetings I'd attended, sent him my updated list of personal contacts, and copied to him the product enhancements they'd asked about.

"Tell them we're already working on most of those and we'll look into the rest ASAP," Mr. Dawes said.

"Bessy already did," I said. "Are we ...?"

"As of my next meeting, yes," Mr. Dawes said.

"A few of these will be tricky, but they're possible. I'll run them by Mr. Tiasan after our call."

"Great," I said.

"We need you in Nebraska in two weeks," Mr. Dawes said.

"The Nebraska Medical Trade Show," I nodded. "What about the Pacific Northwest Medical Research Conference?"

"I'll remind Bessy," Mr. Dawes said. "If you're needed elsewhere, we'll send someone else."

Bessy, Nathan, and I each put in a full day, and then headed to the parking lot together. Summers in Atlanta were hot and muggy, and even inside the underground lot, we were sweating before we reached our cars. Bessy headed out first, and I followed Nathan to the first traffic light, where we lost Bessy. I followed him onto I-75, but halfway to our hotel, I exited onto Old Dixie Road ... just on a whim. I scolded myself at once, but I had a strange feeling, like I was holding my hand over one of three cards. I didn't know Atlanta, except for the exit near the airport, and I was already lost. However, I knew my hotel was south of here, and turned to keep the sun on my right.

Before I found my hotel, I was furious; I'd been driving almost half an hour, following directions on my phone. If I'd stayed on the freeway, I'd be in my room by now ... or possibly Emerson's room. *Emerson was waiting ...!*

Emerson answered his cell phone as I was walking toward the elevator.

"I'm in the hotel bar," Emerson said. "Shall I ....?"

"Stay there," I said. "I'm going up to my room."

"I could join ...," Emerson suggested.

165

"Actually, I need a drink," I said. "I'll drop off my work gear and meet you."

Fifteen minutes later, I sat down on the barstool beside Emerson.

"Black and tan," I said to the bartender.

"Bad day ...?" Emerson asked.

"Just long," I said. "Trying to remember everyone's names and faces is the worst. If you don't remember, they feel insulted."

"Glad I don't have your job," Emerson said.

"I've got some questions," I said.

"Questions safe to be overheard?" Emerson asked.

I frowned. "No."

I glared at him until the bartender set my beer in front of me. I gulped it deeply.

"This is frustrating," I said.

"It won't be for long," Emerson said. "Once I've answered all your questions ..."

"How long will that take?" I asked.

"Depends on how many questions you ask," Emerson said.

"You can be really ...," I growled.

"Life is frustrating," Emerson said. "Magic can't change that."

"No magic you know ...?" I asked.

"Do you know magic I don't?" Emerson asked.

I took another sip. Suddenly the bar cheered. The Rambling Wrecks from Georgia Tech had scored. I glanced around; the same game was being played on every screen.

"Are there other ... tests ...?" I asked. "Wine on mirrors, three cards, ...?"

"Many," Emerson said. "They're all the same ...

learning new ... awarenesses, expanding sensitivity ..."

"I got a strange feeling on the road coming home," I said. "Exited early ... then I got lost."

"These things happen," Emerson said. "When starting, you never know if feelings are real or imagined. Well, no one is ever sure. Even I make mistakes, and right courses can go badly wrong."

"How?" I asked.

"Events are constantly happening," Emerson said. "You set your course, then the course changes, and you arrive where you didn't expect."

"How often does that happen?" I asked.

"The more complicated your course, the more likely it'll happen," Emerson said. "The longer your course, the more variations creep in."

"How long do you have?" I asked.

"I need to leave in an hour and a half to set up my stage," Emerson said.

"Have you eaten?" I asked.

"Not for a while," Emerson said.

"What would you like?" I asked.

"Whatever pleases you," Emerson said.

"You won't have time to eat," I said.

"I can drive through ...," Emerson said.

"Drink up," I said.

Alone in the elevator, we mashed our faces. Emerson pressed me against the wall, and fingernails dug into shirts until the door opened. Inside his room, we started over, and seconds later we were flinging off clothes.

Magic ... three times!

We showered together, but didn't have time to enjoy it fully. No coincidence would delay Emmerich the Amazing's curtain, and I wanted him to have time to eat. I had to dress in the same clothes so I could see him down to the lobby. We kissed before he left.

"You want to see my act again ...?" Emerson asked.

"Not tonight," I said. "I've got practicing to do."

With another kiss, Emerson headed off, and I returned to the hotel bar. To my surprise, Bessy and Nathan were sitting together.

"Wasn't that horrible?" Bessy asked as I sat beside them.

"What ...?" I asked.

"That traffic jam!" Bessy snarled.

"Oh, yes," I agreed.

"You must've gotten stuck way behind me," Nathan said. "We got here half an hour ago."

"In the wrong lane," I said.

"Glad I don't live here," Bessy said.

I sat beside them as they rambled complaints.

Had the feeling that caused me to exit the freeway saved me from an hour stuck in traffic?

"Two lanes blocked ... couldn't have happened just one exit farther ...!" Nathan complained. "Hey, where's your ...?"

"I dropped it in my room," I said.

"I came straight here," Nathan said, nodding to the computer bag at his feet.

We talked shop, glad that the introduction to our product was going so well. Nathan complained about their load-balancers, calling it a 'Jurassic system' and wondering what idiots had installed it. Bessy seemed delighted by his solutions and workarounds, yet both were in such dismal moods that even good news seemed dreary.

"No friend tonight?" Bessy asked me.

"He's working," I said. "Took me to see his act last night; it was impressive. Tomorrow night's his last performance."

"Maybe we should go ...?" Nathan suggested.

"Not me," Bessy said, looking at me. "I don't like magic tricks."

I made a mental note to thank Bessy, then reminded her about Nebraska and Seattle.

"There's really not much left we can do," Bessy said. "Nathan's got their system mostly integrated ... and I've talked to everyone."

"I don't trust anything until it's fully tested," Nathan said. "I've gotten their data to show up, but we need practical testing with real data from remotes."

"I'll talk to Abigail tomorrow," Bessy said. "It'd be nice to close this deal quickly."

"What about training?" I asked.

"Mr. Dawes is doing a series of new training videos," Bessy said. "We'll host remote conferences, show them our videos, and take questions."

"Unless I have to do firewall updates on every site," Nathan complained.

"What about you?" Bessy turned to me. "Are you anxious to get back home ... or stay?"

"I need to clean my apartment," I said.

"A magician in North Dakota ...," Bessy smiled. "I wonder how that will go ...?"

"So do I," I fretted.

I finished my second beer, which Bessy and Nathan thought was my first, and tried to excuse myself, but they wouldn't hear of it.

"Aren't you hungry?" Nathan asked.

"Oh," I said; I'd been eager to get back to my room and practice. "I'm so tired ... I forgot."

"We could eat here," Bessy said. "I'm starving, but needed drinks after that drive ..."

"More like park ... except for one inch every few minutes," Nathan groused.

"Okay, but then I need some sleep," I said.

We stayed at the bar. Bessy ordered another round of drinks, and we ate together. The rest of the bar kept cheering a different game; the local team had fallen behind but was catching up. I ate a bacon-cheeseburger, hoping it would offset the level of alcohol I was drinking. Fortunately, Bessy picked up the tab for all of us, yet she ordered another round of drinks first.

I kept thinking about the feeling I'd sensed which had saved me from being stuck in traffic for an hour.

Would this be happening all the time ...?

Alone in my room, I tried the three cards. I kept failing. I'd drunk too much. Finally I recalled I wasn't supposed to guess the card; I was looking for the coincidence of selecting the ace, not the ace itself. I tried to feel joyful and scanned each card. I succeeded once. However, my next few tries all failed. Frustrated, I threw the cards across the room.

I couldn't concentrate on my book. I turned on the TV, but skipped through lots of nothing. I wondered how Mephistopheles was and phoned mother. She was delighted to hear from me, but reminded me of the time difference; she'd been on her way to bed. Before I hung up, she asked if I'd been drinking. I told her I'd only had a few.

My phone woke me up at 10:30 PM.

"I just got out," Emerson said.

"Oh, um ...," I stammered.

"Did I wake you?" Emerson said.

"I'm in bed alone," I snarled.

"I'll be right there," Emerson hung up.

My phone rang again.

"Where are you?" I asked.

"I've been knocking on your door for a full minute," Emerson said.

Bleary-eyed, I staggered to my door.

"Well, look at you!" Emerson said.

"Clothes off!" I ordered.

Chapter 18

My wakeup call rang. I answered, then hung up on the automated voice wishing me a good morning. I snuggled against Emerson, who winced yet didn't awaken.

My head hurt. I wondered if we'd made love; I didn't remember falling asleep. Yet we had a meeting first thing this morning.

Shower. Soak head. Shampoo and conditioner. Try to wake up.

I kissed Emerson before I left. Despite the noisy blow dryer, he seemed sound asleep.

One meeting passed and I didn't say a word. After a second hour, another meeting ended, and I kept wondering why I was there.

After the third meeting, I sat at my temporary desk and checked my office emails, then my personal emails, and then I played on social media, reading about all the crises my friends thought were important. I didn't social media often and mostly liked the jokes.

That afternoon Bessy approached me.

"Nathan is going to have to visit every remote site," Bessy said. "Some of their firewalls are so obsolete that he can't update them from here without tearing them down completely. However, it looks good."

"The sale is happening?" I asked.

"We've agreed on a three week test period," Bessy said. "They also insisted on a three month buy-out ... in case they try it and can't manage adoption. But we're through here. I've got one meeting this afternoon, but you can go."

"Go ...?" I asked.

"Rosanne is arranging your flight back," Bessy said. "She'll email you the details. If I can, I'll be on the same flight, but we'll see. They're popping champagne corks in Bismarck."

"Are you serious?" I asked.

"I'll see if I can get you an office near mine," Bessy said. "Go be with your boyfriend."

I reached for my phone as soon as she left.

"Rosanne ...?" I asked. "When are you planning to bring me home?"

"Working on reservations now," Rosanne's voice said. "Possibly Sunday."

"Not before then," I said.

"What's going on?" Rosanne asked. "Not another man ...!"

"Rosanne, who do you think I am ...?" I asked, exasperated. "Just make the reservation!"

"I want every dirty detail ...!" Rosanne's voice deepened.

"Good-bye, Rosanne," I said.

I hung up and pushed 'call' a second later.

"We made the sale!" I whispered to Emerson.

"That's great!" Emerson said.

"I'm on my way," I said. "Where are you?"

"At the hotel," Emerson said. "I was thinking of

trying out their hot tub."

"Wait for me," I said.

No traffic jam slowed me. Within half an hour, I was knocking on Emerson's door wearing my red bikini under a hotel bathrobe.

"Wow!" Emerson exclaimed. "Do we have to go tubbing?"

"Didn't you get enough last night?" I asked.

"I did, but you slept through most of it," Emerson said.

"Bessy kept buying us drinks," I said.

"Remind me to thank Bessy."

"Don't you dare!"

"Me ...?" Emerson pretended innocence. "I wouldn't do anything ... special ... after you fell asleep."

"What did you do ...?" I demanded.

"You tell me," Emerson teased.

"No wonder I didn't wake rested," I said.

The hot tub was divine despite that it overlooked a pool filled with shrieking kids, and bored parents resting poolside. We soaked for almost half an hour ... and each of us kept slipping our hands under bubbles where no one could see. I suggested we go upstairs to finish what we'd started, yet Emerson made me wait ten minutes while he sat on the other side of the tub ... so he could walk past strangers without embarrassment.

We showered first, completed our business under hot streams, and then Emerson kissed me long and deeply.

"I love this part of relationships," Emerson said. "Everything is new and exciting. I never want this part to end."

"Nothing's new forever," I said, looking at him.

"We'll just have to find new ways to keep it

exciting," Emerson smiled. "Whatever turns either of us on, any fantasies, secret desires, we tell each other."

"I'll be your sexual fantasy if you'll be mine?" I smiled. "I have to tell you; my work is done. I'll be heading home soon."

"Tonight is my last show ...," Emerson started.

"I know," I said. "Emerson, did you ...?"

"I had nothing to do with your sale; that was all you," Emerson said. "We've got to be respectful; not do anything that might affect the other, not intentionally, without permission. That's a code all magicians follow."

"What do you mean 'intentionally'?" I asked.

"You got a feeling and avoided a traffic jam," Emerson said. "You didn't sense the accident; you felt the good coincidence of an exit, so you took it."

"Will I always feel good coincidences?" I asked.

"It's not that simple," Emerson said. "I'll explain each part as soon as you've learned enough to understand it. However, we've got to trust each other ... and swear to avoid manipulating ..."

"You can ... I can't ...," I said.

"You don't realize how subtle manipulations can be," Emerson said. "Get dressed; I'll change in my room, and we'll go out for a big breakfast ... well, lunch for you."

"How late did you sleep in?" I asked.

"Not long, but I didn't want to get out of bed," Emerson said. "You'll learn about that, too."

"What ...?" I asked.

"Not today," Emerson said. "Today we celebrate. Tomorrow I introduce you to something new. Acceptable?"

"Maybe," I said. "I've got to ask. What are your plans ... post Atlanta?"

"What's the weather in Bismarck?" Emerson asked.

"Atlanta without humidity," I said.

"I'll arrive in a Hawaiian shirt," Emerson said.

"The dark one ... not the gaudy orange ...?" I pleaded.

"If I must," Emerson rolled his eyes.

I can't say it was the finest seafood restaurant in Atlanta, but its prices were outrageous. Few others were there for late lunch, so we sat at a secluded table where no one could eavesdrop.

"Lemonaide, no alcohol," I told our waiter.

"I'll have orange juice," Emerson said, wearing his gaudy orange Hawaiian shirt.

"Did you have to wear that?" I asked.

"You asked me to save the dark one," Emerson reminded.

I ordered my favorite, garlic shrimp scampi, and Emerson ordered a shark fillet. Once our waiter vanished, I risked the big question.

"Why aren't you rich?" I asked.

"Why would I want to be rich ...?" Emerson asked.

"Private planes, mansion, ...," I said.

"Everything has a price ... and money itself has costs," Emerson said.

"What's the price?" I asked.

"Loneliness," Emerson said. "Once you get rich, you're news. People notice you."

"You're a celebrity!" I argued.

"Small-time ... and I keep it that way," Emerson said. "The more you're watched, the less you can do, the less openly you travel, and the fewer you meet, so you need to identify what you want out of life. We're not

177

immortal. When I became a magician, the first thing I did was seek out the oldest of our kind and learn from them; probably the smartest thing I ever did."

"What did they say?" I asked.

"Keep everything simple, quiet, and keep moving," Emerson said. "Try every adventure. Magic isn't forever. Someday you'll be laying on your deathbed thinking back upon your life ... live the life that lets you leave this world smiling."

"Good advice," I said.

"Some magicians I spoke to were on their deathbeds, and some not far from them," Emerson said. "One was a hundred and twenty-two ..."

"Human's don't live that long!" I argued.

"They can, but few follow the paths of coincidences that would let them," Emerson said.

"Are you saying I'll ...?" I asked, my mouth unable to voice the thought.

"Avoiding everything that could kill you, it's possible," Emerson said. "Eat only what extends life. But that many coincidences are virtually impossible, and don't leave much time for enjoyment. Magic can't stop death."

"But ... these things you do!" I whispered. "You could ... fix so many ... bad things!"

"Ah, the superhero calling," Emerson smiled. "End war, solve all problems, rescue the innocent ..."

"What's wrong with that?" I asked.

"Abilities get noticed," Emerson said. "Stage magicians have been kidnapped, tortured, and even killed by fans who believed our tricks were more than deceptions. Also, range matters. To get drug dealers, rapists, or gangsters arrested, you'd need to be near them, and that's never safe."

"What about nonviolent problems ... like exposing cheating politicians?" I asked.

"If you think they're not criminals, then they've deceived you," Emerson said. "Rich people notice who's near them. You might pull it off once or twice, but soon you'll get investigated."

"But no one can prove ...!" I insisted.

"No one can prove God exists, but many have been killed for religious beliefs," Emerson said.

"How does it work?" I asked.

"Suzzannia believes all coincidences are preordained," Emerson said. "Another magician claims ghosts of dead people create possible doors and direct the living through them. I think it's more complicated; I believe time is like a thick rope, multiple strands looping and crisscrossing reality, eternally splitting and rejoining. Alternate universes exist all around us, but they keep branching off, then fading away, or folding back into reality. It's like a carnival fun house; you may go right or left, but every path pressures you to the same destination."

"That's pretty deep," I said.

"I can't prove a word of it," Emerson said.

"Why not tell everyone?" I asked.

"Hangings, witch trials, burnings at the stake," Emerson said. "Don't think those can't happen again."

"Most people can't ...?" I asked.

"Fear kills sensitivity; the paranoid have zero," Emerson said.

"You'd think people would notice," I said.

"That's what stage magicians are for," Emerson smiled. "We convince the world that magic is fake."

Stuffed with seafood, we drove back to the hotel.

"Can I watch your show tonight?" I asked.

"They're sold out," Emerson said. "You could come, but watching from backstage; you can't see anything. Besides, you need to rest up."

"Why?" I asked.

"I was thinking we could do the Atlanta zoo tomorrow," Emerson said.

"You said you'd teach me something new ...," I said.

"Hotel rooms host limited coincidences," Emerson said. "Your next lesson requires animals."

We spent the afternoon lazing, and visited the bar before Emerson had to leave. We were still stuffed from our heavy lunch, but we split a gooey nachos so that Emerson wouldn't be hungry during his last show. I sent him off with a kiss and returned to my room.

I turned on my TV ... and wished that a tropical ocean was splashing just outside my window.

Chapter 19

Asleep, Emerson breathed slowly and softly. I watched him from the light coming through the tiny gaps around the curtains. I couldn't believe my changed life ... he was still so much a stranger, yet we seemed to fit so tightly.

Had coincidence led him to me ... or something greater ...?

Emerson's manners, consideration, intellect, and gentleness thrilled me. Yet one month was too soon. You don't really know someone until you see how they act under adversity, but how can adversity strike someone who controls coincidences?

He excelled in lovemaking. He took longer to be satisfied than any man I'd ever known, although he surrendered quickly when I took charge. His hands were firm, yet his touch tender. He warned me before he tried something new, and seemed thrilled by everything I liked.

What limits restrained his power?
What limits would restrain mine?

Emerson awoke gasping, my head under the covers. I thought it appropriate; the last thing I remembered from last night was his flicking tongue pleasing me. We writhed and squirmed. When we finally collapsed, we pushed back the covers; heat and satisfaction radiated.

After we recovered, we showered together ... and repeated our mutual pleasing.

I'd never known anyone so insatiable!

Hunger forced us to get dressed. He watched me ... and asked if I'd do a striptease. I informed him that no timelines allowed that. We ate in the hotel restaurant, then climbed inside Emerson's sports car, and motored to the zoo.

"Is it a big zoo?" I asked.

"I heard it's world famous," Emerson said.

"You've never been there?" I asked.

"No," Emerson asked. "Why?"

"You're not using a map," I said.

"I looked at one to get the general area," Emerson said. "Best to get started in the right direction."

I stared at him, amazed.

"Feeling sensations is only the first step," Emerson said. "The second step is trusting what you feel."

"How many steps are there?" I asked.

"Depends on how high you want to climb," Emerson said.

Within half an hour, we arrived at the zoo. We laughed at squabbling flamingos, then spent two hours visiting the World of Reptiles, the African Plains and Rain Forest, the Living Treehouse, and the Asian Forest. Everything was wonderful, yet I kept wondering when my next lesson would begin.

In the Boundless Budgies exhibit, as kids ran about and adults watched, Emerson smeared seeds onto one finger and held it up. One of the countless birds flew down from one of the many small, enclosed trees, landed on his hand, and took advantage of his feast.

"Feel it," Emerson whispered pointedly.

I tried to sense it, but felt nothing.

Another bird joined the first and tried to steal its feast.

"Which birds will land on me?" Emerson asked. "There are a hundred birds in here; why these?"

"Coincidence ...?" I asked.

"You tell me," Emerson whispered.

I reached out and tried to sense coincidences, yet still nothing.

A bird with fluttering wings flew past my head. It distracted, yet I kept trying.

"Nothing," I said.

After cleaning his finger of seeds, the birds flew off.

"Everything is coincidence, but some are too unpredictable, too random to sense," Emerson whispered. "If you came here every day, or were in an enclosed room where you felt safe, you might feel them. Even then, they'd be faint, almost imperceptible. Now think about the feelings you had with the cards and wine-drops. Remember what they felt like when it worked. Project your joy there, on that dirt patch beneath that bush. What a coincidence it would be if every bird here suddenly landed on that spot. Project that coincidence ... your joy ... how it would feel."

"I don't know how," I whispered back.

Emerson nodded, then waved his hand at the spot. Two birds flew to land there ... three ... five ... a dozen ...!

"That's enough," Emerson said. "These places

are security monitored, and we can't be noticed doing things zoo-keepers can't explain."

"How did you ...?" I asked.

"We're part of every coincidence we feel," Emerson said.

"How do I make it feel like a coincidence?" I asked.

"How would you feel if all these birds suddenly flew there?" Emerson asked, pointing at the bare spot. "Imagine how you'd feel ... and make your reaction precede the event. Create the sensations inside you, then experience them."

"If you feel it, they will come?" I asked.

Emerson shrugged. I stared at the spot. I tried to focus, yet couldn't. After long minutes, Emerson put his arm around me.

"Don't feel dispirited," Emerson said, nodding to the excited kids. "Hard to concentrate here. Yet I think you've got the idea. Birds are easy... but it takes practice."

"I still miss a lot with cards," I admitted.

"I don't always get it right," Emerson said. "It's an art, not a science. Let's go."

"I want to try again," I insisted.

"One last time," Emerson said.

Again I failed. Emerson laughed at my embarrassment.

"If it was easy, everyone would be doing it," Emerson said. "Most give up after only a few failures. Give yourself time ... months, not days."

We left the zoo. On the way back, we stopped at a chain restaurant for burgers and beers.

"There's no hurry," Emerson said.

"It's frustrating," I said.

"Can you paint like Michelangelo?" Emerson asked. "Oh, that's right; he spent years perfecting his technique."

"It's not the same," I said.

"Not like an author writing their first book?" Emerson asked. "Not like a wrestler competing in his first match?"

"Not at all," I said.

"How so?"

"Because it's about me!"

Emerson laughed.

"I'm scared," I said.

"About what?" Emerson asked.

"Us," I said. "Not the magic; we're happening ... swiftly."

"If you want anything, even to slow down, you need only ask," Emerson said.

"I don't ... and that worries me," I said.

"Worries me, too."

"What ...?"

"Worry is fear," Emerson said. "Maybe we should slow down; I'm introducing this to you too fast."

"I can handle it," I said.

"Worry is evidence that you're not," Emerson said. "Besides, fear reduces sensitivity."

"What can I do?" I asked.

"Stop being in a hurry," Emerson said. "It took me years."

"Maybe if you tell me how you started ...?" I asked.

"I will ... but not here," Emerson said.

"Soon ...?"

Emerson nodded, yet his smile faltered.

"If you're worried about ... us ... perhaps we

should ...," Emerson said.

"No," I said. "I won't sleep."

"When are you going home?" Emerson asked.

Curious, I pulled out my phone. It felt odd; usually I checked my emails at least once every hour. I scanned and found one from Rosanne ... five hours old.

"Tomorrow," I said. "10:30 AM."

"When would you like for me to arrive?" Emerson asked.

"My apartment needs cleaning."

"How many weeks will that take?"

"Friday," I said. "Mid-afternoon, if you can. I can leave work early, pick you up, and we'll have the whole weekend ..."

"Sounds perfect," Emerson said.

"Remember Hawaii ...?" I asked. "When we rapid-fired ...?"

"Here ...?" Emerson asked.

"No," I said. "Tonight."

"As you wish," Emerson said softly, staring into my eyes.

"I'm not a princess bride," I groaned.

"Inconceivable!" Emerson exclaimed.

I slapped his arm.

I felt bad as we drove back. Again we were about to say good-bye, to sunder each other's company for an uncertain future. *Would it always be like this?* Both of us traveled a lot. Separated relationships carried difficulties. Absolute trust would be a constant requirement. We'd enjoy reunions, but in the end, we'd be apart more than was good for lasting relationships.

Would being apart make us grow apart?

When we got settled in my hotel room, we sat facing each other. I took a deep breath.

"When did you first ...?" I asked.

"High school," Emerson said. "I wasn't popular. Jerks always look for people they can bully ... and I was always the 'new kid'. I began looking for ... ways to avoid them."

"You discovered magic on your own?" I asked.

"Just the first part," Emerson said. "I started feeling things ... every time I needed to run away. I began to notice, somehow, where not to go."

"Fear taught you," I said.

"Probably why it took me so long," Emerson said.

"Maybe that's my problem," I said.

"My turn," Emerson said. "Normal relationships have shaky starts. Am I teaching you too fast ...? Should we slow down ...?"

"I don't know," I said. "In Hawaii, I knew something was odd about you. If you hadn't confessed ..."

"You'd have had me arrested ...?" Emerson asked.

"Uneven relationships don't work," I said. "I don't know what limits manipulated coincidences have ..."

"We'll never know for sure if we're manipulating each other," Emerson warned. "There's no way to tell."

"The easier it is to cheat, the more important trust is ...?" I asked.

"Exactly," Emerson said.

"How can we insure trust?" I asked.

"I have to tell you ... my bad stuff," Emerson said.

I stared at him.

"He was an old guy," Emerson said. "Merlin

Melville. He sensed me. He instigated a coincidence so we met. I just happened to be walking by as he was packing up after doing a backyard kid's party. He knew everything about magic, real and fake. He was in his fifties, fat with white hair, and he ... he liked young boys."

"A predator ...?" I asked.

"He wasn't my first," Emerson said. "Growing up in foster care, you meet all types, old men and women who'll do anything for sex. He showed me the magic I could do, over several weeks, at a horrible cost. Once I managed it on my own, I left him ... and my foster parents. I ran away from everyone I knew ... and never went back."

"I'm sorry," I said.

"Lots of kids face the same nightmare," Emerson said. "Eventually I met others like me, magicians, and learned more. But I didn't learn well."

"What happened?" I asked.

"What usually happens when an abused child gains power?" Emerson asked. "I became the bully I'd always hated. I'd suffered so much, I abused my gift."

"You became ...?" I began.

"A monster," Emerson finished. "Yet, there are some among us who watch out, who sense when we're about to be exposed. They seek us out ..."

"You got caught?" I asked.

"I got jailed," Emerson said. "When I got out, I couldn't find money or food. Every girl I approached screamed in terror ..."

"Screamed ...?" I asked.

"Every bad coincidence happened," Emerson said. "I thought my power had backfired. Finally, I was confronted by a force I couldn't combat; her name was

Lucinda. She'd raised a son, and had no patience with bullying. She ... she was far more powerful than I."

"What happened to her?" I asked.

"She lives in Florida near her half-dozen great-grandkids," Emerson said. "I still visit her when I can. She's the closest thing I've ever known to a real mother."

"She straightened you out?" I asked.

"Not just me," Emerson said. "I ... told her about Merlin Melville. She went looking for him. No one ever saw him again."

"She killed him ...?" I asked.

"I don't think so," Emerson said. "She isn't the type, but between equals, battles of coincidence can be deadly. A brick on the top of a building breaks off and falls. A car swerves to avoid a stray cat ... drives onto a crowded sidewalk. Coincidences can kill."

"You never asked ...?" I asked.

"I don't want to know," Emerson said. "My point is, I've led the life you fear I could. It's my greatest regret. It's taken me years to regain my self-respect. I never want to be like that again."

"Wow," I said.

"Don't ask for details," Emerson said. "You're ... too new. You need to know who I am now ... before you learn ... what I was."

"Someday ...?" I asked.

"Only if you insist," Emerson said.

"We'll leave it until then," I said.

"Thanks," Emerson said.

"I ... need to digest this," I said.

Emerson nodded.

I glanced around; my hotel room was small ...

"I could use a soak in the hot tub," Emerson said. "You look like you need a drink. Promise me you

189

won't go farther than the hotel bar ..."

I silently nodded. Emerson stood up, bent to give me a nervous kiss, and left to fetch his swimming trunks.

I sat staring at my empty room, at the mirror that the maid must've cleaned, as it bore no streaks, at my suitcases and things.

Emerson ... had once been a nightmare ...!
I needed a drink!

Emerson had suggested that I go to the bar. *Was he manipulating ...?*

I hesitated. *Suspicions* ... I was doing exactly as Emerson feared, assuming that I was being coerced. He hadn't told me everything, but how could he? Some things take time to digest. All new relationships suffer fears ... sharing intimate thoughts with someone mostly a stranger. Yet ... you have to know someone a short time before you can know them a long time.

Could I hold off my fears long enough to build a relationship?

Those who'd been a bully once were likely to be a bully forever. But not always. Bonnie had the biggest bustline in our sophomore year, when she used and threw away more boys than paper towels. Then, right after high school, she got married, and suddenly disapproved of premarital sex. I'd been no angel growing up, and I'd hated several girls just because they were popular. All I'd known about them was their names, pretty faces, and that they were cheerleaders. I still saw some of them around town, and I wasn't jealous of them anymore; one frequently served me coffee.

Emerson had suffered a terrible childhood ... and become what it had made him. Yet I hadn't seen a glimpse of bad manners since I'd first noticed him in the airport.

> *Magicians were experts at hiding things.*
> *I couldn't let fear ruin what we had!*

Yet ... what was I risking ... *and what would happen if I was wrong?*

Every argument against him faced one irrefutable obstacle: Emerson was a shining beacon in my drab, boring life. I liked him ... I might even love him ... and I wasn't sure if I could leave him.

He'd also shown me a reality I'd never guessed existed. Could I spend the rest of my life not knowing what powers I'd rejected ... because of unfounded suspicions?

I sat there, in my room, for two hours, torn, swaying from fear to lust to suspicion to longing.

> *Was I going to risk losing potential life-long happiness with a fantastic lover because of unproven doubts ...?*

I sat there until nine o'clock, pondering and resolving nothing. I didn't have enough information to make a rational decision, and the only logical course was ...

"Hello?" Emerson answered his phone.

"Are you planning to sleep alone tonight?" I asked.

Chapter 20

"Penelope ...?" Emerson asked.

I groaned.

"Your flight is at 10:30 AM," Emerson reminded.

"What time ...?" I asked.

"It's 6:30 AM," Emerson said. "If you plan to shower, eat ..."

"Five more minutes," I said.

Fingers slid up and down my back. Soft shoulder rubs. A kiss on the back of my neck ...

I didn't want to ...!

Packing. Check out. Rush hour traffic. Arrive two hours early. Stupid security screens. Can't miss my flight ...

I pushed back my covers.

"Do you want me to ...?" Emerson asked.

"No," I said.

"Like Hawaii ...?" Emerson asked.

"Sleep," I said. "No point both of us ..."

"I could do breakfast ...?" Emerson offered.

"Didn't I exhaust you last night?" I asked.

"I could use some more ...," Emerson said.

"We don't have time," I said.

Showered and dressed, I began packing my suitcase. Emerson sat up and turned on a light so I could see what I was doing.

"I can't wait to meet your friends," Emerson said.

"Expect to meet them all right away," I said. "Once they know you're there ..."

"Maybe you could host a party ...?" Emerson asked.

"In my apartment ...?" I asked. "I'm not going to clean it so they can trash it."

"Restaurant ...?" Emerson asked.

"I'll think about it," I said.

All too quickly I was packed. I looked everywhere, but I'd forgotten nothing.

"Going back to your room?" I asked.

"After you've left," Emerson said.

We shared a long good-bye kiss.

"Call me," I said.

"I'm excited about Bismarck," Emerson said.

"I'm nervous," I said.

"I'm nervous, too," Emerson said. "Yet ... you know how I feel."

"How ...?"

"I'll tell you ... inside your apartment."

We shared a long embrace ... and then I had to go.

Traffic was horrible. I had to wait in line to return my car. Security took too long. I sprinted to my terminal. They were boarding as I arrived, yet no line clogged the coffee shop beside the terminal; I boarded last, carrying two fruity muffins and a large, steaming mocha espresso.

With no upgrade, I sat near the tail, aisle seat,

too close to the tiny toilets for my preference. I couldn't sleep during the long flight from Atlanta to Minneapolis. The rows around me were mostly twelve year olds wearing matching jerseys under jackets, and their adult monitors seemed unable to keep them still or quiet. I wished that I could do more with coincidences than sense which card was the ace.

The connecting flight to Bismarck was little better, but shorter.

Bonnie met me at the airport with her youngest son in tow. I let him pull my carry-on while we descended to luggage.

Bonnie knew about my sale; *the Bismarck Express.* Fortunately, she didn't know I'd been with Emerson the whole time. Yet she'd already chosen my next, fancy new car.

"At least let me get paid first," I said.

"Where's the fun in that?" Bonnie asked. "Speaking of fun, where's Mr. Amazing ...?"

"We've talked ... a few times," I said.

"When are you seeing him?" Bonnie asked.

"Who knows?" I answered.

Bonnie's phone rang as she was driving. Before I could object, she invited Lyn to meet us at my place.

Lyn arrived while I was still unpacking.

"I've been watching your boyfriend's website," Lyn said.

"Stalking him ... or me?" I asked.

"Is there a difference?" Bonnie asked.

"His calendar shows nothing for the next several weeks," Lyn said.

"Really ...?" I asked.

"Don't lie," Bonnie said.

"Why should I be evasive?" I asked. "My

195

girlfriends are stalking my boyfriend ..."

"The Bismarck Express stops for no one,"
Bonnie said.

"He'll come here ... eventually," I admitted.

"When ...?" Bonnie asked.

"Ask the Bismarck Express," I said. "Until then,
I just want to pick up Mephistopheles and enjoy some
private time."

"Wash your hands afterwards," Lyn said.

"Ha-ha," I faked a laugh.

I waited until both of their cars drove away
before I started cleaning. Mom arrived with
Mephistopheles while I was vacuuming. We talked only
briefly; I kept the conversation on the business side of
my trip. She had to get back home before her TV shows
came on.

During my leftovers dinner, Emerson called.

"I have a ticket," Emerson said.

"When ...?" I asked.

"Friday afternoon," Emerson said. "I land in
Bismarck at 1:40 your time."

"Until then ...?" I asked.

"I was thinking of driving to Florida," Emerson
said.

"Lucinda ...?" I asked.

"I haven't seen her in a year," Emerson said. "It
might do us both good."

"To talk about me ...?" I asked.

"I keep no secrets from Lucinda," Emerson said.
I swallowed hard.

"Ticket purchased; too late to say no ...,"
Emerson chuckled.

Chapter 21

"The Atlanta South Regency Alms ...?" Rosanne asked with a grin.

"What ...?" I demanded.

"Oh, nothing," Rosanne said. "Just wondering if your ... bed was comfortable."

"Spill ...!" I ordered.

"I talked to Bessy Andrews," Rosanne said.

"Don't tell anyone," I said.

"That depends ...," Rosanne said. "Lunch ... tell me everything. And Mr. Dawes just left, but he wants to talk to you."

I set my laptop on my desk, avoiding Rosanne's stare. *What would she be like when Emerson arrived?* Even minor celebrities were Selena Gomez, Justin Bieber, or Angelina Jolie in small towns. My friends would swarm over him like hornets. The Bismarck Express would chug at full steam.

Emerson was used to being on stage. I wasn't. I didn't like the spotlight and couldn't handle hecklers.

I'd be the train whistle ...!

Ten minutes later, Mr. Dawes walked in.

"My office," Mr. Dawes said.

He interrogated me for an hour. He wanted to hear every detail, every discussion, every nuance and impression. I praised Bessy Andrews and Nathan Qui.

"Excellent," Mr. Dawes said. "You've outdone yourself."

"Glad to hear it," I said. "I know the purchase won't be finalized for weeks. Do I still need to do Nebraska?"

"We need our best presenter there," Mr. Dawes said. "People will be coming from all over."

"Wyoming ...?" I asked.

"Midwest states are underfunded, living off federal grants, but our competition will be there," Mr. Dawes admitted. "We can't surrender market share."

"I'll be ready for Nebraska," I promised.

"How ...?" Rosanne asked as we sat down at lunch. "You meet in Hawaii ... and a week later in Atlanta ...?"

"Lucky coincidence," I said.

"Miraculous, I'd say," Rosanne said.

"Don't start picking bridal flowers," I said.

"Where next?" Rosanne asked. "Here ...?"

"Florida," I said.

"Another show ...?" Rosanne asked.

"Family, I think," I said.

"You didn't make plans?" Rosanne asked.

"We travel a lot," I said.

"You can't leave love up to chance!" Rosanne argued.

"We haven't used that word," I said.

"Are you crazy?" Rosanne asked. "Emmerich must meet lots of pretty girls."

"A one night stand would've ended after

Hawaii," I said.

"Nothing ... permanent?" Rosanne asked.

"Too early to ask," I said.

"You set the hook while the bait's in his mouth," Rosanne said.

"Would you trust a hook baited during sex?" I asked.

Rosanne demanded sexual specifics; I refused. She threatened to announce that I was pregnant to the Bismarck Express.

"I can lie, too," I warned. "About your dancing naked in those college porn movies ...?"

"I n-n-never ...!" Rosanne stammered, eyes bulging.

"The juicier story is always most-believed," I reminded her.

Neither happy, but protected by mutually-assured destruction, we returned to the office. We both had afternoon meetings. I sat through mine bored, unimpressed with next year's predictions. I wondered if I could use coincidences to tell if their predictions were real ...

That evening, I spent three hours cleaning before opening a can of soup and sitting in front of the TV with Mephistopheles demanding attention.

"You don't mind a little company, do you ...?" I asked.

Mephistopheles purred.

Emerson didn't call.

Chapter 22

I awoke before the alarm went off. Tired as I
was, I couldn't return to dreams. Something was
bothering me, something bad. Unable to crush the
sentiment, I rose early, showered, got dressed, and fed
Mephistopheles. I didn't need to leave for work for half
an hour, yet I was awake and felt no reason to stay.
Vaguely I fancied the idea of stopping for coffee and a
scone.

In the early dawn, I walked down the stairs to the
parking lot, ready to get into my car, when I heard a
muffled, pained cry.

"Lillian ...!" I shouted, and I ran to help.

She was laying on the cold sidewalk beside her
fallen walker, her gray hair mussed.

"Oh, Ms. Polyglass!" Lillian gasped.

"Are you hurt?" I asked.

"I don't think so ...," Lillian said.

I set up her walker first, then lifted her aged
frame to lean upon it, trying not to hurt her. As old as
she was, she could've easily broken something.

"How long were you there?" I asked.

"Only a few minutes," Lillian said. "I edged my

walker off the sidewalk. It tilted, and I couldn't ..."

"Are you sure you're all right ...?" I asked.

Twenty minutes later, Mrs. Lillian safe on her couch in her ground floor apartment, I got into my car. She'd seemed shaky but kept insisting she was fine. I'd made sure her phone was working, charged, and set beside her, with orders to call if anything started to hurt. My nerves were afire, yet my fears weren't only for her.

If I hadn't gotten out of bed early then she could've been laying there a long time.

Quite a coincidence ...!

I did stop for coffee and a scone, yet I couldn't shake my suspicions. In Atlanta, I'd taken an unknown freeway exit and avoided almost an hour of traffic jam. The sensation which had been bugging me all morning was gone.

Was I meant to rescue Mrs. Lillian ...?

Coincidences ... *what limits did they have? Did the power to sense coincidences condemn you to running errands for karma?*

I had to ask Emerson. *Was your life truly yours if karma kept summoning you?*

I'd seen Star Wars, yet didn't believe in the Force ... nor did I want to.

Work wasn't exciting. Rosanne was disappointed to hear that Emerson hadn't phoned, and then I suffered her speculations on what he could've been doing. I answered emails, then dug out the company files on Nebraska and began reviewing the only two contacts we had there.

I wasn't looking forward to this trip.

Before I left work, Stacy phoned. She wanted to talk, so I arranged to meet her at our usual place, and within fifteen minutes I got a text that Bonnie, Julie, and

Lyn would be joining us.

After work, I drove straight to Arnold's. Julie had claimed a corner table for us, Rachel already serving her beer.

"Dad took the kids to little league," Julie grinned after I'd ordered. "I don't need to be home until seven."

"Mephistopheles will be furious if I don't feed him before then," I said.

"How's Emmerich?" Julie asked.

"Amazing," I said.

"How amazing ...?" Julie asked.

"I already told you ..."

"Bismarck Express ...!" Julie warned.

She knew ... which meant that they all did.

"I got to watch his act again," I confessed.

"You kept the lights on ...?" Julie laughed.

"Ha-ha," I snarled. "You and Bonnie should be comedians."

"As long as I don't have to listen to any more cartoons," Julie sighed.

"You have wonderful kids," I said.

"I just need someone Amazing to help me raise them," Julie said.

"Not my Amazing," I said.

"Does he have a brother ...?" Julie asked.

Bonnie, Stacy, and Lyn arrived. After forcing me to talk, each spewed the same question.

"I don't know when Emerson will call," I said.

"Phone sex ...?" Stacy suggested.

"On a cell phone?" I asked. "Are you crazy?"

"Video chat ...?" Bonnie suggested.

"No," I said pointedly.

"We could film you, and you could send it ...," Stacy began.

"Not enough in Fort Knox ...," I said.

"Would he like it?" Bonnie asked.

"What man wouldn't?" Lyn asked.

"Never going to happen," I said.

"Prude ...!" Bonnie scorned.

"When have you filmed porn ...?" I asked.

"I take the fifth," Bonnie said.

"After you've drunk a fifth," Julie chided.

To change the subject, I told them about my possible sale. Their imaginations of my upcoming wealth equaled their fantasies of my sex life.

"Build a huge, luxury mansion, and let us move in," Lyn said.

"Open a magician's theater in downtown Bismarck and run it for Amazing," Stacy suggested.

"Take us to Hawaii so I can find a magician," Julie said.

"My raise won't equal more than a few bucks an hour," I tried to rein them in. "I'll be lucky if the full bonus would get me a down-payment on a car."

"Why buy anything when you're traveling the world with Amazing?" Bonnie asked.

"Your plans, not mine," I said.

"Have you made more secret plans to meet Emerson?" Bonnie asked.

"Bring him here!" Lyn insisted.

"Let you four siege him ...?" I asked. "The Bismarck Express will jump its tracks."

"You're embarrassed of us?" Stacy asked.

"Constantly," I answered.

"Send him a photo of you in your red bikini," Bonnie said. "It got him into your bedroom ..."

"And you never thanked us for that," Julie said.

"Have you considered that he might like me for

other reasons?" I asked.

"Nope," Bonnie smiled. "Bikini is more fun."

"How can I bring him?" I asked. "Look how you behave ...!"

"We'll be nice when he's here," Julie said.

"Yea, we just want to know everything about him and tell him everything about you," Bonnie said.

"Don't you dare ...!" I warned Bonnie.

They all laughed.

I cringed. *Emerson would be arriving in less than three days!*

Julie, Lyn, and I ate at Arnolds after Bonnie and Stacy left to cook for their families. Nancy, Kathy, and Brendan joined us. I took some ribbing, but the Bismarck Express had returned to one of its usual tracks, denying the authenticity of the mayor's relationship with his wife. Then Nancy suggested that Gwen and Joel were secretly dating, yet Brendan only wanted to talk about his new truck.

I escaped as soon as I could, and hurried home to Mephistopheles, who whined about being left alone. I fed him right away, then resumed cleaning, stacking, and boxing all my loose paperwork. Then I sorted all my piled DVDs back into their cases and slid them onto their shelf. I folded both couch blankets and shoved unneeded boxes under my bed.

In the middle of cleaning, Emerson called.

"Lucinda wants to meet you," Emerson said.

"Do you need to be rescued?" I asked.

"She grilled me until I'm well-done," Emerson said.

"I'm getting equally roasted," I said.

"Your friends excited to meet me?" Emerson asked.

"You think I told them ...?" I asked. "They'd go insane! No, I'm not giving them days to make plans. They'll learn you're here when you are."

"Sounds risky," Emerson said.

"Risky is trusting them," I said. "A couple of hours' notice ought to be enough."

"Enough for what?" Emerson asked.

"For the Bismarck Express," I said. "Be prepared."

"My sleeves will be stuffed with rosebuds," Emerson laughed.

"You'll be on stage the whole time," I said. "If we don't do it this way then they'll be knocking down my door all weekend."

"We can't have that," Emerson said.

"It would ruin my plans," I said.

"Do tell ...!" Emerson said.

"I'm not giving you days to make plans, either," I said.

"I'll have to imagine," Emerson warned.

"I need to tell you something," I said. "Remember when I took that freeway exit, got lost, and escaped a traffic jam ...?"

"Something happened ...?" Emerson asked.

"I woke up and left for work way too early," I said. "I rescued old Mrs. Lillian in our parking lot ...!"

"Love, cell phones are monitored," Emerson said. "If we don't need to talk about it right now ..."

I caught my breath, unable to speak.

"Hello ...?" Emerson asked. "Still there ...?"

"Here," I said.

"I thought I'd lost you," Emerson said.

"No, you ... surprised me," I said.

"How?"

"You called me 'Love'."

Silence.

"Lucinda ...!" Emerson snarled.

"Is she there ...?" I asked.

"No, but her stories ..."

"Stories ...?" I asked.

"Lucinda tells stories," Emerson said. "She's been regaling me with stories since I told her about you."

"What kind of stories?" I asked.

"You'll learn when you meet her," Emerson said.

"So ... you didn't mean it when you call me 'Love' ...?" I asked.

"I didn't mean to say it over the phone," Emerson said.

"So you meant it ...?" I asked.

"We'll talk when I get there," Emerson said.

"Can't wait," I said.

"You'll have to," Emerson said. "My flight number is A4164."

"I'll be there when you land," I promised.

"I'd better say good-night," Emerson said, "... before I slip up again."

"I don't mind," I said.

"Good-night," Emerson said. "See you Friday."

Chapter 23

Work, meetings, and Rosanne's babble passed in a delightful haze.

Emerson had called me 'Love'!

I went shopping on my way home. My refrigerator was empty, I was almost out of cat food, and I didn't want Emerson thinking I always ate out. Almost by route I trolled each aisle, wondering not so much whether I wanted each item as what Emerson would think when he saw it in my kitchen. For once, my selections were only name brands.

I paused in the wine section. I knew little of wines, and stared perplexed at the countless bottles. What was good? Which one would Emerson like ...?

Quickly I glanced around; no one was looking. If I could blindly pick the ace, king, or queen of hearts, then I could find a bottle Emerson would like. I reached out my hand and sensed for a coincidence. *Would it work?*

I peeked several times to make sure that no one was watching. I slid my hands over the bottles, one shelf and then the next, seeking for anything unusual. Surely one of these wines would impress Emerson, but which one? Hundreds of different bottles stood before me on shelves from below my knees to above my head.

I closed my eyes, letting my senses lead me, feeling for any coincidence. Yet I felt nothing. All these wine bottles ... *which would Emerson choose?*

Crash!

My ankles ...! Wet ...!

Horrified, I jumped back and opened my eyes. A broken bottle lay on the tile floor, red wine pouring out, forming a rapidly-widening puddle.

A manager was summoned; *I'd broken a thirty dollar bottle of port!*

Ten minutes later, I left the supermarket with no bottle of wine, despite having paid for one. My face was scarlet, my shoes wet, and I tried to avoid everyone's eyes, yet knew I was being stared at ...

No more attempting magic in public!

I found my home impressively clean. It hardly looked like anyone lived there. I kicked off my shoes on my doorstep, unwilling to stain my clean carpet.

I fed Mephistopheles, admired my living room, and wished I could keep it like this all the time ... showplace quality ... which I knew I wouldn't. I double-checked to insure that my door was locked; anyone who saw my living room this clean would know I was expecting a guest.

Tomorrow I'd dust and vacuum again.

I plucked Emerson's hat off the living room shelf where I'd placed it on display. I put it on, looked at myself in the mirror, undid the top three buttons of my blouse, and smiled. I looked good, and despite all my doubts, I couldn't wait for Emerson to arrive. I didn't believe in fate, yet I enjoyed how he played me.

I wore his hat for the rest of the evening.

Chapter 24

"Penelope ...!" Rosanne hissed. *"Are you even listening ...?"*

"Sorry ...?" I asked.

"You're thinking about him, aren't you?" Rosanne asked.

"Don't be silly," I said.

"Really ...?" Rosanne asked. "Without looking at your screen, tell me what's on it ..."

I glared at her; *I had no idea what was on my screen.*

"I'm not playing games," I covered my ass.

"No, I don't think you are," Rosanne said.

"You're worse than Bonnie," I said.

"You love him," Rosanne said.

"No, I ...," I started, but I couldn't finish.

"I knew it," Rosanne said. "Not just magical on stage ...?"

"If anyone hears you ...!" I shushed her.

"You're planning something," Rosanne said.

"No ...!" I argued.

"Tell the truth," Rosanne insisted.

I glanced around; Mr. Dawes' office was empty.

"You promise not to tell ...?" I whispered.

"Upon my soul ...!" Rosanne swore.

I hesitated.

"You'll know soon enough," I whispered. "You can't tell anyone: Emerson is coming ... tomorrow."

Rosanne's eyes and smile widened.

"You need to cover for me," I said. "I have to leave early to pick him up."

"Tell me everything ...!" Rosanne salivated.

"Nothing to tell," I said. "I thought we had a problem, but we resolved it in Atlanta. Now he's coming for a visit ..."

"For how long ...?" Rosanne asked.

Color drained from my face.

"Is he ... moving in with you?" Rosanne asked.

"No, he can't ...!" I said.

"You invited him ... with no itinerary?" Rosanne asked. "No ... duration?"

I stared, unable to answer.

"He can't stay forever," Rosanne said. "His magic act ..."

"That's right!" I blurted out. "See? We have an itinerary ...!"

"Really ...?" Rosanne laughed. "What is it?"

"He's ... coming for a visit," I said.

"To meet friends ... and family?" Rosanne asked.

"Yes," I said.

"Sounds like he's here to ...!"

"No!" I interrupted. "We haven't known each other ... I mean, I just met him ...!"

"Less than a month ago?" Rosanne asked.

I bit my lip. *We couldn't be that ... serious ... not yet!* We barely knew each other. *It was too early to be thinking about ...!*

"When do I get to meet him?" Rosanne asked.

"Never ... if you tell anyone," I said. "I'll be taking him to Arnold's tomorrow."

"Into the gamut?" Rosanne asked.

"Better all at once than dribbling all weekend," I said.

"Don't want to be interrupted ...?" Rosanne smiled.

"You read too much smut," I said.

"Think of it as an itinerary," Rosanne grinned.

All the rest of the day I sat worried. *How long was Emerson planning to stay? What would he do on Monday while I was at work? Wasn't meeting the family usually a prelude to ... something important?*

Coincidences happened. Emerson couldn't control all of them ... *or could he?* He'd warned me about suspicions going wild.

Or had he warned me ... to distract me from the obvious?

That argument had sucked me in too often. *I had to keep my imagination from running roughshod ...!*

I left work worrying. I drove straight home ... and found another surprise: three boxes ... outside my door. Mailing boxes ... covered in brown paper. Addressed to me. From a shipping warehouse. I opened my door and carried them inside.

I chose one and peeled off its thick tape. It revealed ... a white garbage bag tied shut. Carefully I untied it.

Orange Hawaiian shirt ... with two other shirts ... in a large resealing plastic bag: Emerson's clothes.

I breathed easy, then looked at the sheer size of each package. *How long was he planning to stay?*

The next resealing bag held socks and

underwear, and another held a toothbrush and paste, disposable razors, and tiny wrapped soaps and shampoo bottles, each from a different hotel. One contained a small steam iron, which explained why none of his clothes ever appeared wrinkled.

I left his other two boxes unopened. *Would he think I was spying?*

I sat fretting. We'd discussed long-term relationships. *Were we already in one? Did he think we were ...?*

Mephistopheles rubbed against the boxes, purring. *Was this a sign?* No, he loved boxes. I had to rein in my suspicions.

I had to stop having suspicions!

After feeding His Majesty, I opened every window and dusted and vacuumed. The breeze blew most of the dust I raised outside, what didn't get sucked up into my bag. When finished, I sat back and relaxed; I was ready.

Emerson would be here in less than a day!

I set his hat onto the shelf where I wanted him to find it.

Bonnie, Julie, Stacy, and Lyn would kill me when I surprised them ...!

I folded my sexiest nightgown, hid it in a plastic bag, and stashed it in a bathroom drawer.

Chapter 25

Work drug by, prodded only by Rosanne's irrepressive smiles. I got nothing done and skipped a minor meeting ... nothing I needed to worry about. I slid my cursor back and forth over my screen and accomplished less than zero.

"See you at Arnold's," Rosanne grinned as I gathered my things.

I shot her a glare, then hurried to my car. Yet no one had asked; for once, Rosanne hadn't told anyone.

The Bismarck Airport was the smallest I knew. Almost all flights were shuttles from Minneapolis or Denver. His plane was listed 'on time'.

I sat nervously.

Unburdened by luggage, Emerson walked into the secured section of the upper floor. I rose from my seat and our eyes met. His smile both warmed my heart and sent chills down my spine. He was wearing a dark gray, lightly pinstriped suit with a red tie. He looked like a software salesman.

"Penelope ...!" Emerson called as he slipped through the spewing throng of passengers.

His face shone, plastered with the smile I'd

dreamed of seeing. I was almost trembling.

We kissed, briefly, unceremoniously, our first G-rated kiss.

"Boxes arrived?" Emerson asked.

"Yesterday," I said.

"Great," Emerson said. "I'm yours. Where first?"

"It's early," I said. "I thought ... well ... we have ... a while ..."

We stepped onto the escalator and descended to the main floor, walked past glass-covered exhibits, and out to the car. I still didn't know how long he was planning to stay.

"I feel guilty exposing you to everyone so quickly," I said.

"I'm used to crowds," Emerson said.

"Perhaps my mother's," I said. "Just to get you prepared."

"Fine," Emerson said.

We climbed into my car and I pulled out my phone.

"She doesn't know I'm coming ...?" Emerson asked.

"No one knows you're here," I said.

"What're you planning?" Emerson asked.

"Giving them as little ammunition as possible," I said.

"Ammunition ...?" Emerson asked.

"Stories about me," I said.

"I want to hear everything," Emerson said.

"No, you don't," I said. "That's an order."

"Shall I salute?" Emerson asked.

"I'll tell you when," I said.

I called mom and informed her that Emerson

had come for a visit ... and her voice grew so loud Emerson could hear her without my phone on speaker.

"He doesn't care how the house looks," I said. "Do you want to meet him or not ...?"

Twenty minutes later, I parked in her driveway.

"Where's your father?" Emerson whispered as we got out of the car.

"Passed away years ago," I whispered back. "Let mom mention him first ... if she does."

Mom was breathing hard as she opened the door; her living room looked cleaner than I'd seen since Christmas.

"Mom, this is Emerson," I introduced them.

Mom welcomed him inside, ushered him into the kitchen, and I wasn't surprised to smell biscuits baking and coffee brewing.

Emerson was polite and genteel. To my amazement, he described our meeting in Hawaii as a mystery, describing each coincidence as an author might twist a plot, leaving my mother guessing what would happen next.

I hadn't felt that way at the time!

He didn't mention my red bikini.

After an hour of stories, I phoned Bonnie and asked her to meet me at Arnold's. My revelation that Emerson would be there evoked shouts that made me smile. She'd planned to make a big dinner and now wouldn't have time to cook it.

She was pleased that I'd called her first. I didn't mention it was because she had the biggest mouth; through her Julie, Stacy, and Lyn would know within minutes.

I quickly went back to mom and Emerson, unwilling to leave them alone. Mom was describing a school play I was in.

"Mom, that was in junior high," I complained.

"It was on stage," mom pointed out. "Emerson works on stage."

"Penelope helped me on stage," Emerson said, and he began the story of my joining him for his finale.

I bit my lip and let them talk. *Worse would come;* diaper stories and countless embarrassing moments from my childhood, yet when we got to Arnold's, Bonnie, Julie, Stacy, and Lyn would reveal my worst.

Mom kept refilling coffee cups so they were always full. Finally, I suggested that we needed to leave. Then mom asked the worst question of all.

"How long are you staying?"

"That depends," Emerson said, glancing at me. "We both work on the road, so sooner or later, one of us will be called away."

"We'll let you know," I promised mom.

As we said good-bye, Emerson waved his hands and presented mom with a rosebud. She acted as delighted as if he'd given her a diamond.

Five minutes later we were driving to Arnold's.

"Your mom's nice," Emerson said.

"I'm surprised she didn't ask where you were sleeping," I said.

"She knows you well ...?" Emerson asked.

"I'm not that kind of girl," I said. "Not where she's concerned."

I swerved to distract from any retort and cuffed him when he wasn't expecting it.

Arnold's was packed. I had to park by the kitchen door, so every face stared as we passed by windows. We entered like visiting royalty celebrating their birthday. Rachel met us at the door, vigorously shook Emerson's hand, then led us to the centermost table. Bonnie, Julie, Stacy, and Lyn were waiting there ... with two chairs empty.

They could've been paparazzi, with Rosanne needing a photo of the two of us, and then more cameras came out. Questions rapid-fired, compliments flew, and queries on magic tricks seen online were expertly side-stepped. Emerson whispered into my ear, asking who my best friends were, and a minute later each of them held a rosebud. People applauded his tricks and begged until Emerson promised to show them one trick. Emerson drew out a plain deck of cards, had five people each choose a card at random, and then shuffled those five and blindly dealt them in numerical order, lowest card first. Then he let others shuffle them ... and again blindly dealt them in numerical order.

The entire restaurant exploded with applause.

Emerson was coerced into repeating the story of our meeting. He used his stage voice, not loudly, but so clearly that everyone in Arnold's heard. He kept them spellbound, yet when he got to our meeting by the pool where he was making balloon animals for the kids, Bonnie asked him what I was wearing.

"She was wearing red," Emerson said.

"Just red ...?" Bonnie asked.

"She'd just finished bodysurfing; she had a robe and a towel," Emerson said. "Yet when she saw me ..."

Emerson skimmed the rest of the story, ignoring Bonnie's failed attempt to embarrass me. I should've known; he frequently handled hecklers. He hadn't lied; I'd had a robe and a towel ... I just wasn't covered.

Stacy kept ordering us drinks, making sure that I never had an empty glass. I switched to lemonade, determined not to get drunk, and too late realized my mistake. I spent half an hour trying to not need a bathroom, only to hear Stacy laugh when I told Emerson where I was going.

"So, how long are you in town ...?" Rosanne stepped up as I walked away.

I peed dreading what they were saying to each other.

"I got started young," Emerson was saying as I returned to his side. "Magic just interested me, and I started learning how it works. I stepped onto my first stage at seventeen ... in a seedy bar I couldn't legally be in."

"You must've been nervous," Lyn said.

"Terrified," Emerson said. "Still terrified, you know. A lot can go wrong. One card in the wrong pocket can ruin your show. But ..."

Emerson pulled a quarter out of Lyn's ear, tossed it into the air, caught it in his mouth, and appeared to swallow it. Everyone stared at him as if he was crazy.

"It's gone," Emerson said.

"No, it isn't ...," Lyn said.

"Anyone here a dentist?" Emerson asked.

Emerson opened his mouth, turned his head so we could all see, and lifted his tongue.

"You swallowed it!" Julie exclaimed.

"That would be painful," Emerson said. "But ... believe what you want ..."

"You won't tell us?" Lyn asked.

"If everybody knew, it wouldn't be magic," Emerson said.

"He'll tell me later," I promised them, and everyone laughed.

Emerson put his arm around me. Rosanne smiled and took another photo.

"I hate to say it, but I haven't eaten since early this morning," Emerson said.

"Okay, everyone, we need food," I announced.

"Second act after dinner," Emerson smiled.

Another table scooted against ours, and the usuals joined us: Bonnie, Julie, Stacy, Lyn, Gwen, Nancy, Kathy, Joel, and Brendan crowded. Only Emerson opened a menu; the rest of us knew it by heart.

Rachel was stuck behind the bar. Katie came and took our order; she was the manager and wanted to meet Emerson. She asked if she could take a photo of him by the bar.

"Not right now, but I'm sure I'll be back when it's less crowded," Emerson said.

"It's like this every Friday and Saturday night," Stacy said. "Bismarck isn't LA or New York."

"Some places have too much happening," Gwen said. "People get wrapped up in entertainments and forget to get wrapped up in each other."

"Is that what Penelope's for ...?" Bonnie asked Emerson.

"Ow!" Julie exclaimed, reaching down to protect her shin.

"Sorry," I frowned. "I was aiming for Bonnie."

"Some questions only Penelope should ask," Emerson answered Bonnie.

"But asking questions I shouldn't is fun ...!" Bonnie argued.

"Answers are a magician's bane," Emerson said.

"Don't worry," I told Bonnie. "I'll tell him what he needs to know."

"You want me telling stories ...?" Bonnie warned.

221

"I know every story you have ...!" I warned.

"No fighting," Julie said. "Emerson, where does your family live?"

Emerson began a Disney version of his childhood traumas. He was still talking when food arrived.

"I'm so sorry," Lyn said.

"Hey, who didn't have a rotten childhood?" Emerson asked.

Guilty faces shared the same expression.

"You forget where you're at," I told Emerson.

"North Dakota is the heart of suburban America," Stacy said.

"My father drank a lot," Lyn said. "He still does ... but he never hit me ..."

"I had a few good foster parents, but never for long," Emerson said. "The other kids, ADHDs, drug users, victims of abuse; they acted out, rebelled louder, got more attention. Bad foster parents are nightmares."

"Terrible ...!" Julie said.

"Let's change the subject," I said. "Something happy."

"So ... would you say you and Penelope are long-...?" Bonnie began.

"Something else!" I interrupted Bonnie.

Emerson laughed, and asked if any of them had been to Hawaii. None had, but Bonnie told about her cruise to Alaska, Julie about both her trips to Disney World, and Lyn complained that she'd never been anywhere.

Emerson took over. He briefly described France, England, Japan, Singapore, South Africa, and Latin America. He amazed them with the same amusing banter he used in his show, which had the blessed effect of avoiding more questions. He paused to eat only when someone related a similar experience. Yet he was still talking when all our plates were empty.

"I do hope I'll get to see all of you again while I'm here," Emerson said to everyone.

"We're here all the time," Gwen said.

"Well, I hate to beg your apologies, but traveling can be exhausting," Emerson said.

"Oh, you can't ...!" Bonnie began.

"I'll bring him back," I promised.

"Some of us can't just hang here anytime," Julie complained.

"It would be inexcusable to not spend more time with you ... when I'm rested," Emerson said.

I smiled; *Emerson was a master at manipulating a crowd.*

Escaping took almost an hour. We had to stop at every table to say good-bye, and others blocked the aisle to prevent us from leaving without talking. I was part of this group and expected nothing less. Finally Katie invited us to come back soon.

"I'm so sorry," I said after we climbed into the car, having waved at the smokers standing outside.

"Demanding audience," Emerson chuckled. "I hope I put on a good show."

"What happened to the quarter?" I asked.

"I swallowed it," Emerson answered, and he smiled at my expression. "Not a real coin; a sugar crystal with a gray candy coating. Tastes terrible. They cost a dollar each. Don't tell."

"Your secrets are mine," I said. "I'm just glad to be out of there."

"Quite a circus you live in," Emerson said.

"People celebrate whatever they can," I said.

"I prefer private celebrations," Emerson said.

"We're headed ... home," I said.

"Problem ...?" Emerson asked.

"Jitters," I said. "Again ... moving so fast ..."

"Want to slow down?" Emerson asked.

"No, it's just ...," I didn't know what to say.

"Penelope, if you want me sleeping on your couch, at least for tonight, I won't argue," Emerson said.

"It's not that," I said. "We ... want the same thing. We're just ... getting there faster than expected ..."

"I won't force ...," Emerson said.

"I know that," I said. "No ... for the rest of tonight ... you're mine."

Emerson liked the placement of his hat on my shelves. I gave him the one-minute tour of my apartment, and then kissed him.

"Time for bed," I said.

"Are you tired ...?" Emerson asked.

"No."

After Emerson brushed his teeth, I kicked him out of the bathroom and pulled out my surprise. Soon I was wearing only two sleeveless layers of sheer black lace brushing the floor. As I stepped into the bedroom and dimmed the lights, I became shifting shadows, revealing, then hiding every pale curve. I walked around my bed with Emerson's eyes fixated on me.

"There's a word we've been avoiding," Emerson whispered.

"Love," I whispered.

"Love isn't a choice we make," Emerson smiled. "Love is a power that overwhelms us ... or it isn't love."

I climbed on top of my blankets and overwhelmed him.

Chapter 26

Sated, we climbed out of bed long after we awoke. We showered long together, then had to rinse off quickly when the water got chill. We dried each other, then I dressed in pajamas, and I slid my pink robe onto Emerson. He complained, yet I only laughed at him, then offered to make him breakfast. I suggested eggs, bacon, sausage ... anything he liked. He sealed his socks and underwear from last night into a bag marked 'Dirty', dropped them into one of his boxes, and asked for toast.

"I try not to eat too much," Emerson said. "I can't afford to replace my rhinestone suit."

"You didn't mail it here, did you?" I asked.

"No, I sent it to storage ... with all my props ... except my wren, which stays with its trainer," Emerson said. "I wash everything before I pack it, and log it in my book. My shipping company takes delivery by mail, and stores boxes by number. When I ask, it ships them for me ... to any address."

"Where ...?" I asked.

"Tucson," Emerson said. "I've never been there. Susan used to use them."

"Suzzannia the Sorceress?" I asked. "Were you and her ...?"

"Are we revealing our pasts?" Emerson asked.

"My friends will tell you mine," I said.

"Susan and I were enemies," Emerson said.

"Seriously ...?" I asked. "She seemed to like you ... a lot."

"It's a long story," Emerson said. "You need to progress farther before it will make sense."

"Magic ...?" I asked.

"There's a lot more to it than you know," Emerson said.

"I want to know," I said.

"You've just started sensing coincidences," Emerson said. "You've been affected randomly at least twice."

"At least ...?" I asked.

"Natural coincidences happen every day," Emerson said. "Forced coincidences are consciously driven. Yet some, like Susan, don't believe in natural coincidences. She thinks all coincidences are the Predetermined Will of the Supreme One."

"God ...?" I asked.

"Creator, Universal Consciousness, Fate ...," Emerson scowled.

"You don't believe ...?" I asked.

"Everyone has their own perspective on reality, what made it, how it works," Emerson said. "Magicians don't have any better idea than anyone else."

"Can't you use your senses ...?" I asked.

"Most try," Emerson said. "They trace all coincidences to find ... guess what?"

"Exactly what they wanted to find ...?" I grinned.

"Every time," Emerson shook his head.

"Have you tried?" I asked.

"I found nothing ... exactly what I expected," Emerson said. "We all have preconceived notions. Susan thinks our notions are divine gifts. Lucinda thinks our notions combine to form the Universal Consciousness. I assume it's an unknown form of physics."

"So ... magicians don't have 'special connections' to God?" I asked.

"Some are gifted at music," Emerson said. "Some calculate complex mathematical problems. We sense coincidences."

"But we control them," I said.

"Everyone tries to control the world around them," Emerson said. "I think all timelines are short and eventually merge ... one washes over others. Susan thinks I'm crazy. She uses prayer ... it works for her."

"Religions are unprovable by default," I said.

"Yet undeniable to the faithful," Emerson said.

"How should I ...?" I began.

"Continue with what you're doing," Emerson said. "Eventually you'll sense multiple coincidences. For example, you may sense that, on your way to work, you'll witness an accident. You'll also notice a coincidence where you don't; where you leave one minute later. By comparing their feelings, you choose when to leave for work."

"We sense the future?" I asked.

"What's 'near-future' but the outcome of innumerable coincidences?" Emerson asked.

"So, our power to manipulate ... is choosing between existing coincidences?" I asked.

"Not all coincidences can be manipulated," Emerson said. "If you could only prevent an accident by

throwing fistfuls of money into the air, and you don't
have fistfuls of money, then you can't affect the
accident."

"So we can't affect just anything," I said.

"Also, coincidences happen quickly," Emerson
said. "Sometimes they're over before we can choose."

"I've watched friends make terrible choices," I
said.

"You may be able to sense your friend's mistakes
before they happen, but you couldn't stop your friends
before; what makes you think you can stop them now?"
·Emerson asked.

"Maybe I'll find the right words ...?" I suggested.

"And maybe, while you're sensing for those right
words, they'll run out and make those mistakes without
you," Emerson said.

"That's what happens now," I said.

Emerson laughed.

"What's planned for the day?" Emerson asked.

"I didn't have an ... itinerary," I said, recalling my
conversation with Rosanne.

"I'm sensing something," Emerson said. "You
don't like that word ...?"

"I don't want to ... talk serious now," I said. "But
I'm still wondering ... how long are you ... what your
plans are ...?"

"How long I'm planning to stay ...?" Emerson
asked. "Until you ask me to leave."

"But ... how ...?" I asked.

"Secrets between magicians are difficult,"
Emerson said. "I've got scheduled performances.
You've got work ..."

"Where would you go?" I asked.

"Exploring," Emerson smiled. "Sometimes I just

head off with no plans, let the winds blow where they may. I can vanish whenever you want ... if you don't want me gone for long."

"What will you do while I'm at work?" I asked.

"Practice," Emerson said. "You don't just learn tricks and walk up onto a stage. Magicians practice everything a hundred times, not only our tricks but our banter. Do you have a deck of cards?"

I fetched one from a cabinet in the living room. Emerson drew out four cards and examined them.

"Center of each cushion," Emerson said.

Standing in the kitchen, Emerson threw each card like shurikens ... into my living room. Two landed center on my couch cushions, two on different chairs.

"Wow!" I exclaimed.

"Not magic," Emerson said. "It just takes years of practice."

"Like sensing coincidences," I said.

"When it gets easy, you learn more difficult tricks," Emerson said. "Once you can manipulate timelines, why control wine drops on mirrors?"

"Where should we go ...?" I asked.

"Anywhere you want," Emerson said.

"Bismarck isn't a cultural center," I said. "We have a zoo ..."

Emerson looked at his pink robe.

"I'd prefer to wear something else."

"Your boxes are in my closet," I said. "I need to change, too."

"You could wear the black thing from last night ...," Emerson suggested.

"Better than the red bikini ...?" I grinned.

"Only when I'm watching," Emerson smiled.

Although a fraction of the size of the Atlanta zoo,

the Bismarck zoo was nice. We walked holding hands like young lovers, watching kids run about. One parent was trying to stop their son from crying as we walked past. Emerson drew a yellow balloon out of his pocket, waved it before the crying child's eyes, and moments later, he stopped crying as Emerson handed him an inflated yellow sword. The parent thanked him, and Emerson tipped his hat, which he'd insisted on wearing, and we walked away.

"You like doing that," I said.

"It makes people happy," Emerson said. "It's also good advertisement. When I was just starting out, it got me lots of birthday parties."

"You like being the center of attention," I said.

"Me ...?" Emerson laughed. "Never ...!"

We walked the length of the zoo, stopping at most exhibits. Before a group of grazing antelopes, we noticed that we were alone.

"These guys look like good subjects for you," Emerson said.

"Can I make them do something?" I asked.

"Anyone could," Emerson said. "The key is knowing what to do to get the result you want."

"Sense ...?" I asked.

"Not yet," Emerson said. "What do you want them to do?"

"I don't know," I said.

"Would you like to see them dance a chorus line?" Emerson asked.

"Can I ...?" I asked.

"No timeline leads to choreographed antelope routines," Emerson chuckled.

"So, I need ... something likely?" I asked.

"The more likely, the easier," Emerson said.

"What if I just want them to ... step closer?" I
said.

"What would make them approach ...?"
Emerson asked.

"If we had food ...," I said.

"So ... the easiest method would be non-
magical," Emerson said. "Non-magic is usually best.
What if ... they simply thought you had food?"

"That would work," I said.

"What must it feel like to the antelopes ...when
their feeders arrive?" Emerson said. "They love their
feeders. Sense their love in you."

I closed my eyes and concentrated.

"Antelopes aren't any different than cards or
wine-drops," Emerson said. "Don't sense actions.
Experience the feelings that cause the reaction you want.
Let your mouth salivate in anticipation ..."

I'm happy to see my feeder!

I imagined the sensations: *the creak of the food
cart as it neared, its wheels crunching grit, the click of the
door opening, the scrape of the scoop digging into food
pellets, expectancy as I step forward, hungry for ...*

Every antelope lifted their head and looked at
me ...!

"Incredible!" Emerson said. "Well done!"

"They didn't move," I said.

"They sensed you," Emerson said. "You made a
connection. For a first try, this is fantastic."

"But ... I lost concentration ...," I said.

"Don't startle when you see the effect you
desire," Emerson said.

"Should I try again?" I asked.

"Expectations ruin repeats," Emerson said. "For
now, try once. No point making it harder."

Most of the antelopes stared at me for a full minute before they resumed grazing. I waved at them, content with my success.

"What's the biggest coincidence you've ever caused?" I asked.

"Bad subject," Emerson frowned.

I stared at him.

"Before Lucinda found me, I went to Las Vegas," Emerson said. "I had three dollars. I left the casino with nine thousand."

"Big win," I said.

"Big mistake," Emerson said. "I got robbed, and almost beaten to death. Someone called an ambulance. I awoke in the ER with no idea how I'd gotten there."

"What did you do?" I asked.

"I ... I wasn't a nice person back then," Emerson bowed his head. "I was an angry brat looking for revenge against the unorphaned world. I went hunting for the guys who beat me up."

"Did you find them?" I asked.

Emerson nodded.

"Did you ... hurt them ...?"

"I got beat up again," Emerson said. "There was no timeline where I cornered them and got my money back. Only, this time, Lucinda found me ... unconscious, with two black eyes, a skull fracture, and three broken ribs."

I didn't know what to say.

"Penelope, I'm trying to be as honest as I can," Emerson said. "What I'm teaching you ... it's dangerous. Better than I have been seduced by power."

"Power corrupts ... and manipulation is power," I agreed.

"We can't control every outcome," Emerson

warned.

"You manipulated me in Hawaii," I said.

"No, I didn't," Emerson said. "I learned which flight you were taking. I learned which hotel you'd use. Then I made reservations; no manipulation."

"But ... we kept running into each other," I said.

"I searched for you ... then went where I felt," Emerson said. "The only manipulation I used in Hawaii was on Mr. Jenklie to pick you; he was looking for a team-building activity for specific merchants. It didn't take a lot; he liked your butt. I was startled to see you in your red bikini ... that was pure coincidence."

"You should hear what my friends said when they saw pictures of you," I said. "On second thought, maybe you shouldn't ..."

"Again, no magic required," Emerson grinned. "From what you described, they'll tell me ..."

After the zoo, we found a bar with outdoor seating. We ordered a sampler of four appetizers; potato skins, wings, nachos, and fries. Crows cawed nearby; Emerson threw some fries near the fence, and the crows dove upon them. Then he held up one french fry and dropped it close to our feet.

"Try now," Emerson whispered. "Bring one of those crows over here to get that fry."

I tried to focus, but before I even got started, the crows flew away, taking their treats.

"That happens," Emerson said. "Sometimes you don't get the chance ..."

My phone rang.

"Bonnie," I read the screen before I pressed answer.

"Where you at ...?" Bonnie asked.

"Lunch," I said.

"How long is Emerson staying?" Bonnie asked.

"We haven't decided," I said.

"Last night; I want every detail ...," Bonnie said.

"Emerson can hear you," I said.

Emerson chuckled; *I hadn't put my phone on speaker.*

"Party, your house, tomorrow afternoon," Bonnie said.

"One condition," I said. "No one bothers me until then."

"See you at 1:00," Bonnie said.

"1:00 PM ...!" I stressed.

I'd barely hung up when Stacy called.

"David and I want to invite you to dinner tonight," Stacy said.

I rolled my eyes.

"We've got plans tonight," I said. "Bonnie will be calling you about tomorrow."

"Please, Penelope ...?" Stacy asked. "David won't allow it on a work night."

I sighed heavily. Emerson shrugged.

"All right, but you have to tell Bonnie you begged me," I said.

"I am begging you," Stacy insisted. "Thank you!"

"I'm sorry," I told Emerson.

"We'll have plenty of private dinners," Emerson said.

"She wants us as a buffer," I said.

"Forced conversation is my specialty," Emerson said.

All the way to Stacy's, my apprehension grew. Her first husband, Nathan, was still a drug addict. They'd been stoned the day they met ... and the day they married. They were divorced three months after his inheritance ran out. With our help, Stacy pulled herself out of Nathan's world. David, her current husband, was no prize, yet a genius compared to Nathan. I just couldn't stand the pompous ass.

Stacy opened the door when we were halfway up her driveway.

"Come in!" Stacy cried. "So good to see you!"

Stacy grabbed Emerson and drug him in front of the TV. David was stretched out on the sofa, feet propped, and never once looked up. He was older than Stacy by ten years, with dark hair, still wearing business clothes, coat and tie thrown over the back of the couch. Their dog was on the sofa beside David; at least the dog seemed aware of our presence.

"Emerson, this is David," Stacy said.

"Pleasure to meet you," Emerson said.

David frowned, then looked him up and down.

"You're a magician ...?" David asked.

"That's what my card says," Emerson smiled. "Ever see a magic act?"

"No," David said. "I sell restaurant supplies."

"Have a seat," Stacy said to Emerson. "I'll get you a beer. David's a great salesman; he holds the state record for packets."

Emerson sat in a recliner with a long blanket hanging over its back. The old dog jumped off the couch to sniff him. Emerson petted him.

"Packets ...?" Emerson asked.

"To-go supplies," David said. "Ketchup, mayonnaise, mustard, salt, pepper ..."

"Big money ...?" Emerson asked.

"Volume sales," David said. "Reliable. Also, equipment, and everything kitchens need. Not fancy like stage-work."

"Stage-work isn't reliable," Emerson said. "That would be magic."

"Got a rabbit in that hat?" David asked.

"Not this hat," Emerson said, taking off his hat and accepting the cold beer Stacy handed him. "I have one that holds birds, and a rosebud up my sleeve, but every magician has those."

Stacy locked her hand on my wrist and pulled me into the kitchen. I wanted to hear what Emerson and David said, yet I let her drag me away. I stopped in the doorway where I could still watch.

"Thank you ...!" Stacy whispered.

"No arguing," I hissed softly.

"I just want a nice, peaceful meal," Stacy said, checking a pork loin roasting in the oven. Three pots were on her stove, two boiling, one of mashed potatoes. Carefully she examined each.

"About five minutes," Stacy said.

"Did Bonnie call?" I asked.

"Yes, but I may have to work tomorrow," Stacy said. "How's Emmerich?"

"Emerson," I corrected her. "Amazing. We're moving too fast, but it feels right."

"Never too fast when it's right," Stacy said, and then she frowned.

The table was set, not fancy, yet two tall white candles stood in the middle. Stacy set the hot food on the table and lit the candles.

"Bring your beers," Stacy called. "Supper time."

Emerson and I sat across from each other at a round, stone-top table. Their house was well-furnished; David made a good living. Stacy was a cashier and could never afford this lifestyle on her own. We bowed our heads while she said grace. Then we loaded our plates with pork, potatoes, asparagus, and corn nibblets.

"Looks delicious," Emerson said.

"It does," I added.

"Thanks!" Stacy said.

David grunted.

"Are any of your local restaurants dinner-theaters?" Emerson asked.

"No," David said. "I doubt if there's one for two hundred miles."

"The Palace has a stage," Stacy said.

"That's for music, and only Doug's band plays there," David said.

"Doug's been playing there every Friday and Saturday night for six years," I said. "It's a bar that serves pizza."

"Thinking of putting on your act?" David asked Emerson.

"Always looking for new venues," Emerson said. "Occupational duty; you can't rely on the same places."

"That's for sure," David said. "Damned internet is stealing half my business."

"It's good for advertising, but too many magicians reveal tricks," Emerson said. "Fortunately, most of our act is banter."

"Alcohol must help," David said.

"Yes, but we don't get a cut of the bar," Emerson said. "Serious drunks are a problem, but the ones who don't drink are the worst; they're just watching to spot how your tricks work."

"I don't use tricks," David said. "Salesmanship is real."

Emerson smiled; I don't know how he kept from reacting. Most of the tricks magicians did were well-

237

known. Performing them was the ultimate salesmanship.

"You have a lovely house," Emerson said to Stacy.

"We're proud of it," Stacy said. "We decorated it together. David installed the strip lights."

"Stacy knitted those blankets," I nodded to the blankets on the chair and couch.

"Nice colors," Emerson said.

I hated banal conversation. No one was smiling. We'd be finished eating too quickly.

"We went to the zoo today," I said.

"I haven't been there in years," Stacy said, and she looked at David. "We should do that sometime."

David grunted again, never lifting his eyes from his plate.

"You won't believe what Penelope tried to do when we were little," Stacy began a story about me offering mud pies at our lemonade stand.

"We were seven," I told Emerson when he laughed. "No one bought them. Stacy liked horses, had a friend that used to take us riding, and she always fell off."

To my surprise, Emerson had never ridden a horse. Yet he listened intently and spoke politely, trying to keep up the conversation as best he could. David seemed determined to stay silent.

"David and I are huge Vikings fans," Stacy said, which was no surprise as two purple pennants decorated their kitchen.

"Follow football ...?" David asked Emerson.

"I'm on the road more than they are," Emerson said. "I enjoy watching, but work keeps me busy."

"Ever had a man's job ...?" David asked.

Stacy and I froze.

"I've made a lot of money gambling," Emerson answered. "Some casinos don't let magicians play."

"You cheat ...?" David asked.

"Not that I'd admit," Emerson said. "I definitely can ..."

"Do you like dogs?" Stacy interrupted.

Half an hour later, we thanked both our hosts and said good-night. David had quickly retired to the couch to watch an important baseball game, and turned the volume up loud enough to make talking uncomfortable. He waved at us as Stacy opened the door.

"I'm sorry," Stacy whispered in my ear.

I gave her a knowing glance. David was a prick, and Emerson and I were just dating; *she hadn't done me a favor.*

"I'm sorry," I said as I started the car.

"It was exactly as you warned," Emerson shrugged.

"I never want to be like that," I said.

"I try not to get angry ... and avoid being bitter," Emerson said.

"I'm angry enough for both of us," I said.

"You'll end up a David," Emerson said.

"How can you be so mellow?" I asked. "He called you ...!"

"If he's an example of manliness, I don't want it," Emerson finished. "Besides, if I got angry, bad things could happen; what would that make me?"

"Like David ...?" I asked.

"Screw David," Emerson said. "We helped Stacy. She seems nice."

"Could we help her?" I asked.

"We showed her that not every man's a David," Emerson said.

"Can you sense their future?" I asked.

"Don't need magic for that," Emerson said. "He's angry. Maybe he knows why, maybe not. He's making her miserable because he is."

"You should be a psychiatrist," I said.

"I've seen the world his way," Emerson said. "Anger only makes the world worse."

"Did Lucinda teach you that?" I asked.

"Lucinda's a story-teller, not a teacher," Emerson said.

"I can't wait to meet her," I said.

"Got vacation time ...?" Emerson asked.

"I can't use it now," I said. "Between Atlanta, Nebraska, and Seattle, I need to be in the office ... until my sale is confirmed."

"Let's stop for a drink," Emerson suggested. "Anywhere but Arnold's."

Most of the local watering holes were depressing, hideaways for people looking to lose themselves. I chose a chain restaurant with a small bar in back; it was crowded, yet we found a table near the kitchen. Emerson noticed that they had mud pies on their desert menu, and ordered one to split. I laughed and tried to put our dinner-disaster behind us.

"How do you decide when not to ...?" I asked.

"When things can hurt others," Emerson explained. "I take risks; others shouldn't suffer because of my choices."

"How bad can things get?" I asked.

"Coincidences can kill," Emerson said.

"Kill ...?"

"Unintentionally ... yes."

Two white wines and a mud cake arrived.
Emerson took a drink and offered me a fork.

"How 'unintentionally' ...?" I asked.

"Timelines have short spans, but many variants,"
Emerson said. "Each may lead to unexpected
consequences."

The chocolate pie was gooey and decadent and I
liked it way too much.

I liked Emerson way too much!

"What ...?" he asked.

"Are you ... reading me ...?" I asked.

"If I could read minds then I wouldn't have to
ask," Emerson said.

"Too many thoughts ...," I confessed.

"Rapid-fire ...?"

"No. I was ... wanted to apologize again ... about
dinner ... love this pie ... thinking about that word ..."

"From last night?" Emerson asked. "While you
were wearing ...?"

"Quiet!" I hissed, glancing at the booths near us.
"The Bismarck Express is everywhere."

Emerson licked the chocolate off his fork.

"No reason to fear," Emerson whispered.
"Pretend that I used that word again ... right now."

Sex that night reminded me of our last night in
Hawaii. We barely spoke ... not with words. Never had
I peaked to such slow tenderness.

"I ... I have to know," I whispered between gasps
as paradise wavered in afterglow. "What ... made you
decide ... you wanted a ... permanent relationship?"

Emerson stared at me, then tried to roll away. I
grabbed his arm and pulled him back.

"I ... I ... telling you would ...," Emerson

241

stammered.

"I need to know," I said.

Emerson sighed. "It's not pretty."

I stared at him.

"You were my first ... in a year," Emerson said. "When I told you how easy it was to find vulnerable girls ... I wasn't kidding. But ... my power grew ... I started sensing their pain. Girls who'd been rejected. Girls with abandonment issues. Girls with low self-esteem. They were seeking something ... real. Near the end, I understood that ... and I wasn't real."

"You ...?"

"It wasn't worth it," Emerson said. "I could sense their shame ... saw myself from their eyes ... what they thought about me ... for days afterwards. Lucinda had been right."

"You felt guilty," I said.

"I want ... good sex," Emerson said. "I like dirty ... yet I ... I'm not a slimebag ... treating girls like ..."

"Like Merlin Melville ... and foster care ... treated you ...?" I asked.

"We've talked enough ... for now," Emerson said.

"I just need to know ... you're serious," I said.

"I've never had a real family," Emerson said. "I'm ... hoping ... I want one ... to belong to a family."

I hugged him, then rolled on top and refused to get off. We started to wrestle ... and he got excited.

I won!

Chapter 27

Morning sex is the best part of new relationships.
Despite all my reservations, Emerson and I were
in a relationship. Alarms clanged in my head, yet I
ignored them. Relationships aren't perfect, yet
everything feels wonderful when love's new. Yet time
reveals differences. David once felt to Stacy like
Emerson feels to me; *I couldn't let us end up like them.*

We made a grocery run and got everything we'd
need for the party, including a dozen new unbloomed
roses, which Emerson needed for his sleeves. Back
home, while he trimmed, dethorned, and inserted
rosebuds, I grilled hot and spicy sausage, started
spaghetti sauce, and set out my biggest pot for boiling
noodles. I half-filled the pot with water, added salt and
spices, including my secret; just a bit of curry to boil into
the noodles. *Everyone asked what special spices I added
to my sauce, but my secret was to spice my noodles.*

While everything was simmering, I started
vacuuming. As I'd cleaned so fully for Emerson, my
apartment didn't need much. Emerson objected, yet I
insisted on displaying his hat on the shelf in my living
room.

"You gave it to me," I reminded him.

"That's a classic Stetson fedora!" Emerson objected. "It's white, but it's exactly the same model Humphrey Bogart wore in The Treasure of the Sierra Madre ... 1948! You can't just leave it on a shelf!"

"The girls will be expecting it," I insisted. "Do ... you know all the Bogart movies?"

"Of course," Emerson said. "Why?"

"I know he was in Casablanca."

Emerson's eyes rolled.

Had I just found a difference ...?

Bonnie, Julie, and Lyn showed up within minutes of each other.

"Stacy can't make it," Bonnie said.

"She warned me she might be working," I said as I dumped thin noodles into spiced boiling water.

"So, Emerson, what'd you think of David?" Lyn asked.

Emerson and I exchanged glances.

"He seems ... set in his ways," Emerson said.

"We don't like him either," Julie said.

"He's an ass," Bonnie said.

"We put up with him for Stacy's sake," Julie said.

"I hope I'm not ... tolerated," Emerson said.

"Not so far," Bonnie grinned. "What did he say?"

"He doesn't have high opinions of magicians," Emerson said.

"He doesn't have high opinions of anything," Lyn said.

"We're not here to trash David," I said from the kitchen, sliding a tray of garlic bread into the oven.

"No, we're here to interrogate Emerson," Bonnie

announced, and everyone laughed.

"I'm protective of my friends, too," Emerson said.

"So, you know how difficult long-distance relationships are ...?" Julie asked.

"Julie ...!" I almost screamed.

"When you have no home, all friendships are long-distance," Emerson said.

"Being on stage, you must sleep in lots of hotels ...?" Bonnie asked.

"Bonnie ...!" this time I screamed.

Emerson shook his head.

"I didn't know this would be third degree ...," Emerson said.

"We've been friends for most of our lives," Lyn said.

"All I can offer are promises, and it's possible you've known too many bad men to believe in any ...," Emerson said.

"Far too many," Bonnie assured.

"I'm condemned ...!" Emerson lamented.

"I'm the only judge that matters!" I reminded.

"Ladies, I give you my full permission to enact any revenge you desire if I hurt Penelope," Emerson said.

"You may regret that," Bonnie said.

"Now, what if Penelope dumps me?" Emerson asked.

"No problem there," Lyn smiled, and she winked at Emerson flirtatiously.

"Lyn ...!" I screamed.

"Will you stop screaming?" Bonnie asked.

"Stop interrogating Emerson!"

Bonnie, Julie, and Lyn laughed.

245

"I think that's why they're here," Emerson said.

"Besides, Penelope doesn't need to worry about Lyn," Julie said, smiling wickedly. "So, Emerson, do you like kids ...?"

"Out ...!" I ordered all three of them, but only laughter followed.

"They can't leave," Emerson said, grinning. "I haven't heard any embarrassing Penelope stories ...!"

I blushed all through lunch. Every terrible moment of my childhood flashed by, and Emerson lapped it up and joined in their laughter. I revenged myself by telling how loose Bonnie was before she got married, how Julie once loudly farted on a crowded school bus, and how Lyn lost her virginity to the father of a child she'd been baby-sitting. Yet Emerson kept reverting the conversation back to me.

"You know what he's doing?" I finally asked. "He wants us to talk about anything but him. Maybe you should ask him ... about Suzzannia the Sorceress ...?"

Every woman demanded to hear this story.

"All right," Emerson shook his head. "Suzzannia is the magician I went to Hawaii to replace while she was occupied with family matters. Now, you understand, magicians rely upon our reputations for employment ... so the general reputations of magicians matters to all of us. Well, I was young and foolish ... and by the oddest *coincidence,*" Emerson stared at me, "Susan ... Suzzannia ... was playing Atlantic City the same week I was there. Well, I needn't tell you what young men are like. I was in my early twenties and performed in bars where lots of drinking occurred ... much of it by attractive women. Magic tricks work wonderfully well on the intoxicated, and Susan thought I was taking advantage of girls who were too drunk to choose wisely.

In retrospect, she was right; I was too young and dumb to realize it. Anyway, I almost died that week ... by several unexplained *coincidences*, and I began to think these accidents were caused by Susan ... Suzzannia."

"She tried to kill you ...?" Lyn asked.

"Murder requires much the same skills as stage magic," Emerson said. "Deception, misdirection, hidden exits, traps; if any profession could regularly get away with murder, it would be magician. Of course I couldn't prove anything, so I set up my own trap ... not realizing that any good magician could easily avoid it."

"You tried to kill her?" Julie asked.

"I tried to expose her trying to kill me," Emerson said. "I didn't succeed. She had a pet monkey she used in her act. I wasted film on an hour of her monkey flipping me his middle finger. Afterwards, Susan snuck into my hotel room and set a trap for me ... not a fatal one. She set up my stage lights and movie camera in front of my bed. Late that night, when I brought another drunk girl to my hotel room, we were both surprised."

"The girl thought you wanted to film her ...?" Lyn asked.

"Yes, but Susan's plan backfired ... as such plans usually do," Emerson said. "The camera excited this girl, and she made me film her ... and eventually, us; I'd been drinking, too."

Bonnie, Julie, and Lyn broke out laughing.

I stared, uncertain how I felt about this.

"What happened?" Bonnie asked.

"Suzzannia," Emerson sneered. "When we woke up, the camera was gone."

"She stole the film ...?" Lyn asked.

"Video tape, actually," Emerson said. "She later returned it ... but only after I endured a long lecture and she extracted unforgivable promises."

"You stopped picking up drunk girls?" Julie asked suspiciously.

"I had to promise to go to Florida ... to see someone else," Emerson said.

"Did you?" Lyn asked.

"No," Emerson confessed. "And that was my big mistake. That person came looking for me. Her name is Lucinda, a retired magician, and she put the fear of magicians into me."

"Where's the tape?" Bonnie asked.

Emerson blushed as the girls laughed.

"In rare instances, arson can be a blessing," Emerson said.

Bonnie and Lyn looked disappointed.

"You could always make another," Julie suggested, glancing at me.

I glared daggers at her.

Plates of spaghetti became replaced by glasses of red wine as we sat in my living room. Lyn felt obliged to relate the story of my drunken return from Hawaii, during which I repeatedly interrupted with unheeded objections.

"So, when's your next performance?" Bonnie asked.

"Two weeks from last Friday in Las Vegas," Emerson said. "I've got a two week contract, then a week off before I need to be in Chicago. Of course, emergency fill-ins happen all the time ... at the last minute."

"You're on the road a lot," Julie said. "Long-distance relationships can work ... until kids ..."

I glared, horrified.

"We haven't discussed kids ...!" I objected.

"Then this is a good time ...!" Bonnie started.

"End of party!" I announced.

"Just when it's getting good ...?" Bonnie asked.

"I do think that's a conversation we'll have alone," Emerson said, "... but I promise I'll tell you as soon as Penelope thinks it proper ..."

"That'll never happen!" Lyn argued.

"Penelope isn't as proper as she pretends," Bonnie said.

"Really ...?" Emerson asked. "Now there's a topic ..."

"No ...!" I insisted.

Despite my objections, again the popular topic became my past.

Bonnie and Julie had to be home in time to make supper for their kids. Lyn volunteered to stay, to continue my embarrassment, yet the glare in my eyes threatened. With peals of laughter, each had to hug Emerson, welcoming him to our 'family', and then they stole Emerson's Stetson and took turns trying it on. I snatched it back and forced them out my door. We could hear them laughing all the way down the stairs.

Emerson bore an amused smirk on his face.

"We're never doing that again!" I seethed.

"It wasn't my idea," Emerson said.

"Fine," I said. "No more ideas." Then I paused. "What you said about Suzzannia ... Susan ... was that true?"

"It was ... the Reader's Digest version," Emerson said.

"I understood that," I said. "I wish you hadn't told them."

"Why?" Emerson asked.

"They know me ... well," I said. "I don't want

them noticing *coincidences."*

"That would be best," Emerson held out my wine glass. "Maybe you should have more ...?"

I grabbed my glass and drank.

"Their stories were exaggerated," I said.

"Most stories are," Emerson said.

"I hate how complacent you can be," I said.

"I'll try to be less complacent."

Some days all men needed their noses punched!

Chapter 28

The world's most annoying alarm clock went off. I crawled out from under Emerson's arm, overheated from cuddling all night. I hit snooze and gently slid back against him.

After the third snooze, Emerson groaned. I rolled over, grimaced, and slid my feet toward the floor. Thirty minutes later, I leaned over and kissed him. Then I left.

Rosanne was grinning at me before I sat down.

"No," I said.

"Just the juicy ...!" Rosanne whined.

"No."

"PG version ...?"

"You met him on Friday."

"And how many orgasms have you had since then ...?"

I docked and turned on my laptop, trying to ignore Rosanne's guesses ... which implied I'd not slept, left the house, or worn clothes since Friday night. By the time she reached triple digits, I wished a magical coincidence would drag her away from her desk ... yet none happened. She already had every photo she'd taken on Friday added to her work screensaver, and showed me each.

This Friday I'd be leaving Bismarck, headed to a grueling weekend at the Nebraska Medical Trade Show. *What was Emerson going to do all week while I was at work ... and what would he do after I left ...?*

Before lunch, Mr. Dawes called me into his office for a chat. He asked about our Nebraska contacts, and I fumbled to recall them.

"What's the matter?" Mr. Dawes asked.

"Nothing ... I started studying them on Friday, but had a crazy weekend ... family stuff," I said.

"Well, as long as you're prepared by Friday," Mr. Dawes said. "Atlanta looks good, but we could use another, even a small sale."

"I'll do my best."

Back at my desk, I opened all the relevant files and began reviewing them again, shocked at how much I'd forgotten. Not having a personal life helped me focus on work; *I couldn't mess up while the Atlanta sale was pending!*

"Lunch ...?" Rosanne asked. "I'm buying ...!"

I couldn't refuse a free lunch.

"Still *magical ...?"* Rosanne asked.

"No sex talk," I said firmly.

"Gotten serious ...?" Rosanne asked.

"I ... think so," I said.

"Permanent ...?"

"I wouldn't object ..."

"Marriage ...?"

"Too far."

"What's the problem ...?"

"No problem."

"All relationships have problems."

"Only ... moving too fast."

"Sounds scary."

"A little."

"Is he scared ...?"

"He acts like we're perfect. We've only been dating ..."

"Sleeping together ..."

"One month."

"Romance fading ...?"

"Last night was romantic."

"Lucky ...!"

"How long can it last ...?"

"You worried ...?"

"Yes."

"Then you have something to talk about tonight."

I stared incredulous. *How could I broach that subject without ruining what I was trying to protect ...?*

Rosanne smiled and sipped her coke.

Back at work, the company files on Nebraska hovered: The Renault Medical Enterprise, an importer of medical suppliers, and The Equality Medical Group, a small consortium named after the Nebraska State Motto: 'Equality before the law'. I'd always wondered about that motto. Yet they were a friendly bunch. Of course, most were men, and last summer's trade show had been so hot my sweat-drenched silk blouses became virtually skin-tight; no orders, but plenty of invitations.

Only cotton shirts this time!

Before I left work, I'd reviewed all their data and gone to their websites to look for changes and any new photos. Then I packed up, said good-bye to Rosanne, and hurried home.

My TV could be heard from the steps; a girl

screamed as background music swelled. I opened the
door to find Emerson doing yo-yo tricks, a giant butterfly
made of balloons atop my shelves, and playing cards
scattered everywhere. Emerson's hat was in the middle
of the living room floor, upside down, and filled with
playing cards.

"Hey!" Emerson cried, and he hurried to turn
the TV down. "You gotta see this!"

Emerson pulled off the yo-yos, set them on my
end table, and collected all the cards from out of his hat.

"*Mephistopheles ...!*" Emerson called.

He stepped back into the kitchen, flung a card
through the air, and I watched it drop into his hat. At a
run, Mephistopheles ran out of my bedroom, to the hat,
and stuck a paw into it. Emerson repeated his stunt with
mastery, sending each card flying toward his hat. I had
no doubt each would've landed inside his hat, but
Mephistopheles seemed determined to bat away each
card as it flew toward him. Some still landed inside the
hat, but most fell onto the carpet beside it.

"New assistant," I smiled, hanging my keys on
their hook.

"We played for hours," Emerson said, throwing
a last card.

Mephistopheles remained guarding the hat while
Emerson kissed me. I gave him a long hug, until I felt a
feline rival for attention rubbing against my leg.

"*Mephistopheles ...!*" I complained.

Forced to pick him up and pet him, Emerson
asked if I wanted to sit down and rest. I obliged, and was
halfway down when Mephistopheles jumped from my
hands and ran into the kitchen.

"His bowl is full," Emerson said.

"Dry food; he wants a can, but not until dinner,"

I said. "You look like you've had a productive day."

"Practice or lose it," Emerson said, and he started picking up cards from all over the room, even two that were balanced on the painted molding above the door. "Mephistopheles doesn't like balloons."

"What have you practiced?" I asked.

"The usual," Emerson said, and he held up his open palm, fingers squeezed together. "Can you see the card?" He arced his hand from waist to head height. "Magicians need to be able to hold the card so it can't be seen from any angle."

I hadn't even known he was holding a card. He snapped his fingers and a four of diamonds appeared pinched between his index finger and thumb.

"Very nice," I said.

"Enough of me," Emerson said. "How was your day?"

"Routine," I said. "My days are panic or boredom. It depends on sales ... or loss of a customer."

"That must suck," Emerson said.

"I was distracted ... by a question ...," I said.

"Sounds scary," Emerson said.

I startled and stared at Emerson.

"Did you just ... do magic ...?" I asked.

"Not that I know of," Emerson said. "Why?"

"Rosanne said ... exactly the same thing," I said.

"Not a coincidence," Emerson said. "You must've said something scary, and by your expression, the tone of your voice, I responded the same."

I sighed heavily.

"I'm sorry," I said. "It's ..."

"Easy to suspect a magician," Emerson finished. "I give you my word, when I do magic, I'll let you know ... if I can. If not, I'll tell you afterwards ... when we're alone."

"I'm sorry," I said again.

"What's bothering you?" Emerson asked.

"Fate," I said, speaking plainly. "Emerson, do you believe in fate?"

He eyed me suspiciously.

"Before I answer, what do you mean by fate?" Emerson asked.

"Predestination," I said.

"Long term or short term?" Emerson asked.

I didn't know how to answer this.

"Long term is absolute fate, what must happen," Emerson said. "No, I don't believe in long term fate. The world is chaotic. Futures are made by random circumstances and conscious choices. However, certain short term fates are testable."

"How?" I asked.

"It's like swimming in a river every day," Emerson said. "Once you know the currents, you know how the river flows."

"We swim in coincidences?" I asked.

"Every day, especially for those who are insensitive," Emerson said. "Most people get washed about by the same currents day after day."

"What current are we in?" I asked.

Emerson smiled.

"A comfortable one," Emerson said. "I've no idea where it's going, but it feels right. I'm used to currents, so I trust them."

"Can I sense currents?" I asked.

"What do you feel?" Emerson asked.

"Anxious ... worried," I said.

Emerson paused, then gestured for us to sit on the couch.

"You're worried about us ...?" Emerson asked.

I nodded.

"I've seen ... relationships go south," I said. "We're still almost strangers. There's much we don't know ..."

"It's your fault," Emerson said. "You figured out I was hiding secrets before I wanted you to ..."

"You're too calm!" I said. *"How can you be so calm?"*

"Relationships are risky," Emerson said. "Maybe we won't work out; some people are incompatible. But fear of incompatibility is poison."

"I know," I said. "Everything seems so ... easy, yet the more we learn ..."

"The less easy it'll be," Emerson said.

I glanced at the muted TV; someone was creeping through a graveyard.

"What are you watching?" I asked.

"Rerun; Buffy, the Vampire Slayer," Emerson said.

"Are vampires real?" I asked.

"Not that I know of," Emerson said. "I like the characters ... and it's good business to know what non-magicians call magic."

"I never liked this show," I said.

"See ...?" Emerson asked. "Exactly what you're afraid of; there's a difference. Now watch how I fix it ..."

Emerson grabbed the remote and clicked my TV off.

"I watch Jeopardy," I smiled.

"Couples tolerate differences or avoid them," Emerson said. "I can watch Buffy when you're at work ... as long as you don't make me watch any reality TV."

"Agreed," I said.

"Here's another; you don't have a lot of books ...," Emerson said.

"I have a Kindle," I said.

"I tried that," Emerson said. "I prefer paper. But you don't have room ..."

"I'll clear a shelf for books," I said.

"This is good," Emerson said. "Hard conversations rather than hidden grudges. I'm trying to be honest. You need to be honest, too."

I nodded.

"Okay," I said. "I'm honestly hungry."

"Do you want to go out ...?" Emerson asked.

"I'm not hungry for food."

Chapter 29

Mr. Dawes grilled me for an hour the next day, forcing me to recite everything I knew about our Nebraska contacts. Fortunately I answered all his questions. Afterwards he stared at me long and hard.

"Well done, Penelope," Mr. Dawes said.

"Sir, I've done a lot of these," I said. "Is there something about this expo I should know?"

Mr. Dawes exhaled heavily.

"It's not Nebraska," Mr. Dawes said. "Devonshire-Slate Medical is likely going through. Bessy Andrews and Colin Mendale wanted me to test you. As far as I know, you've never been in charge of a team, have you?"

"No, but I think I could ...," I answered.

"That's the problem," Mr. Dawes said. "I once knew a great computer programmer who wanted to be a manager. He was our best programmer, so we gave him the promotion. Six months later, we fired our best programmer because he wasn't a good manager. We can't lose our best salesperson, but if we make this sale, we'll be able to do twice as many expos, events happening simultaneously, and hire several new sales positions ..."

"Expanding," I said.

"You'll still be doing the main expos, but simultaneously managing others at smaller venues," Mr. Dawes said. "Managing takes an entirely different skill set."

I stared at him, knowing what this meant.

"It's no coincidence that I make big sales," I said.

Mr. Dawes nodded his head.

"This decision is above me," Mr. Dawes said. "Bessy Andrews favors you, but there're several who barely know your name who must approve."

"Who would I be reporting to?" I asked.

"Bessy," Mr. Dawes said. "This sale requires a new paradigm shift; more promotions than yours depend upon it."

"Will we be rivaling Medicorps International?" I asked.

"No, but we'll become the second largest in two major markets," Mr. Dawes said. "We'll need to expand our service representatives, too. We may need an office in Atlanta. Of course, none of this is to be mentioned outside this office."

"We never discussed it," I said.

"Rosanne is making your Nebraska reservations," Mr. Dawes said. "Best of luck."

I ate lunch alone, thinking over everything Mr. Dawes had said. I'd no doubt that I could manage people, especially with my new sensitivity.

Back at my desk, I answered a few emails, wished a developer happy birthday, and found myself with nothing else to do. I opened the files I'd read yesterday and skimmed them again, glad that I'd known enough to answer Mr. Dawes' questions.

I reached into my purse and drew out three playing cards, an ace, a king, and a queen. Rosanne was on the phone and scrolling through a spreadsheet. Shuffling the three cards under my desk, I dealt them out and held my hand over each. I glanced about to make sure no one was watching, then closed my eyes. My hand slowly waved back and forth and I sensed for any difference. My goal was the ace; odds were three to one that I'd select the right one. Yet all three felt the same. I hesitated over each.

If I chose this one, would it be a coincidence?

The odds were random. To choose the ace on my first attempt would be pure luck ... or an amazing ...

I turned one card over. It was the ace.

"What're you doing?" Rosanne asked.

"Nothing!" I said way too guiltily, as I snatched up the cards and dropped them back into my purse.

"Training to be a magician's assistant?" Rosanne asked.

"No," I said. "I ... Emerson showed me a trick ... and I'm trying to figure out how he did it."

"Ask him," Rosanne suggested.

"Figuring it out would be more impressive," I said.

"Marked cards ...?" Rosanne asked.

"No, and he doesn't wear glasses or contacts, so it can't be chemical," I said.

"Magnetic ...?" Rosanne asked.

"How ...?" I asked.

"Magnetic dust in the card," Rosanne said. "If he wore an iron ring, magnetic, the card would jump into his hand."

"I hadn't considered ...," I said. "Emerson doesn't wear rings, not that I've seen, but he could easily

261

palm a magnet."

"Look online," Rosanne suggested.

"There're a thousand card tricks," I said. "I'd never find the right one."

"Too bad," Rosanne said. "You'd look good ... in a rhinestone tuxedo and hot pants!"

"Never!" I insisted.

I left work with airline and hotel reservations. I halted just inside my front door. A rainbow covered my living room, brightly colored streams of silk.

"Hey!" Emerson said. "You're home early."

I closed my door.

"What's this?" I asked.

"Silk scarf," Emerson said, stuffing the bright silk into a small plastic case. "Thirty feet long. It fits in this case; you just have to pack it tightly."

"Why did you have to be a magician ...?" I sighed.

"What would you rather I be?" Emerson asked.

"Something that let my living room look normal when I come home," I said. "When you're done, we need to eat out."

"The refrigerator's not empty," Emerson said.

"I don't feel like cooking," I said.

It took Emerson ten minutes to stuff his rainbow silk back into its container. Five minutes later, we headed out.

"Any place but Arnold's," I said. "Since I'm leaving on Friday, I want to drag you back there tomorrow."

"Why not on Thursday?" Emerson asked.

"On our last night together ...?" I smiled. "I'm not sharing you."

Emerson smiled.

"What are you going to do while I'm gone?" I asked.

"Oh, I thought I'd hang around, throw wild parties in your apartment, and hear more embarrassing stories about you," Emerson chuckled.

"North Dakota has lots of places to hide a body," I warned.

"Las Vegas has a magician's club," Emerson said. "I have friends there."

"I hate being apart," I said.

"I'll be back whenever our schedules allow," Emerson promised.

"Look, I'm ... not who my friends described, or the person the Bismarck Express gossips about," I said. "I don't date two men at the same time."

"I've never really dated," Emerson said. "You're my first steady relationship."

"It would hurt me if you slept with ...," I started.

"I'm in a relationship with you ...!" Emerson assured.

After thirty minutes, we arrived at a small, out of the way Italian bistro. The neon sign out front shined 'Luigi's'.

"This place has the best food," I said. "Stacy introduced me to it. They're a chain; one of David's biggest customers."

"I'll try not to hold it against them," Emerson said.

The atmosphere was romantic, dim with indirect lighting, filled with colorful vases, fake marble busts of classical figures from history, and dark, decorative wood framing. It was the middle of the week, yet most of the tables were filled.

I'd made a reservation; we were ushered in at once. Our small, circular booth had a bright light beaming upon our table, yet left our faces in shadow. We accepted menus from our waiter, ordered our drinks, and before drinks arrived, selected our dinners.

"I'm going to miss you," I said.

"Nonsense," Emerson said. "I'll phone as often as I can. We'll compare schedules and get together often."

"Work is running me ragged," I said. "The more I sell, the more they expect me to sell. Is there any way managing coincidences could help?"

"Start small," Emerson suggested. "Baby steps. Half of learning is discovering what you shouldn't do."

"How does it work?" I asked.

"Depends on what coincidences are," Emerson said. "All magicians have different opinions."

"Who's right?" I asked.

"Me, of course," Emerson chuckled. "What's a coincidence?"

"A random, unlikely occurrence," I said.

"Every single moment is a coincidence," Emerson said. "That's a quote from Douglas Coupland."

"Magician ...?" I asked.

"Artist," Emerson said. "I've never been lucky enough to meet him. Real magicians don't advertise ourselves, so no one knows how many we are."

"Why not?" I asked.

"Salem witch trials," Emerson said. "We'd end up in labs with wires attached to our skulls."

"Governments can't prove coincidences," I argued.

"Coincidence is the word we use when we can't see the levers and pulleys," Emerson said. "Emma Bull

said that."

"But every decision's a lever ...!" I argued.

"It is such a complex matter we live within, it is impossible to track logic and decision making really, so therefore each choice can actually only be seen as coincidence," Emerson said. "Alva Noto."

"Enough quotes," I whispered.

"Happiness is always a coincidence," Emerson said. "Jose Bergamin."

"You must have some idea ...," I inquired.

"I have ideas, Susan has ideas, and Lucinda has ideas," Emerson said. "Different definitions."

"So ... magic works ... regardless of definition?" I asked.

"If uniform understanding was required, we couldn't all do it," Emerson said.

"I just assumed ... like laws of physics ...," I began.

"If you figure out Laws of Coincidence, you'll be the wisest magician ever," Emerson said.

"Hasn't anyone tried ...?" I asked.

"Many," Emerson said.

"If all of you communicated, maybe you'd find Laws of Coincidence," I suggested.

"If Laws of Coincidence exist, why would we need them?" Emerson asked. "We don't keep lists of magicians because we can't afford to be on lists ... we don't want to get arrested or have our movements tracked."

"That's why you pretend all magic is illusions ...?" I asked.

"It keeps the Cotton Mathers away," Emerson said.

"But ... with coincidences, we could avoid Salem

witch-hunters," I argued.

"ID checks, facial recognition software ...," Emerson warned. "You wouldn't escape for long."

"But ... if we're not abusive ...," I started.

"Evil hides in the pretense of goodness," Emerson said. "They'd brand us as evil. Then they could do whatever they want."

Chapter 30

I felt stuffed all day; we should've split an entrée rather than take doggie bags home. After refusing to answer Rosanne's queries, I lunched on lemonade and a small salad. Several email arguments kept flashing onto my screen, one between four managers, another between programmers. It took time to make sense of both. Yet I was reading them for more than form. If I was called into Bessy's or Colin Mendale's office, I needed to know what was going on.

I did take a few minutes to call Bonnie, Julie, Stacy, and Lyn. I told them I'd be flying out on Friday, and Emerson would be leaving on Thursday. We agreed to meet at Arnold's.

I left work early. Emerson had washed his dirty clothes and sealed two of his boxes.

"I'll need you to drop these at the post office," Emerson said.

"I will," I said. "Unfortunately, I've got to take you back into the fire."

"Arnold's ...?" Emerson said. "I kinda enjoy it."

"Center-of-attention lover," I smiled.

"I ran away from foster homes, spent almost a decade being a jerk, and travel all the time," Emerson said. "It feels good to belong to a group. That's why I hang out with other magicians."

"Are there stage magicians who can't sense coincidences?" I asked.

"Many," Emerson said. "It's not a light switch; sensitivity exists at countless levels."

"What level do I have?" I asked.

"When you reach your limit, you'll know," Emerson said.

"What if my abilities excel yours?" I asked.

"Then you'll teach me," Emerson smiled.

We drove to Arnold's in silence. *Leaving;* I feared to ask what he was thinking.

Stacy, Lyn, Gwen, Nancy, and most of the crowd were already at the bar, Rachel serving drinks.

"Bonnie and Julie are running late," Stacy said after the crowd cheered Emerson's entrance. "They'll be here soon."

"Emerson, you're leaving us?" Gwen asked.

"At least for a while," Emerson said.

"I'm flying out Friday," I said. "Emerson would be alone ..."

"He could hang with us ...!" Lyn grinned.

"That's why I'm shipping him out," I said.

"Where are you going?" Joel asked Emerson.

"Las Vegas," Emerson said.

"Got a show?" Nancy asked.

"Two week engagement," Emerson said.

"Wish we could see it here," Gwen said.

"Shipping my stage props here would cost two hundred dollars," Emerson said. "However ..."

Emerson pulled out a plain, unopened deck of

cards. He shuffled with mastery few could repeat, then asked Rachel to place five empty plates on the bar. From ten feet away, he tossed ten cards; two landed on each plate.

Applause exploded. Then Emerson tossed a card to land atop the heads of several in the bar. More applause.

Finally he collected his cards, had Brendan shuffle them, then lay them out on the bar in three stacks. Kathy cut each pile, making six stacks. Nancy selected one stack, drew a card from it, and showed it to all of them ... everyone except Emerson and me. Emerson set aside the remaining piles, then had Kathy scatter the six cards in her last stack onto the bar, in any order, while he turned his back. Once done, Emerson held his hand over each, as he'd taught me to do. When he finally touched one with his finger, he asked them all.

"What card was selected?"

"Jack of spades," several answered.

Emerson turned over the card; jack of spades.

Everyone demanded to know how he'd done it. Emerson waved off their queries.

"If I tell you, it won't be magic," Emerson insisted.

I smiled; *he'd demonstrated real magic, but none of them believed.*

Emerson pocketed his cards and ordered a beer.

Usual conversations began, groups broke off, and old memories dredged up. Brendan and Nancy started arguing about the baseball game on TV. Kathy described a magic trick she'd learned for a school play. Bonnie and Julie arrived.

"Why leaving so early?" Brendan asked. "We'd love it if you stuck around."

"It takes hours, sometimes days, to prepare a stage for a magic act," Emerson said. "Penelope won't be home until Monday or Tuesday, when I'd have to leave."

"We'll keep you entertained ...," Julie promised.

"That's what Lyn said," Emerson smiled. "But I want Penelope rested, and she won't ... until I'm safely aboard my airplane."

Julie pretended innocence ... and everyone laughed ... except me. Julie and Lyn were two of my best friends, yet no cute, decent, single man was safe around them ... and married men were only slightly less endangered.

Bonnie had big news; her eldest daughter won the county prize for uneven parallel bars, and was going to compete against the rest of North Dakota in the State finals. If she won, she'd compete at Nationals. Big news, yet Bonnie and I sat beside each other, sipping beers, virtually unseen in the crowd. Crowds always focus on the newest novelty.

"Are you sure you don't want to be his assistant?" Bonnie asked me. "You could keep a close eye on him."

"I'm not a magician's assistant," I said.

"You'll get jealous," Bonnie said.

"I'm more mature than that," I said.

"Don't lie," Bonnie said.

"Suspicions kill relationships," I said.

"You're basically separating!" Bonnie said. "Long distance relationships ...!"

"What other kind of relationship could I have?" I asked. "Even if he stayed here, I'd be doing conventions."

"He could go with you," Bonnie said.

"Hawaii, maybe, but Nebraska?" I asked. "What's he to do while I'm working?"

"Go fishing," Bonnie said.

"I don't think he's ever been fishing," I said.

"Camping ...?" Bonnie asked.

I shrugged and took a drink.

"Sounds like ... you don't know him as well as you think you do," Bonnie said.

"We're new," I said.

"All sex, no talk ...?" Bonnie grinned.

"We talk."

"About what ...?"

I couldn't tell her: 'about real magic'. Yet she was right; when we talked, it was usually about magic. *Did he like anything ... besides magic and sex?*

"Well ...?" Bonnie asked.

I had to say something; Bonnie never let a subject drop.

"We talk about ... magic ... his show," I said.

"He tells you how his tricks work?" Bonnie asked.

"Not all of them," I said. "I had to promise not to tell ..."

"You trust me," Bonnie said.

"I do," I said to Bonnie. "But I need Emerson to trust me."

The only way to handle Bonnie when she got bossy was to never let her get her way. Yet her concerns bothered me.

I knew too little about Emerson to be in a permanent relationship.

Bonnie got tired of my stonewalling. Rachel poured us new beers. Bonnie had to drink quickly; she had to cook dinner for her husband and kids. Finally

271

she assured me that she'd eventually wheedle the answers from me, finished her beer, and started saying good-bye. She gave Emerson a big hug, and I saw her whisper something into his ear, yet I couldn't tell what she'd said.

Julie had dropped her kids off at her mother's, so she could stay later than usual. She joined those circled around Emerson, entranced by his every word. All were girls; the men sat at nearby tables, eyes glued to the baseball game, cheering or cursing in unison. I forced a smile, walked up behind Emerson, and slid my arms around his waist. Unsurprisingly, the eyes of every girl, so attentive to his words, dropped to watch my hands wrap protectively around him.

"Hecklers are part of every magic act," Emerson told them. "Books on stage magic have whole chapters on hecklers. Usually they're just drunks, and common tricks exist to embarrass them. If they get really loud, you make them part of your show ... get the audience laughing at them."

"Darling, I'm getting hungry," I said, asserting dominance.

"I'd better wash first," Emerson said.

Emerson excused himself and headed for the men's room. I smiled at the girls, receiving dark glares.

"You're so lucky," Julie said. "Cute, smart, and interesting ...!"

"Meeting him was a coincidence," I grinned.

"I need a coincidence like that," Julie said.

Emerson returned. I flagged down one of the waiters, Mike, and he took our orders. Stacy came to say good-bye; she had to cook for David. She wished us both safe trips, then slid toward the door. At my request, Lyn and Julie joined us at our small booth; I trusted them more than the others.

Emerson described all the tricks he used in his act. He also described a few I'd never seen, which he'd dropped for one reason or another. Then Mike brought our bacon cheeseburgers, and Emerson complained that he knew virtually nothing about either Lyn or Julie. I grinned; he wanted them talking so we could eat.

Lyn glossed over her life's history, but Julie described herself in depth, especially the type of man she was hoping to meet ... in case Emerson should run into any single magicians. Lyn jumped in, also hoping to meet a single man, and Julie quickly described Ivan, the soldier who phoned Lyn once every month. Lyn obviously didn't appreciate this tactic.

Emerson and I ate and let them argue.

"When we're finished, I'd like to go home," I whispered in Emerson's ear.

He nodded.

Lyn and Julie looked ready to fight, cats with claws extended. I suggested that Emerson should conjure up new magician-boyfriends for each of them. He promised to do his best, which mollified their spat.

We managed to slip out after only twenty minutes of good-byes and half a dozen posed photos. Ignoring my glares, several girls, including Kathy and Nancy, had to give Emerson good-bye hugs that could've passed for a physical.

"Thanks," Emerson said as we got into my car. "I was afraid for my prostrate."

"That was Nancy ... and she'd have done more if I wasn't there," I said.

"There're plenty of guys around," Emerson said.

"Half of them have cheated on every girlfriend they've had," I said. "Some are just boring. In towns like

Bismarck, new prey is pounced upon."

"One girl makes the kill and others suffer?" Emerson asked.

"*Kill ...?*" I asked.

"Animal kingdom reference," Emerson said. "Prey ... pounced upon ...?"

"And devoured," I said.

"Lyn and Julie ...?" Emerson asked.

"She-tigers ... if ever there were," I said.

"Glad I didn't meet them first," Emerson said. "What about you? Are you a she-tiger?"

"Queen-tiger."

I paused to check both ways before I drove out of the parking lot, then I spoke up.

"Rapid-fire ...?" I asked.

"Here ...?" Emerson asked.

"Do you like camping?" I asked.

"Never been," Emerson said. "Other kids in Mississippi and Wisconsin talked about it, but foster parents never took me."

"What do you like to do?" I asked.

"Going to shows," Emerson said. "Concerts, live theater, dances, other magic shows; entertainers swap free tickets. I wouldn't mind trying camping, just to see what it's like."

"What about ... guns?" I asked.

"What about them?"

"Ever own a gun?"

"No, although I've shot a few ... long stories," Emerson said. "Traveling with guns is complicated ... time-consuming. I avoid places where I might need one."

"So ... probably no hunting, then," I said.

"What brought this on?" Emerson asked.

"Bonnie thinks we don't know each other," I said.

"Bonnie doesn't leave questions unasked, does she?" Emerson grinned.

"Not since kindergarten," I said.

"Other questions?" Emerson asked.

"Yes, but I can't think of what," I said. "When we talk, it's mostly about magic ..."

"Something we have in common," Emerson said.

"Must have other things ...," I said.

Emerson nodded. "All right, but let's get to your place first."

We drove in silence the rest of the way home. I parked, led the way upstairs, then locked the door behind us, then stood ... waiting. Emerson noticed my expression and seemed to suffer a dry throat.

"Our relationship is moving fast," Emerson admitted. "You haven't spent years trusting coincidences. I trust that you're perfect for me. I'm trying to be perfect ... for you ... and not blow it."

"I feel like I'm being forced," I said. "I don't want to be controlled ... by fate or anything."

"I'm not trying ...!" Emerson started.

"Look at it from my point of view!" I couldn't help shouting. *"You 'coincidentally' chose me, stalked me, deceived me, got me drunk, slept with me ...!"*

"How do you tell someone about magic on a first date ...?"

"That's not the point!" I couldn't lower my voice. *"You chose me! I didn't choose you!"*

Emerson bowed his head and said nothing while I breathed heavily. I started to say something else, but he raised his hand.

"You were only in Hawaii for one week,"

Emerson said. "What should I have done?"

"*Something else ...!*"

"What ... exactly?"

We stared through thick tension. *I had no idea what I wanted ... how else he could've ...!*

"*Shut up!*" I suddenly shouted.

Emerson nodded and crossed his arms. *He was so infuriating ...!*

Unfortunately I had no answer. *Again I felt out of control ...!*

"*Well ...?*" I demanded.

He rolled his eyes.

"Can I talk now ...?" Emerson asked. "Few couples arrive at the same point simultaneously. One of us believes that our relationship is still in the tentative stage and the other thinks it's farther along."

"How far ...?" I asked, but Emerson looked away. "*How far ...?*"

"I'm hoping it's ... permanent," Emerson said. "Isn't that what you want ...?"

"*I want to make my own choices!*" I said.

"Okay," Emerson said. "Choose."

"*You can't be in charge of everything!*" I said.

"You've been in charge of everything," Emerson said.

"You arranged for my big sale so you could ambush me in Atlanta!" I accused.

"I sensed you'd be sent to Atlanta, I didn't know why," Emerson said. "I didn't arrange your sale ... and I just called a friend at The Illusion Emporium and asked if they could use me for a week."

"And what about the magician who otherwise would've been performing that week ...?" I asked.

"His name is Malcolm, and he wanted the week

off anyway," Emerson said. "He was using magic to find someone to replace him. Don't you see? My wanting to replace him was *his coincidence* ...!"

I stared dumbfounded.

"He ... was manipulating you?" I asked.

"No one's manipulating ...!" Emerson said, seeming exasperated. "Coincidences happen every day, to everyone; we're all affected. That's how life works ... always been that way. Only, now that you understand 'coincidences', suddenly they're 'manipulations'.'"

"You make it sound like 'The Force'," I said.

"That would be manipulation," Emerson said. "The Force controls people's minds, moves objects, and has magic sensors."

"You're not manipulating me?" I asked.

"Not any more than you're manipulating Bonnie to not be bossy, or Stacy to tolerate David," Emerson said. "You nudge friends toward paths that you think are best for them ... everyone does. They nudge back. Suddenly you consider it 'manipulation' ... even though you've always done it ...!"

"You're ... not using coincidences to control me ...?" I asked.

"What you're voicing are suspicions," Emerson said. "If you want to choose, choose."

"Just like that ...?" I demanded. "You want me to decide ... my entire future ... right now?"

"Everyone does, every day," Emerson said. "Most don't realize it. You could drive me to the airport now, make me sit there all night, and fly out of your life tomorrow. You could drag me to your bedroom. You could kick me out and leave me standing in your parking lot. You could make me sleep on your couch. Or, like most people, you could choose not to decide anything, and eventually a coincidence will occur; I can't say what. Then another coincidence, and another, and we'll be swept along whatever current we randomly fall into. Who can say where that leads? I can't. A choice will be made, by you, me, or by random chance."

"What is random chance?" I asked.

"Chance and coincidence differ only slightly," Emerson said, and he pulled out a quarter. "I could flip this coin. Odds of it being heads or tails is fifty percent. That's chance. What values you apply to it, what happens if it lands on heads, that's coincidence."

"What if I choose to ignore it?" I asked.

"Most do," Emerson said. "People's lives are crazy because they let random chance make their biggest decisions."

"So ... I finally get to choose," I said.

"You chose to take me to Arnold's," Emerson said. "You chose to show me off to your friends. You chose to eat there. You chose when we left. You chose to let me come to North Dakota. You chose for us to eat at Stacy's. You chose when I met your mother. Now we're here, having our first argument, because I'm choosing everything ...?"

"Because you could ,,,!" I insisted.

"So could you," Emerson said.

"I haven't mastered ...!" I said.

"You will," Emerson shook his head. "Then I'll have to trust you."

"I'm supposed to trust a magician ...?" I asked.

"I'm supposed to trust a salesperson ...?" Emerson asked. "We both present to our audience what we want them to see ... to get them to believe what we want them to."

I frowned. *That is how sales works ...*

"I'm trustworthy," I said.

"I'm trying to be ... as a boy scout," Emerson said.

We stared at each other.

"So ... I need to choose."

Emerson nodded. I took a deep breath.

"What if I choose to be ... your ultimate queen ... and order you to serve me?"

Emerson smiled.

"Sounds like your king is going to enjoy his new job."

"Pour me wine ... now ... naked," I ordered.

Emerson's smile widened, and he began to unbutton his shirt.

"Yes, my queen."

Chapter 31

My alarm went off at 6:30 and I shut it off, still unable to think, feeling like an Olympian exhausted from running a marathon. Emerson lay unmoving on the pillow beside me, looking equally worn out from our long, passionate night. A sheet covered us; he must've recovered it from the floor.

We had to say good-bye today.

We showered together, but didn't have time to make it enjoyable. Our relationship had reached the level where we bowed to practicality; his plane left at 10:00 AM, and I'd be late to work after I'd dropped him off. We didn't have time to eat, so we brushed our teeth, and Emerson sealed the last of his clothes in a box, which he addressed to Sorcery Magnifiquie, Las Vegas.

"I'll mail it today, but it won't arrive for days," I said.

"I called my storage company on Monday while you were at work and forwarded my stage props ... packed in clean clothes," Emerson said. "I'll have to wash these when they arrive." He handed me some cash. "This will cover the mailing costs." Then he paused. "I feel that I should leave my hat."

"No more suspicions," I promised, and I set his hat upon his head.

Dressed, we loaded his boxes and my computer into the car, and headed for the airport.

"Was my queen satisfied with her king ...?" Emerson asked.

"Imperially!"

All too soon, we arrived at Bismarck's airport. At the curb, Emerson and I kissed, and then he got out.

"Call me tomorrow night," Emerson said.

"I will," I promised.

"Penelope, I love you."

"I'm glad you tricked me into loving you," I smiled widely.

Emerson laughed, tipped his hat, and closed the door.

Confident, I drove away.

I was already late for work, yet I stopped at the post office to drop off Emerson's boxes, paying with the cash he gave me. By then I was really late.

Rosanne startled when she saw me. As I sat down, she wheeled her chair over to my desk.

"Details ...!" she demanded.

"Of what ...?" I asked.

"You never smile in the morning," Rosanne said.

"We said good-bye last night ... again and again and again ...!"

Rosanne's face seemed to expand as if she'd explode from not laughing out loud.

"Tell me everything ...!"

"All I can say is ... this smile is from Emerson."

Rosanne started listing sexual acts. Normally I'd

refuse to answer, but I said 'Maybe' to each. Most we'd done, and the rest I'd always been afraid to try, but they now seemed appealing. Rosanne didn't need to know which, however, I kept a mental note of her list, wondering if Emerson would enjoy them.

By the time that Rosanne rolled her chair back to her desk, eyes wide and breathing hard, she looked like she'd had the wild night. Yet she only grabbed some paperwork and rolled back.

"New copies of your reservations."

I glanced them over; *I needed to pack.*

"If you meet any cute magicians ...," she whispered.

"I have all I need," I said.

Rosanne stuck out her tongue.

I read through a long string of emails, mostly conversations by program managers, debating how to approach a new appointment logging option, then brought up the Nebraska files for one last review.

My phone rang.

"Hello, Penelope speaking."

"Ms. Polyglass, this is Colin Mendale. Can you come by my office?"

I caught my breath.

"I'll be right there."

"Thank you."

I rose at once and turned to Rosanne.

"Colin Mendale," I said, and Rosanne's eyes widened.

"What did he want ...?" Rosanne asked.

"Me ... in his office. How do I look?"

"Pale ... and you're not smiling anymore."

I took a deep breath; *I had to look professional.*

Everyone knew where Mr. Colin Mendale's

corner office was. I'd never been inside it. I considered bringing a notepad, yet didn't want to look like a secretary. I glanced down at my clothes and hurried toward his door.

If I'd known I'd be meeting him, I'd have worn something nicer.

His door was partway open.

"Mr. Mendale ...?"

"Please, come in ... and close the door."

I sat at one of the two soft, comfy, straight-backed chairs facing his desk. He was an older man, brown hair going gray, large bald spot, shelf full of golf trophies displayed before his wide window.

He was Bessy Andrews' boss.

"We haven't spoken much, but I've heard a lot about you," Mr. Mendale said. "We're excited about Devonshire-Slate Medical and all the other business you've brought in. So much, in fact, I'm considering expanding our sales division. Frederick Dawes is managing too many departments to take on acquiring and training a new team."

He paused and looked at me.

"I agree, sir," I said. *Always agree with the boss!*

"Ms. Polyglass, may I call you Penelope?"

"Please do."

"Penelope, Frederick and Bessy Andrews speak highly of you," Mr. Mendale said. "They think you should head this new team. Unfortunately, you've no management experience ..."

Mr. Mendale picked up a piece of paper on his desk which looked like my resume from years before ... when I applied for the sales job. He scanned it closely.

"However, I need someone in your position that can do your job ... and keep doing it," Mr. Mendale said.

"There are enough conventions to hire two more people who can do the job you do. Could you continue selling software equally as well ... and train, hire, and lead a new team?"

"I can," I said with confidence.

"You'd have to hire two good, experienced salespeople, and get them up to speed on every aspect of our business, without dropping your current responsibilities," Mr. Mendale said. "I'd like for each to speak an additional language."

"I'm sure I can find the right people," I said.

"Ms. Penelope, I'll be honest with you," Mr. Mendale said. "We can't afford mistakes. Devonshire-Slate Medical is giving us a chance to step up, to claim a larger national market share, and we can't afford a team that doesn't produce results. If our sales don't rise thirty percent within the next calendar year, we may have to scrap the new team."

"A larger team will allow us more chances to sell," I said.

"That's another aspect of management; getting us into new trade shows," Mr. Mendale said. "Mr. Dawes will be handing that responsibility to you."

"I already know most of the trade show managers," I said.

"This is a huge responsibility," Mr. Mendale said. "Do you think you're up for it?"

"I do," I said.

"We need to start planning right away," Mr. Mendale said.

"I'm flying to Nebraska tomorrow," I said.

"Wherever you are, you'll have to coordinate with Bessy Andrews," Mr. Mendale said. "I've spoken to the board. They've assigned me the responsibility of choosing the head of the new team. That makes me personally responsible for our sales quotas for the next year. Do you understand how serious I am?"

"I do, Mr. Mendale," I said. "Thirty percent."

He looked at me hard, then dropped my resume onto his desk. He picked up a 9x11 white envelope and handed it to me.

"Ms. Penelope Polyglass, I'm offering you this chance," Mr. Mendale said. "I needn't say what will happen if our quotas aren't met ...?"

"No, sir," I said.

"Take that home, read it, and if satisfactory, return it to Bessy Andrews," Mr. Mendale said. "Thank you for your time."

"Thank you, Mr. Mendale," I said.

He stood up and held out his hand. Anxiously, I rose and shook it, and he thanked me again for my sales. I thanked him, uncertain what he meant. *Had I gotten the job ...?*

Uncertain, I walked toward my desk. Rosanne would want answers. I slipped into a bathroom, checked that every stall was empty, and opened the envelope.

A new employment contract; *the title read 'Sales Manager'!*

I slid my eyes down the long list of responsibilities.

Compensation ... almost twice my current salary! And my sales bonus!

I almost fell over. My fingers were trembling.

I reported directly to Bessy Andrews!

I fell back against the wall, scanning the paper again and again, unable to read it clearly.

I needed to be alone; I'd come to work late. Sadly, it was too early for lunch.

I put the new employment contract back in its envelope, closed it, and stared at myself in the mirror.

I looked like a deer caught in headlights ... or a contestant on a game show!

Several deep breaths later, I wiped the smile off my face and put on my best stoic expression. I left the ladies' room and headed straight to Mrs. Bessy Andrews' office. She was on the phone, yet her door was open, and when she saw me, she waved for me to wait.

"That sounds good," she said into her phone. "Look, I've got someone here and need to go. All right ... Wednesday by the latest. Good-bye."

She hung up. I stepped inside her office and closed the door.

"You understand; announcements of promotions must come from upper management," Bessy said.

"I do," I said.

"Is the offer acceptable?"

"It is," I said, *although I'd no idea what others at this level made.*

"You fly out tomorrow?" Bessy asked.

"Yes, early," I said.

"Perhaps you should go home, spend the rest of the day getting ready for your trip," Bessy said. "We've got lots to do. By Monday, I want a list of requirements and responsibilities for the new sales positions. We can't afford to hire the wrong people."

"I can do that," I said.

"Email it to me by the end of the weekend," Bessy said.

"You'll have it," I promised.

"Is that your contract?" she gestured to the white envelope in my hand.

"Yes," I said.

"Read it carefully, make a copy for yourself, and bring me the signed original when you get back." Bessy instructed.

"I will," I said.

"Congratulations, Penelope," Bessy said. "I hope you know what you're getting into."

"Thank you, Mrs. Andrews," I said.

I stepped out of her office feeling dazed. I walked back to my desk. Rosanne stopped typing and looked at me.

"What did Colin Mendale want?" she asked.

I stared at her.

"I can't say ... and I can't do lunch," I said. "I've got to go home, get ready for ... Nebraska."

"Get ready ...?" Rosanne asked. "You've never had to ..."

"I have to now," I said.

"Does that mean ...?" Rosanne asked.

"I can't say ... and neither can you," I emphasized.

"I don't know a thing," Rosanne promised.

In a fog, I gathered everything I'd need for the show, including my newly-printed reservations. My display monitor and signs were in my work case back home, so I didn't need much. I collected my computer and left without a word. I forced myself to remember where the parking lot was.

I was promoted ...!

I sat in my car ten minutes before I turned the key. *Never drive in a daze!*

Before I knew it, I was parking in front of my apartment, taking my usual things ... and the white envelope ... upstairs.

I dropped down onto my couch and opened the

envelope again, this time reading every word. Mephistopheles came investigating, doubtlessly awakened by my unexpected early return, yet I ignored him and focused on my contract.

Never in my life had I made this much money!

After the third complete reading, I slid the contract back into its envelope. *I had to make a copy of it.* I had a scanner and kept a flash drive plugged into it. I extracted the contract, scanned it, then put it back. Tingling with excitement, I opened my laptop and plugged in my flash drive.

Login. Click. Double-click. The contract opened on my screen. I read it again.

I set my laptop aside, not bothering to close it or plug it in. I stood up.

Suddenly I started dancing.

If Emerson was here I'd try everything on Rosanne's list ...!

Everything looked hazy yet sparklingly bright. Most days suffered drudgery.

Lives turned on days like this!

I glanced at the clock; Emerson was in the air. *I couldn't tell him.*

Upper management makes the announcement; *I couldn't tell anyone.*

The Bismarck Express would jump tracks and plow through its station!

If I told anyone, my whole company would hear; *my promotion would be at risk.*

I could only tell Emerson ... but not until tonight!

I had to stay home. If anyone saw me, especially Bonnie, they'd notice how excited I was. I had to wait until the paperwork for my promotion had gone through ... and the announcement made.

Mephistopheles demanded food, yet I'd given him fresh dry this morning, and he didn't get his can until dinnertime. I needed to drop him off at mom's; I could take his cans and feed him there.

I still needed to pack, but I had hours. I glanced at the clock again, suddenly realizing how long I'd been dancing; at least half an hour.

I needed to eat.

I wanted to eat out. *Managers ate out.* Yet I feared running into anyone I knew; *keeping this secret would be challenging.* Reluctantly, I microwaved leftovers for lunch. *I couldn't risk messing this up!*

Luckily, I'd be in Nebraska all weekend!

Around 4:00 PM, I called mom, drove Mephistopheles over, and didn't stay long. I stopped at my favorite French restaurant, got take out, and headed home to celebrate in private. At 7:00 PM, I could wait no longer; I phoned Emerson and practically screamed my news at him.

Emerson was delighted, but his news wasn't good; the magician who accepted delivery of his mailed packages had gone to a party, and wasn't answering his phone. We didn't talk long, yet he congratulated me on my promotion, and promised we'd celebrate in style when we saw each other. I almost asked if he'd like one of the positions on Rosanne's list, decided against it, and said 'I love you' instead. He said it back to me, then we hung up so he could keep trying to find his clothes.

I couldn't wait to see Emerson again!

I was a sales manager ...!

Chapter 32

Still excited, I arrived at the airport early. I'd brought my Kindle and had downloaded a new mystery novel. Yet I was too excited to focus on fiction.

Should I stay in my apartment? Buy a house? A new car ...? Get an investment manager?

Dreams and visions flashed past in increasing audacity. However, I had to focus on navigating the airport, not get in the wrong line and miss my flight. Bessy probably made more money than I did, and she didn't live like a millionaire. I needed to make choices wisely.

Emerson had seemed excited. *Were we a couple ...?* I wanted a long-term, permanent relationship. Yet ... *was I ready to commit ...?* We'd grown comfortable with the 'L' word, but no mention of the 'M' word ... I certainly wasn't ready to talk about it.

I scorned myself; *how many times had I prayed for what he'd described?* I was uncomfortable with how fast our relationship had cemented, yet he was so hot that I couldn't stand sleeping alone. He'd virtually forced himself into my social circle, met my family ... how could this be some devious plan? *No, those were suspicions.* If he'd just wanted a quick fling, he would've never called after Hawaii.

Besides, with his magic, he could have anything he wanted.

He wanted me.

I took in a deep, warming breath.

I wanted him.

I wished he'd been with me last night so I hadn't had to celebrate alone!

The flight to Minneapolis was uneventful, a small jet for maybe fifty passengers, two on each side. Then I transferred to my flight to Nebraska, where the plane wasn't much larger.

I noticed kids in the row ahead of me randomly clicking through all the free options on the little screens on the backs of the seats in front of them. One of them flashed on a free Disney movie. I was feeling adventurous; I closed my eyes and focused on them.

Coincidences!

I opened my mind, allowing myself to stretch out, to feel for the coincidences of their screens. *Which buttons would they push? What video would they choose?* I sensed for their choices. *Could I align them?*

I couldn't focus. The speed at which they were clicking, the movements of the person next to me, flipping pages on her magazine, the constant coughing of someone two rows behind me; all added up to too much distraction. Finally I gave up.

Hours later, the plane landed. My mind was still a blur. I pulled out my reservations to review; the freeway south of the Lincoln Airport was dotted with hotels and restaurants. I had to check into my hotel first, which was right across the street from the convention center.

After luggage pick-up and car rental, I drove to my hotel in minutes. My room was small and sparsely decorated with one framed print of men fishing in a stream before small, rugged mountains.

Emerson wouldn't be visiting this room.

TV didn't relax me. I flipped open my laptop and reread my new contract ... it made me smile, but didn't calm me. I closed my computer and took it with me to find dinner.

The hotel restaurant didn't look appealing. The painting by its entrance was the same picture framed in my room. There were lots of restaurants in Lincoln, and I headed for a local Mexican favorite.

In the bar, I sat at a table. I considered a margarita, yet I had to be bright and cheery tomorrow; I ordered lemonade and a small burrito. The salsa that came with the chips was hotter than I liked, yet I indulged anyway.

Opening my laptop, I scanned my contract again, focusing on my raise. Then I minimized it ... so I would stop rereading it. I considered reviewing the Nebraska clients again, but couldn't. Frustrated, I clicked my network icon, found a free WIFI, and opened to Emerson's website. His image evoked a smile. I didn't think I'd feel complete until I saw him.

By Monday, Bessy expected a list of requirements and responsibilities for my former position. This was easy; I kept all files, including every version of my resume, whenever I applied anywhere. Dragging it up, I found the ad I'd answered when I applied to this job. Copying it to a new file, I scanned the internet for medical software sales jobs, found several that sounded challenging, and copied those as well. Slowly I merged them together, staying with the original

format. I didn't know if Bessy had written my
requirements, but someone in the company had, so the
format had been acceptable. I combined it with a few
ideas of my own.

I let the waitress take away the remains of the
burrito that I hadn't been able to finish, yet kept the
chips and hot salsa. I glanced up; several pairs of eyes
stared directly at me. The bar was full, mostly men,
muted talk overwhelming the samba music playing over
the speakers. It was Friday night in Lincoln, Nebraska,
and I was sitting alone in a bar ... glad that I was wearing
more than my red bikini. I asked for the check, left cash
on the table, and hurried out.

Back in my hotel, I returned to Emerson's site,
and left his photo onscreen. The sun was setting, yet it
was still early. Before Emerson, I'd been content to
watch TV, think about Mephistopheles, and wonder
who was the topic of the Bismarck Express. Now none
of those mattered.

Cards; I drew out the deck I'd brought. I took
out three cards, then two more, and noted that one of
them was the king of clubs. I shuffled, dealt the cards
face down, and searched for the king. Feeling nothing, I
recalled Emerson's instructions and tried to clear my
mind, test each card individually, and notice which felt
different. Choosing the king would be a coincidence.
Yet I felt nothing.

Emerson was my king.

Joy: as soon as I thought of joy, I knew the right
card. I flipped over the king and smiled. Then I
reshuffled and tried again with equal success. Focusing
on Emerson, I somehow knew I'd always pick the king.

Within half an hour, I was shuffling ten cards
and still picking the king. Suddenly it felt easy, almost

too easy; I wished I could try more. I wondered if Lincoln had a zoo, and regretted that I wouldn't have time to visit it. I'd love to test my skills against antelope again.

I upped the volume on the TV. I tested myself again; choosing the king was much harder with distracting sights and noises. The sensations I needed were subtle. How Emerson managed magic onstage was a mystery. I struggled, but sometimes I overturned up to four other cards before I found the king. I practiced most of the night with the TV on, with limited success. Focusing on subtle sensations amid distractions took intense concentration; I wondered how many months or years it had taken Emerson to manage it.

My beeping phone startled me. *Emerson!*

"Hello!"

"Guess where I am ...?"

"Vegas ...?"

"Minneapolis," Emerson said. "I was trying to save money; I'm on standby."

"I was just there!"

"Sorry we didn't meet ..."

"Until when ...?"

"Tomorrow at 5:00 AM ... maybe."

"Sorry about that," I said.

"What're you doing?" Emerson asked.

"Cards ... alone in my room," I answered.

"Best place for it," Emerson said. "I said don't try too much, but I couldn't stop once I'd learned the basics. Be careful."

"I will," I said. "I wish you were here."

"I'd rather be with you than anywhere ... especially here," Emerson said.

"What are you going to do?" I asked.

"Sleep in the airport ... again," Emerson said.

"Why didn't you use coincidence ...?" I asked.

"I tried," Emerson said. "No timeline existed that would get me into an empty seat."

"Couldn't you ...?" I asked.

"Make someone else miss their flight so I can get their seat?" Emerson asked. "Is that what you're suggesting?"

"No, I guess not," I said.

"Good, because that could ruin someone else's trip and make me ... someone you wouldn't like," Emerson said. "I'm not late for my show."

"I understand," I said.

"Please tell me something interesting," Emerson said. "I'm so bored."

"I'm naked," I said.

"That's the sweetest lie I've ever heard," Emerson said. "Keep going."

"I don't do that over the phone," I said.

"I couldn't ... react accordingly ... here," Emerson said.

"I want to be there when you're aroused," I said.

"I'm always that way ... near you," Emerson said.

"Tease ...!" I accused.

"You're lucky I can't speak freely," Emerson said.

"I don't know if I could listen," I said.

"We'll see," Emerson promised. "Unfortunately, not tonight."

"Depends on what my dreams are," I said.

"Tell me tomorrow night," Emerson said.

Chapter 33

The Nebraska Medical Trade Show started empty; twenty minutes before start time, only a handful of vendors had arrived. I found my booth number on a chart taped to a table just inside the door, found my location, and set up my display with no one in sight. Finally I walked to the end of my row and found two men setting up a backdrop and a large bowl of candy beside a stack of brochures.

"Where is everyone?" I asked.

"No one shows up on time," one man said. "We just drove up from Austin, got here sooner than expected."

"I'm Mike ... and this is Dan," Mike said. "Hospital equipment."

"Penelope," I said, looking at a picture of a CT scanner on their brochure. "Down the aisle. Medical software."

"Were you in Hillsborough last weekend?" Dan asked.

"No, but I'd like to hear about it," I said.

Mike and Dan were a treasure box of information. I walked back to my booth holding one of their brochures with the names of four new medical conventions written on its back.

At five to nine, more vendors started streaming in.

I couldn't stop smiling. I found the booth on one side of me setting up a fancy table and chairs, the sign behind them reading Apex Consolidated Supply.

"Were you at Hillsborough last week?" I asked.

"I wish," the old woman said, while her younger helper opened and unpacked a plastic crate. "We were stuck in Vermont."

"What was the name of that one?" I asked, scribbling on my brochure.

The Nebraska Medical Trade Show had been open for almost half an hour before the first customers walked by. Many vendors were still setting up, and a few had not arrived.

I smiled and batted eyes; every man stopped to talk to me. I recited my speech, answered a few questions, and they didn't walk away while I talked. Unfortunately, two hours later, the 'early crowd' was gone, and I stood looking only at other vendors. Most were visiting each other. I unplugged my display, so that my laptop screen wouldn't show to everyone, and typed in all the information I'd gathered. I also emailed Bessy the job requirements she'd asked for. I scanned my emails, saw nothing important, and restored my display. As no more customers appeared, I took a pad and pen and went to siphon more information.

A second rush came by around lunchtime. We returned to our booths, and for a few hours it felt like a real convention. I spied one of the contacts I'd researched and called them over. We shared a long conversation, and I wrote some notes as they walked away. Then the crowd thinned to a trickle, and we were left staring at each other again. I used the time to add three new medical conventions to my list.

One vendor had a fresh cookie oven, and we gathered around their booth. I knew a few of the vendors from the next row, and we traded stories about Hawaii and my sale in Atlanta. Many vendors knew each other, and several suggested we go out for dinner together. I chimed in, as I didn't want to end up the only single girl in a Mexican bar again.

At 4:00 PM, the doors closed ... the customers were already gone and half of us were packed and ready to go. They assured me that the doors would be locked and armed security would be there all night, so I packed only my laptop and display monitor. Locking them in my trunk, I drove a group to BBQ.

By quarter to five, we filled tables in a bar hosting eight different BBQ sauces ... from Jamaica Lickin' Sweet to Black-Charred Satan-Tongue. We ordered pitchers of beer and lots of wings, since they'd only had one food truck at the convention and all it served was hot dogs and pop. When bone-in wings started arriving, we attacked them. Within twenty minutes, BBQ sauce painted our fingers and lips, and we were laughing at practically anything.

One woman, Vanessa, had accompanied me to the magic show after the Hawaiian convention. Despite her questions, I rolled my eyes and insisted that Emerson wouldn't tell me how his big finale worked. This prompted a few questions I wasn't ready to answer.

"When did you speak to him?" Vanessa asked.

"After the show," I said.

"You were escorted back to your hotel," Vanessa said.

"We ... met ... later ... in the hotel bar," I said.

The vendors exchanged glances.

"And ...?" an old lady asked.

"He was mighty cute ...," Vanessa said.

I took a big swig of beer.

"We may have ... dated," I confessed.

Laughter erupted. I felt myself blush.

"Dated ...?" the old lady asked.

"In Hawaii ... and Atlanta ... and Bismarck."

Cell phones came out, searches were made, and soon everyone was watching Emerson's videos.

"He's in Las Vegas doing another show," I said, defending myself. "He calls me every night."

"Has he taught you any tricks?" a man asked.

"No ...," I said.

"Show us a trick!" they urged.

"I can't do them," I said. "He practices all the time. I came home and found cards and silk scarves all over my living room."

I described how he could throw cards anywhere, and no one believed me. My story about my cat defending his hat was laughed at. Then Dan found an old video of Emerson tossing cards, and everyone had to watch.

Rather than have a meal, people kept ordering appetizers and sharing. Before eight, I was stuffed and feeling no pain.

My phone rang. *Emerson!*

I shoved it against one ear and stuck a finger in the other.

"Emerson ...?"

"Thank g..., where are you?"

"In a restaurant," I said. "With a bunch of vendors."

"I don't ... can you talk?" Emerson asked.

"Barely," I said. "It's noisy here."

"I'm still in Minnesota," Emerson said.

"What ...?" I asked. "You were supposed to ...!"

"Got bumped this morning and again at 4:30," Emerson said. "They've promised me a flight near midnight."

"Oh, my sweet!" I exclaimed.

"Is that Emerson ...?" Vanessa asked.

I shushed her, yet she only laughed.

"Everyone, say hi to Emmerich the Amazing!" Vanessa urged.

"Hi, Emmerich ...!" everyone shouted.

"Sounds like you're having fun," Emerson said.

"I never should've told them about you," I said.

"I'm kinda glad that you did," Emerson said. "I hated being your secret."

"I've no secrets left," I said.

"We'll keep a few just between us," Emerson said.

"Have you slept?" I asked.

"Not well, but I'll sleep on the plane," Emerson said.

"I'm so sorry," I said.

"Perils of cheap travelers," Emerson said. "You're busy ...!"

"I can leave," I said.

"No, we can talk tomorrow," Emerson said. "By then maybe I'll have something nice to say."

"Get some sleep," I said. "I love you."

"Nicest thing I've heard in years," Emerson said. "I love you, too. Good-night!"

Chapter 34

Sunday was dead. The number of visitors in the convention never exceeded the number of vendors, and I sat bored. A few of the vendors sat talking to each other, yet none voiced enthusiasm.

"Where is everyone?" one vendor asked.

"Golf course, most likely," another vendor said. "Sunday. No one checks to see if they're here."

The vendor across from me was drinking coffee to stay awake. His eyelids drooped. He worked alone, his display of surgical equipment behind glass, unread fliers on his table.

I felt sorry for him, yet I sensed something else. Something subtle tingled at the edge of my awareness. Slowly I imagined him dropping his head onto his desk, sound asleep. At the same time, I also sensed him standing and walking around, stretching his arms to stay awake. Yet he did neither, just kept drinking coffee.

His hand was shaking. I wondered if he'd drop off and spill his coffee.

Could I make him spill his coffee ....?

I closed my eyes and expanded my senses. *Coincidences swirled around us.* It wouldn't be unlikely;

303

he could easily spill without meaning to. He looked half-asleep. As with the cards, the coincidence I wanted to evoke was already there. I just needed to find it.

I reached. I felt. *Feelings. Joy.* I opened my senses to every thread, every outcome I could grasp. I understood limitless possibilities, likelihoods naturally the strongest. Paths led, yet I disregarded all, save paths of deep slumber.

I became his boredom, his weariness, his numbness of thought. My head tilted, drooping, my sight and thoughts dim. My hand; I pushed it forward, abruptly jerking ...

"Aaahhh ...!" he cried.

I opened my eyes; he was wide awake, his cup overturned, coffee soaking his fliers.

I'd done it!

I grabbed a box of Kleenex and ran to help. Another vendor had paper towels. He thanked us, taking our offered papers to soak up his mess. We dismissed his embarrassment; any of us could've fallen asleep.

I stood back as they finished cleaning up the mess, throwing away the drenched fliers.

I'd ... forced a coincidence ...!

Or had I ...?

How could I know?

This coincidence could've happened without me. How did Emerson know which coincidences he arranged and which he just stumbled upon?

He didn't ...!

Yet I felt certain that I'd done it ...!

What else could I do ...?

I looked at all the vendors. They had no idea what'd just happened. They wouldn't believe me if I told them ... which I couldn't do.

I sat back and stared at them. *My life had just changed.*

I was a magician ...!

The accident woke up everyone on our row. Moments later, doldrums resumed. No customers were visible, strolling up other rows, or sitting by the door. None of us had any business being here.

Except me ...

No one was looking at me. I reached out again, stretching my senses as far as I could. Coincidences swirled around me. I was free, swimming, flying in swirls of currents I'd never known existed. *Time ... nature ... truths ... flowed like tides.* I felt ... *sighted* ... after a life of blindness.

I had to try again.

What should I do ...? I looked around. Everyone was bored. I didn't want to spill another coffee. I wanted to test myself ... flex my newfound ability. But what did I want ...?

A reason to be here.

This event was boring, yet there were a few customers; stragglers walking in pairs, talking sports or trends ... whatever took their minds away from work. Few cared or even glanced at the booths they walked past ... or the direction their feet carried them.

Random chance steered them.

I could steer random chance!

I sat on my chair, rested my arms on my table, and closed my eyes. I took in a deep breath. I had to relax, be ready to not only challenge myself, but seek beyond me farther than I'd ever dreamed. Nerves and fear killed sensitivity. I had to remain calm.

Joy!

Possibilities branched out in every direction. Every occurrence was mapped, thick, four-dimensional cloth ropes woven in threads leading off at every angle. I was its center. The thickest weaves composed cords of likelihood. The lighter cords spun around knots of vendors trapped in their booths. Yet I was their center. I pulled, drew in, and gathered all threads to me.

I attracted them!

I felt them ... every coincidence ... as a part of me. Like the fine hairs on my arms, they rose and spread ... until I gathered, twirled, and banded them.

Noise ...

I opened my eyes.

Customers walked into view at both ends of my row. Each seemed surprised to see a crowd at the other end. Yet both sides came forward. Most glanced long at me, although if this was because I'd pulled them, or because they were mostly men who always stare at pretty girls, I didn't know or care.

I was Penelope the Magician!

At the end of the day, I declined offers to dine with other vendors. Like most, I was packed and ready to go an hour before time ... when a messenger came around telling us that the last customers had departed. The event was over.

I called Emerson within seconds of closing my hotel room door.

"I did it!" I almost shouted as he answered.

"What ...?" Emerson asked.

"Magic!" I squealed. *"I did it!"*

"Congratulations!" Emerson said. "Hold on. I need to get somewhere ..."

I could hear noise, music, and voices. Then the

volume cut in half.

"Where are you?" I asked.

"Nightclub," Emerson said. "Back of a magic club. The show starts in forty minutes. Tell me everything."

"I was at my convention ... and it was dead," I said. "No customers, nothing to do. The vendor across from me was falling asleep in his booth, a cup of coffee in his hand. I was bored, so I started experimenting. I reached out, sensing everything. Emerson, I made him spill ...! He dropped his head and coffee simultaneously! I found the path, willed it, and made it happen!"

"You made someone ... spill their coffee ...?" Emerson asked.

"It went all over!" I was almost shouting. "It soaked into his sleeves and all his papers ...!"

"Wow ...," Emerson said, yet his voice was flat and hesitant. "That's ..."

"What ...?" I asked.

A long moment passed.

"Listen, Penelope," Emerson said. "I'm glad for you. Moreover, I'm proud of you. I know what this means. But ... think what you did. You spilled a man's coffee. Of all things, why that?"

"It ... no, it wasn't like that!" I said. "I wasn't trying to be mean or anything. He was already falling asleep. It was likely he was going to spill it anyway ..."

"So it was easy," Emerson said.

"Well, I felt ... I didn't think I could handle a big thing ... not at first, but then ...!" I said. "I made all the customers come toward me ...!"

"Come to you ...?" Emerson asked.

"They were wandering blindly around the hall," I

307

said. "I just ... sensed for them ... pulled them ... and they came. I emptied out all the other aisles."

"That's sounds great!" Emerson said, suddenly enthusiastic again. "That one I'm proud of ...!"

"Wait ...," I said. "Did I do ... something wrong?"

"Not ... wrong," Emerson said. "Everyone starts out differently. Lucinda made a boy wreck his bicycle and fall down. He got hurt; she's ashamed of having started that way. Suzzannia drew in huge ocean waves no one expected; she's lucky no kids got swept out to sea. It ... it doesn't matter."

"What about you?" I asked. "How did you learn ...?"

"Do you promise not to tell?" Emerson asked.

"Yes ...," I said.

"I was a city boy, living on the streets," Emerson said. "I started out playing ... with pigeons. I made them land, fly, chase food ..."

"That's not so bad," I said.

"I made it bad," Emerson said. "I hung out in front of banks with cash machines, waiting for people to walk away still holding money. I sent pigeons flying at them. They swarmed and attacked them. If they dropped their money, fighting off the birds, I'd grab it and run."

Emerson paused.

"You were ... just a boy," I said.

"You're learning as an adult," Emerson said. "That's an advantage; you already have a moral center. You mustn't let power corrupt ..."

"It was just a cup of coffee," I said.

"I know," Emerson said. "It's impressive you've learned to do magic so quickly. But be careful, or at least mindful; bad beginnings lead to bad places."

"I'm not Lex Luthor," I almost laughed.

"Luthor started out as Superman's friend," Emerson said. "You're strong, yet we're all susceptible; humans have failings. Once I'd mastered the basics, I snuck into casinos, bet on baseball games, and attended boxing matches. A single coincidence, a roll of seven, a wild pitch, or a dropped defense seems a minor influence ... but its influence on you is far greater than your influence upon it."

"I'll be more ... selective," I promised.

"Glad to hear that ...," Emerson began, but then the loud music and voices returned. "Look, it's getting crazy here. I got to Las Vegas early this morning and only woke up an hour ago, I'll call you tomorrow night. Keep practicing ... safely."

"I will," I said. "I love you."

"I love you, too. Good-night."

Chapter 35

Strange dreams; I awoke late and had to hurry to check out in time. My flight home wasn't for hours, yet I quick-packed everything into my suitcases, returned my room key, and went searching for breakfast.

All through pancakes I sat wondering. Emerson was sweet to be protective of me, yet I wasn't a child. His foster-upbringing was a nightmare, and had made him its equal. He was lucky to have escaped the traumas he'd suffered. I was a grown woman in control of myself and knew what I was doing.

I'd never purposefully hurt others.

I'd nowhere else to go, so I drove to the airport. Good thing I did; the line to return my car was out the door. I stood waiting, but the only clerk was a girl who looked barely out of high school. Twice she messed up and had to start over, and when she wasn't screwing up, she was answering the phone or trying to be 'personable' while a dozen customers stood glaring.

Half of the customers were returning, the others picking up cars. The person in front of me kept shouting that they were going to miss their flight.

She could go faster ... all she needed was the

right coincidence ...

The setting was chaotic, full of angry vibes and foot-tapping. I tried to block it out, to concentrate, to ignore the powerful sensations around me, and focus on the subtle. I reached out, searching for the flow surrounding her. A monkey could do her job. My intercessions could only improve her efforts.

I sensed nothing.

I tried again, clearing my mind. The coincidences were there ... waiting to be found. I just had to seek harder, to locate ...

The man behind me coughed. Several 'tsk's and heavy sighs reached my ears. Someone near the front asked if her manager was onsite.

Emerson could do magic here. He'd affected prize-fighters while sitting amid cheering, bloodthirsty crowds. I had to push through.

Again and again I failed. Slowly I shuffled my luggage to the front with small, disgruntled kicks, unable to sense a single coincidence. I frowned, more angry at my failures than her incompetence. When I finally set my keys on her counter, I couldn't look her in the face.

She messed up entering my data and had to start again.

Frustrated beyond reason, I stormed out, past a line only half as long. I must've arrived at the worst time ... yet it wouldn't prevent me from telling Rosanne to never use this car rental company again.

Walking across the street to the airport proper did nothing to lighten my mood. I was early, and still stuffed with pancakes. I checked in my suitcases, then stopped at a store before I wandered toward security. I thumbed through several paperback mystery novels in a store, yet not one enticed. I had a new mystery on my

Kindle. I wondered if my Kindle could download books on magic.

Why had I failed ...?

Frowning, I went and stood in the security line, which wasn't long. Yet the longer I stood, the worse it seemed; *America's biggest waste of time.*

Again I reached out, trying harder but with less anger, and sensed the subtleties around me. All these people felt the same as I, annoyed at pointless searches designed to profit only the paranoid and those already rich.

My earlier attempt had been too complicated. Coincidences had to be likely, not impossible, not even near-improbable. I needed to start with easily attainable goals.

Yet, if there wasn't a physical reaction, how would I know if it worked?

Actions by others could be just as telling as overturning coffee cups. If I could ... make people act in a certain way ... like Emerson's pigeons ... then I'd know success when I saw it.

Ahead of me were two dozen people, waiting while ICE officers scanned passengers and carry-ons. These people looked safe, unlikely to rebel. However, the ICE agents actively searched ... and must be frustrated by their constant failures. They wanted to find something, anything, to earn the respect of their peers, to be the heroes that they imagined they were. Perhaps they'd even get rewarded, fame and promotions ...

They didn't even need to actually find anything! A suspicion would do ...!

I chose a likely suspect, loading their shoes, belt, and camera into a bin. I focused on him. I seized him with my will. I concentrated ...

313

I suspected him!

"Stop!" shouted a uniformed ICE agent. Another pushed a button and an alarm sounded. Red lights flashed.

The man looked startled as ICE agents charged him. Hands grabbed and threw him down; the man cried out as arms were twisted, warnings shouted, and everyone watched.

I'd done it again!

Trays holding his belongings were seized and carried in his wake as they dragged him off. Everyone looked shocked.

I smiled. He didn't look like a terrorist, and had probably never even touched a bomb; they'd realize they'd overreacted and release him with embarrassed apologies. No harm done ... and I'd proven myself again.

Soon I regretted my foolishness. The chaos closed one line, and made our searches even slower. By the time that I'd humiliated myself, being photographed by their see-thru cameras, my departure time was close; I wouldn't be able to eat again before flying.

My terminal was disembarking when I found it, and I crowded into the back of the line. By the time I reached my seat, no spaces were left in the overhead bins near me. A stewardess took my laptop case and carried it halfway to the back of the plane where bins were still open. I had a middle seat between a guy frequently sneezing and an elderly woman reeking of cheap perfume. I sat down, buckled my seat belt, pinched my nose, and wished I'd used my miles to upgrade to first class.

I was trapped and the flight looked full; coincidences wouldn't help.

I tried to distract my discomfort by thinking about my victory. The ICE agents had jumped on that guy like cats on a mouse. Stuttered protests were ignored as they dragged him away.

I'd made that happen!

Yet the more I thought about it, the less good it seemed. Emerson would be furious. I'd been seeing if I could affect people, not thinking how it affected them. That poor man could've been strip-searched. He could've missed his flight, upset his job or ruined his vacation. He could've missed connecting flights and spoiled expensive plans.

This was exactly what Emerson had warned me against.

I wasn't a child playing with a new toy!

I couldn't tell Emerson about this! I'd get another lecture.

For the first time, I wasn't looking forward to his phone call.

Hours later, I transferred in Minneapolis. I attempted no more magic.

The best thing about the Bismarck Airport was the safe parking; my car was waiting exactly where I'd left it. I was early enough to pick up Mephistopheles, where I asked my mother not to tell anyone I was home. I waved off her questions as a bad convention, which spoiled my mood, then hurried home. I didn't want to talk to anyone.

My apartment looked empty. I didn't even have Emerson's hat on my shelf. Mephistopheles jumped from my arms and ran toward the kitchen. I dropped my luggage and collapsed onto my couch.

My mood didn't lighten before my phone

beeped.

"Hello!"

"Hi."

"You okay?" Emerson asked.

"Terrible event," I said.

"Looks like we both had bad trips," Emerson said. "No sales ...?"

"Barely any fish and not even a nibble," I said.

"You had a party Saturday night ..."

"A bunch of drunk vendors," I said. "You had the party ..."

"Same problem as before," Emerson said. "The magician holding my boxes got lucky. He wasn't home, his ringer was mute, his door locked, and I'd been wearing the same clothes without a shower since Friday."

"Poor baby ...!"

"I showered, slept naked, then had to redress in dirty clothes to go get my things, when he finally turned his phone on around noon ... after only a few hours of sleep. That after more than two days in Minneapolis ...!"

"Sounds like we both need a rest," I said.

"You managed magic," Emerson said. "That must've been big."

"Yes, but I did it wrong ...," I said.

"Don't feel bad," Emerson said. "You made a novice mistake ... first time is the definition of novice."

"I ... never want to do that again," I said.

"Accidents happen," Emerson said. "Be careful. One magician was driving and sensed a deer was about to run out in front of his car ..."

"Did he hit the deer?"

"No, the horn of the other car must've scared it off ... when he wildly veered into the wrong lane."

I didn't know whether to feel shocked or

terrified.

"You know, maybe we both need to sleep a while before we enjoy chatting," I suggested.

"All right, but I expect some interesting conversation tomorrow," Emerson said. "Nine o'clock your time ...?"

"I can't wait. Love you!"

"Love you!"

I'd lied to Emerson. I felt awful.

Chapter 36

Applause erupted as I stepped inside the office. Two dozen donuts sat on my desk wrapped in a pink ribbon with a bow. The sign over my desk read 'Congratulations'.

My promotion ... I'd forgotten!

Hugs and back-pats showered. I forced a smile; *this was a great thing!* However, I was at work; I plastered on my professional face and forced my way through, opened the donuts, insisted that everyone have one, and acted delighted. The one skill every salesperson needs is the ability to appear enthusiastic.

However, the party wasn't over. Rosanne took my arm and pulled me into Mr. Dawes' office. He wasn't there ... the name on his door had been removed, and the pictures of his children were gone from his desk and walls.

"They announced it yesterday!" Rosanne almost cheered. "Mr. Dawes has a new office. This is your office!"

I stared at it ... dumbfounded.

My first office ...!

"I cleaned it up ... boss," Rosanne said.

319

"*W-what ...?*" I asked.

"I report to you," Rosanne said. "They told me yesterday morning. I'll still be making reservations and legal filings for Mr. Dawes, but I answer to you."

I fumbled for words to say ... which evoked a few chuckles.

"Okay," Rosanne announced to the crowd. "We're busy. Back to work."

Grabbing extra donuts, everyone retreated to their desks, still smiling. Rosanne closed the door behind them.

"Congratulations," Rosanne said again.

"My office ... my desk ...?" I asked, looking around.

"I'm your staff," Rosanne said.

"I've ... never had ...," I said.

"They're going to convert your space into two small cubes," Rosanne said. "Rumor says Mr. Mendale wants two new sales people hired by the end of next month."

"This is ... big," I said.

"What's the matter?" Rosanne asked. "You knew about this Thursday ...!"

"I know ... just overwhelmed," I said. "Nebraska was a waste of time."

"No new contacts?" Rosanne asked.

"Nobody sold anything," I said. "Vendors went out for drinks afterwards ... no one wanted to go back. Spent Sunday talking to each other."

"Sorry," Rosanne said. "How's Emerson? Did he show up in Nebraska?"

"No ...," I looked at her.

"Vegas ..?"

"He got bumped, spent most of his weekend in

Minneapolis ... sleeping in the airport," I said.

"That sucks!" Rosanne said.

"He'll be in Vegas for two more weeks," I said.

"But ... then you'll leave for Seattle ...!" Rosanne said.

"Don't remind me," I said.

"No more magic 'till then ...!" Rosanne said.

"What ...?"

I caught myself – *she was talking about sex!*

"No," I said. "I guess not."

"Guess ...?" Rosanne's eyes widened. "Do you have another ...?"

"No, I ...!" I glared at her. "You should wash that brain of yours!"

"Is that my first order from my new boss?" Rosanne laughed.

"Yes," I frowned. "Now ... get out of my office."

"Right away, Ms. Polyglass," Rosanne chuckled as she walked back to her desk.

I got up and closed my office door.

My office door ...!

I surveyed my new office; the carpet was worn, nail holes in the walls, and my small window looked down upon dumpsters in the alley behind our building. I examined Mr. Dawes' desk ... *my desk* ... and noticed the scuffs and dents all over it. This office was hardly the best ... yet it was mine. I could close the door and sleep and no one could see me ...

I opened my drawers, found them empty and unexpectedly spotless; Rosanne must've cleaned them. A smile started on my face, too strong to hide. I had an office ... and a ... subordinate. I was management ... in charge of sales.

Thirty percent increase in sales within a year ...

or I could lose all this ...!

I opened my laptop and logged on, then printed my new contract. I had to click 'print', then hurry to the printer so that no one saw it. I'd left the original at home, but she was unlikely to notice, so I took it back into my office and signed it so I had something to give to Bessy. Then I slid it into a desk drawer and went back to my old desk to start moving my things.

"Can I help?" Rosanne asked.

"I can manage," I said.

Twenty minutes later, I carried my signed contract to Bessy Andrews' office. She was on the phone, I laid it on her desk, and she gave me a thumb's up and kept talking.

I walked back to my office. On the way, I received more congratulations. I thanked everyone nicely and begged them to come take a donut off my old desk 'before the sharks gathered'. Several were parents; I suggested they come by at end of day and collect all leftovers for their kids. The last thing I wanted was Mephistopheles munching on a week's worth of stale donuts, and tracking sprinkles all around my apartment.

I reviewed the list of new conventions I'd compiled in Nebraska. I googled each, got dates, locations, website addresses, and how to sign up for attending. I quickly scanned their requirements; most conventions have the same rules, set-up and break-down times, electrical availability, no leaving before end of the event, etc, ... most of which I knew by heart.

Bessy Andrews came by and congratulated me again, asking if I was comfortable in my new office. From her office, she'd just emailed back my edited job advertisement for my experienced sales positions with requirements. She asked me to review her few changes and, if acceptable, to contact Steve Johnson, and have it posted on the company website. I promised to get to it today, and showed her my new list of medical conventions we weren't doing, telling her I was still compiling opportunities for the new sales force. Bessy approved, and thanked me for taking my responsibilities so seriously. She promised to tell Colin Mendale at lunch, and then she left. I wasn't invited to join the other managers for lunch. I couldn't expect to be instantly included.

I lunched with Rosanne instead, although I silently wondered if I should. What was the protocol for social meetings with people who reported to you? I didn't know, yet I'd no doubt details like this were described online; I just had to find the right source. However, I didn't want Rosanne to think I couldn't be friends with her anymore ... that I was one of those bosses every employee hates.

Rosanne made me promise not to fuel the Bismarck Express, then spoke in whispers. Last Friday, in Arnold's, Rosanne had met a local guy, and spent a long night drinking with him, thinking that he might be an acceptable interest. Unfortunately, after he left, two of his ex-girlfriends and one waitress came over to talk to her. Small towns have advantages and disadvantages; quickly learning a guy's dating history saves you long-term, but costs a lot of second dates.

On the seat beside me was a copper penny, probably dropped out of someone's pocket. I wondered if I could control how it flipped; I snagged and stuck it in a pocket.

Back in my office, with the door closed, I pulled out the penny. I held it in my hand, wondering if I could manipulate how it landed. I tossed it into the air.

Tails ...

I recognized the sensation of coincidence; like choosing between two equally-familiar driving routes. You'd arrive at your destination at the same time whichever route you chose, so you let your feelings rule ... yet never before had I examined those unimportant, unconscious choices. One route may be faster, another have fewer stops, one drives past a favorite restaurant, the other has less chances of being blocked by an accident. Subconsciously, your brain considers all these factors, but consciously, you just make a quick decision and steer.

Coincidences felt like that. Focus, concentrate on subconscious impressions, and open your mind to new, subtle sensations. Remember joy, and forget your desire; search for the coincidence.

Yet mathematics didn't change. The coin landed on heads. Perhaps I had to focus harder.

Which side a coin lands on is entirely random chance. To have it land on your preference was always a coincidence. But ... if you could identify which coincidences tend to cause one side ... I concentrated:

Heads!

I closed my eyes, sat perfectly still, and shut out everything else. Then I opened myself to every impression.

"Heads!" I whispered.

I opened my eyes and flipped the coin again. It dropped to my desk, bounced, clattered lightly, and landed showing heads.

I'd done it!

Yet one toss didn't prove anything. I'd have to do it a lot, at least a hundred times, and I couldn't expect perfection.

My new office wasn't the place to try.

I put my penny away, and started reviewing emails, writing replies. Bessy's edits were adequate; some things I'd have worded differently, but my goal was to attract qualified resumes and make my new boss happy. I'd choose the applicants worth interviewing. I double-checked to make sure that I'd added Mr. Mendale's request for multiple languages. Bessy's email included the approved requisition numbers for both positions, so we were ready to hire. I forwarded her email to Steve Johnson with instruction to post it.

I spent the rest of the day researching the new medical conventions. Planning events, avoiding scheduling conflicts, and estimating size was tough. I looked for photos of past events; usually they were the best predictors of attendance, yet they were hard to find. Few photos usually meant a poor event.

Countless factors decided an event's popularity. Nearness to airports, major cities, and total of listed vendors were clues. Facebook doesn't delete old events, so you could compare past years to see if events were expanding or declining. By the end of the day, I'd chosen six more events we should have a booth at.

Mephistopheles was still demanding I pet and feed him when Bonnie called.

"Where the Hell are you?"

"Home," I answered.

"You got home yesterday," Bonnie said. "Was your phone dead?"

"Tired."

"Where's cutie ...?"

"Las Vegas."

"Pity," Bonnie said. "What's your plan?"

"I got a promotion," I said.

"Oh, and how long have you been sitting on that information?" Bonnie demanded.

"This is the first time we've talked," I said.

"Dinner at my house ...?" Bonnie asked.

"Not tonight," I said. "Emerson's calling."

"You could talk in my bedroom," Bonnie said. "Needs more action in there anyway."

"Husband problems ...?"

"No, but boyfriends are more adventurous."

"Naughty thoughts...!" my phone beeped. "Stacy's calling. Should I ignore ...?"

"Nah," Bonnie said. "Arnold's. Tomorrow. After work."

"See you tomorrow." Soft clicks. "Stacy ...?"

"Penelope!" Stacy said. "Glad you're home."

"How's it going?" I asked.

"I wish I knew," Stacy said.

"David ...?"

"Haven't seen him in two days."

"Any idea ...?"

"No, but I know where he'll be tomorrow," Stacy said. "The owner of Luigi's dines there every Wednesday night."

"Meet him there," I suggested.

"He'll be working," Stacy sounded fearful.

"At least you'll see him," I said.

"I need to know why," Stacy said.

"Share a nice, romantic dinner," I said. "Maybe he needs it."

"We haven't been romantic ... in a long time," Stacy said. "No, I'll just wait ..."

"I'll drive you," I said. "We'll meet tomorrow at Arnold's. Be early and wear something nice. If it works out, then you can drive home together."

"But what if ...?" Stacy began.

"Let me do the worrying," I said. "I've got a little pull on 'what ifs'."

We hung up, and I glanced at the clock; over an hour until Emerson phoned. Mephistopheles was hiding, but the slightest whirr of the can opener would summon him. I went into the kitchen to find something to eat.

On time:

"Hello!"

"Good to hear your voice," Emerson said.

"I've been penny-flipping," I said.

"Excellent practicing method," I could hear Emerson's smile.

"The rest ... I don't know," I said. "Everything seems to be going right ... except for Stacy ... something feels wrong ..."

"In what way ...?" Emerson asked.

"Well, it's kinda like Alice in the Looking Glass," I said. "Only, when I look at myself in the mirror, my image looks at me and says 'That's not my life' ..."

"Sounds normal," Emerson said. "You built a firm grasp on reality, then learned that you grasped only half."

"When will I learn the rest?" I asked.

"After you unlearn," Emerson said. "Don't be in a hurry. Fixed world-views hurt when they break."

"How can I trust coincidences?" I asked.

"Experience," Emerson said. "You'll get there ... eventually."

"In the meantime ...?"

"I'm a phone call away."

"Sadly impersonal," I said.

"That's why I came back to my hotel room to

call you," Emerson said. "I'm unbuttoning my cuffs."

"Your cuffs ...?"

"Long sleeve shirt," Emerson said. "There. Now I'm undoing my top button."

"We're not doing this," I said.

"Next button."

"Emerson ...!"

"Going down ... getting lower ..."

"This is a cell phone!"

"Fine," Emerson said. "Penelope, and whoever else is listening, I'm taking off my shirt."

"Why should I believe you ...?"

"You don't have to believe me," Emerson said. "Just imagine ..."

"I'm going to hang up ...!"

"Too late," Emerson said. "You might as well stay for the whole performance ... you'll be thinking about it all night ..."

"How was your day?"

"Hard," Emerson breathed. *"Very ...!"*

"That's enough ...!" I warned.

"Never enough ...!" Emerson sighed.

"Call me tomorrow," I said. "Maybe you'll have something interesting to say."

"This doesn't interest you ...?"

"I love you, Emerson," I said. "Good-night."

"Pleasant dreams ...!" Emerson said. *"Dream about me ...!"*

I hung up.

Frustrated, I stared at my phone.

Was he pretending ... or really ...!

No, if I started thinking about it ...!

I won't imagine ...! I won't ...!

Damn you, Emerson ...!

Chapter 37

My first manager's meeting began at 8:00 AM; Bessy Andrews, Colin Mendale, Mr. Dawes, Maria Saviano, George Wilber, and Mr. Brown. Introductions were made; I knew them all ... even those I'd rarely spoken to.

"Frederick ...?" Colin Mendale asked. "How fares your team?"

"Advertising is preparing a new campaign," Mr. Dawes said. "We've only had one meeting, but we're consolidating ideas to increase market share. I'll do a presentation as soon as we have a concrete platform."

"Excellent," Colin Mendale said. "Mark ...?"

"Finance is studying possible methodologies for the new acquisition in Atlanta," Mr. Brown said. "With a marginal lowering of stock values, we can take out a three year loan, and cover the rest in capital to open, with a starting headcount of eight, without disrupting other payments."

"How much of a lowering?" Colin Mendale asked.

"Stock values should bottom at $190, yet when we announce the expansion, we should recover most of it," Mr. Brown said. "We're looking at other finance options, too."

"Keep me informed," Colin Mendale said. "I've got a meeting with Mr. Sloans on Monday morning, and I'll need an update before then."

"You'll have it on Friday," Mr. Brown promised.

"Bessy ...?" Colin Mendale asked.

"Working with Penelope on setting up the new team," Bessy said. "The ad's posted, resumes have started coming in. She's found a list of new venues ..."

"How many?" Colin Mendale asked, and Bessy turned to me.

"Nine confirmed possibilities, looking at more," I said. "Some are opposite current conventions. We need to apply as soon as we have personnel."

"Do you have a list of expectations for interviews?" Colin Mendale asked.

"We're meeting on that later today," Bessy said.

I noted to thank Bessy for answering for me.

Maria Saviano answered a bunch of legal questions and reported on outstanding applications for patents. George Wilber reported on our software development teams; he droned on for twenty minutes. I tried to keep track of everything he was saying, yet all of it was new. Bessy and Mr. Brown looked as if they didn't care.

Colin Mendale again welcomed me, ended the meeting, and was the first out the door.

Rosanne was busy; I ate lunch alone.

Afterwards, Bessy and I met briefly. She told me to devise a strategy and checklist to tell if an applicant was qualified, including two lists of questions; one for her and a second for Colin Mendale.

"He's not a salesman and knows nothing about

330

our job," Bessy said. "Not giving him pertinent questions would leave him staring at the applicant with nothing to ask. Bad idea letting your boss feel stupid."

"I'll give him good questions," I promised.

Alone in my office, I thought about Stacy. I felt sure Stacy was correct that David would be at Luigi's. Yet he'd be working; if I took her there, would David be in a romantic mood ...?

I closed my eyes and opened my senses. I'd never tried anything this big, yet I wasn't trying to affect anything, just gain information. I envisioned Stacy, hopeful to restore romance between her and her husband. I wondered if I could sense David, hopefully to give myself a little guarantee this might work.

Sensations flowed around me, too many to identify. I knew Stacy's every secret; her feelings came easily. Yet I didn't like David; searching for him was like seeking an itch before it begins. Focusing on irritations disgusted me, yet through her I traced him ... what I felt was him. Yet his current emotions weren't as sick as I expected. He felt ... happy. Perhaps he was just pissy around me; I hadn't seen him happy since he and Stacy were newlyweds.

This might work!

Bonnie's car was parked at Arnold's when I pulled in.

"There she is!" Bonnie shouted from the bar as I walked in.

A light cheer came from Kathy, Joel, and Brendan as they spied me.

"I'm not here for long," I warned.

"You should've called me Monday night," Bonnie said.

331

"I was exhausted," I said.

"I could've told you about your promotion ...!" Bonnie said, and then she glared at my lack of reaction. "You already knew ... *and didn't tell me ...?!?*"

"I couldn't tell anyone ...," I began.

"I'm not anyone!" Bonnie raised her voice. *"We built our first snowman together ...!"*

"The Bismarck Express could've derailed my promotion," I argued. "Who do you know hasn't fueled it ...?"

"Come on, Bonnie; you're the Bismarck Express' main depot," Joel said.

"No excuse!" Bonnie complained emphatically.

"Where's Mr. Magic?" Kathy asked, obviously to change the subject.

"Las Vegas, preparing for his show," I said.

"Talk to him lately?"

"Every evening."

"Phone sex ...?"

"No ... and I wouldn't tell you if we had," I said.

Kathy scrunched up her face. Bonnie scowled and acted insulted.

"You should tell me everything!" Bonnie argued.

We drank and chatted until Stacy arrived. She wore a long coat despite the warm day. I suspected a sexy dress lay hidden underneath; she wanted to be prepared but not obvious.

Fifteen minutes later, Stacy and I climbed inside my car. She paused to peel off her too-warm coat; I hadn't seen her wear her red miniskirt since college. Her white blouse was tight, a black lacy bra clearly visible beneath it.

On the long drive, she chickened out every ten minutes, yet I refused to turn around.

"I have a good feeling," I said. "The Blue Stag hotel is nearby; you and David should spend the night there."

We arrived sooner than I expected. Then we sat in the parking lot for another ten minutes before Stacy agreed to go inside.

"They're probably done with dinner by now," I said.

"Li Chin likes drinks after dinner," Stacy said.

"Li Chin ...?" I asked. "It's an Italian bistro ...!"

"Li Chin is the real owner of the whole Luigi's chain," Stacy said. "Don't let that news board the train."

Finally we got out of the car and walked past the neon sign. Stacy suggested I leave, yet I wasn't going anywhere until I saw her sitting with David. We walked into Luigi's together.

Emerson had loved Luigi's.

Air-conditioning and indirect lighting were always welcome. A huge fern sat by the doorway opposite the reservation desk; Stacy hurried behind it and peered inside. Colorful vases and decorative wood framing filled the dim dining hall, which was buzzing with dozens of muted conversations.

I walked up behind her. *David wasn't to be seen.*

"Li Chin prefers the back, out of sight," Stacy said.

"I'll stay discreetly behind," I whispered.

Stacy proceeded into the dining room. More than a few pairs of eyes widened as she appeared; despite her age, she could still wear that scandalous outfit. Yet she ignored them and walked around the main partition to the back area.

My mouth fell open as I turned the corner.

David was holding hands and drinking wine with a beautiful, light-brown skinned young woman who was dressed a little more evocatively than Stacy. They were pressed tightly together in a round booth made for two, so focused on private whispers that they saw no one else ... and coy smiles displayed intimate familiarity.

"*David ...!*" Stacy shouted.

"*Stacy ...?*" David's face paled.

The young woman beside him stared at Stacy in surprise.

"*Who's this ...?*" Stacy demanded.

"*A ... a friend ...!*" David stammered.

"*Friend ...?*" the young woman exclaimed, looking at Stacy. "*Who's this ...?*"

Stacy held out her left hand, showing her gold band.

"*I'm his wife ...!*" Stacy screeched, silencing every conversation in Luigi's.

"*Wife ...?!?*" the young woman screamed, and she pushed away from David. "*You told me you were divorced ...!*"

"*Divorced ...?!?*" Stacy screamed.

The young woman jumped up, looking furious.

"*She's lying!*" David shouted, not specifying which woman he was accusing.

The young woman stared from Stacy to David and back again. Then she snatched her drink off the table and splashed it into David's face.

"*He has three large moles right above his ... tiny dick!*" she seethed, glaring at him. "*He calls it his Bermuda Triangle ...!*"

With a last glance at Stacy, the young woman stormed out, walking the other way to stay out of Stacy's reach. In seconds, she was gone.

Stacy's red face crinkled with murderous rage. I wondered what she'd do ... keep screaming at David or follow his betrayed lover ...?

Stacy looked down at the dinner of a nearby elderly diner, snatched his dirty steak knife off his plate, and charged David, screeching and aiming high.

David jumped back, and ran around an empty table, keeping it between her and him, like a child playing keep-away. Both screamed too incoherently for accusations or excuses to be understood. Yet Stacy kept darting one way, then the other, frantically trying to get to David, slashing her knife to block his retreats.

Customers ducked and stared, waiters aghast, the manager dialing the police. I ran to Stacy, grabbed her from behind, and pulled her away. She was screaming, wailing, and slicing the air with her steak knife, aimed at David, who was, luckily, out of reach.

I dragged her backwards out the front door.

Forcing her into my car, I gunned it, squealing out of my parking space, then slammed on the brakes as a white Mazda suddenly stopped in my path, completely blocking the exit.

A woman got out of the Mazda; *David's secret lover!*

The young woman walked up to the passenger side and held up a business card, looking down at Stacy. As she didn't appear threatening, I inched down Stacy's window.

"I'm a lawyer," she said, poking her card inside the gap. "Call me ... *we'll take that lying bastard for everything!*"

Stacy just stared at her. I reached over and grabbed her card.

"We'll call," I promised. "Probably not today."

She nodded, and moments later, she peeled off and raced toward the freeway. It was the only route home; I had no choice but to follow ... so I drove slowly. Stacy sat sobbing, still holding the knife and ignoring the beeping seatbelt alarm.

"I'm sorry," I said, and I reached over and plucked the dirty steak knife from Stacy's grasp.

Chapter 38

I was awake long before the alarm clock buzzed. I'd used my power successfully, yet drawn the wrong conclusion ... *David had been in a romantic, receptive mood ... just not for Stacy!*

Could I have avoided this ...?

Stacy snored beside me; I'd made her stay close, as I didn't trust her to not leave in the middle of the night. She'd cried until 2:00 AM, and then passed out exhausted. I didn't tell her I felt just as bad.

I was responsible!

David's cheating didn't surprise me. I'd expected no less. I'd hoped not, for Stacy's sake, yet knew better; Bonnie predicted he'd cheat the day they came back from a long weekend together in Detroit haggard, hung over, and unexpectedly married. Their elopement was champagne for every rider on the Bismarck Express.

Finally the alarm buzzed. I showered, dressed, and fed Mephistopheles, and then called my mother. After a quick explanation, I drug Stacy out of bed, forced her into her skimpy outfit and coat, then drove her to mother's. Mom came outside in her robe and slippers and helped Stacy stumble inside her door without a word, just sad, knowing glances. I nodded to her, handed her Stacy's cell phone, which I'd turned off, then sped to work.

No coffee in the world could be strong enough!

Forty-one new emails, each with an attached resume.

Unable to keep track, I printed each and stacked them on my desk. Blindly I scanned them, unable to concentrate on anything. Two of these could be my first salespeople, upon whom my future as a manager would be decided. I had to find the right people ...!

I couldn't stop thinking about Stacy ...!

I set them aside and began compiling a list of questions I'd expect to be asked if I was applying for the job. I'd been on enough interviews to know what they were like; questions to see if they could sell, understanding of software production, medical knowledge, web experience, philosophy as a salesperson, reasons for leaving past jobs, problems with other employees, availability for travel, thinking outside the box ...

"Penelope ...?" Rosanne asked. "Are you doing lunch?"

"What ...?" I asked. "Lunch ...?"

"It's afternoon," Rosanne said.

Disbelieving, I stared at the tiny clock on my screen.

"I had no idea ...," I said.

"You okay?"

"Rough night ... with a sick friend," I said. "She can't be on her own; I dropped her off at my mother's."

"Sorry," Rosanne said.

"Have you had lunch?" I asked.

"I just asked ...," Rosanne said.

I told her everything over burgers.

"Please, don't tell," I begged.

"I don't power trains," Rosanne promised. "Well, not this time."

"I was trying to help ..."

"David cheated, not you," Rosanne said. "Call the lawyer. Don't wait for Stacy."

"Is that legal?" I asked.

"Ask the lawyer," Rosanne said. "If Stacy objects, sic Lyn and Julie on her."

"Not Bonnie?"

"Sic Bonnie on David."

"I owe Bonnie too much to put her in jail," I said.

"She won't kill him ... probably," Rosanne said.

Back in the office, I closed my door and dialed Ms. Alexandria Tempest, Attorney at Law.

"Hello," I said when she answered. "I'm ... Stacy's friend."

A momentary pause ...

"Thank you for calling," Alexandria's voice said, unexpectedly calm. "To be honest, I didn't know how I'd ... deal with her."

"She didn't know what he ... was ...," I said.

"He told me he was divorced ... dating no one else," Alexandria said. "I hope you understand ... I'd never have ...!"

"David lied to everyone," I said.

"I'm looking at half a million plus legal fees," Alexandria said. "I need ... her ..."

"Stacy ...," I said.

"I need her to sign a form for me," Alexandria said. "If she can get her hands on his tax forms, any legal documentation for his business ... and get it quick, before he destroys it ..."

"I'll get ... her ... to do it tonight," I promised. "I made her sleep at my place."

"The less that she talks to David the better," Alexandria said.

"I can assure that," I said.

"Will she ... stay with him ... take him back ...?" Alexandria asked. "I don't want to waste my time ..."

"I'll let you know tomorrow," I said. "Here's my email address ..."

Less than a minute later, we hung up. I dialed another number. *I had work to do.*

"Bonnie ...?" I asked. "Do you have time ...?"

"I'm a bit busy," Bonnie said. "How about I call you back ...?"

"David cheated on Stacy."

"He's dead!!!"

"She's at my mother's," I said.

"Details ...!" Bonnie demanded.

"I'm at work," I said.

"I'll drive over to see her now," Bonnie said.

"Mom will appreciate that," I said.

I smiled; *Bonnie would handle it!*

I got more coffee.

Before I left work, I had three lists of questions, one each for Colin Mendale, Bessy, and me. I also had two ideas for cold sales pitches, so that we could get a feel for their sales-style. More important was their dependability and personal sense of responsibility, which resumes couldn't convey. I still hadn't read all the resumes; they lay printed and stacked on my desk.

Tomorrow I'd have to invent sorting standards ... and if Bessy dropped by, I had my three lists to prove that I was working on her project ... *my project.*

I phoned Bonnie before I left work, and then drove straight to mom's. Julie was already there. Stacy wasn't crying yet looked too fragile to touch without breaking.

At 6:00 PM, Emerson phoned. Despite objections, I fled into mother's bedroom and closed the door.

"Hello," I said.

"I tried calling last night ...," Emerson said.

"I know," I said. "Stacy caught David cheating. By the way, you didn't ... you know ...?"

"Me ...?" Emerson asked. "We talked about this ... I won't interfere unless you and I discuss ..."

"I'm sorry," I said. "We're all upset. I was taking care of her all night. I couldn't talk in front of her. We're at my mother's; all Hell is breaking loose."

"Bonnie ...?"

"She's lighting torches and sharpening pitchforks."

"You may want to give her a wide berth," Emerson said.

"I can't," I said. "The girl David was cheating with; she didn't know. He lied to her ... and she's a lawyer ..."

"Lawyer ...?" Emerson almost laughed. "She can really screw him ...!"

"She already has ... and hopes to do it again," I said.

A fist hammered on the door.

"Tell Casanova we say hi ...!" Bonnie's voice boomed.

"He heard!" I shouted. "Go away!"

"Look, you're busy," Emerson said. "Time differences; my show starts tomorrow night, so if I call when I'm done, it'll be almost midnight at the earliest. If you can, call me during the day ... after lunch; I'll be on a late-night shift."

"I'll try," I promised. "I love you so much."

"Not being with you is incredibly frustrating," Emerson said.

"I'll make it up," I promised.

"Can't wait," Emerson said. "Love you!"

I waited until my call ended, then returned to the madness. I'd printed out Alexandria's form, but had yet to tell them that I'd called her. Bonnie called and told her husband to start making dinner, and Julie had to leave to feed her kids. I wished Lyn would arrive. Once we all knew, then we could start considering real plans ...

Mephistopheles would be starving by the time I got home.

Chapter 39

I awoke early and alone. Lyn had taken Stacy to her apartment for the night. I'd given Lyn Stacy's cell phone; in private we'd turned it on, saw multiple calls from David, and shut it back off. Lyn planned to call in sick and I had to go to work.

I hadn't cheated on anyone! I had no reason to feel guilty!

Work was frustrating. Reading resumes gave me a headache. Most looked impressive, the same claims, sales numbers I could never verify, accomplishments of dubious successes. I sorted them into piles; travel, education, medical knowledge, software background, computer experience, direct sales.

Rosanne asked about lunch yet I declined. I needed to think, not talk.

After Rosanne left, I called Lyn. Julie was also there. Stacy was still there but had demanded her phone. Lyn insisted Stacy put his messages on speakerphone and spent every minute since convincing her that David was lying to her again. Stacy was insisting that she had to take him back; she couldn't intrude on friends forever, and she had nowhere else to go.

I had Lyn put me on speaker so all could hear. I told them about my call to Alexandria Tempest. I told them how much she was planning to sue David for ... and that I had the form she needed.

"I want my house," Stacy said.

"She'll be glad to add that, I'm sure," I said.

"Should we call her back ...?" Julie asked.

"Not yet," I said. "I'll come over after work ..."

"I won't be here," Julie said.

"Stacy, do you ... think you could talk to her ... without ...?" Lyn asked.

No answer.

"We'll call her when Stacy's ready, not before," I said. " Stacy, you need to stay away from David."

"He won't get in here, but I have to work tomorrow," Lyn said.

"Drop her off at Bonnie's on your way to work," I said. " Stacy, I'll call you tonight."

With a few muttered thanks, I hung up. I was starting to get mad ... David had screwed all of us.

I phoned Emerson. He barely said 'hello' before I exploded, deluging him in the whole story, from when we walked into Luigi's to my phone call with Alexandria Tempest. I unburdened myself of everything ... yet I said nothing of my searching coincidences; I didn't want to bring magic into the mess. I ended with a rant of name-calling.

"I'm sorry, but it's probably best you were there," Emerson said. "If not, Stacy would be in jail."

"I still have their steak knife," I said.

"Let the lawyer handle it," Emerson said. "She knows what she's doing ..."

"And she's motivated," I said.

"I feel awful," Emerson said.

"Why?"

"I used to be like ... well, I didn't lie to women, but I wasn't ... nice ..."

"You were a kid," I said. "David is an adult ... a married adult."

"Still ...," Emerson said.

"Are you ready for tonight?" I asked.

"My show ...?" Emerson asked. "My wren just arrived, props are inventoried, and I'm heading to set them up after breakfast."

"Oh, time difference!" I said. "Did I wake you up?"

"Yea, but I needed to get up anyway," Emerson yawned.

"Are you still in bed?"

"Magic acts start late in Vegas."

"Adjusting your clock," I said. "That's the worst part of traveling."

"You at work?" Emerson asked.

"Yes," I said. "Why?"

"I sleep naked ..."

"I'm at work!" I almost shouted.

"Where is my hand reaching ...?"

"Good-bye. I love you."

"Love you!"

After work, Bonnie had us meet at her house. Stacy and Lyn were already there, and I had to repeat my conversation with the lawyer.

"Tempest ...!" Stacy scowled. *"With a name like that ...!"*

"Who here hasn't been lied to by a man ...?" Lyn asked.

"Did you demand proof the last time you dated a divorced man?" Bonnie demanded.

"Please, whatever her name, she wants to take David for half a million ... at least!" I said.

"He doesn't have it," Stacy argued.

"You need to decide," I said to Stacy. "Do you want David ... or your house?"

"Do you think ...?" Stacy began.

I pulled out the form and a pen I'd brought. Stacy stared at both.

"Why her ...?" Stacy seethed.

"She's a pissed off lawyer he lied to and cheated with," Lyn said. "Sign the form."

"Sign it," Bonnie ordered.

Reluctantly Stacy signed. I put the form back in my computer bag.

"Call her," Bonnie said.

"Later ...," I said, but both Bonnie and Lyn argued. "All right ... but Stacy: you let us handle this!"

I pulled out my phone and called.

"On speaker," Bonnie insisted.

Rings ...

"Alexandria Tempest," her voice answered.

Stacy started to say something, but Bonnie grabbed and shook her arm.

"This is ... Stacy's friend," I said. "She signed your form."

"Excellent," Alexandria said. "Can you fax it?"

"As soon as I can," I promised.

"I'll take care of the rest," Alexandria said.

"I'll fax any tax or financial records we can get, too," I said. "Call this number when you want to talk."

"You're sure she won't reconcile ...?" Alexandria asked.

"No, she won't ...!" Bonnie shouted, but I waved for her to shut up.

" Stacy wants to keep their house ... in her name," I said.

"I'll add it," Alexandria said. "What's your name?"

"Penelope Polyglass," I said.

"Thank you, Penelope," Alexandria Tempest said. "You'll be hearing from me soon. Fully document any contacts ... Stacy ... has with David ... especially any threats. His last wife reported that he threatened her."

"Last wife ...?!?" Stacy screamed.

A brief silence passed.

"I searched his legal history," Alexandria said. "You're not his first."

Stacy looked shocked.

"Thank you," I said, staring at Stacy. "Expect my fax soon."

"Thank you. Good-bye."

From Stacy's expression, we knew that the final coffin nail had been driven into her marriage.

"David was divorced ...?!?" Stacy screamed.

"We don't know that," Bonnie said. "She could've died ..."

"You met David's family," I said. "Didn't they tell you ...?"

Stacy shook her head.

"He threatened her ... whoever she was," Lyn growled. " Stacy, you're living with me ... from now on."

"Don't listen to his phone messages, and don't delete them," I said. "Your lawyer may be able to use them."

"She's ... my lawyer ...?" Stacy gasped.

"David encouraged her to win," Bonnie quipped.

Bonnie's kids came home for supper, and we left. Lyn took Stacy and invited me to join them for dinner, but I declined, claiming that I had work to finish. I really wanted to be alone.

After feeding Mephistopheles, I pulled out the penny I still had, focusing on trying to control what side it landed on. I got several right, more than half, but then I was wrong eight tosses in a row. I stopped, cleared my mind, reached out fresh for the coincidences, tried to dredge up some joy, and got the next six tosses correct.

I worked on tosses for nearly an hour, then fetched the cards Emerson had given me. I traded off which card I wanted, and managed to find each more often than not.

I was a magician.

If I was going to get good, I needed lots of practice.

I wondered what David was doing now.

Thinking about David spoiled my sensing. Anger intruded, even when I tried to block it.

He deserved to be hurt!

I glanced at my clock, wondering if Emerson was doing his magic act.

I wished he'd left his hat!

Chapter 40

I awoke early, although I didn't need to. I wished Emerson was here; Saturday mornings with nothing to do left me more aware of his absence than ever. He was probably still asleep, or he'd call to talk. My pillow wasn't nearly as much fun to cuddle.

I still hadn't gotten my first paycheck with my new manager's salary. No mention had been made of the bonus I was hoping for, yet the final sale wouldn't happen until the trial period ended. I wondered if I could afford a brief Hawaiian vacation for two ... I needed it ... and I couldn't imagine going without Emerson.

Breakfast. Shower. Car. Zoo.

I felt self-conscious, paying for a solo admission. The zoo had just opened, and every other adult in line had a string of excited kids around them. Yet this was where Emerson and I had practiced manipulating coincidences ... and I needed more practice.

The ducks were eating, and my attempts to make them move elsewhere proved useless. However, I stopped trying to force unlikely coincidences and tried the highly likely. I plucked at vibrations of suspicion, dominance, and protectiveness; I wanted specific ducks to feel that their breakfast was being threatened by another duck. Before long, several fights began, loud-squawked complaints leading to fluttering wings batting others away, and bigger ducks chasing smaller ducks. My victory caused a ruckus; I left the warring ducks to sort out their noisy disputes before zoo-keepers arrived.

Avoiding the crowds, I reached the otter pool. These incredible swimmers darted quickly and easily. By the time I could pluck a coincidence, it vanished; the otters had changed direction and were swimming away. None of my attempts worked in time, so I had to try something else.

I stared long and hard. My targets were swift, almost musical, their smooth, dark skins, sad eyes, and whiskers darting underwater with inhuman speed and dexterity. I couldn't anticipate changing directions. I had to find another way.

I targeted a tall, flat rock. One had climbed out of the water, stopped atop that rock, then slid off and dropped back into the water as if it were a game. I realized my mistake; I needed to stop trying to control them. I needed to control their destinations.

I focused on the rock. Nothing affected it. Yet coincidences weren't only changes; it mattered how others perceived it. I expanded my senses, focusing on the place. It was a high place, a place of strength and importance, where there might be food. It was the place all otters wanted to be ...

Waters splashed. Otters climbed up, jumping onto the high rock, fighting for a place there, pushing others off. The ones who made it barked and stood tall, each claiming the feelings of superiority I'd placed there.

A dozen laughing children came running up to

the rail, cheering the squabbling otters.

I smiled and walked away as tired mothers hurried to catch up with their offspring. I'd come to practice magic, not to have it observed.

More families arrived; typical Saturday at the zoo, and I tried to avoid as many as I could.

I briefly found myself facing a pen of four bears with no kids watching. These bears had recently eaten; tongues were still licking thick-toothed muzzles. Three were adults, one a cub.

I cleared my mind and expanded my senses. I felt for them, reached beyond everyday sensations into the randomness all of us live in. Strings of chance and possibility surrounded us, the bears and I. I didn't know what I wanted. I reached out and tested the strands swirling about me. The strongest strands revealed themselves. I extended my thoughts ... and plucked one.

Something burst out of me, a held breath, a puff of life. I'd never felt it before. I plucked the same strand again. Something deep inside me popped out, a long, slow sigh. My mouth opened ... a sound came out, soft and droning.

What was I doing ...? The timeline I'd plucked: it wasn't bears. It affected ... me.

Song ...!

I'd made myself sing ...!

I glanced around. No one was nearby, no one looking.

I turned back to the bears. I plucked the string again, allowing it to happen.

I began to sing.

No words came, only a slow, loud melody, barely changing. I sang gently; I was no great singer, had failed dramatically at karaoke, yet I needed to trust the future I chose. I closed my eyes, inhaled deeply, and kept singing, not loudly, but clear and strong.

When I opened my eyes, all four bears were as close to me as they could be, inside their pen, staring at me. The young cub was standing on its hind legs, reaching toward me with waving paws. One of the adults sat unmoving, yet their dark eyes never left me.

I needed no magic. The key to manipulating this coincidence was within me all the time. I just had to manipulate ... myself.

One of the adult bears let out a long, moaning, soft roar. It knew what I was doing. It was connecting to me. We sang together.

I sensed a disturbance; the bear stopped singing. I stopped. Moments later, I heard footsteps; a zoo-keeper came running up behind me.

"What's going on here?" a man no older than I asked. "Are you feeding those bears?"

"No, sir," I said. "I was ... singing to myself; they just came over."

"Oh, that's fine," the zoo-keeper said. "Animals hate people standing frozen. People want to see them move, but the best way is to entertain them. You want to see them excited; dance to your own song. Animals love a show."

With a smile and a nod, the zoo-keeper walked away.

I sang good-bye to the bears, and two of them waved at me. I nodded to them and walked on. I wondered what the bears would do if ... but I wasn't going to dance in public.

I wandered the little lanes, looking at the animals, yet ever more aware of the humans. Eyes were everywhere, preventing me from practicing more. The zoo had grown too crowded to practice magic.

I drove to a restaurant for lunch and selected a table in the back, away from any patrons. I ordered a coke and a burger, then called Emerson.

"Perfect timing!" Emerson said. "I just ordered breakfast!"

"Where are you?" I asked.

"Casino," Emerson said. "Not a big one, but the magicians' club is nearby. We patronize a sleazy hotel behind it. It's not a place for tourists."

"Are you alone?" I asked.

"Just me and social media," Emerson said. "Two of my friends left yesterday; they're doing an act in Detroit next week, and I don't know the new lady."

"Lady ...?" I asked.

"Lady Legerdemain," Emerson laughed. "She's quite pretty. Jealous?"

"I get even, not jealous," I said. "Besides, my red bikini holds more magic than coincidences."

"Oh, the mental picture I'm seeing ...!"

"Don't make me hang up ...!"

"I won't," Emerson said. "She showed up last night, we all introduced ourselves, and she sat with the other magicians at my show. By the time I'd packed my props, she was gone."

"How many magicians are there?" I asked.

"Three live here, but they have families and go home after their shows," Emerson said. "There're usually four or five others on contract."

"Sounds more friendly than here," I said.

" Stacy and David ...?"

"The Bismarck Express will soon know."

"Will you be on it?"

"Eventually," I said. "And when I ride, you do."

"Hopefully it'll derail before I get back," Emerson said.

"When will that be?" I asked.

"An eternity," Emerson said. "Thursday after next."

"I'll count the seconds," I said.

"Then I'm yours for a month," Emerson said. "Assuming I don't get an emergency fill-in."

"Don't," I said. "Sleeping alone sucks."

"Now you're getting me started ...," Emerson said.

"Don't," I said. "I'm having lunch."

"Enjoying your promotion?" Emerson asked.

"Between work and Stacy, I've had little free time," I said.

"Are you practicing?"

"Trying to," I said. "It feels different, like ... like harp strings all around me ... and I just have to pluck the right ones."

"You're bringing your senses into focus," Emerson said. "Like I said, at this point, each magician needs to find the way that works for them."

"Let's not use the 'M' word in public," I said. "It's ... crystalizing."

"Excellent," Emerson said. "You truly are 'M'."

"How did your show go?"

"Fine, as usual. Thinking of switching out some old tricks for some new."

A pause followed.

"Long distance relationships suck," Emerson said.

"I agree, but ...," I said.

"We'll make it work," Emerson said. "I'm already planning something special for our reunion."

"What?"

"Secret."

"You're going to make me wonder for two weeks?"

"Yep."

"Worst boyfriend ever. I love you."

"Love you, too."

"I can't wait."

"Neither can I."

My phone beeped. I glanced at it: Bonnie.

"Bonnie's calling."

"Do you want to answer?"

"I want to spend the day talking to you."

"I know ... but talking without touching ... I don't have much new to tell you. Go have fun."

"I'll be thinking of you ... tonight."

"Say hi to everyone for me."

Reluctantly I switched to answer Bonnie.

"Where are you?"

"Talking to Emerson."

"Dirty talk ...?"

"We're both in restaurants."

"Too bad. I'm headed to Lyn's. Come tell us about him."

"I'll be there in an hour."

I ate in peace, enjoying my success at the zoo. I was sensing deeper, reaching feelings I formerly didn't know existed. Trust was building. I hadn't told Emerson yet ... wasn't sure I wanted anyone to know. I was becoming different ... powerful. I started to wonder how I'd ever lived so blindly.

I knocked on Lyn's door with one hand and opened it with the other. I could hear Stacy crying from outside ... inside was worse.

"It won't last," Julie whispered to me. "She was laughing hysterically twenty minutes ago."

I hugged Stacy, and she effused on how lucky she was to have good friends. I forced a smile and didn't wipe her tears off my cheek until she looked away. Lyn and Bonnie both looked exhausted.

Although it was only noon, I suggested wine.

Thirty minutes later, Stacy was on her feet cursing me for not letting her stab David.

"He deserved it ...!" Stacy shouted.

"We agree ...!" Lyn assured her, trying to calm her down.

"We could still do something nasty to him," Bonnie suggested.

"Let's ...!" Stacy agreed.

"Not yet," Julie suggested. "Let the lawyer take him for as much as she can ... and then we'll take everything he has left!"

"Good plan ...!" I added, hoping Stacy would be cooled off by then.

By the time she was refilling her wine glass, Stacy had reversed again.

"But what am I going to do ... divorced and alone ...?" Stacy whined.

"You haven't been alone since you met us," Julie said.

"Penelope found a great guy ... and look how many losers she dated," Bonnie said.

"Hey ...!" I complained.

"Gotta agree," Lyn said. "Emerson can't be the only one."

"You three have needed good husbands since high school," Bonnie said.

"Oh, shut up!" I said. "Stacy, every guy we've

dated was a test to see if we could make a marriage work; David was just another failed test."

"You're closer to a real marriage than me," Julie said. "Two kids ... and I've never had a proposal ...!"

"Your kids are your family ...!" Stacy argued.

"Enough of that!" I snapped. "Real friends are family!"

Arguments lasted until Stacy suggested David's cheating was her fault ... and then we all started shouting.

Finally I drove home, glad to escape the madness my life had become. For the attempted murder in Luigi's, Stacy's divorce would eventually become a permanent new trestle. My name would get dragged in; I'd be a cattle car. Of course, once aboard, my new relationship with Emerson would be revisited, additional spice on the gravy train that would cruise around Bismarck for a month.

Chapter 41

"*Mephistopheles, no ...!*"

I glanced at the clock; almost ten and I was still in bed.

Cold floor. Hallway. Kitchen. Bag. Pour into bowl.

I staggered back to the bedroom with my cat eating breakfast rather than trying to perch on my head.

I had to go back. Bonnie and Julie had kids; I couldn't let Lyn suffer Stacy's tirades alone. Yet I didn't want to spend all day there.

I wanted to experiment more.

Every caregiver knows exhaustion. Dealing with a friend's breakup is almost as difficult as suffering one yourself. I couldn't believe how tired I felt.

Better to get it over with. I reached for my phone.

"Lyn ...?"

"Yea ...?" she sounded like I felt.

"I just got up. Want company?"

"Sure."

"I'm not moving quick. I'll be there when I can."

Washed and dressed, I was in my car less than

an hour later. I drove slowly, not delighted yet determined; *they were my friends.*

Stacy met me at the door, wide-eyed and smiling brightly. She yanked me inside and hugged me tightly. She seemed overjoyed. I suffered her enthusiasm confused, like Minnie Mouse was welcoming me to Disneyland in North Dakota.

I glanced at Lyn, who shrugged.

"Ms. Alexandria Tempest, Attorney at Law!" Stacy laughed. "I looked her up; she's successful! Owns her own law office! I'm going to get my house ... maybe retire ...!"

I smiled and nodded, yet I silently knew she was crazy. David didn't have the money Alexandria wanted. Even if Stacy got the house, she'd need income ... her house wasn't fully paid for.

"Congratulations!" I forced myself to say.

"No more uniforms, cash registers, or stupid bosses!" Stacy effervesced.

I kept smiling. Lyn rolled her eyes.

"Have you eaten yet?" I asked. "I haven't."

"Let's go out for lunch!" Stacy said.

"No argument, but I'm not ready," Lyn said.

"Get dressed," I said. "I'm buying."

"Big raise with your promotion?" Lyn asked.

"Enough for one big lunch," I said.

As I waited, I heard Stacy singing to herself, and wondered how long this mood swing was going to last ... and what would come next.

Someone knocked on the door.

"I'll get it," I said. "Who else is coming ...?"

I opened the door.

David ...!!!

"Where is she ...?" David demanded.

"Not here," I said.

"I followed you from your house ...!" David shouted. "Bonnie and Julie wouldn't ...!"

Stacy's scream of rage filled Lyn's apartment.

"*Stacy ...!*" David shouted.

I tried to close the door; David pushed halfway inside. Lyn and Stacy were both screaming.

"*9-1-1 ...!*" I shouted as loudly as I could. "*9-1-1 ...!*"

"*She's my wife ...!*" David shouted.

"*This is Lyn's apartment ...!*" I shouted back.

David burst inside, using all his weight. The door slammed hard against my side. I fell onto the carpet, stunned, unable to stop him.

"*Cheater ...!*" Stacy screeched.

"*Get out ...!*" Lyn shouted.

"*You have to listen ...!*" David shouted.

"*Liar ...!*" Stacy shouted. "*Cheat ...!*"

"*Shut up, all of you!*" barked a strange, deep voice outside the door.

"*Mr. Langrick ...!*" Lyn shouted.

Standing just outside the open door was an old man, eyes ablaze, wild white hair, with only half his brown teeth remaining, wearing a bathrobe ... and carrying a pistol.

"*Everyone, hold your places ...!*" Mr. Langrick warned. "My wife's phoning the police; hold your screams until they get here."

"*That's my wife ...!*" David shouted, pointing at Stacy.

"*This's my apartment ...!*" Lyn shouted. "*He broke in!*"

"None of my business ... unless someone starts swinging fists, and then I'll settle it!" Mr. Langrick said, waving his pistol. "We wait for the cops!"

David glared at each of us.

"I'm not waiting ...!" David snarled.

"Then you'd best get going," Mr. Langrick said.

With a curse, David stormed out the door, past Mr. Langrick, and his stomps practically ran down the stairs.

"Thank you, Mr. Langrick," Lyn said.

"Will you be all right ...?" Mr. Langrick asked.

"Yes," Lyn said. "We'll wait for the police."

"Fine," Mr. Langrick pocketed his pistol. "Knock on my door if you need anything."

"I'm sure the cops will want to talk to you," I said.

"I'll be watching the game," Mr. Langrick said, and he walked toward the next door down the hall, which was still open.

We watched him go, and then Lyn ran forward, closed her door, and locked it. Stacy burst into tears. I shook my head, yet grinned.

Alexandria Tempest was going to love this!

My arm and ribs were clearly bruised, and my butt felt sore from being knocked onto the floor. Cops took our names, details, and I had them photograph the darkening bruise on my arm. Stacy told them everything about David, and they spoke long with Mr. Langrick. Lyn declined to say if she would press charges for breaking and entering, and I replied the same for assault charges against me; we wanted to talk to Alexandria Tempest first. The cops gave us a reference number to get their report, and we thanked them. Within half an hour, they were gone.

We were preparing to go get lunch when Emerson called. Upon insistence by Stacy and Lyn, I put him on speaker and we told him about David's invasion.

"He had a gun ...?!?" Emerson exclaimed.

"This is Bismarck," Lyn laughed. "Most households have guns."

"Did anyone get shot?"

We finished our story before Emerson interrupted again.

"You should be talking to that lawyer right now," Emerson said.

"We were going to ... but you called," Stacy said. "How's the show?"

"Show's fine; nobody's pointed a gun at me," Emerson said. "Penelope, did David just show up or was this a ... coincidence ...?"

"He followed me here, trying to find Stacy," I said.

"He's dangerous," Emerson said. "You all need to be careful."

"He probably knew Bonnie wasn't here," Lyn said. "She'd still be punching him."

"Stacy isn't going anywhere without one of us," I said.

"I need my things ...!" Stacy insisted.

"Julie knows a cop ... intimately," Lyn said. "We'll get him to help Stacy get in and out of her house."

"I wish I was there," Emerson said.

"We've got it under control," I said. "We'll see you when you get back."

"Bring some cute single magicians ...!" Lyn added.

"I'll do what I can," Emerson replied. "Penelope, until tomorrow ... usual message."

"What message ...?" Stacy asked. "You can talk in front of us."

"Usual reply," I answered. "I'll call tomorrow."

Stacy and Lyn erupted with giggles before I could hang up.

By the time that we reached the restaurant, Stacy was crying again.

"David and I used to say 'I love you' every day ...!" she wept.

"No more eavesdropping on Emerson and I!" I ordered.

We calmed her down enough to find seats and order burgers.

"We need to call the lawyer," Lyn said.

"Later," I said.

"I'm okay," Stacy said.

"You broke apart talking to Emerson," I said.

"Still ...," Lyn said.

"Let me go to the bathroom first," I said.

In the bathroom, I pulled out my phone.

"Alexandria, this is Penelope," I said. "David tried to see Stacy."

"Did he ...?" Alexandria asked.

"Saw her, but didn't talk," I said. "He forced his way into Lyn's apartment, where Stacy's staying. He hurt me. A neighbor showed up with a gun. Cops came."

"Did they give you a case number?"

I read the number to her.

"I'll have a restraining order on him first thing tomorrow," Alexandria said.

"Thanks," I said.

Lyn and Stacy were pissed that I'd called Alexandria, yet I didn't care.

"We don't need another scene," I said. " Stacy,

you need to hold it together. We will get through this."

"I say road trip," Lyn said. "A weekend, the five of us; we could visit the Mall of America."

"Soon ... before Emerson gets back," I said.

"Let's go!" Stacy said.

"What about Bonnie and Julie's kids ...?" Lyn asked.

"My mom can babysit for one night," I offered.

"When Stacy's settlement comes through we can vacation in Hawaii," Lyn said.

We ate lunch making wild plans. By the time our burgers were finished, we'd decided that Emerson would meet us in Waikiki and bring magical boyfriends for Lyn, Stacy, and Julie ... and a muscle-bound, well-oiled masseuse for Bonnie.

Bonnie couldn't join us, so we diverted over to Julie's when she got off work. While she cooked for her kids, we regaled her with our plan; she laughed.

Chapter 42

Mondays deserve their reputation. Thirty-eight new resumes had arrived. Crappy jobs were plentiful but, despite inflation, the economy was still booming, so even those working were applying in the hopes of better.

My smallest pile, my best prospects, looked perfect, yet you can't trust resumes. So many factors couldn't show on a resume; travel requirements, availability, health, appearance, and professionalism. One of my questions had to be if they'd ever been on a 'No Fly' list or been refused a passport; this job required air transportation.

Bonnie phoned; Alexandria Tempest had secured a restraining order against David for Stacy. Bonnie must've found Alexandria Tempest online and called her, and I didn't have time to waste arguing with Bonnie. I thanked her for calling and got back to work.

Ecstatic, Rosanne came in; the Bismarck Express was running entirely upon the attempted murder of an unfaithful husband at Luigi's. Fortunately, no names were known except 'David', but everyone was guessing. I told her that I knew several Davids, yet I knew my deflection wouldn't last. The gossip train's ears were

367

everywhere.

Rosanne's tale of the crazed wife attacking her husband with a steak knife was far from the truth; the Bismarck Express had him running around the whole restaurant, through the kitchen, and his life was saved only by a strange woman who appeared seconds before the death-blow. She'd knocked out the crazed woman with one punch, and carried her outside after the cheap tramp that he'd been cheating with had fled in tears, shouting that she was pregnant.

I smiled; *the Express embellishes everything.*

Yet I couldn't bear it; I had to work with Rosanne. She trusted and worked for me. I couldn't ruin our work relationship over facts she'd know soon enough. I insisted that we take an early lunch far outside of the office.

"Rosanne, I have to tell you something," I said. "This is friend-to-friend, nothing related to work, and you have to swear ... upon your soul ... not to tell anyone."

"What do you know?" Rosanne demanded.

"Everything ... but if I hear anything I tell you on the train tomorrow, I'll never trust you again ...!"

Despite doubting Rosanne's solemn promise, I told her everything, even David's pushing his way into Lyn's to try and see Stacy. Rosanne's eyes blazed. She ate every word. I added a few fake details, gold-glitter eye shadow on Alexandria, a huge diamond ring on her hand, and the thrown drink was now a strawberry margarita; if the Bismarck Express carried these details then I'd know who blabbed.

We returned to the office to find another twenty resumes had arrived.

I called Bessy and told her that I had enough

resumes, and she agreed that we should pull the ad from the website. I called Steve Johnson and asked for it to be taken down.

After closing my door, I phoned Emerson.

"Lyn and Julie are at work; Stacy's with Bonnie, and the lawyer got a restraining order," I told him. "Yet that's not what I want to talk about. I went back to the zoo."

"Practice ...?" Emerson asked.

"Success," I said.

I told him, unable to keep the excitement from my voice. I described the hungry ducks, how I caused their squabbles, about the otters, how I got them to all climb onto the high rock, and about the bears, how the coincidence I plucked caused me to sing ... and how the bears responded.

"I felt my own coincidence!" I whispered. "When I plucked the strand, it reacted ... within me!"

"We're always part of what we do," Emerson said. "You knew that, but now you've experienced it; that's why we can only learn so much from each other."

"I understand now," I said.

"Understanding isn't enough," Emerson said. "You've felt the power we wield. You have to learn to respect it."

"I do," I said.

"You caused ducks to fight," Emerson said. "The irresistible force that made you sing; they felt that, only ... it wasn't friendly."

"I didn't hurt them ...!"

"Timelines are inherently complex," Emerson said. "I once saw Lucinda make a mistake ... and she's more powerful than I'll ever be. A hundred timelines surround us every minute, and sometimes the consequences of one pluck can't be felt for months or years. Every pluck endangers timelines beyond count; hundreds for each person, and each animal, spawning, separating, swirling around us, eternally merging and branching. Please be careful."

"I will," I promised.

"I just don't want you to live with regrets like I do," Emerson said. "Now ... what are you wearing ...?"

"I'm naked ...!"

"You're at work ...!"

"I have an office now," I said. "My door is closed ...my finger moving ..."

"You wouldn't do that in your bedroom with me watching ...!" Emerson laughed.

"Enough of that," I said. "How are you doing?"

"Bored, until now," Emerson said. "You know what it's like; traveling for business."

"Nothing to do?"

"I've toured the casinos and resisted the urge to gamble," Emerson said. "They'd catch me if I won big ... I'm probably still on a file somewhere."

"Youthful indiscretions ...?" I asked.

"Childish foolishness," Emerson said.

"I really hate sleeping alone," I said.

"If I was in my hotel room ...!"

"You're not in your hotel ...?" I asked. "Where are you?"

"Sitting at a bar ... drinking iced tea," Emerson said. "I'll call from my room this time tomorrow."

"I can't wait," I said.

A long pause followed.

"Emerson ...?" I asked.

"I'm here."

"What ...?"

"I'm worried," Emerson said. "Your voice, your tone, even the things you're saying ... and where you're saying them ..."

"I'm fine," I said.

"No, you're not," Emerson said. "It happened to me. It happens to all of us. Penelope, I'm worried about you."

"Nothing's wrong ...!" I insisted.

"If you say so," Emerson said. "Just ... stay aware. Compare what you're thinking now ... to how you thought before we met. Power changes people ..."

"So do relationships ... and trust," I said.

"You ... trust me ...?" Emerson asked.

"I love you," I said.

"I love you," Emerson said. "Yet, even though I know I shouldn't, the temptation to grab some dice and shoot craps ... and cheat ... is incredibly tempting. I'm only human, susceptible to weakness. So are you ..."

"I'll rein it in," I promised. "I won't let you down."

"Call me this time tomorrow," Emerson said. "I'll be naked ... and waiting."

"Good-bye."

I got called to a meeting ten minutes before I'd hoped to leave. Colin Mendale announced that Nathan Qui had finally succeeded in upgrading all of Devonshire-Slate Medical's servers, and our software was powering their business. However, Nathan Qui wouldn't be returning; offices had been rented near Devonshire-Slate Medical, and Nathan would be moving to Atlanta. Mr. Dawes was no longer leading the advertising department; he would be joining Nathan as the head of our Atlanta branch.

We all congratulated him. He nodded and

expressed thanks. I'd never seen him look so happy.

The meeting lasted more than an hour; I had to silence my phone because Bonnie kept calling. My only report was that I was still selecting the best applicants. I was starving by the time that the meeting ended.

I called Bonnie from the car.

"Late meeting," I explained.

"Lyn took Stacy to Julie's for the evening, but she'll be sleeping at Lyn's," Bonnie said. "Julie wants to help, but she can't risk David breaking in while her kids are asleep. Lyn and Stacy are babysitting while Julie goes to Stacy's house to get her things."

"What if David's there ...?" I asked.

"Julie isn't alone," Bonnie said. "She's friends with a cop ... I think she's sleeping with him. They have a signed letter from Stacy granting them access and permission to collect a long list of Stacy's things."

"Do you need me?" Penelope asked.

"Not today, but you'll need to take Stacy tomorrow night," Bonnie said. "None of us can."

"I'll take care of her," I said. "I've got some work stuff I need to catch up on tonight ..."

"Earning your big promotion?" Bonnie asked. "You still haven't told me how much you're getting paid now ..."

"And that's not an accident," I said. "Call if you need me."

"I will."

I stopped for take-out Mexican on the way home. Mephistopheles would claim to be starving, yet I had a quick drink while waiting. I considered playing with the people in the bar, yet decided not to; Emerson's warning still rang in my ears. I needed practice, so I waited impatiently. I had all evening to master coincidences.

Finally Mephistopheles was fed, petted, and slunk off to sleep. I finished half of my burrito and slid the remainder in the fridge, turned off the TV, and fetched my penny. I held it in my hand and stared at it, opening my awareness, searching for the barest sensations of possibilities. Everything held energy, active or potential. I was part of that energy. All I had to do was command it.

"Heads."

I flipped the coin.

When it hit my table and stopped rattling, Abraham Lincoln's profile faced me.

I practiced with the coin at least twenty tosses, failing only a few times.

I stared at my empty chair, focusing on it. I thought about Mephistopheles. It took almost fifteen minutes, yet Mephistopheles finally came into the living room, sniffing about as if hunting, and cautiously jumped up onto the chair and sat down.

Test after test I experimented with Mephistopheles, yet it became too easy. I started reaching out farther, exploring whatever I found.

Careful not to touch anything, I searched beyond my walls. Neighbors surrounded me; I could sense them in their apartments, aware of their presence and the possibilities swirling around them. From some, I got feelings ranging from happiness to distrust. Mrs. Lillian was sleeping, dreaming; I left her be. I sensed excited kids playing video games. A lady I'd never spoken to was reading, her emotions burning hot ... passionate. A young couple was arguing.

I felt dizzy, stretched, and tried to draw back into myself. My head spun; I feared I'd vomit. I'd never explored so far. I almost felt I'd lost myself ... or come close to it. I'd risked too much ... delved into the unknown.

I had to stop. I shook my head, then walked into the kitchen and poured myself some wine.

Hours later, I felt recovered, slightly tipsy from drinking too fast. I chastised myself; Emerson had told me to be careful. I had to go slow, test each step, not go randomly exploring.

Just to prove I still could, I flipped my penny again, and forcing it to land on tails.

Tails!

I grinned; *I was learning fast!*

Where would it end? How much farther could I push myself? What would I eventually discover ...?

It was almost ten o'clock. I had work tomorrow; I needed to get ready for bed. Yet I wanted one more test ... just one, and then I'd quit.

I thought about Stacy, of checking on her, yet Lyn would be taking care of her. Bonnie was probably watching her late-night shows. I could possibly wake up her kids, just to annoy her, but they had school and needed sleep.

There was one person who deserved harm. I reached out, wondering where David was. I'd sensed him before, from a distance, when he was at Luigi's. I had no idea where he was and wondered if I could find him. I knew his feeling now, more than before. I leaned back, let my head rest on the back of my couch, and closed my eyes. His feelings were out there ... somewhere.

He wasn't hard to find. However much she might hate him now, Stacy's connection to David was strong, yet mine to Stacy's was even stronger. I detected, focused on him, and felt his turmoil. His twisted familiarity sickened me. Dark possibilities surrounded him, yet I couldn't tell where he was or what he was doing. His thoughts burned angrily, yet nervousness bubbled throughout him; I sensed fear. He felt like hunted prey backed into a corner: *dangerous.*

No pity welled. He'd hurt Stacy. He'd hurt me, slamming Lyn's door into my side and knocking me onto my butt. He didn't care. All David cared about was himself.

Numerous possible timelines swirled around him. Most were vengeful, some hopeful of escape, others looming like manacles. Some painful. None regretful.

I needed to break my connection; I didn't want him sensing me. Yet I couldn't resist. Just before I broke free, I plucked one of the timelines, a single swirling thread knotted around him; a thread of pain.

"Aaarrghhh ...!" I bent over, clutching the pain in my chest.

Yet it wasn't my pain; it was David's. I pulled away, releasing my connection. It was just a brief pain, and it faded when my concentration broke.

I'd hurt David!

I shouldn't feel good ... but Stacy was my friend. *I'd avenged her!*

Chapter 43

Bessy Andrews called me into her office, asking me to bring the five resumes I'd selected, and minutes later she was reviewing them while I sat quietly.

"We need these candidates vetted," Bessy said. "Forward their emails to Marsha Kendal. She reports to Maria Saviano. If they pass Marsha Kendal, we'll have Rosanne set up interviews."

Her laptop beeped.

"Oh, damn," Bessy said. "Another meeting ... in ten minutes. We're both on the invite."

"What's this meeting?" I asked.

"Mark Brown ... new Atlanta office," Bessy said. "We'd better get coffee."

Ten minutes later, armed with caffeine, we were shown a PowerPoint of the new office, given its address, and descriptions of the general layout. I tried to pay attention, yet constantly wondered why I needed to know this.

Again Bonnie phoned in the middle of a meeting. I didn't answer. My phone was silent, yet every few minutes its screen illuminated; Bonnie must really want to talk. However, she finally seemed to give up.

Mark Brown was in the middle of describing long term cost-benefits of the new office when a knock came to the door: Rosanne.

"Excuse me," Rosanne said in an oddly weepy voice. "There's a ... phone call for Penelope. I think she should take it."

We all looked surprised. I was horrified; I was the junior manager, and to step out of a meeting wasn't professional. Yet Rosanne's face was ghostly pale, her voice tremulous. I quietly rose and stepped outside. Rosanne was holding her phone in one hand, yet she grabbed my arm and drug me into the printer and supplies room. Then she handed me her phone.

"Hello?" I asked.

"Penelope ...," Bonnie's voice.

"This better be important," I said.

"Penelope, shut up and listen," Bonnie's voice. "This is serious. There's been a death."

"Death ...?" I asked, almost amused, but then I saw tears glistening on Rosanne's cheeks. *"Wait ...! Who ...?"*

"You'd better come," Bonnie said. "We're at Lyn's."

"We ...?" I asked.

"All of us," Bonnie said. "I just got back. I had to ... identify ..."

"Who ...?" I demanded.

"Calm down," Bonnie said. "We're okay. It's ... it's David. They found his car this morning ... in a ditch. Penelope ... David's dead."

"Dead ...?" I gasped.

"He was driving late last night, swerved off the highway near Mandan," Bonnie said. "No one saw it ...

not until it got light this morning."

"*How ...?*" I demanded.

"They don't know," Bonnie said. "Drunk, sick, or maybe he just fell asleep. They won't know until the autopsy."

"*Autopsy ...?*" I asked. "*When did it happen ...?*"

"The cops think it was right after ten o'clock," Bonnie said. "That's when his watch broke."

I staggered.

Rosanne caught her phone as it fell from my grip, and my arm as I started to fall. I stumbled back against a tall metal cabinet, crashed loudly, and slid to the floor. Rosanne was shouting my name.

Several faces appeared in the doorway.

Spurred by Rosanne, hands grabbed and lifted me to my feet, led me to the nearest desk, and lowered me to sit. I heard Rosanne talking to Bonnie, but I had no idea what she was saying.

Ten o'clock ...!

David had been driving ...!

I'd caused him pain ...!

Sounds of concern floated around me ... yet I couldn't understand a word.

I'd killed David ...!

Walking. I was helped outside, to Rosanne's car, and loaded into the passenger seat. My purse was set in my lap. Voices spoke. Someone leaned over me. My seat belt was buckled. Rosanne got into the driver's seat and started her engine.

Streets. Traffic lights. Other cars.

We arrived at Lyn's parking lot.

Rosanne unbuckled me and helped me out. Hands clenched my arms. At the main door, Bonnie and Julie came out and helped carry me, and thanked Rosanne for bringing me. We stumbled up two flights of stairs and into Lyn's apartment. Rosanne came with us.

Stacy was softly crying, her face and eyes red.

We hugged ... somehow ... and then I was set onto the couch. I felt ... floaty ... unreal.

"Penelope ...?" Lyn asked. "Are you all right ...?"

"Do you want to lay down ...?" Julie asked.

I couldn't answer.

I was a murderess ...!

"Penelope!" Bonnie shouted, and she shook me.

"I ... David ... last night," I whispered. "I ... wished him ... bad ...!"

"You're not responsible," Bonnie said. "Wishes can't cause accidents."

She didn't know how wrong she was. *I did!*

"You're not alone," Stacy said. "We've all been angry at David, me the most."

"She's in shock," Rosanne said. "You've known for hours. Give her time."

"Here's some water," Lyn forced a cold plastic bottle into my hands.

I took several deep breaths before I drank. The water tasted artificial. Nothing seemed right.

David was dead ...!

Hands held me for twenty minutes before my mind started to clear, to accept the impossible. I trembled uncontrollably. Coincidences couldn't be proven. The cops wouldn't even guess I was involved.

Images of iron bars and jail cells filled my mind.

Emerson would know!

I couldn't hide this. Even if I didn't tell him, he'd learn when he got back.

Would Emerson want a murderous bride ...?

"Penelope, snap out of it," Bonnie said. "He was Stacy's husband. We brought you here for her."

"I'm all right," Stacy said, tears in her voice. "Take care of her."

Stacy sat beside me and hugged me. Her arms felt like needles. I didn't respond; she clung to me, but I'd betrayed her.

I'd killed her husband!

"We ... should pray for him," Rosanne stammered.

Julie led us in prayer. I shivered deep inside.

Hell ...! Murderesses went to Hell ...!

I wasn't sure if I believed in Hell until this very moment.

I prayed hard, the familiar words like old friends. We all recited.

The words mocked me.

I had to pull myself together. I couldn't tell them what had really happened.

They wouldn't believe me anyway.

A strange thought permeated my brain.

I'd never know if I'd killed David ...

Car wrecks happen every day. Coincidences happen without magicians. Someone could've driven him off the road. A tire could've burst ... brakes failed. David could've had a heart attack. *I'd seen him drink and drive ...!*

No matter what ... I had to say nothing!

Words began to penetrate my brain. Bonnie was talking about the accident scene. No tire marks showed where he'd left the asphalt, only tracks through weeds leading to a wide, deep ditch. Only part of his trunk and bumper could've been seen from the highway ... once the sun rose. Some morning semi-truck driver had noticed and reported it to 9-1-1.

"Who ... who talked to him last?" I asked.

"We don't know," Lyn said. "The last anyone saw him, he was leaving here."

"He has several customers in north Mandan, but he never stayed out until ten ... except with Li Chin ... I mean, ... Alexandria," Stacy said.

"Not what we should be thinking about," Julie said. "The police will discover where he was. William will tell us when they do."

"William ... your cop-boyfriend ...?" Bonnie asked.

"Just friend, but he's a cop," Julie said.

"How long have you two ...?" Bonnie asked.

"We haven't," Julie said. "We talked about it. He doesn't want kids ... no family ties."

"Give him to Lyn," Bonnie said.

"I want kids ...!" Lyn argued.

"David never wanted kids," Stacy said.

Although guilty twice-over, slowly I recovered. Even if I'd killed David, I should be consoling Stacy.

"Stacy, I'm sorry," I said.

She hugged me again.

"Not your fault," Stacy said.

"Stacy, pizza or Chinese?" Bonnie asked.

"Thai," Stacy said. "David always liked Thai."

Bonnie called for home delivery.

"Let's turn on some news," Lyn suggested. "It may be on TV ..."

The fatal car accident on I-94 was headline news. We watched fascinated and horrified; mostly they kept showing the roped-off ditch surrounded by cop cars with flashing lights and a tow truck standing by. A police officer described a single-car accident and reported no evidence of a cause and what a tragedy late night driving could be. Then the bubble-head announcers kept trying to talk about it, obviously strapped for things to say.

"Has anyone called his parents?" I asked.

"The police did," Bonnie said.

Lyn logged online and found the story on local news websites, yet we learned nothing new.

"Penelope, your purse," Julie said.

I looked; a light was flashing inside my purse. My cell phone. *Emerson ...!*

I couldn't talk to him.

"Mother," I lied. "I'll call her later."

How could I tell Emerson?

Still on silent mode, I shoved my phone deep into my purse and clicked it closed.

Food arrived, Swimming Rama, Black Pepper Vegetables, Pnang Curry with Beef, and Pad Thai. Lyn set out plates and we shared everything, eating the spicy food with our eyes glued to the TV.

Constantly-repeated news spared us conversations we didn't have. Soon we had the story memorized, yet we kept watching, being promised another police announcement ... hours later, the announcement still hadn't come.

No one said what we were all thinking. David had been cheating ... no divorce was needed now. Stacy would get the house and everything, no need to go to court. Yet no alimony; after she got everything, no income would follow. Stacy couldn't retire.

After dinner, Bonnie gave me a ride to my office so I could retrieve my car. I thanked her, drove home, and hurried inside. I grabbed and hugged Mephistopheles despite his cries of starvation. I was so torn I didn't know what to think.

David was a terrible person ... but I hadn't meant to kill him!

I'd made Stacy a widow ...!

I could never use magic again ...!

Chapter 44

All next morning, condolences were offered. Everyone had seen the news, and I had to explain who David was ... from my reaction, everyone assumed that we were close. I nodded and didn't contradict them. I told them that Stacy needed condolences more than I.

I had to search my emails for the names of each candidate and forward them to Marsha Kendal, and cc'ed Rosanne so I wouldn't have to do it twice. Then I had nothing to do, so I went online and made lists of contacts for the medical conventions we weren't attending, and compared those dates against other events. I also needed to verify the events I was scheduled to attend before Mr. Dawes left for Atlanta.

I had to call Emerson. Perhaps after lunch ...

Rosanne and I went out again. She wanted to hear everything, and pressed me for my relationship with David. I told her that I didn't have one, but lied ... told her I'd encouraged Stacy to marry him, and my concern was for her.

Rosanne had known Stacy for years, although not as well as I. Bismarck was like that. We repeated all the details of his death ... yet those were well known. I slid our conversation to Stacy inheriting everything, and we discussed her finances in detail.

After lunch, I closed my office door and phoned Emerson.

"I left messages ...!" Emerson started.

"I heard them ... Emerson, please listen," I said. "You're not driving, are you? Are you sitting down?"

"What's wrong ...?" Emerson's voice grew serious.

"There's been a death ... car accident," I said.

"Are you all right?"

"It wasn't me. David ... Stacy's husband ... he drove into a ditch ..."

"Hurt ...?"

"Worse."

"Oh, my ...! How's Stacy?"

"Emotional rollercoaster dragged through a wringer," I said. "She'd once loved him, then hated him, and now he's ... dead. She feels guilty, horrified, but also relieved, and maybe ecstatic. All her problems just ended ... yet she's emotionally twisted."

"Poor girl ...!" Emerson said.

"Emerson ... I'm scared," I said.

"Why ...?"

My hand holding my phone was shaking. *I couldn't tell him!*

"I ... I'm worried for Stacy," I lied. "She's really upset."

"Is she alone ...?"

"No, we're keeping her with one of us ... around the clock. She's staying at Lyn's."

"Why are you scared?"

"I ... I don't know, but this is why I didn't answer yesterday ... I was with them. I'm sorry."

"Don't worry about me," Emerson said. "The worst I have is boredom and crappy room service in this fleabag hotel."

"I'm still sorry," I said.

"You've nothing to be sorry about," Emerson said. "Wow. This is a lot to take in."

"I'm sorry," I repeated. "It's all over the local news ... probably didn't make it out there."

"Look, what we were planning ... we can do that anytime," Emerson said.

"I listened to your messages, but it just wasn't appropriate ... and then you were doing your show ..."

"I understand," Emerson said. "My last performance is a week from tomorrow. I'll be coming home ... your place ... assuming I'm still welcome."

"My home is yours," I said. "Our place ... oh, wait; the Pacific Northwest Medical Research Conference ...!"

"When is it?"

"I'll have to leave Tuesday after you arrive."

"We'll have a weekend. How long is it?"

"Wednesday through Sunday."

"I'll be there when you get back."

"I love you so much."

"I love you, too."

I could barely hang up. I'd lied to Emerson ... again. I loved him ... yet I was constantly lying to him ...

What was I going to do?

Hours later, Bonnie called.

"Meet us at Arnold's," Bonnie said. "Come straight from work."

"Us ...?" I asked.

" Stacy and I," Bonnie said. "You're not going to believe this."

"What ...?"

"I'll tell you when you get there."

Bonnie had barely hung up before Rosanne burst into my office.

"Guess what ...!" Rosanne looked excited.

"What ...?"

"Your friend Stacy ...!" Rosanne exclaimed. *"I just heard ...!"*

"Heard what ...?"

"You don't know ...?" Rosanne asked. *"The Bismarck Express is on overdrive! Your friend went to the bank this morning to get some money ... the banker showed her all of David's other accounts ...!"*

I stared unblinking.

"David was rich!" Rosanne shouted. *"He had secret accounts that she knew nothing about!"*

I arrived a few minutes early and hurried inside Arnold's.

"Bismarck Express ...!" I said before Bonnie and Stacy could shout their news.

"Damn!" Stacy cursed. "Everyone knows ...?"

"Emerson doesn't ... until tomorrow," I said.

"Who blabbed ...?" Bonnie asked.

"Rosanne heard before lunch," I said.

"That blabbermouth bank teller ...!" Stacy scowled.

"As loud as you screamed ...?" Bonnie laughed. "Every customer in the bank heard you."

"How much ...?" I asked.

"Almost seven hundred thousand dollars ...!" Stacy said.

Gwen, Nancy, Brendan, Rachel, Katie, and Mike cheered as if on cue. Those not working raised glasses.

"That's good, but you can't live off it," I said to Stacy. "She needs to invest."

"We agreed to that before you found out," Bonnie said.

"Lyn and Julie can barely afford rent," Stacy said. "I've got this big house. I was thinking of letting them rent rooms ... Julie and her kids can have the whole downstairs ... I'll charge them half of what they're paying now."

"Have you asked them?" I asked.

"We've been sitting here talking in front of Gwen, Nancy, and Brendan," Bonnie said, giving them a stare. "They may already know."

Each protested their innocence.

"Sounds like a good idea," I said.

"Beer ...?" Rachel asked.

"Lemonaide," I said.

"Since when ...?" Bonnie asked.

"Since now," I said.

"Scotch is what Emerson drinks," Stacy laughed.

"He called my place 'home'," I smiled.

"Congratulations!" Bonnie smirked.

"Here," Rachel said, setting my lemonade on the bar. "On me."

"Thanks!" I said.

"Anyone who brings cute magicians here deserves it," Rachel said.

I gave Stacy a short speech on wise investing, not blowing her newfound excess, but Bonnie objected.

"That's no fun!" Bonnie complained.

"Decide on a set amount," I suggested. "A small amount to spend; no more. Go to Hawaii ... lay on a beach."

Stacy liked that idea, yet wanted to take all of us.

I told her that she was crazy; she should take one person, tops, and no more. Bonnie insisted that she should go ... to take care of her. I didn't argue; no one could take care of anyone like Bonnie, and I wouldn't go to Hawaii without Emerson.

I ate at Arnold's. Stacy changed her plans from Hawaii to a cruise to Alaska to New York City to London and Paris. Soon she was talking about a Caribbean cruise.

"Penelope, will you lend her your red bikini?" Bonnie asked.

"I'll buy her a new one," I promised. "Mine has memories."

"It's lucky ...!" Bonnie insisted.

"Any girl can get lucky in a red bikini," I said.

"Or out of it," Kathy laughed. "Right there on the sand ... right, Penelope?"

I scowled and wished I was drinking beer.

All night I sat staring at my walls, my TV on, yet I had no idea what I was watching.

Had I killed David ...?

Probably ... but I'd never know. I was terrified ... unsure what scared me most. Every priest's description of Lakes of Fire blazed through my mind ... although I hadn't meant to kill him.

Chapter 45

Rosanne asked about 'Rich Stacy' before I even sat down.

"She's not rich," I said. "She could pay off her house or buy another, but then she'd be broke."

"Is that what she's going to do?" Rosanne asked.

"No, she's going to take a short vacation to celebrate, then come back," I said. "It's not enough to retire; she'll have to do something for income."

"Maybe she'll meet someone cute in Hawaii ...?" Rosanne said.

"Maybe ...," I agreed just to get to my desk.

Meetings lasted all morning and beyond. They brought in lunch boxes; sandwiches, chips, a pickle, and a bottle of water each. I tried to look excited, yet the plans were basically more about administration in Atlanta and prospects for finding additional customers in the Southeast. I promised to research new conventions in Tennessee and below. For the rest of it, I chugged coffee and struggled not to yawn.

Back in my office, I checked my plans for the Pacific Northwest Medical Research Conference. Rosanne had my tickets and reservations, but hadn't printed them yet. Seattle was a hotbed of medical research; I had to review lots of potential customers.

I chastised myself every time my mind wandered. I hadn't killed anyone ... at worst, it was an accident.

Was his death really a bad thing? I'd saved Stacy months, possibly years of legal battles, a divorce that could've ended up costing her everything. She was totally free now, and hopefully wiser, and wouldn't make the same mistake again.

Well, not as big a mistake; Stacy wasn't the brightest ...

Maybe I could help her ...!

No, I thought sternly. That part of my life was over. Good or bad, what I'd done was wrong.

I had to tell Emerson ...!

Yet I no longer feared that. He'd made mistakes; he'd understand.

Pain ... I'd felt David die.

Chapter 46

"Lyn and Julie are moving in with Stacy," Rosanne said.

"Do you live on the Bismarck Express ...?" I asked.

"I've got guest quarters in my mother and sister's private car," Rosanne said.

"Doesn't sound very private," I commented.

Without meetings, work flew by. Rosanne and I ate lunch together, and she acted offended when I asked what rent Julie would be paying for Stacy's basement, and whether or not Julie was sleeping with her cop-friend.

"Julie's dating a cop ...?" Rosanne gasped.

I bowed my head; *I'd just fueled the gossip train.*

"You didn't hear it from me," I said.

Julie would never forgive me!

My phone beeped.

"Hey, sexy," I answered.

Long pause.

"Can I speak to Penelope?" Emerson asked.

"Ha ha," I grinned.

"I'm not complaining, just surprised," Emerson said.

"I can't wait to see you again," I said.

"If I'd known you'd be like this I'd be in my hotel room," Emerson said.

"Your loss," I said.

"I know you're in your office," Emerson said.

"Yes, but my door is closed," I said.

"So what does that mean?" Emerson asked.

"It means I'm alone ... thinking about you," I said.

"I see ...," Emerson said.

"I'm wearing a red silk blouse," I said. "It has very small buttons. My fingers slide slowly across it, slip inside. I feel skin ..."

"I'm never going to sleep tonight," Emerson said.

"Dream about me," I breathed heavily. "I'm tracing the curves of my bra, feeling its lacy edge ..."

"You're torturing me!"

"Slipping underneath, nipple searching ...!"

"Oh, my dear soul!"

"So soft, firm and round ..."

"Penelope ...!" Emerson hissed. "I'm at the magic club! We're going out to lunch in ten minutes! I can't go ... aroused ...!"

"Nipple found ... squeezing ...!"

"Aaaarrgghhh!" Emerson moaned. "Penelope, please ...! Don't make me hang up ...!"

"Feels so good ...!"

"This isn't the time ...!" Emerson pleaded. "Penelope, I love you, and I'll prove that as soon as I see you ... I swear! I'm going to hang up now ...!"

"Oh, a tiny button came undone ...!" I said. "I can see ... all the way down ...!"

"Good-bye, tease!"

Emerson hung up.

I laughed ... and glanced down at the buttonless pullover dress I was wearing ... properly concealing.

Horny men are so easy to manipulate!

By freedom hour, I'd reviewed the last of our Seattle contacts and returned to researching new medical conventions. Seattle was a huge venue; I could probably get a long list of new sales events from the vendors there. I wondered if I could get a giant wall calendar to keep track of everything, rather than use my tiny screen for tracking dates.

Most of the other managers had two large monitors. Before I left, I stopped by Bessy's office and asked if I could get some. She promised to look into it.

I drove home, carried my purse and laptop up my stair, then froze.

Someone was sitting on an old, large suitcase, blocking my front door. An elderly black woman ...

"Hello, Penelope," she said.

"I-I'm sorry," I stammered, taken aback. "Have we met ...?"

"Not formally ... but I've been watching you," she said. "I'm Lucinda."

"Lucinda ...?" I asked, and then I remembered. *"Emerson's Lucinda ...?!?"*

"A pleasure to meet you," Lucinda said, and she stood up. "May we go inside ...?"

I stared disbelieving.

"Lucinda ... from Florida ...?!?"

She didn't smile, just stared at me. I fumbled for my keys and unlocked my door. She waited until I entered and held the door for her.

"Do I need to carry this in ...?" Lucinda asked.

"I'll get it," I said.

I grabbed her heavy suitcase; with both hands I lifted it inside, wondering how she'd managed. Lucinda stepped inside my apartment and walked across my living room. Before I closed my door, she was sitting on my couch, staring at me.

"Does ... Emerson know ...?" I asked.

"Why would he know anything?" Lucinda asked. "Don't get me wrong; he's straightened himself out nicely. You're the first good decision he's ever made."

"Thank you," I said.

"I told him that in Florida," Lucinda said. "Now I'm not sure."

Unable to speak, I stared at her.

"Emerson never murdered anyone ...!" Lucinda accused.

Time seemed to stop, yet my mind was too blank to notice.

Mephistopheles ran into the living room, glanced at Lucinda, and jumped up onto her lap. She scratched and petted him thoroughly.

"Enough pointless silence," Lucinda said. "This little guy needs to be fed, I could use a beer, and you need to tell me what happened."

I stepped into the kitchen, brought her out a beer, and went back inside. Usually the can opener was Mephistopheles' siren song, yet even after I dropped his dish to the floor, he hadn't appeared. I went back into the living room to find Mephistopheles on his back getting his tummy rubbed.

"Go eat," Lucinda said.

Mephistopheles flipped over, jumped down, and ran into the kitchen.

"You have ... an amazing gift with cats," I said.

"Animals like me," Lucinda said, and she sipped her beer. "I'm waiting."

"Waiting ...?"

"What happened ...?"

I stared at this old woman. Her skin was mottled brown, sagging and wrinkled, and several moles dotted her face and neck. Her hands were thin, fingers long. Despite the warm weather, she wore a faded white, knitted shawl around her shoulders, and the skirt of her flower-printed dress fell to only a handspan above her ankles. Yet she had the eyes of a prosecuting attorney.

"I'm just learning," I said. "Trial and error; I make mistakes."

She didn't react at all.

"I'd never tried this before," I said. "I didn't know he was driving. I was here ... practicing, experimenting ... to see what I could do."

She didn't move.

"He was mean to Emerson ... to everyone," I said. "He cheated on his wife. I've still got bruises he gave me. He hurt everyone. I just wanted ... a tiny bit ... to hurt him back."

Lucinda sighed and sipped her beer again.

"Would you invest money in a company you'd never heard of?" Lucinda asked.

"N-no," I said.

"Yet you twanged a fate-path when you didn't know where it went?"

I bowed my head.

"How do I tell where it goes?"

"You follow it!" Lucinda snapped, and then she took a deep breath. "I'm sorry, child, but this is serious."

"How serious ...?" I asked.

"We'll know that before I leave," Lucinda said. "I trust you have no plans tonight?"

"No, I ... I'm still in a bit of shock," I said. "I don't know what to do."

"Good," Lucinda said. "Someone who could ... do what you did ... and feel no remorse; that would show a lack of heart I couldn't abide."

"What should I do?"

"Start from the beginning," Lucinda said. "Tell me everything."

"Well, I had just left Lyn's and was driving home," I began.

"No, child, not the killing!" Lucinda exclaimed. "I want your story."

"Oh, well, when Emerson was here, we ate dinner with ..."

"Is that where your story begins ...? Did you exist before you knew Emerson ...?"

"Oh, but ... what ...? You want my life-story ...?"

"There's only two of us here ... and I know mine," Lucinda admonished.

"Okay ... *why* ...?"

"How will I know your reasons for what you did if I don't know where your reasons originated?" Lucinda asked. "Start at the beginning. We'll stop for dinner when you're hungry."

"This could be ... a long story," I said.

"The best stories are," Lucinda said.

"No, I mean it could take hours ... all night," I said.

"I don't care if it takes days!" Lucinda snapped. "Start talking, and when you're done, I've got stories for you."

"*Days* ...?" I asked.

"Yes; I'm your house guest."

I wanted to argue, but felt it futile; Lucinda didn't seem the type to back down. All this was happening too fast, yet her dark-eyed stare sent shivers through me. Mephistopheles, still licking his teeth, came running back into the living room, jumped into her lap, and started purring.

"I was born here ... in Bismarck ...," I began, and I kept talking for more than an hour.

As I ended telling about elementary school, my stomach growled.

"What do you have for dinner?" Lucinda asked.

"Here ...?" I asked. "I've got lots ..."

"Let's see what you have," Lucinda said.

She rose with creaky movements, yet managed well enough without aid. She proceeded me into the kitchen, and examined the contents of my refrigerator and most of my cabinets.

"Thorns of roses, child, don't you have any food ...?" she asked.

I stammered; *my kitchen was full ...!*

"I-I could heat up soup ...," I said.

"Your vegetable crisper is empty!" Lucinda scorned.

"I could make spaghetti ...," I said.

"Do you have tomatoes?" she asked.

"No," I said.

"You can't make spaghetti sauce without tomatoes."

"I have ... Mrs. Ragatini's," I said.

"Well, unless she's a neighbor with fresh tomatoes, we can't have spaghetti," she said. "We don't have time for grocery shopping tonight. We'll go tomorrow. Is there a good French restaurant in this

399

town?"

"French ...?" I asked.

"What, you think I eat hog jowls and jambalaya every night?"

"No, I didn't ...!"

"What can we have delivered?"

"Pizza ... Chinese ... maybe Mexican ...," I said.

"Do your steak houses deliver?"

"I don't think so."

"Chinese ... I like lots of shrimp and brown rice. I'll cook tomorrow. You do have pots and pans ...?"

"Under the counter," I pointed.

She bent low and examined my cookware with audible displeasure. I tried to ignore her and reached for my phone.

I ordered for both of us as she searched my kitchen in vain.

"No tea kettle ...?" she asked.

"No ... I just ... microwave," I said.

"Very well," she sighed. "I see you have teabags. Would you like some tea?"

"Ah ..., sure," I said.

She was so old that I was surprised she knew how to use a microwave, yet she chose two mugs, filled them with water, started them at a minute and a half. I suggested that she add the teabags before they heated, and she looked at me like I was crazy.

"Let's get back to your story," Lucinda said. "I believe you liked your sixth grade English teacher? Good looking, by the sound of your voice."

I hadn't described him and wondered how she knew ... and how much more she understood than I was telling her. I continued, regaling her with stories of summer picnics at multiple parks.

Lucinda started interrupting me with questions, a few at first, but by the time I was in college taking Classical Literature, the major I'd dropped in my second year, I felt like I was being grilled. Most of her questions were personal, so much that I didn't want to answer. Thankfully, our food arrived before I outright refused.

"You're a bad storyteller," Lucinda said as we ate.

"What ...?" I asked.

"Your stories are unrelated," Lucinda said. "You say what happened, but never why."

"Is 'why' part of the story?" I asked.

"'Why' is the only story," Lucinda said.

When we resumed, I tried to answer her more fully. Yet her questions grew increasingly intimate. I tried to skip over my first lover, yet she wouldn't be gainsaid.

"Your life's just starting to get interesting," Lucinda smiled and petted Mephistopheles, who'd resumed his place in her lap. "Tell me more."

"He was ... I thought he was everything ... my future happiness," I said.

"Aha!" Lucinda grinned. "If all you've told me is true, that was your first decision based upon your own beliefs."

"Are beliefs important?" I asked.

"To know your beliefs is to know you," Lucinda said.

"I'm Catholic," I said.

"Faith is what you were taught by others," Lucinda said. "Beliefs are what we teach ourselves."

I stared at Lucinda, uncertain what she meant, yet certain that she was right. She was deep, wise beyond years I'd never known. She looked thin and frail, yet in her I sensed a strength I couldn't imagine.

"I surrendered to him on a couch in his parent's basement," I said. "He wanted it so badly ... I think I did, too."

Lucinda smiled widely.

"Details ...?"

I kept nothing back. I described how deeply in love I was ... until I discovered that I wasn't the girl he'd asked to the next dance. Weeks afterwards I'd cried. Bonnie marched to the dance and told his date what he'd done; she screamed at him and stormed off, abandoning him in front of the entire school.

My former relationships amused her. Stories of graduating college irritated her; I'd done it because my parents insisted, not by choice, and to this day I'd never thanked them, as Lucinda was quick to point out.

Years of good and bad dates caused frequent shakes of her head. My lifelong friendships with Bonnie, Julie, Stacy, and Lyn impressed her; their lives were intertwined with mine. My stories were constantly interspaced with stories about them.

Late that night, my description of Emerson during an unwanted Hawaiian cab-share made her laugh.

"You know, I would appreciate compensation for my stories," I said.

"Stories of Emerson ...?" Lucinda asked. "You may not like them."

"Now I want them even more ...," I said.

"You'll have them," Lucinda promised. "More than anyone, you need to know."

I took her assessment with no small foreboding. I told her everything about my tropical week with Emerson, my avoidance, and eventual surrender, and about our worrisome good-bye.

My first attempts at magic without Emerson made Lucinda lean forward. Her constant questions and interruptions turned my story into an interview. She demanded to know every nuance of my wine-dripping, card-finding, and information-sensing. My vocabulary troubled her; what I called coincidences and random chance she called fate-paths and secret happenings.

My first success at sensing David, not knowing his romantic feelings weren't for Stacy, made her scowl. She shrugged when I described controlling animals at the zoo, even when I experienced magical feedback for the first time. Yet when I told her how I'd plucked a single timeline of David's, one which felt painful, she shook her head.

"Enough," Lucinda said.

"But ... you don't understand ...," I argued. "What happened after ..."

"I sensed David's death as clearly as you," Lucinda said. "Not a word has escaped your mouth since then I haven't heard, not a sight I haven't seen."

I stared, shocked for the first time since I'd found her on my doorstep.

"You've been spying on me ...?" I asked.

"It's time for sleep," Lucinda said. "Forgive an old woman, but I can't rest these bones on a couch or floor. Would you mind resting out here? I'll need your bedroom."

"Of ... of course," I stammered.

"Fine," Lucinda said. "A good night's sleep and dreams to sort out our confusions are exactly what we need." She stood and looked at her suitcase. "Would you mind, my sweet?"

Numb from shock, yet wanting to appear polite, I carried her suitcase into my bedroom and set it on the foot of my bed. I quickly gathered the things I'd need, pajamas, extra blankets, and one of my pillows. I wished her good-night and left her sorting through her things.

Mephistopheles ran into the bedroom before she closed my door.

Traitor cat ...!

Chapter 47

My phone woke me up.

"Where were you last night?" Bonnie demanded.

"Here ... my place," I said.

"I called you four times!" Bonnie said.

"My phone never rang," I said. "Hold on."

I checked my history. Bonnie, Stacy, Lyn, and Julie had each called many times.

"You left messages but my phone never beeped," I said.

"Lyn and Julie are moving in with Stacy," Bonnie said.

"Rosanne told me that on Friday," I said.

"Rosanne's a conductor on the Bismarck Express," Bonnie said. "We're moving them next weekend."

"I'll help ... if I can," I said.

"What does that mean?" Bonnie asked.

"I have a houseguest," I said.

"Emerson ...?"

"No. She's sort of ... *Emerson's stepmother.*"

Bonnie laughed.

"Come to check you out?" Bonnie asked.

"Bonnie, this is serious," I said. "I don't think Emerson will stay with me ... if she disapproves."

"I'll let the others know," Bonnie said. "When can we meet her?"

"I don't know," I said. "I just ... found her on my doorstep. I didn't know she was coming. I've no idea how long she'll stay ... but it may be some time."

"Good," Bonnie said. "Invite her to Arnold's ..."

"Bonnie, she's old, she's stubborn, and she's the closest thing Emerson has to family," I said. "I can't promise anything ...!"

"You've done nothing to be ashamed of, have you?" Bonnie asked.

I didn't know how to answer.

"What've you done ...?" Bonnie demanded.

"I can't talk ... now," I said.

"If she doesn't come to us, eventually ...," Bonnie began.

"Please don't," I said. "I need to handle this."

"All right," Bonnie said. "Call if you need help. And don't forget ... you will tell me what happens."

No coffee. Yawning, I walked into the kitchen, reaching for some cola when Mephistopheles came running in. I fed him dry, then heard Lucinda in my bathroom. I slipped into my room and fetched clean clothes.

Lucinda glanced at my cola and hissed pure displeasure.

"Groceries before stories," Lucinda said.

Before we left, Lucinda explored my kitchen and, without asking, threw out a lot of my stuff, including old spices and anything past its expiration date. When we got to the supermarket, she led the way up and down every aisle, scowling at almost everything, and spent eternities selecting chicken, meat, rice, eggs, fruits, and many vegetables, which soon comprised most of our cart. She wiped spice jars with a clean Kleenex and then sniffed each, choosing the best by the smell of their bottles. Checkout totaled to over $160, more than I'd ever spent on groceries, yet I didn't argue. I only hoped she knew how to cook all this food; I couldn't even name half of it.

I carried up all the bags while Lucinda cooked breakfast. Thirty minutes it took her, yet then I ate the best meal of my life; eggs rich with spiced vegetables glazed with a sauce like none I'd ever known.

"This is fabulous!" I exclaimed. "This recipe must be worth a fortune!"

"Life is made to be lived, not bought ready and microwaved," Lucinda said.

"It's mostly a priority of time," I said.

"Time shouldn't be your only priority," Lucinda corrected me. "Our time is limited; what we choose to do with it isn't."

"What should I be doing ...?" I asked.

Lucinda looked long at me, and then her voice suddenly softened.

"A sailor once loved the sea," Lucinda said. "He delighted to tell everyone he drank with about the ship that he'd someday command, and happily his brother sailors drank to his great dream. He worked hard, caught many fish, saved his money, and finally bought the ship he most-desired. Bursting with pride, he quit his job and sailed off, determined to never again work for any master but himself. He quickly succeeded. His skills and the sea provided all. He sailed to distant ports to sell valuable catches. Yet, alone on the sea, many years passed where he laughed not once. Finally the sailor sailed home, sold his boat, sought out his former master, and resumed his old job. Again he worked for a master, yet every night he laughed and sang with his brothers, immensely happy."

Lucinda stared at me expectantly.

"Well ...?" she asked.

"Emerson said you were a storyteller," I said.

"What did you think of my story?" Lucinda asked.

"Nice," I said.

"Nice ...?"

I hesitated, fearful of insulting.

"It's a simple story," I said. "A sailor thought he wanted more; found out that he was wrong,"

"Is that all my story means to you?" Lucinda asked.

"What more should it mean?" I asked.

"Have you never wanted something, then found that you desired something else?" Lucinda asked.

"I wanted to escape Emerson, then I didn't," I said.

"What changed your mind?" Lucinda asked.

"I got to know him," I said. "We slept together. I still wonder if he arranged that ..."

"Who paid for your drinks that night?" Lucinda said.

"I ... don't remember," I said.

"You wanted to escape Emerson; my sailor wanted his own ship," Lucinda said. "You both learned something, didn't you?"

"Not the same way," I said. "I wasn't looking for Emerson ..."

"You didn't want a relationship?" Lucinda asked.

"I thought Emerson was stalking me," I said.

"So, what did you learn that the sailor didn't?" Lucinda asked.

"First impressions can be wrong," I said.

"Who's first impressions?"

"Mine," I said. "I learned ... that I can be wrong."

"I've told that story many times," Lucinda said. "Each listener sees in it a reflection of themselves, and learns something different."

"But ... I already knew that I'm not perfect," I said.

"You strummed a fate-path without knowing what effect your involvement would cause," Lucinda said. "If you knew that you weren't perfect, why did you do it?"

I bowed my head.

"Lectures don't teach," Lucinda said. "I tell stories; what you learn from my stories you learn from yourself."

"Thank you for helping me learn," I said. "But how do I discover the consequences of ... plucking a fate-path?"

"My sailor got his boat; only then did he learn," Lucinda said.

"So I must ... fail first ...?" I asked.

"Fate-paths shouldn't be toyed with blindly," Lucinda said.

"You're the most powerful magician, aren't you?" I asked. "Emerson said you're ... like a leader."

She looked at me and smiled.

"A wealthy man once lost his beloved wife," Lucinda said. "In his grief, he sought relief, offering great reward for succor. He traveled far and visited holy men, yet none cured his anguish ... so he kept his gold to

409

himself. Finally he came to a village to seek a legendary holy man, but their wise one had died weeks before. Without their leader's aid, the village had lost its way, and lacked the means to survive. Their children were starving. Feeling pity, the wealthy man purchased them food, spending all his gold to alleviate their suffering, and used his wisdom to help them restore their way. The gratitude of the people cured his grief forever, and he remained with them happily for the rest of his days."

She smiled and looked up at me.

"The healing that he needed was helping others," I said.

"But ... what if he'd arrived at the village before their wise one died?" Lucinda asked.

"Then he would've ... never been healed," I said.

"Think of that before you look up to leaders," Lucinda said.

I nodded. Lucinda looked contented.

"We'd better wash these dishes," Lucinda said.

"I have a dishwasher," I said.

"That would save you time, but which will clean your dishes best?"

I washed our dishes in the sink and she dried. However, as soon as we finished the dishes, she began slicing vegetables.

"We just ate ...!" I said.

"These need to simmer for hours," Lucinda said.

Half an hour later, Lucinda suggested we leave.

"To where?" I asked.

"To help your friends," Lucinda said. "Lyn and Julie are packing, are they not?"

I didn't bother to ask how she knew that. I called Bonnie and told her where we were going, then stopped at a local liquor store to collect cardboard boxes. We got ten large boxes; no more would fit in my car.

Julie thanked us and welcomed Lucinda. I described her as part of Emerson's extended family, and she offered to help wrap glasses and plates. Her kids stared; old black women weren't commonplace in North Dakota, yet she smiled at them as she worked.

I took several boxes and the kids into their room and helped them pack their toys. Julie attacked a closet stuffed to the ceiling.

Hours later, we stopped for a break.

"We need to get back," Lucinda apologized to Julie. "We left something simmering."

"You're a godsend," Julie said.

We left them standing before a wall of stacked, sealed boxes, and drove back to my apartment.

"That went well," Lucinda said.

"Yes," I said, glancing at her. "Why ...?"

"To avoid talking," Lucinda said. "Like a good meal, stories take time to properly digest."

"The sailor story or the old man seeking healing?" I asked.

"Yes," she said. "It's also important you learn to trust me. Support from your family will make that easier."

"We're not related," I pointed out.

"Families of friends are more important than family or friends," Lucinda said.

"What if they're family and friends?" I asked.

"How are they not included in 'families of friends'?" Lucinda asked.

We hurried up to my apartment, and Lucinda rushed into the kitchen. Her simmering pot filled the air with a savory seasoning, as if walking into a fog of steamy, rich soup. To my surprise, she pulled out more pots, rinsed brown rice, and pulled a paper-wrapped package of large shrimp out of the refrigerator with a sigh.

"Florida has better shrimp than North Dakota," Lucinda said.

"We have better steaks," I said.

"That's for dinner," Lucinda said.

Half an hour later, Lucinda's lunch topped her breakfast.

"You eat like this every day?" I asked. "I'll gain twenty pounds!"

"Not on my cooking ... unless you eat until you're stuffed," Lucinda said.

"But it's so good ...!" I said.

"Then I'll cook smaller portions," Lucinda said. "Always eat like a bird if you hope to fly."

"My heart will break out of sympathy for my stomach," I said.

"Unlikely," Lucinda said.

"Can I have another story?" I asked.

"Are you finished contemplating the last two?" Lucinda asked.

"I'm not sure," I said. "Perhaps we could just talk."

"About what?"

"About magic."

"You killed someone ... and want me to teach you more ...?" Lucinda asked.

"I didn't mean to," I insisted.

"If you learn to put on a parachute, are you ready to jump out of a plane?" Lucinda asked.

"Well, you need to know how to land, too," I said.

"However, you learned how to sense a fate-path, and without hesitation decided to strum one," Lucinda said.

"Emerson taught me," I said.

"Would you let one child teach another child how to shoot a gun?" Lucinda asked.

"I should've come to you," I admitted.

"You should've explored every step fully before you took the next," Lucinda said. "You trusted him more than you should've. Ah, that's always been Emerson's worst failing; he jumps blindly."

"Like ... into relationships?" I asked.

"I can't track records that don't exist," Lucinda said.

"He told me that I was his first ... long-term," I said.

"Long-term ...?" Lucinda chuckled. "He may call two months long-term. Why do you ...?"

"I told him that we were going too fast," I said.

"You deferred to his thinking because he knows magic?" Lucinda asked. "Who's more experienced in long-term relationships?"

"My longest was almost five years," I said.

"Still short-term to my mind," Lucinda said. "However, your knowledge is greater; you should've made him comply."

"Emerson seems so ... in control of everything," I said.

"The best stage magicians do," Lucinda said. "It's their most-important illusion."

After lunch, we hand-washed the dishes again. My mouth was still dancing from the taste of shrimp. I couldn't wait for dinner.

My phone rang. *Emerson.* I put it on speaker.

"Be careful what you say," I warned Emerson. "I'm not alone."

"Bonnie ...?" Emerson asked. "Lyn ... Julie ...?"

"Good to hear your voice, Emerson," Lucinda said.

"Lucinda ...?!?"

"You remember my name," Lucinda grinned at me. "A pity you didn't remember my stories ..."

"I do ...!" Emerson insisted.

"Then you should've taught them to her," Lucinda said.

"I'm not a storyteller," Emerson said.

"Then maybe you shouldn't be teaching," Lucinda said.

"What didn't I teach?" Emerson asked.

"Patience," Lucinda said.

"I told her to go slow!" Emerson insisted.

"What proofs had you that she learned ...?"

Silence ...

"Penelope, tell him," Lucinda said.

I hesitated, unwilling, but she lowered her brows.

"David's death ...," I confessed. "I ... I did that."

More silence ...

"Accidentally ...!" I added.

Dead silence ...

"Lucinda, you're not there to ... *evaluate* ...?" Emerson's voice sounded frightened. "She's a good girl! I love her!"

"Then you should've listened to her!" Lucinda said. "Love ...? You can't teach what you don't know!"

"I'm ... doing the best I can," Emerson said.

"Stalking ...? Seducing ...?" Lucinda asked. "Love is neither. Your failure made me come here ... to clean up your mess."

"Please, be nice to her ...!" Emerson begged. *"Please ...!"*

"You've left me a lot to undo," Lucinda said. "Now you must learn patience. Penelope will call you after I depart."

"When will that be ...?" Emerson asked.

"Good-bye, Emerson," Lucinda said.

Lucinda gestured for me to hang up.

"Penelope, I love you!" Emerson shouted as I held my finger pointed at 'End'.

I glanced at her. She repeated her gesture. I pushed the button and hung up.

"That boy needs hard lessons," Lucinda said.

"What is ... *evaluate?*" I asked.

"That's why I'm here," Lucinda said. "Others have abused what Emerson taught you. He abused it himself. You knew that, yet you trusted him."

"It's ... complicated," I said.

"Sleeping with your teacher usually is," Lucinda said.

"He was the only teacher I knew," I said.

"You met Susan, I believe," Lucinda said.

"Emerson seemed determined to keep us apart," I said.

"And that wasn't a red flag ...?" Lucinda asked.

I bowed my head and said nothing. Lucinda sighed deeply.

"A man sat at a bar where deep discussions were common," Lucinda said. "He analyzed and deconstructed everyone's arguments using what he called 'logic'. One night, a woman told him that she'd taken 'Logic 101' in college, and this man's idea of logic wasn't valid. He argued, saying that he didn't need to take a college course to understand logic. So she asked him to solve a simple trigonometry equation, since he could obviously come up with the right answer whether he'd studied trigonometry or not."

I ran her story through my head several times.

"I don't get it," I confessed.

"In this story, are you the woman ... or the man?" Lucinda asked.

My heart sank.

"The man," I admitted.

"Doubtless the man knew a general definition of logic ... which hardly made him an expert," Lucinda said. "Before he attempted to analyze the arguments of others, what should he have done?"

"Fully learned what he was doing," I said. "You're right; I shouldn't have tried magic I didn't fully know. I should've let you teach me."

"I'm no teacher," Lucinda said. "Teachers infuse facts, not wisdom. I'm a storyteller. I make you judge what you think you know; wisdom is learned from within."

"I'll learn your stories," I promised.

"No more tonight," Lucinda said. "Three in one day; you've enough to think about. Would you mind if we watched Jeopardy?"

"Sure," I said, and I reached for the remote control.

Lucinda's thin-sliced, blackened steaks were so delicious I might've been tasting meat for the first time. Yet we had almost no conversation. I described my relationship with Emerson in greater detail, hoping she'd forgive me.

Mephistopheles spent the evening in her lap, ignoring me.

I feared her evaluation.

Chapter 48

My anticipation of another perfect breakfast heightened when I awoke to find Lucinda in the kitchen wearing a green nightgown and robe. The oven was on, and something smelled delicious. When she opened it, she took out two steaming pastries.

She set one pastry before each of us. The bread was toasty brown, steaming, and the fruity topping cupped in its middle bubbling hot. Yet both looked tiny.

"Begging your pardon ... is this all?"

"Always eat like a bird ...," Lucinda repeated.

"... if you hope to fly," I finished.

"I would rather not be guilty of your unwanted pounds," Lucinda said. "Besides, I would not wish you so full as to snore in church."

"Church ...?" I asked.

Lucinda looked surprised.

"Each to their own," Lucinda said. "Our beliefs construct the Universal Consciousness, not just magicians; everyone."

"Emerson told me you'd say that," I smiled.

"His memory is spotty," Lucinda said. "Sieves hold more water."

"Emerson isn't without ... virtues," I said.

"Virtues ...?" Lucinda laughed.

"He has a good side," I said.

"You love him ...?"

"I ... can't name a man I've cared so strongly for," I said.

"He does have natural charms ... under which too many have fallen," Lucinda said.

"He believes we are ... fated, he and I," I said.

"He takes the wrong lesson to heart," Lucinda said. "Fate is our plaything. Magicians may see better, yet only the watchful choose their way. If his beliefs lead him to be an honest husband ..."

"We haven't talked marriage," I said.

"Emerson has never been one to do anything halfway," Lucinda warned.

I swallowed hard.

"If you wish to attend church, we'd best hurry," I said.

"If you wish to avoid a subject ... you need only say so," Lucinda grinned.

We ate quickly and left the dishes on the counter. I fetched clothes, then vacated my bedroom so that Lucinda could dress.

At ten o'clock, we attended a Catholic mass. Lucinda was Southern Baptist, yet she didn't care; she wanted an hour to dwell upon the Universal Consciousness that she believed each of us contributed to. I sat beside her, ignoring my silenced phone, which kept lighting up with calls from Lyn.

After church, we sat in traffic for ten minutes to escape the parking lot, then headed home. While waiting, I returned Lyn's calls; she wanted to meet Lucinda, and overhearing, Lucinda suggested that we help her pack today. I conveyed this to Lyn and she thanked us.

We changed clothes, and then stopped at two different stores to get more boxes, and then drove to Lyn's. She welcomed us with cold beers and greeted Lucinda as she would her own grandmother.

"So honored to have you here," Lyn said.

"Any friend of Emerson is my kin," Lucinda said. "Whatever an old woman can do ..."

"Your company is enough," Lyn said.

"No, these old bones need work to keep them moving," Lucinda said.

Lyn's apartment was smaller than Julie's, and she had no children, yet she owned no less. She and I cleared a space to stack newly-packed boxes, and still we walked down aisles of piles. Within three hours, every box that we had was packed full, and her piles were only halved. Yet we had two new large piles of bags; garbage and recycling.

"Stacy is cleaning her place," Lyn said. "She's talked to David's parents, and she's sorting his things for anything they might want. She also asked about his first wife."

"What did they say?" I asked.

"They learned that he was married only when his first wife sued him for divorce," Lyn said. "They never met her."

"David liked secrets," I said.

"Secretive men make untrustworthy husbands," Lucinda said.

"He proved that," Lyn said. "I think I'll take a load over there and empty some boxes tonight."

"We need to go home and eat lunch," I said.

"Julie is getting off work in an hour," Lyn said.

"Bonnie will be done with her son's soccer by then. Maybe we should all meet at Arnold's?"

"I think we need to eat soon," I said.

"I'm willing to eat at Arnold's, if we don't wait," Lucinda said.

"They won't mind," Lyn insisted. "Don't wait for me; I'll be there before them ... and I'll call to make sure they hurry."

"Are you sure?" I asked Lucinda. "Arnold's food can't equal yours."

"We wouldn't have time for what I'd want to cook," Lucinda said.

"Go," Lyn ordered me.

Ten minutes later, Nancy, Kathy, and Joel cheered as we entered.

"Lucinda!" Nancy held out her hand. "So good to meet you!"

"You know me ...?" Lucinda asked.

"She's unfamiliar with the local train," I said.

"We heard about you from Julie," Kathy said.

"Shall we sit with your friends?" Lucinda asked me.

"I can't ask you to sit on a barstool," I said to Lucinda.

"I've been doing that since before you were born," Lucinda asked. "Iced tea first."

Katie was behind the bar, not Rachel, and she had Lucinda's iced tea on the bar before she climbed atop her stool; Joel and I stayed poised to help if she needed it, yet she managed expertly. I asked for a beer and menus.

Everyone was happy to meet Lucinda and, after we ordered, Nancy asked how she knew Emerson.

"I met Emerson shortly after he started doing his

magic act," Lucinda said. "He was far too young to be in any bar, one a most disreputable hostelry. When not getting into fights, he was tall and handsome; drunk women threw themselves at him, and he was headed for a life of gambling and depravity. Yet I sensed something worthwhile in him. We started to talk every day. He tried to avoid me, but coincidences kept bringing us back together. Eventually he began to listen, and we grew close."

"When did he begin his magic act?" I asked, trying to keep the conversation away from *coincidences.*

"He always knew some card tricks, and was clever with sleight of hand," Lucinda said. "He'd briefly known a magician who'd taught him several tricks. One night an entertainer, a juggler, I believe, became violently ill, and couldn't perform. Emerson had been making cards appear and disappear for a ... mostly-undressed dancing girl. The proprietor offered to cover his bar tab if he'd do his act for everyone."

"That must've been some show," Kathy said.

"I'm more interested in the mostly-undressed dancing girl," Joel grinned.

"No more beer for you," Katie reached for his glass, but Joel snatched it off the bar.

"I took him to a magic shop not far from the Vegas strip," Lucinda ignored Joel. "I wanted to channel his ... proclivities ... into something constructive. He liked attention and fooling people; the tricks I bought him let him do both. After that, he just ... succeeded. Word got around, and another bar offered to pay him more than free drinks."

Our food arrived and our fast ended.

"Forgive us," I said, starting to eat. "We were helping Lyn pack this morning."

Jay Palmer

Nancy, Kathy, Joel, and Katie kept the
conversation going, giving us time to eat. Unfortunately,
my promotion was now well known, and my personal
corporate ladder was their new favorite topic. Between
mouthfuls, my denials fell unheeded on their plans for
my sudden wealth, and with Emerson at my side, soon
they had me elected mayor of Bismarck; even Lucinda
laughed.

Lyn walked in, and not much later, Julie arrived
with her kids, Bonnie with hers, and Stacy strode in
wearing a new red leather vest.

Finished eating, Lucinda and I abandoned the
bar to sit with them at Arnold's largest table.
Introductions were made, and Bonnie and Stacy
welcomed Lucinda to our family. Mike fetched their
kids waters and a basket of french fries and began taking
orders from the colorful kid's menus.

Nancy, Kathy, and Joel joined us. The afternoon
became a party, cell phones came out, and within an
hour, Arnold's was packed, every table filled and
whispers impossible to hear. Mike ran about frantically,
and Katie called in two more waiters to deal with the
unexpected crowd. Everyone wanted to meet Lucinda,
and I could barely get near enough to hear what they
were saying.

In the early evening, we snuck out and drove
home.

"You have wonderful friends," Lucinda said.
"Their loyalty to you ... to each other ... is refreshing."

"They're the world's best pains-in-the-ass," I said.

"I miss small towns," Lucinda said. "I love my
family, but living in Florida ... it's too hot."

"Our summers are no picnic," I said.

"Still, where people treat you like family; that's

422

home," Lucinda said.

"When do I get another story?" I asked.

"At dinner," Lucinda said. "You haven't tasted what I can do with chicken."

My mouth watered.

Fifty minutes after I got home, I sat down to a spicy pineapple and red peppers baked chicken that tasted divine. I almost refused to eat her brussel sprouts, which I'd never liked, yet I risked a bite and found them more than acceptable. I surprised myself by eating them all.

"I love Bonnie and Julie's kids," Lucinda said. "Do you hope to have children someday?"

"I've ... never discussed it with Emerson," I said. "Wow! Sorry for that presumption. I do want ... a family."

"Once there was a village that, every summer, sent its oldest children to die in a Valley of Dread," Lucinda said. "Chosen by their village chief, each child was taken by warriors and abandoned there. While the valley was rich with fresh fruits, it was dangerous. Monsters roamed it, constantly chasing the children. Fortunately, the monsters were slow and easy to evade. However, eventually each child grew tired of running, picked up a stick or stone, and turned to fight. When this happened, they were captured by the monsters, who carried them back to their Fortress of Terror. There the monsters removed their disguises; they were really warriors of the village. As each child had found the courage to fight, they were welcomed and blessed. They were trained in combat skills and given secret knowledge, and finally these brave children were appointed warriors. After serving their time hunting and protecting the borders of their land, these warriors were released to return to their village, where they would marry and raise children of their own."

I paused to consider my response.

"Children must ... be given the chance to find their way," I said.

"Only children ...?" Lucinda asked.

"I didn't mean to kill David ...!" I shouted. *"Those kids were given training ...! I wasn't ...!"*

"How would you suggest magicians be trained?" Lucinda asked.

"I don't know ... a school, a book, ...!" I said.

"Our only protection is secrecy," Lucinda said. "Imagine if professional criminals learned what you could do, and threatened to kill your friends if you didn't work for them. It's happened before."

"What happened ...?" I asked.

"The criminals shot each other," Lucinda said. "Quite a coincidence ..."

"What about the magician they captured ...?" I asked.

"He never used his power again," Lucinda said. "The point is: the more we're visible, the greater our risk."

"Emerson's highly visible," I said.

"Emerson maintains our illusion that magic is false," Lucinda said. "You should hear the first story I told him."

"Oh, please tell ...!" I said.

Lucinda smiled.

"A star shined bright in the sky," Lucinda said. "It's light gleamed across the universe, yet it was sad, feeling unnoticed, lost among the millions of other heavenly glows. To gain attention, the star exploded, a super-nova so bright that it dimmed every star near it.

Countless eyes looked up to see its brilliance shine throughout its wide galaxy. Then it was no longer sad, nor joyous, nor seen. No one ever noticed it again."

"Did your story help Emerson?" I asked.

"It helped open his mind," Lucinda said. "Minds are like flowers; they can't remain closed and bloom."

"You had a good effect on him," I said.

"I'm surprised you two have lasted this long," Lucinda said. "You're the first girl he's been serious about."

"He's ... been surprisingly nice," I said. "Lyn and Julie dream about meeting a man like him."

"A young man once dreamed of the perfect girl," Lucinda said. "He knew everything about her, from the bright red of her hair to the hazel-green of her eyes, the freckles on her cheeks, her favorite book, favorite song, and even what fashions she preferred. She was wise and skillful in many arts. She loved theater and music. Every night, as he drank, he'd describe her to his friends, who laughed and claimed that she didn't exist. Yet, one day, perfect in every detail, she walked into his life. She was everything that he'd dreamed of, and matched his description impeccably. In front of his friends, he jumped up and introduced himself, and she was quite startled when he correctly described her many accomplishments, passions, and pastimes. He swore to her his undying love. Yet she asked him only one question: 'Such a woman as you describe, what qualities would she desire in the man of her dreams?' Here the young man fell silent, aghast, for he'd only dreamed of his desires, and done nothing to make himself worthy of hers. She thanked him for his introduction, and then turned and walked out of his life forever."

"Ouch," I said. "Will you tell Lyn and Julie that

story?"

"You can," Lucinda said. "I'm more worried about you."

"Me ....?" I asked.

"You know why I'm here," Lucinda said. "You killed a man ... yes, accidentally. However, in all the time I've been here, you've never once expressed any sorrow for what happened."

"I am sorry ...!" I insisted.

"Are you ...?" Lucinda asked. "You didn't like him ..."

"Nobody liked him!" I said.

"Stacy must've ... at one time," Lucinda said.

"Yea ... *when he was lying to her!"* I said.

"Some magicians think we're better than everybody else," Lucinda said. "That type of thinking causes dangerous, hurtful magic ...!"

"I don't think ...! I'm not ...!"

"Would you say that to fighting ducks ... or a man you made spill his coffee? What about the man who missed his flight because you had him strip-searched?"

I swallowed hard, unable to reply.

"Three men once claimed to be the bravest and the best," Lucinda said. "One was a swordsman, and no greater blade-swinger walked any land. Another was the fastest gun, who never once missed his target. The third was massive, with more muscles than the other two combined, and no man had ever out-wrestled him. These three met to challenge each other, yet none would accept, for only in their own fighting style would any accept a challenge. Tired of their boasts, the king commanded that whoever challenged another must duel in the style of he who was challenged. That night, all three fled the town, and departed the kingdom forever, each to a different land. Their names became objects of scorn. All three were branded cowards ... which they were."

"I don't think I'm the best," I argued.

"Not yet," Lucinda said. "Yet ... power is insidious. People change, get too big for their britches."

"Not me," I said. "My friends would stomp me if my ego got too big."

"Once, seven women formed a knitting club," Lucinda said. "For nearly three years, they got together every Tuesday, watched old movies on TV, and knitted. One day, they decided to formalize their friendship. They took a group photo, chose a name, and decided to hold an election to choose their official president. Two women wanted the title, and each spread vicious rumors about the other. The next week they voted, one woman won, and the other stormed out and left their club forever. The new president asked for volunteers to be secretary and treasurer. When two women reluctantly agreed to take those offices, the president assigned them laborious duties. They met only two more times as a club, spent both days arguing, and then these life-long friends broke up and never spoke again."

I stared as she finished her story. I feared to respond. She matched my glare.

"Should I start getting ready for bed ... or are you throwing me out?" Lucinda asked.

"What are you going to tell Emerson ...?" I asked.

"Why would I tell him anything?" Lucinda asked.

"That's why you're here, isn't it?" I asked. "To evaluate me ...? To decide if you're going to break up

427

our relationship ...?"

"That's not what evaluation is," Lucinda said.

"What's evaluation ...?" I asked.

"I told you, the magician who was captured by criminals never used his power again," Lucinda said. "I didn't tell you why: he was killed."

I stared as she bowed her head.

"Are you here to kill me ...?" I asked.

"Do you know how much damage one cruel magician could cause?" Lucinda asked.

"It was an accident ...!" I screamed.

"Put yourself in my shoes," Lucinda said. "What would you do if Lyn learned our power ... and used it to hurt people? We must police our own; no one else can do it."

"I'm not a monster!" I said.

"Most of my stories are about people who changed because they gained power," Lucinda said. "Seven brothers once grew to manhood, working their father's farm. The oldest was the smallest, yet he worked no less than his brothers, for their father was a hard-working man who demanded all chores be shared equally. The family grew wealthy and bought many adjoining farms. Then the father died. In his will, he left the farm to his eldest son. The eldest chose the easiest chores for himself, assigning the hardest work to his brothers. Finally he ceased working altogether. Angry, his brothers abandoned him, and soon his farm fell to ruin, and his wealth was squandered. The vast family farm was sold for a pittance, and the elder son walked away, forever blaming his younger brothers for murdering their family."

Lucinda looked up at me.

"Bonnie would sit on me and make me eat dirt,"

I said. "Yes, she once did that."

"I trust you were both young," Lucinda said.

"We were fighting over Barbie dolls," I said.

"Your extended family is why I'm still undecided," Lucinda said. "I like you, Penelope. I think you're a good person. I think you're good for Emerson. I'm just not sure if you're going to stay good ..."

"I'm trying ...!" I said.

"I think I should go," Lucinda said.

"Have you ... *evaluated me?*" I asked.

"No," Lucinda said. "But I think you've evaluated me. Excuse me; I'll go pack."

"You don't have to," I said.

"I think I do," Lucinda said.

She stood up, nodded to me, and walked into my hall toward my bedroom.

I stared dumbfounded.

What would she do ...?

I grabbed my phone and started to dial Emerson, but then I stopped; he was onstage, doing his act. *I couldn't disturb him ...!*

Lucinda wasn't long. I was still standing in the same spot when she emerged, lugging her heavy suitcase.

"You don't have to go," I insisted.

"Sleeping under the same roof is difficult when both think the other may kill them," Lucinda said.

"I'm not going to kill anyone!" I said.

"All things considered, that's hard to believe," Lucinda said.

"Before you go, please tell me," I said. "How do I explore ... fate-paths?"

"I'm a storyteller, not a teacher."

"Please ...?"

Lucinda sighed deeply.

"The same way you explore anything," Lucinda said. "You expose yourself to it. You examine it fully ... without strumming anything. Search and discover every facet ... including how your presence affects it. Touch nothing until you're sure. Now, thank you for your hospitality, but just by coincidence, an empty cab is about to drive by."

"It was ... until now ... a pleasure meeting you," I said.

She nodded to me, opened my door, and walked out of my apartment. My door closed like a falling guillotine blade. I stood helpless ... ego decapitated.

She was gone!

Chapter 49

Alarm. Slowly I reached over and shut it off.

I hadn't slept a wink. I'd considered calling Emerson several times, but what could I say? I'd hoped to convince Lucinda that I'd be a great wife for Emerson. Now I wondered if I'd live to see another sunset.

After feeding Mephistopheles, I opened my refrigerator and stared at all the food Lucinda had chosen. *Did I dare eat any of it?* I grabbed a can of soda and drank.

Never had I driven so defensively on the way to work. The slightest coincidence could plow a distracted driver into me.

Could she do to another driver as I'd done to David ...?

Doubtlessly.

I wanted to stop for coffee, but I didn't trust any drive-through.

At first I parked in the rear of the parking lot, but then I thought of the long walk, unprotected, so I parked as close as I could, then almost sprinted to the front door.

"Good morn ...!" Rosanne said as I dashed into

my office.

I set my laptop on my desk and leaned against it, breathing heavily. I was almost shaking.

"Penel ...?" Rosanne asked.

I jumped so hard I scared both of us.

"What's wrong?" Rosanne demanded when she caught her breath. "Is it ... Lucinda?"

"How do you know ...?" I started to ask, but I already knew the answer. "She's gone. She left last night."

"Oh!" Rosanne sounded disappointed. "I wanted to meet her ...!"

I didn't bother contradicting her.

Meeting Lucinda carried risks.

"I've got to get some work done," I said.

Rosanne gave me an odd look, then returned to her desk. I sat at my desk, docked my laptop, and stared at my small screen, unable to focus on anything. Finally I went for coffee, wondered if I could trust it, decided that I had no choice, and hurried back to my desk.

I couldn't concentrate. I scanned emails I needed to focus on, yet their letters seemed jumbled, and I marked them unread.

My eyes kept glancing at the clock. Emerson was still asleep.

I needed to talk to Emerson!

I got up to close my door. The less that I saw ...

"Penelope ...?"

I startled as Bessy appeared in my doorway. Her eyes widened.

"Are you okay ...?"

"Sorry," I said. "Deep in thought, I didn't expect ..."

"That's all right," Bessy said. "I just wanted to tell

you; I spoke to Colin about your new monitors. He's approved, but it may be a week or two ..."

"New monitors ...?" I asked. "Oh, yes! Thank you."

"You look like you need coffee," Bessy said.

"Just got some," I said.

"Fine," Bessy said. "I'll let you know when I hear more about your monitors."

"Thanks," I said.

Bessy left, and I closed my door. My heart was pounding. *All I could do was wait.*

At 10:30, I phoned Emerson.

"H-hello ...?"

"Emerson ...!" I couldn't hide the tears in my voice.

"Penelope? Where ... what happened?"

"Lucinda left."

"When?"

"Last night ... while you were onstage. She didn't leave well."

"Are you all right?"

"She threatened me ... sort of."

"Sort of ...? What does that mean?"

"She ... accused me ...!"

"Wait, I just woke up. Take me through everything ... slowly. How ... tell me about David ..."

I began with how I'd stopped for Mexican food on my way home to practice flipping my penny. I told how, right before bed, I'd tried to sense David, wondering if he'd hurt Stacy again. When I found him, I sensed a coincidence that would cause him pain ... and I'd just plucked its strand lightly. I didn't know what it would do.

Emerson kept quiet, letting me speak. I told him

how I'd learned of David's death, feared that I'd killed him, and then how Lucinda unexpectedly appeared. I told him everything she'd said, all her stories, and how she'd arranged to meet my friends, and then accused me and left without any warning whatsoever ...

"I don't know if I killed him ...!" I whispered.

"Calm down," Emerson said.

"She threatened to kill me ...!" I hissed, lowering my voice so Rosanne wouldn't hear.

"Did she ...?" Emerson asked. "Did she really threaten ...?"

"Well, not specifically ..."

"She scared you," Emerson said. "She's good at that. She was born in a shack in Mississippi ... her mother practiced obeah."

"What's obeah?" I asked.

"A Haitian form of voodoo," Emerson said.

"Voodoo ...?" I hissed.

"Don't worry," Emerson said. "It's ... a leftover from slavery. She's older than she looks, and she remembers stories of her mother and grandmother; it's incredible that any of them survived. The conditions of blacks in the Deep South didn't improve for a century after they were freed ... and their stories are terrible."

"Is she going to kill me?" I asked.

"I don't think so," Emerson said. "I'll talk to her. She's been watching over me for six years; she'll listen."

"What if she doesn't ...?"

"Let me deal with her. You need to stop worrying ..."

"How can I ...?"

"Scared people overreact ... and terrible things usually happen because they overreacted," Emerson said.

"I'm scared ...!"

"Obeah counts on that," Emerson said. "You need to relax. I'll call her son and leave a message; he'll call me when she gets back. He's reasonable; we'll work this out."

"But ...!"

"Being afraid puts you in danger ... more than threats," Emerson said. "You've got to trust me."

"I trust you ..."

"Good," Emerson said. "This'll blow over. I'll talk to Lucinda ... find out what she knows ... and how she knows it. As far as I know, no one can tell a manufactured coincidence from a natural one ... it's not possible."

"She hates me ...," I said.

"I'll fix everything," Emerson said.

"Thanks," I said. "I love you, Emerson."

"I love you, Penelope. Don't worry. I've already got my plane ticket. I'll be in Bismarck Friday afternoon."

"I can't wait," I said.

My nerves calmed down by lunch time. Rosanne had brought her lunch, but I offered to buy her anything; she jumped to join me. I drove to a nice restaurant, and we took a booth apart from others.

"Tell me ...!" Rosanne urged.

"Lucinda is an old, black woman from Florida; sorta like Emerson's adopted mother," I said. "She left in a huff. I don't think she likes me."

"Mothers never like girls stealing their sons," Rosanne said.

"She's Emerson's only family," I said. "I fear ... to become family with me, he'd have to give up the only family he's known."

"Give him time," Rosanne said. "I've never yet seen a man turn away from sex."

"That's not Emerson's only reason," I hoped.

"Smart men always have more than one reason for everything, but basically ... they're all men," Rosanne said.

Knowing what she meant, I shook my head.

Some men were more than what they seemed ...!

Back at the office, I called Bonnie.

"How could she not like you ...?" Bonnie demanded. "She seemed so sweet ...!"

"Emerson said he'll talk to her," I said.

"I'll do more than talk to her ...!" Bonnie said.

"You can't beat up an old woman," I said.

"I can growl at her," Bonnie said.

"I don't think she's the 'intimidatable' type," I said. "No, let Emerson handle her."

"What are you doing after work?" Bonnie asked.

"Lyn's ... or Julie," I said. "Packing, hauling boxes. Emerson will be here Friday ..."

"Loverboy's coming home?" Bonnie grinned.

"And I don't want to spend all weekend helping them move," I said.

"I know what you want to spend all weekend doing ...!"

"I'm at work. Fantasize on your own time."

"I always do. Bye!"

Lyn and I made three trips from her house to Stacy's, hauling ten boxes each time. Stacy helped us unload; she was babysitting Julie's kids so that Julie could keep packing. Another pile of boxes already stood in a corner of Stacy's house; David's stuff.

"His parents will be here on Sunday," Stacy said,

looking sad, yet healthier than I'd seen her in a year. "They want to look through his things."

"Do you want company?" I asked.

"I think I need to face them alone," Stacy said. "They always seemed like nice people. They're heartbroken, yet they seem ashamed of David's ... indiscretions."

After dropping Lyn at her apartment, I drove through fast food burgers and fries and headed home. I felt exhausted. I fed Mephistopheles, then turned on an old movie, then kept flipping through channels, disgusted by everything. The old movie finally came back onscreen.

Just my luck; *The African Queen, ... a Bogart movie.*

Chapter 50

Meetings all morning, vague plans for expansion, and I really didn't care.

Lucinda had judged me unfairly ...!

I wasn't a murderess. I'd been given a gun without full instructions; someone was doomed. *I hadn't meant to ...!*

Lucinda's injustice could cost me the first decent relationship I'd ever had. Even if Emerson was wrong, he believed that I was his perfect life-mate; *who was Lucinda to tell him I wasn't ...?*

The Atlanta office had been leased; it was all Bessy Andrews, Colin Mendale, Maria Saviano, George Wilber, and Mark Brown could talk about. Nathan Qui joined us on speaker. Mr. Dawes was absent; he was busy selling his house and packing to move. I listened uncaring during most of it. We never even discussed the salespeople I was trying to hire.

Rosanne and I went to lunch with Michelle; a cute girl who was newly hired to be George Wilber's new secretary. She seemed nice enough, enthusiastic, yet I was glad because she muted Rosanne's intrusive inquiries. The one time Rosanne asked about Lucinda,

I quickly changed the subject to our crappy choices of insurance plans.

When I got back to the office, I saw emails to Rosanne and I; Rosanne had to schedule interviews for the resumes I'd selected. I was to interview each, and if I thought anyone likely, then we'd bring them back for secondary interviews, where Bessy and Colin would meet them.

I closed my door and phoned Emerson.

"Did you talk to Lucinda?" I asked.

"She's probably still on a bus headed home," Emerson said. "Her son, Charlie, said he'd call me the instant he sees her."

"A bus ...?" I asked.

"She hates to fly ... or drive," Emerson said. "She has flown, on emergency, but ... she's old; you can't convince her of anything."

"That doesn't bode well."

"I know how to handle her."

"Who appointed Lucinda?" I asked.

"Appointed ...?" Emerson asked.

"She was chosen by the last enforcer," Emerson said.

"Enforcer ...?" my voice grew shrill.

"Watcher, monitor, call it what you want," Emerson said.

"She told me about the criminals who kidnapped a magician," I said. "She killed all of them."

"She didn't kill anyone ... I don't think," Emerson said. "From what I heard, she tried to rescue the magician, only it didn't work. One of them saw him trying to escape, shot and killed him, and the others were furious. They got into a gunfight ... I don't think anyone survived."

"Not how Lucinda told it," I said.

"Storytellers takes liberties," Emerson said. "She accused me of getting you drunk and seducing you ..."

"Didn't you ...?" I asked.

"You weren't that drunk," Emerson insisted.

"I knew what I was doing, but I'd never had done it without a few drinks," I said. "You were pretty tipsy ..."

"No more than you," Emerson said. "I haven't gotten seriously drunk in years ... it's made me a lightweight."

"So, Lucinda just takes it onto herself to be ... what ...? Moderator ...?"

"Mentor, mostly," Emerson said. "She's retired, has plenty of time."

"How did she know that David had been killed, or that I'd had any part of it?" I asked.

"She's more than three times my age," Emerson said. "She's been doing it longer ... has skills I don't."

"I don't appreciate being spied on," I said.

"You spied on David ... twice," Emerson said. "That's why we need mentors; magicians with no scruples could cause irreparable, wide-spread damage."

"What about a school ... or a manual?" I asked.

"What if the wrong person reads it?" Emerson asked.

"Don't write it like instructions," I said. "You do magic onstage to convince people there's no magic. Write a fictional story describing how it works; no one will believe it."

"Risky," Emerson said. "Think how many people have tried to Force-choke someone since Darth Vader first appeared ..."

"More risky than letting amateurs learn by trial and error ...?" I asked.

"Maybe you should publish that book," Emerson suggested.

"Maybe I will," I said.

"How will you keep non-magicians from reading it?" Emerson asked.

"Crappy writing and lousy characters," I said. "Only those who know it's a manual will finish it."

"Let me read it first," Emerson said.

"I will," I said. "Are your critiques brutal?"

"Real writers love red pens," Emerson said. "They'd rather errors get caught before publication ..."

"Your sex life will get a red pen!" I warned.

"Kinky," Emerson said. "Speaking of which ...?"

"We have to wait until Friday," I said. "What time are you getting here?"

"Let me look," Emerson said. "Flight 3276, arrive local time 2:30 PM."

"I'll pick you up," I promised.

"And take me home," Emerson said. "By the way; expect some boxes soon."

"I'll bring them in," I promised.

"Love you!"

"I love you!"

I hung up, partly reassured.

I couldn't wait for Friday!

I coordinated with Rosanne to schedule preliminary interview dates only after I got back from the Pacific Northwest Medical Research Conference. I allotted an hour for each person, probably thirty to forty minutes talking, plus time to write notes. If I could get them all done on one day then I could take them to Bessy right away.

I also set up a private Sales Events calendar, and entered into it the dates of every medical convention, including location. I color coded all the ones I'd attended yellow, and all the others green. Conflicts became obvious.

Before I left, I felt that I'd really done a full day's work. This was my respite; once I had additional salespeople, I'd be responsible for keeping them trained and busy. Soon I'd look back on these days with longing.

Julie had several friends, including her cute cop friend, helping at her house, but she welcomed me and let me help her pack clothes. William seemed a nice guy, and good-looking, but too busy to talk. We hurried, and each box was whisked to a waiting car, including mine, as soon as it was taped shut.

Taking her kids, we drove three cars and a pickup truck to Stacy's. She wasn't home; Julie told me she had to see a lawyer, not Alexandria, about some legal forms concerning deeds and stocks with only David's name on them. Julie had a key.

Before dinnertime, each vehicle was unloaded, and the men promised to be back Saturday morning to move her furniture. Julie invited me to have dinner with her and her kids, yet I declined, claiming that I had tasks to finish from work.

I went for Chinese food and ate in the restaurant. I hadn't done magic since David. Yet Lucinda's one lesson stuck in my mind.

Expose yourself to it. Examine it fully ... without strumming anything. Search and discover every facet ... including how your presence affects it. Touch nothing until you're sure.

As I picked at my fried rice with chopsticks, I closed my eyes, calmed myself, and opened my senses. Everything looked normal, yet for every movement at every table, I knew a dozen other movements were possible, each in separate timelines. One family was trying to keep their three kids still. One woman was reading a thick paperback that looked like a romance novel. A young couple seemed to be arguing in whispers. Servers were walking around, carrying dishes and pouring tea. I could hear a clatter from busy cooks talking from the kitchen.

Kids were the most antsy, probably the easiest to get feelings from. I focused on the youngest child. She was a fussy little girl, and as I focused on her, I seemed to push into her, her childish wants and aggravations. I let my vision unfocus, reaching for outside influences surrounding her. I felt tiny movements flow around me, around her. She was facing me; her view of me was affecting her, although I was far from her focus of the chair that she wanted to get out of, and the food her parents were trying to force her to eat. I felt numerous timelines ... heart-strings ... fate-paths. Each was similar yet unique; one had her slipping out of the chair, down under the table. Another had her screaming, crying at the top of her lungs. One had her tipping her chair over backwards; I avoided all those and moved on.

Careful not to pluck anything, I examined a thread I liked, where she gave in and ate her dinner. As I'd never tried before, I clamped onto that thread, following it in both directions. One end was its origin; she was hungry, yet she wanted the candy in her mother's purse, not the hot food on her plate. She also hated the TV; it was showing a baseball game, and she wanted cartoons. She liked to dance, which she only did when she was alone, as her mother didn't like it, and punished her for dancing, as she tended to knock things over.

I startled, amazed I'd never thought to sense this deeply on any thread. I suspected that her mother didn't hate dancing, just only noticed it when something broke.

I could resolve some serious parenting issues by telling her parents, but how could I explain knowing ...?

I sensed the other end of the thread; the little girl didn't want to go to bed. Her bedtime was early, not long after dinner, and she equated eating with being put to bed, which she didn't like ... not without a story.

She didn't have the maturity to tell her parents what she wanted.

I felt a disturbance; a new thread appeared. It was ... *me!*

I drew away from her, releasing my senses. She'd noticed me looking at her, and that bothered her; she'd started to cry. Her parents tried to distract and quiet her with a slice of **BBQ** pork; *only I knew how futile their attempt would prove without candy.*

Averting my eyes so that I wasn't looking at her, I focused on the woman reading. She was a middle-aged Asian woman, possibly as old as my mother, and intent upon the novel she was reading. She seemed unlikely to notice me staring at her.

I stared at her and opened my senses. The cords swirling around her were strong, vibrant, and strangely flitting. They seemed shorter, shooting past and ending, with new cords spontaneously creating. Something about them felt familiar, and I chose one at random.

Hot sex ...!

She was spread out on her huge, four-poster bed, surrounded by lace, barely able to breathe in her tight corset. Above her loomed the man who'd thrown her down. He pushed through her thin curtains, his demanding glare staring down at her half-clothed helplessness. His powerful masculinity struck her, breached her reservations, and evoked irresistible yearnings. She couldn't cry out; servants would hear, her mother investigate, and their secret romance be revealed ...! His strong hands seized her, flipped her over, her smooth face pressed deep into her feather pillow and thick quilts. He unlaced her long, stiff corset with unbridled haste. She knew what he wanted, what he craved ... *to end my virginity ...!*

This thread wasn't hers! The book she was reading was a romance novel! She was so engrossed in it that nothing distracted her. I took a deep breath and slid along the thread to its beginning, where I saw a dozen bawdy women, from other romance novels, all seduced and surrendered, and yet each face slowly became hers. Then I sensed real lovers, past sexual memories, and ongoing lusts for more.

With great effort, I slid away from her past triumphs, worried about how easily I could get caught up in fantasy carnal desires, and sought the other end of the thread. Again I saw a bed, only modern, shrouded in darkness, draped in absolute quiet except for a small, soft mechanical buzz emitting from under her thick rose-colored bed spread ...

Pleasure ...!

I released, drawing back, out of her, into myself. My breaths were heaving, my pulse racing; I'd too willingly succumbed to her thread. I didn't want to see more.

Lucinda had been right; I should've explored each sensation completely before I involved myself.

Had I done this, David would still be alive ...!

Chapter 51

"Why are you smiling?" Rosanne asked.

"No reason," I said.

"Excited that Emerson's coming home ...?"

"Relieved that Lucinda didn't break us up."

"Was that a possibility?"

"Ever been hated by a boyfriend's mother ...?"

"She can't hate you," Rosanne said. "What could you've done to earn that?"

"Nothing," I lied.

The Pacific Northwest Medical Research Conference was huge, with representatives from all over the country, including Seattle's own large medical community and the University of Washington Medical Research Department. I spent the morning familiarizing myself with names and faces, most of whom I recalled from other events. We had dozens of contacts I'd need to remember; I'd be incredibly busy.

Rosanne bought me lunch; payback for Monday. I took us someplace less expensive; Rosanne couldn't afford what I could. I'd checked my bank account before lunch; my first paycheck with my new raise had deposited, yet I didn't want to mention it; too many were already curious about what my new salary was. I let her pay; I'd make it up to her later.

"Anything special planned for Emerson's return?" Rosanne asked.

"Nothing I want traveling by train," I said.

"I keep secrets!" Rosanne argued.

"So does everyone else in Bismarck," I reminded her. "Of course, a few deep, never-revealed stories from your past could prove that ..."

Rosanne glared at me. "It's supposed to rain next week."

"I'll be in Seattle, where it's usually raining," I said.

"And Emerson will be here ... all alone," Rosanne warned.

"It's a good thing North Dakota has excellent hospitals," I grinned warningly.

Back in the office, I closed my door and phoned Emerson.

"Tomorrow night's my last performance," Emerson said.

"Hope it goes well," I said.

"We've had packed houses," Emerson said. "But it'll be good to come home."

"Did Lucinda call?" I asked.

"No, but Charlie did," Emerson said. "She got home late last night. He told her to call, but she hasn't."

"Bitch ...!" I mumbled.

"Don't say that," Emerson said. "I told you: I'll handle this."

"All right," I said. "So ... what are you planning to do while I'm in Seattle?"

"When ...?"

"I fly out on Tuesday," I said. "I won't be home until Monday."

"Rent a car," Emerson said. "Maybe I'll check out Minneapolis, see the Plains states ... I've never been to Sturgis ..."

"Sturgis looks like any small town except during its festival," I said. "The Dakotas are great for biking, fishing, and hunting. Do you ...?"

"It's always time to try something new," Emerson said.

"Try fishing."

"You don't trust me with guns and motorcycles?"

"Not for a second," I said. "Joel and Brendan ride and hunt; go with them, if you want to learn. Only fools hunt alone."

"I'll ask," Emerson said.

"Fine," I said. "Just be warned: Rosanne, Julie, Lyn, Gwen, Nancy, and now Stacy; Bismarck's full of lonely girls who know I'll be out of town ..."

"You don't trust me ...?"

"I trust you to avoid ... coincidences ... which might leave you alone with them."

"No fixing flat tires ...?"

"Not on dark, lonely roads," I said. "Nor helping them move heavy boxes, nor investigating strange sounds outside their houses ... not when they're alone."

"Warning received," Emerson said. "You behave in Seattle."

"If I'm in the same hotel as last year, I can walk from my room into the convention center without going outside," I said.

"Good," Emerson said. "Only you'll be two hours behind me; our schedules suck."

Something on my screen flashed.

"Oh, damn," I said. "I just got a meeting invite."

"Right now ...?" Emerson asked.

"No, but I have to read this whole email thread before I go," I said.

"I'd better sign off," Emerson said. "I love you ...!"

"Love you, too. Bye!"

My meeting was with Bessy; we reviewed the resumes of the candidates I'd interview, and created new questions.

Before I left work, I called Stacy.

"How's it going?" I asked.

"David's parents want to spend Sunday night here," Stacy said. "I'll have Lyn and Julie and her kids ..."

"Must they ...?"

"End of the month," Stacy said. "They've already given notice ... and it's a school night."

"Maybe Lyn could sleep downstairs with Julie and the kids ...?" I suggested.

"Something has to happen," Stacy said. "What about you ...?"

"Emerson will be here," I warned.

"An intrusion ...?" Stacy sounded disappointed.

"Definitely," I said. "We haven't ... in weeks. I want them mostly moved before the weekend so I can be with Emerson. Who needs more help?"

"Not sure either does," Stacy said. "Most of their boxes are here."

"Great," I said. "Don't call me on Friday."

"Not even to chat ...?"

"I'm gonna hang up on you!"

Stacy laughed.

"Good-bye!"

On the way home, I stopped for cash for my trip, not wanting to waste time going to the bank while Emerson was here. My new balance; over a thousand more than my usual balance at the end of the month. I drove to the grocery store. Lucinda had filled my kitchen with healthy foods, yet I didn't know how to cook most of it, and wanted frozen pizzas and plenty of beer and wine.

This time I kept my eyes open as I let coincidence choose a good wine. I didn't want to repeat my last disaster.

Back home, I fed Mephistopheles and stared at my TV more frustrated than entertained. I knew how to search coincidences, yet I needed to know more, and that meant practice. I turned off my TV, annoyed that I could still hear muted TV from my neighbors. I turned on some soft jazz, just enough to drown thunderous explosions from one neighbor and bursts of canned laughter from another.

Anticipations; I cleared my mind. Bismarck was the capital of North Dakota, not New York City, but large enough to have millions of random timelines. I reached out, sensing for anything, letting coincidence guide me. At first I felt nothing, yet a whisper seemed to be out there, sensed more than heard. I opened myself fully, letting sensations reach me.

Suddenly, as if breezes had become visible, I sensed coincidences. They were dim, subtle, yet surrounding the city like a fog of ... translucent strings ... moving, writhing, reaching everywhere. I held that level of awareness, as if doing yoga, feeling only my slow breathing. Foggy lines, flowing and wriggling, passed around everyone, penetrating buildings, walls, and cars. Wherever people breathed, coincidences swarmed.

The sheer uncountable vastness of timelines overwhelmed me, yet I didn't break contact. I wasn't trying to touch any of them, just uncover, learning all that I could.

A powerful thread drew my attention. Somehow it felt familiar; I followed it.

Bonnie!

Small surprise; I was connected to Bonnie by almost two and a half decades. Every timeline of hers was connected to mine, however distantly. I traced her thread; she could call someone ... someone I didn't know ... yes, her cousin ... who was thinking about her ... and their friendship would be renewed. Yet that thread writhed untouched; Bonnie wasn't going to call anyone. The sensation aborted; the timeline vanished. She hadn't taken it, and her cousin probably wasn't thinking about her anymore.

I wondered how many of my friends' timelines I could reach. I abandoned Bonnie's, and reached out for other threads, hoping to find my other friends. With practice, I could spy on them.

One thread was intensely strong, but it couldn't be a friend; it was close, very close. It shined above the others, swirling tightly around me, and finally I realized why: it was one of my timelines. I focused on it, a strong, bright coincidence, almost sparking with energy. Strangely, it ended with me breaking all contacts, stopping sensing altogether. I wondered why. I traced its sensations backwards, seeking its origin.

I'd never felt anything so powerful. The thread felt thick, almost as if it was two simultaneous coincidences, both strong as a physical presence. I traced and felt its origin, yet it wasn't a coincidence ... or an occurrence ... or a random chance ...

It was a person ...

Lucinda ...!!!

I startled out of contact, breaking all connections.

Lucinda was spying on me ..!

Had she always been watching me ... since the moment she'd left? Since she'd first learned of me ...?

I sat frozen ... save for soft trembles.

I was being spied upon ... by a powerful, experienced magician ... and there was nothing I could do to stop her!

Chapter 52

The next day I couldn't focus on anything. I tried to list Bessy's suggestions for interviewing each candidate, and couldn't ...

I could almost feel Lucinda watching me.

I didn't dare sense for coincidences. I dared not confront her, and I couldn't stop her from watching me.

Rosanne and I ate lunch late. She had my reservations for Seattle, and I asked her to hold them until Monday.

"Who cares about Seattle ...?" Rosanne asked. "Emerson's coming back! You two seem to be a permanent pair!"

"We're dating ... that's all," I said.

"Looks like more than that," Rosanne said.

"We've only known each other two months ..."

"Have you discussed life-goals?" Rosanne asked. "Kids: lots, few, or no kids ...? Live in Bismarck ...? Buy a house ...?"

"Hoping to choose my gown and veil ...?"

"Can I ...?"

"Jump that gun any higher and you'll break a leg," I said. "We're not engaged ..."

"Would you like to be ...?" Rosanne asked.

"Would you ...?"

"I would be if any boyfriend asked!" Rosanne said.

"How long has it been, over a year ...?" I said.

"Way too long," Rosanne said. "But you know men; they're best if we do their thinking."

"Emerson's pretty smart," I said.

"So, if he asked ...?"

"Depends upon how he asks."

As soon as we got back to the office, I phoned Emerson.

"Hi," Emerson said. "Please hold on."

I sat waiting for two minutes. I heard him talking.

"Sorry; at the post office," Emerson finally said. "I did my laundry yesterday and had to mail these off today. Did my boxes arrive?"

"Not yet," I said.

"I hope they get there today," Emerson said. "Sucks to arrive with no clean clothes."

"Emerson, I don't care about clothes," I said.

"I like the sound of that."

"No, I mean I'm scared ...!"

"Scared ...?"

"Lucinda ...!" I almost shouted. *"Lucinda's watching me ...!"*

"What do you mean ...?"

"I was sensing ... generally, you know, just seeing what I could randomly feel, not touching anything," I said. "I traced down the strongest threads I could find, thinking they'd be my friends ... but I saw ... her! Lucinda ...!"

"Seriously ...?" Emerson asked. "That's quite a coincidence; searching coincidences and randomly striking a ..."

"I don't think it's a coincidence!" I said. "She's spying on me!"

"Look, I wasn't going to say anything, not over the phone ...," Emerson said.

"What ...?"

"I talked to Lucinda ... early this morning," Emerson said. "She's worried, and she doesn't worry easily."

"Why's she worried ...?" I asked.

"About you," Emerson said. "She doesn't think I've taught you correctly ... or that I should've taught you at all."

"Why not?" I asked.

"Most magicians stumble onto their powers," Emerson said. "Some we find, but few get trained from scratch. Most magicians think only those who find magic themselves should be taught."

"Then, why did you teach me?" I asked.

"You figured it out," Emerson said. "What would you have done, in Atlanta, if I hadn't told you?"

"I'd have assumed that you were stalking me ... and never spoken to you again," I said.

"I couldn't allow that," Emerson said. "Look, I think we should talk about this in person."

"Okay."

"And I think you should hold off ... on doing any magic ... until I get there."

"Why?"

"I can't tell you."

"Why ...?"

"To be honest, I'm worried," Emerson said.

457

"You don't think I can handle it?" I asked.

"No, I'm worried for you," Emerson said. "Lucinda can be ... dangerous."

"Did she threaten me?"

"No, but she ... has serious reservations."

"What kind of reservations?" I demanded.

"The kind I don't agree with," Emerson said. "You have a mother; you know what they're like. I argued with her ... we said things I can't say over the phone."

"She said it over the phone, didn't she?"

"Yes, but she can make sure that no one's listening in."

I gritted my teeth. *How powerful was she?*

"Very well," I said. "I'll check your flight schedule and pick you up at the Bismarck airport."

"I'll make it up to you, I promise," Emerson said. "Just ... stay muggle until I see you. Lucinda will come around. Believe me."

"I love you ... and I want to believe you," I said.

"I love you, too," Emerson said. "See you tomorrow."

I hung up disgruntled.

I'm not supposed to do magic ...?

Yet ... what could I do if Lucinda attacked me?

Rosanne cc'ed me on the confirmation emails with my candidates. I ignored them, and tried to focus on reviewing the customers I'd be seeing in Seattle. Still, my thoughts kept falling back on Lucinda.

What would I do if Emerson sided with her ...?

I called Lyn and Julie. Both were mostly packed but needed more boxes.

Leaving work, I stopped at two liquor stores to get enough boxes to fill my car. I dropped half off at each apartment. Both were kneeling on the floor sorting 'junk to save' from 'junk to throw away'. Each babbled over how tired they were and how happy they'd be if they got their full damage deposits back. I was polite but didn't stay and listen to either for long.

I dropped by Stacy's to see if she needed anything. She was frantic, sorting through David's things. Half of her house was spotless, cleaned for David's parents, the other half a mess, piled high with boxes.

"Can you help ...?" Stacy begged.

"Sure," I said, and she pointed me to a tall stack of papers.

"I'm searching for legal forms," Stacy said. "Titles of Ownership for the cars, things like that."

"David kept them?" I asked.

"He said that he did," Stacy sorted through a box of paperwork, one sheet at a time. "Never said where ..."

I attacked a full box, finding bills long paid, mailed advertisements, and newspaper clippings of strange stories.

"I want to have everything when David's parents get here," Stacy said.

"David would've stored them someplace safe," I said.

"I've been through his desk, all of his files, and everything in his office. I found the house papers, everything for our appliances and his power tools, yet nothing for cars."

"Garage ...?" I suggested.

"I hope not," Stacy said. "There're shelves of boxes in there and I've no idea what's in them."

We each sorted into two piles; possibly valuable and recycling. After I finished with one, I started on another, yet with little hope. Eventually Stacy and I finished; we'd found nothing.

"The state has records; you can get copies," I said.

"I don't know where ...," Stacy said.

"Department of Motor Vehicles ... or the place where you buy your tabs ... start there," I said.

"I will," Stacy said.

"Are you looking forward to Lyn and Julie ...?" I asked.

"We'll see how it works out," Stacy said. "Bonnie suggested that we schedule a meeting; a year from now, we'll get together and decide if it's working or not. I'll let them stay at least until then."

"Good idea," I said.

"And if I find a guy they don't like, this time I'll listen," Stacy said.

I didn't bother to mention that Bonnie and I had been equally outspoken about David.

"You need to calm down," I said. "Let's find food."

I called Bonnie to see if she could join us, but she'd already started dinner for her family, so she was stuck at home. I frowned. I'd wanted to see each of them right before Emerson arrived; I only had a few nights before I had to fly away.

We walked into Arnold's to find Rachel alone behind an empty bar. It was unusual, so Stacy and I joined her and ordered beers.

"When's cute magician coming back?" Rachel asked.

"Tomorrow," I said.

"Eager ...?"

"How would you be?"

"Spread-eagle naked atop the sheets with a can of

whipped cream."

"*Rachel ...!*" Stacy squealed, laughing.

"*No ...!*" I stated firmly.

"Try something new," Rachel laughed. "He might like it."

"Sounds wise to me!" Stacy chuckled.

"Smart people never confuse wisdom with sex," I said.

"Smart people need to get laid more," Rachel said.

"Hoping to fuel the Bismarck Express ...?" I asked.

"Better vicariously than none at all," Rachel laughed.

"Find your own man," I said.

"If a real man ever sat at my bar, I would," Rachel said.

"Not if I take him home while you're still working," Stacy laughed.

I shook my head. Lots of men came in here, but most were nightmares. Many only looked at boobs to decide if women were acceptable, and the rest might as well still be surgically-attached to their mothers. Were women any different? After a girl's fifteenth failed relationship, I had to wonder ... *who was the real problem?*

Of course, since high school, I'd had more than my share ...

Stacy and Rachel began comparing and disparaging most of the men we knew. I laughed, but stayed mostly quiet.

Emerson had asked me to stop practicing magic. Whose side was he on ...?

461

Jay Palmer

Chapter 53

Work passed in a miasma of fears, dreams, and distractions. Rosanne told Bessy about Emerson returning, and I confessed that I'd be sneaking out early to pick him up at the airport. We had lunch in; Colin Mendale provided lunch for everyone as a good-bye to Mr. Dawes, who'd be flying to his new position as lead of the Atlanta office. His furniture had been shipped and he'd sold his house. This would be the last time most of the office saw him.

We ate pizza and salads, drank sparkling cider, said good-byes and best wishes, and then went back to work. I didn't close my door. Emerson was flying. The next time that we spoke would be in person.

Rosanne came in to chat right before I left, yet she mostly giggled and wished me the night of every woman's dreams. I packed up early, then slipped out. The airport wasn't far away; I wanted to be early.

I sat for over half an hour in the lobby before Emerson's plane arrived. He came out wearing his white suit, which I hadn't seen him wear since the first day we'd met, his white hat perched on his head. He smiled when he saw me. I had to wait until he could slip through the line exiting. We kissed and hugged long, and I clung to Emerson desperately.

As usual, he had no luggage; I'd moved his boxes into my living room. We walked straight to my car.

"How was your show?" I asked.

"Two weeks, no complaints, and I got paid in full," Emerson said. "There were a few problems; one night I didn't get all the rings linked, but otherwise everything went well."

"What happened to the rings?" I asked.

"My fault," Emerson said. "Rings require expert alignment. Sometimes fingers slip; magicians are still human. Yet I blew it off as a failed marriage and made a risqué joke; more improper than I usually use. The crowd loved it."

"Shame on you," I said.

"I've a lot to tell," Emerson said. "Two old friends showed up on Tuesday; we ate most of our meals together. They've got new ideas on magic ... but we'll talk about that later."

"Why later ...?" I asked.

"It's complicated," Emerson said. "It's going to be a long, serious conversation. I assume we're going to your apartment ..."

"Our place," I corrected.

Emerson smiled widely.

I reached over, plucked his hat off his head, and dropped it onto mine.

"Looks better on you," Emerson said.

Our door was barely closed before we were kissing desperately. Hands fumbled with buttons and zippers, and clothes dropped. Topless, I grabbed his head, shoved his nose between my breasts, and shimmied. Delighted beyond words, Emerson picked me up and carried me to our bedroom.

Our bedroom ...!

I ravished Emerson as I'd never done before. I kissed things I'd never thought I would and encouraged fingers to places no man had ever touched. I'd always been rather prudish, yet no limits stopped me; we rolled and bounced and gasped until we collapsed ... and then we did it again.

Exhausted, entangled, and satiated, we lay afire, our sweaty skins aglow.

"I ... need to go back ... to Vegas," Emerson gasped.

"Why ...?" I breathed.

"So I can come home ... and we can do that again!"

I smiled and traced my fingers across his chest.

"Hungry yet?" I asked.

"I'm scared to answer."

"I could use some food."

"I haven't eaten in hours."

"Shower first ...?"

The shower started everything all over again. Soapy fingers slid and willing flesh yielded. We tried to be quiet, but I felt certain my neighbors knew I wasn't alone. Emerson took advantage of the shower head and pinned me into the corner until I bit back screams. Then I pushed him into the stream and forced him to surrender.

Gorged, dried, and dressed, I drove Emerson for steaks. We tried to hide our telltale smiles, yet even the waitress commented on how happy we looked. We ordered drinks and food, then sat smiling at each other.

"I can't believe how changed you are," Emerson said.

"Me ...?" I asked.

"Nevermind ..."

"No, what do you mean?"

"Well, we've done a lot of things ... but nothing like that," Emerson said. "That was incredible!"

"Are you complaining?" I asked.

"Thrilled beyond words," Emerson said. "I just ... didn't expect ...!"

"Too much for you?" I asked.

"You seem to have survived," Emerson said.

"Maybe we should go home and try again," I said.

"Your bed might not endure," Emerson said.

Our drinks arrived, and we waited until the waitress left.

"So, you didn't tell me about your friends," I said.

"Raphael and Anna," Emerson said. "They're from Austria. They have an entirely new concept of ... what we call coincidences. They don't think they're coincidences at all."

"Not coincidences?" I asked.

"Not even possibilities," Emerson said. "Not alternate realities ... or timelines. They're opportunities ... variations that magicians make happen. Our sensing ... what we're sensing is ... our own predictions, created by what our subconscious' think might happen, and our beliefs affects them greatly. We, magicians; our real talent is that we cause deviations in the natural timeline, which branches because of us, our knowledge of them, and then we drive reality toward our preference."

"Is that possible?" I asked.

"As much as any explanation," Emerson said. "Who knows what's true?"

"I wish it were," I said. "Maybe I could keep Lucinda from spying on me."

"She's not spying," Emerson said.

"You haven't told me what she said ... except 'serious reservations'."

"She's worried," Emerson said. "She doesn't think I had the right to teach you ..."

"You should've told me," I said.

"There're no rules," Emerson said.

"Lucinda disagrees," I said.

"I had every right," Emerson said. "Our only requirement is that we can't make our abilities public."

"What if someone did ...?" I asked.

"We'd all go after them," Emerson said. "Not at once. Chances are Lucinda would go first ... probably wouldn't need a second."

"What would she do?" I asked.

"Try to talk to them," Emerson said. "Undo the damage, admonish the mistake."

"What if they refused ...?" I asked.

"Magician's Challenge," Emerson said.

"Fight with magic ...?" I asked.

"It hasn't happened often, but ... as you learned, we can be dangerous," Emerson said.

"As I learned ...?" I asked.

"Don't take offense," Emerson said. "Lucinda's old; you can't convince her of anything."

"Lucinda said *'as I learned'?*"

"Not exactly ..."

"What ... exactly ...?"

"This isn't the place ...!"

"What did she say ...?"

Emerson started to speak, hesitated, then lowered his voice.

"She's worried you're ... abusive," Emerson said.

"Abusive ...?" I was shocked.

"You know what happened ...!" Emerson whispered.

"That was an accident!"

"She blames me, too," Emerson said.

"So ... is she going to spy on me forever?" I asked.

"Only to see if you're doing ... you know," Emerson said.

"I'm not allowed to do ... you know ...?" I asked.

"Well, I wouldn't put it that way ..."

"How would you put it?"

Emerson bowed his head.

"Do you really need it?" Emerson asked. "You got along fine without it ..."

"Why should I stop?" I demanded. "Just 'cause some old woman disapproves ...!"

"Not for long ...!" Emerson said.

"How long?"

"I don't know. Enough for her to cool off."

"For the rest of her life ...?"

"Not that long," Emerson said.

"How do you know?" I asked. "Gonna use 'M' against her?"

"She's ... like my mother ...!" Emerson said.

"You expect me to stop doing ... 'M'?" I demanded.

"I'll change her mind," Emerson insisted.

"Sounds like you're trying to change mine," I said.

"No, I'm on your side!" Emerson said. "I just want ... a peaceful solution."

"Well, if she's spying on me, I hope she got her

jollies this afternoon," I said.

Emerson's eyes flew wide; he obviously hadn't suspected that Lucinda might've watched everything we'd done.

Chapter 54

Waking up beside Emerson, still wearing my lacy nightgown, felt disappointing. We needed as much time together as we could get; the dangers of long-distance relationships deserved to be feared.

Nothing as unsettling as your first night of only-sleeping.

How could I not do magic? Now that I knew about magic, I'd always miss it. I felt like a blind person suddenly gaining sight ... then asked to walk around blindfolded.

Emerson should be supporting me!

Infinitely slowly I turned my head, trying not to wake him. His mouth hung open limply as he breathed. Even unconscious he was cute; I wanted to play with him like a sculptor with wet clay ... and I wished we hadn't argued.

Two weeks I'd been waiting to have sex with him ... only to ruin our first night!

I couldn't quit magic. I was a magician. The newest, not the best, but I was learning.

If they'd wanted me to avoid mistakes then they should've instructed better ...!

I stared at Emerson for nearly an hour. Then I slipped out and started the coffee pot.

While it brewed, I turned on the TV and put it on a music station, hoping the noise would awaken Emerson. I wasn't a great cook, yet I knew enough to melt butter in the skillet before I added eggs. Emerson still wasn't awake; I stepped back into our bedroom long enough to kiss his cheek. Emerson moaned and began to roll over.

"Breakfast ...!" I whispered in his ear.

Emerson groaned; he worked evenings and was used to sleeping in, and travelling messes up everything. I'd have to leave on Tuesday; I didn't have time to waste.

"Eggs in the skillet ...!" I licked his cheek, and then hurried back to keep the eggs from burning.

I was setting our plates onto the table when Emerson zombie-walked into the kitchen, wearing only boxers, and yawning.

"Coffee ...!" Emerson growled, and I poured the cup in front of his chair and dropped two slices of bread into the toaster.

I felt bad; Emerson obviously needed more sleep. He was only eating breakfast to please me. I smiled; we were trying to get past this.

The coffee helped, but only slightly. Emerson smiled, yet looked haggard. He ate his toast yet only nibbled at his egg.

"Jet lag?" I asked.

"Circadian rhythm," Emerson said. "I rarely got out of bed before you called."

"That would be three hours from now," I said. "You can go back to bed, if you want."

"Will you come with me?" Emerson asked.

"Still love me?"

"Always."

"Let's go."

Snuggling is its own form of heaven. Emerson smiled as he cuddled, yet fell back asleep almost at once. I kept staring at him until I drifted to join him ...

I awoke with Emerson kissing my shoulder as lightly as a breath. We made love as I loved most; slowly, softly, intensely.

We showered together again, mostly kissing under streams of hot water.

Emerson opened all his boxes and dressed while I was still picking out clothes. Then he decided I needed a back-rub, which slowed me even more. He laughed; anything that kept me from putting on clothes he considered a blessing.

I pushed him down onto my bed and gave him a show. I chose some clothes, then dressed like a stripper in reverse, shaking and flexing what I had, to show off every curve. Emerson loved it ... yet he looked concerned.

"What ...?" I asked.

Emerson shook his head.

"Let's not ...," he started, but I cut him off.

"No secrets," I warned.

"Well, I asked you to do that ... in Hawaii ... and in Atlanta," Emerson said. "Remember what you said?"

"We were still new," I said.

"Have you ever done that, or had sex like we did yesterday, before ...?" Emerson asked.

"You seemed to like it," I said.

"Yes, but you used to not like it," Emerson said. "You've become ... more aggressive."

"Is that bad?" I asked.

"It's wonderful, but think what it means,"

Emerson said. "You didn't do these things before you learned magic. Now you do."

"What're you saying ...?" I asked.

"That you're human," Emerson said. "I went through it; every magician does. Abilities are power, and power changes people."

"I've ... changed ...?" I asked.

"You don't need me to answer that," Emerson said.

"Is that what Lucinda said?" I asked.

"In part," Emerson said. "She thinks our power corrupted you."

"I'm not corrupt ...!" I said.

"I don't believe you are," Emerson said. "Yet ..."

"Yet ...?"

"I don't want to keep secrets ... and I hate this one ..."

"What ...?"

"I'm trying to protect you," Emerson said. "Lucinda told me ... either I keep you from practicing magic ... or she will."

"Is that a threat ...?" I asked.

"It sounded like one," Emerson said.

"Could you stop using magic ...?" I asked.

"Probably not," Emerson said. "I've been practicing since I was too young to legally drink. It's second nature now."

"Yet you expect me to quit ...?" I asked.

"No," Emerson said. "I hope you'll ... take a break, stop doing magic ... long enough for me to convince Lucinda that you're trustworthy."

"Lucinda will never like me!" I said. "You call her your mother; mothers don't like women stealing their sons!"

"I'll phone her again today," Emerson said. "Consider my predicament; I'm trying to protect my girlfriend from my step-mother."

"Sucks," I agreed. "Who are you going to choose?"

"You, but I'm trying to fix it so I don't have to cut the only mother I've ever loved out of my life," Emerson said. "Please ... just give me time."

His choice of pleas drove deep.

"I'll try," I said. "However, I can't promise ..."

"I don't want promises ... not that kind," Emerson said.

"What kind do you want?"

"We can discuss promises after Lucinda rescinds her threat."

"What until then?" I asked.

"I've got a month before my next show," Emerson said. "I have to practice my stage magic, a bit every day, yet otherwise I'm yours."

"You may regret saying that," I warned.

Emerson paused to stare.

"My new, aggressive self may think of some novel ways to use you," I smiled.

Emerson suggested going to Arnold's; I agreed. David's parents arrived tomorrow, and Lyn and Julie were moving furniture, so Stacy was busy. Bonnie was either helping them or busy with own her kids, so I knew we'd be safe.

Arnold's was packed; Saturday afternoon brought kids' sports teams, workers enjoying the weekend, and baseball fans needing shots, beers, and wings. We stood behind Gwen, Joel, and Brendan, who had seats at the bar, while Rachel, Katie, Mike, and the rest ran frantically to keep up with orders. It wasn't unusual; Arnold's had more customers than seats.

Emerson posed for photos with locals; the Bismarck Express had celebrated his new residency and everyone wanted to know him. Emerson loved attention; why else would anyone choose to work onstage? He smiled, shook hands, and after a dozen pleas to see magic, Emerson drew out a pack of cards.

He had a woman draw a card from his deck and write her name on it. Then he folded her card in half, quarters, put a paperclip on it to hold it closed, and slipped it into Joel's shirt pocket. He shuffled, drew the wrong card, then flipped it over and showed it was the right card, with her signature still on it. He shuffled and sent the card to the bottom of the deck, tapped the top of the deck; the card appeared there. Then he folded it like the other card, waved his hands and made it disappear, and then reached into Joel's pocket, pulled out the original folded card, and unfolded it. It was the wrong card. Then, out of Joel's other pocket, he pulled out another folded, paper-clipped card, and unfolded it. It was the right card ... with her name still written upon it.

Everyone cheered. Emerson gave her the card as a souvenir, and she hugged him while several were still applauding. I joined in the applause, no idea how he did the trick, but certain he'd known which card she'd choose ... although I couldn't guess how. Yet everyone knew it was a trick, not real magic. Their limited knowledge of slight-of-hand confirmed their belief that all magic was fake.

If I wanted to, I could amaze them ... then I'd get all the attention. Yet I couldn't; I understood the one restriction on real magic ... and agreed with it.

There weren't a lot of places to go in Bismarck. I suggested a movie, but neither of us knew what was playing now and nothing looked exciting. Emerson suggested ballroom dancing, but the Elk's Club only held a few dances a year, and the only local dance venues were seedy bars or ballet schools for kids. One tavern had a live band; Emerson suggested we check it out, but it didn't start until nine. Other than a few museums, the zoo, and two malls, there was no place to go.

We went to the bigger mall, walked around for a few hours, and just had fun. I liked Emerson best when we were doing nothing. He held every door for me, walked holding my hand, and suggested I try on outfits from every window displaying fashions only teenage girls wore. By the time we'd walked half the mall, I knew he was just joking, yet he suggested it so playfully that I could only laugh.

I wondered what he'd do if I'd agree to try on one of those skimpy, flesh-showing outfits ... just to tease him ... and decided it wasn't a good idea. He'd probably buy it, and even the new, aggressive me wouldn't wear teenage fashions in public.

To appease him, I agreed to let him drag me into Victoria's Secret. He liked everything see-through, and I only got him out by suggesting that he could see whatever he wanted if he didn't make me buy anything today.

We headed back, but suddenly I stopped. Emerson did, too. We glanced at each other; *we didn't want to go on.*

"Coincidence ...?" I asked.

"Clearly," Emerson said. "We don't want to ... well, let's go into another store."

We walked into a store selling videos. I let Emerson lead; he walked past the New Releases and Adventure straight to Comedy and Classics. I wanted to see what he liked, so I watched him closely. He scanned through videos row by row, and I ran a finger down each row, looking mostly to see what caught his eye. He also paused and scanned all the Disney videos.

"Animated ...?" I asked.

"You probably saw all these when you were little," Emerson said. "I don't know how to explain this; I've always felt I was robbed of my childhood. I enjoy watching kid's movies ... makes me feel I'm ... getting back at the foster care system."

"Pick one," I said. "My treat."

"Only if you pick one," Emerson said.

We left with four videos, a romantic comedy, a Bogart movie, and two classic Disney films.

"Path clear?" I asked.

"Do you ...?" Emerson started. "Sorry. I don't feel anything."

"What do you suppose it was?" I asked.

"No idea," Emerson said. "Could've been a possibility that never happened ... because we were supposed to be a part of it, and we went shopping instead."

"How am I supposed to not do something that comes naturally?"

"I don't know," Emerson said. "I've known Lucinda a long time. I've never known her to be unreasonable before."

"So, you think she's being unreasonable ...?" I asked.

"Of course," Emerson said. "But I'm no match for her. Neither are you."

"You're worried for my safety ...?"

"Scared to death."

I wanted to have sex with him right there.

Back at our house, we cuddled on our couch and watched a Disney movie. Emerson got frisky, but I refused ... *not in front of Disney!*

Afterwards, Emerson suggested that we eat in. I took him into my kitchen and showed him all the stuff Lucinda had bought; Emerson knew less than I did about cooking, so we decided to eat out and hear the band.

"Can your friends cook?" Emerson asked.

"Are you kidding?" I asked. "You tasted Stacy's cooking. Bonnie's a master chef. Lyn and Julie are virtually gifted ..."

"Be a shame to let all this food go to waste," Emerson said. "Let's drop it off at Stacy's; they'll know how to cook it."

I kissed him, and half an hour later, we carried five bags into Stacy's front door. Julie was already cooking, yet they gladly accepted the food. Their furniture had been moved in; the house was a wreck, yet everyone was smiling. They invited us to stay, but we begged off; this was their first night living in the same house. I told them that we had to get to the bar early to get good seats, and they were still arguing as I pulled Emerson outside and back to my car.

We didn't dance much. To be honest, the band sucked. The food was second rate. The bar stank of stale beer and cigarettes.

We went home early, showered together, and then made love for hours.

Jay Palmer

Chapter 55

I let Emerson sleep until 10:00 AM, and then crawled under the sheets and awoke him in perfect girlfriend style. He reciprocated, and we didn't shower until after 11:00.

We ate English muffins with butter and fresh strawberry jam.

"No one can outcook me with a toaster," I smiled.

"What's the agenda today?" Emerson asked.

"Anything you want," I said.

"What are our options?"

"That's the problem with North Dakota. We don't go places ... we get together with friends and family."

"And do what ...?"

"You really don't get Bismarck. We don't do; we become involved in each other's lives."

"Oh, okay," Emerson said.

"Try it before you judge it," I said.

"I'm ... not objecting," Emerson said. "I'm just ... inexperienced."

"City folk are into lots of fast, short-term

relationships," I said. "I know old couples that have been married sixty years."

"Lucinda's the oldest friend I have," Emerson said. "I've known Suzanne nearly as long, but I've only been to Hawaii four times."

"Most of your friends are magicians?" I asked.

"We run into each other when we're doing shows," Emerson said.

"You've never had a close, long-term friend?" I asked.

"Yes, I have!" Emerson argued. "You!"

"We've known each other for less than three months!" I exclaimed. "And we've been apart for half of that!"

"For me, that's a long relationship," Emerson said.

"Look, Emerson, I love you, but we need to talk," I said. "You said you wanted 'a long, possibly permanent relationship'."

"You memorized that ...?"

"I'm a girl. I'm just not sure if you know what a permanent relationship is."

"I'm willing to learn ..."

"It's not just a partnership," I said. "It's a joining."

"Look, I don't have the small-town experience, but I know what I want," Emerson said.

"What do you want ...?"

"I want to know, positively, where I belong in this world," Emerson said. "I don't want my life to be an endless churn of ever-changing coincidences. I want family ... roots ... a home where I belong ... with you."

I stared at him dumbfounded.

"You really are innocent," I said.

"Me ...?" Emerson looked incredulous.

"I'll prove it," I said, and I reached for the phone.

"Lyn, what're ... oh, sorry! Call me when you get off work. Julie ...? I'll call now."

I hung up and redialed.

"Julie, what's up for today? Really ...? Want company? We'll meet you there,"

I hung up.

"Where ...?" Emerson asked.

"The zoo," I grinned. "It's about to close for the year, so Julie is taking her kids. She's in a hurry to get them out; David's parents just arrived. Bonnie may join us later."

"Doesn't Bonnie have kids?" Emerson asked.

"Yes, but they're older than Julie's and hate family outings," I explained.

"I love zoos," Emerson said.

"Let's get dressed," I said. "We need to be there in thirty minutes."

"Shower ...?"

"No time for fooling around," I warned.

"What ...?" Emerson complained. "Not taking advantage of wet and naked is a crime against nature and humanity!"

Twenty minutes later, we locked my door and hurried down the stair. We reached the zoo only a few minutes later. We found Julie and her kids waiting for us just inside.

Most of our day was following Julie as she shouted at her over-excited kids. Emerson held my hand as we walked, yet he looked confused.

"Are all kids like this?" Emerson whispered in my ear.

"No," I whispered back. "Few kids are this well-behaved."

Emerson looked shocked.

We approached the antelopes' pen and I pulled Emerson to the side.

"Really, what's Lucinda going to do?" I asked. "If I do magic, will she kill me?"

"I doubt it, but bad coincidences happen," Emerson said. "I advise you don't."

"Will you be angry?" I asked.

"You're not seriously thinking about it?"

"What's the worst that could happen?"

"I'm afraid to wonder."

"I'm not going to let an old woman rule my life."

"I don't want her to spoil our life."

"We can't let her bully us," I said.

"You know what she's like," Emerson said.

"Maybe you should call her again," I said.

We went to see the otters next. I stared at the tall rock, remembering how I'd lured them all up there. I'd just visualized food up there, that height was the place to be. I closed my eyes, remembering.

Suddenly all the kids began cheering, adults snapping photos.

"Stop ...!" Emerson hissed, and he grabbed my arm.

I opened my eyes; four otters had splashed up onto the tall rock, fighting to dominate it.

I shook my head, clearing my mind.

"I'm sorry!" I said. "I didn't mean to ...!"

All four otters dove off back into the water.

"If you want something, let me do it," Emerson whispered.

I nodded, yet frowned.

"I shouldn't have to ...," I grumbled, yet I acceded.

We sat in the outdoor dining area sipping lemonades while Julie took her kids to stand in the longer line for soft-serve ice cream.

"I'm not really sorry," I said. "I feel like I'm being punished."

"I'll call Lucinda when we get home," Emerson said. "Unless you want me to call now ...?"

"No, later'll be fine," I said.

"So ... how long do relationships go before they discuss ... kids?" Emerson asked.

I stared disbelieving; Emerson seemed so cosmopolitan in a crowd, so masterful on stage ...yet he really knew nothing about relationships.

"There's no time limit ... but not at the zoo," I said.

Emerson nodded as if I'd recited an unspoken rule.

We said nothing more until Julie and her kids joined us with dripping cones.

"There you are!" boomed Bonnie's voice.

To our amazement, Bonnie strolled up with two of her kids in tow.

"You got them to come!" Julie smiled.

"I didn't tell them where we were going," Bonnie said, and her kids frowned. "You can't play video games all the time!"

"Why not ...?" her youngest complained.

They joined us, and once her kids got ice creams, they calmed down. We sat while Bonnie dominated the conversation, covering her weekend of kid's sports, shopping, cleaning, cooking, church, and bowling.

"Bowling ...?" Emerson asked.

"Yea ... bowling," Bonnie said. "My eldest girl's on a team."

"I thought she did uneven parallel bars," Emerson said.

"She goes to state next week, and she's been in a bowling league for three years," Bonnie said.

"I haven't been bowling in months," Julie said.

"You're welcome to join us," Bonnie said. "Emerson, when were you last bowling?"

"Me ...?" Emerson asked. *"Bowling ...?"*

"You've never bowled ...?" Bonnie asked.

"I once went to an amusement park," Emerson said. "I won three hundred dollars in a pot to pay for it."

"A pot ...?" Bonnie asked.

"My foster parents liked to gamble," Emerson said.

"How old were you?" Julie asked.

"Twelve," Emerson said. "Six Flags was my birthday present to myself."

Bonnie, Julie, and I exchanged horrified looks.

"Twelve years old ... winning a three hundred dollar pot ...?" Julie asked.

"What ...?" Emerson asked, obviously missing the point. *"I didn't cheat ...!"*

"Bowling ... 7:00 o'clock tonight," Bonnie insisted.

"Definitely," I said, and I tried to smile at Emerson. "We'll make a small-towner out of you yet."

"You poor man ...!" Julie exclaimed.

Emerson looked confused.

Back home, Emerson took out his phone, then looked at me.

"I'd better do this alone," Emerson apologized. "She'll know if you're listening."

I nodded, and Emerson pushed 'dial' as he walked into my bedroom. I petted Mephistopheles, wondering what they were saying. I could almost hear him for the first five minutes, and then his voice raised and I could hear him clearly.

"You can't ...! Look, Penelope's special ... I won't mess up! Yes, I remember the girl in Atlantic City ... that was three years ago! She's not like that! No, I'm not choosing her side! Blame me ... I trained her ... and then went away for two weeks. David was my fault. No, no, I'm not saying that ...!"

I resisted the urge to rush in there and shout at Lucinda. She was Emerson's surrogate mother, and I'd already infuriated her once. I'd only make matters worse, so I stayed with Mephistopheles and tried to eavesdrop. Unfortunately, he lowered his voice, and I could only hear him pace back and forth with over-heavy stomps.

When Emerson came out, his face was flushed.

"That bad ...?" I asked.

"Worse," Emerson said.

"She refused ...?"

"She threatened ... not casual threats," Emerson said. "She's serious. Penelope, I'm ... frightened ... and guys don't say that lightly."

"What can we do ...?" I asked.

"We've no choice," Emerson said. "She won't do anything if you stop doing magic."

"That's not fair!" I shouted.

"I told her that a dozen times!" Emerson said. "She won't listen!"

"I'm not going to have Lucinda tell me how to

live!"

"I don't want you ending up like David!"

We stared at each other.

"She'll ... kill me ...?" I asked.

"She sees your timelines, plucks a bad feeling ... who knows what happens?" Emerson said. "That's what you did ... and ...!"

"I didn't know what I was doing ...!" I shouted.

"Lucinda does," Emerson said. "My fault; I was teaching you ... and then abandoned you ...!"

"What else could you do?" I demanded. "Did Lucinda forbid you to use magic ...?"

"I can't," Emerson insisted.

"I don't think I can, either," I said.

"So ... what do we do?" Emerson asked.

"Can we stop her?" I asked.

"A Magician's Challenge against Lucinda?" Emerson asked. "Even together, we'd lose."

"What if she doesn't know?" I asked.

"She knew that we went to the zoo ... and she knows we're going bowling tonight," Emerson said.

"How can she ...?" I asked.

"She's good," Emerson said. "She examines every thread ... usually they vanish before she's done."

"She told me to do that," I said. "That's how I found her ..."

"I'm not good at that," Emerson said. "I just try to flow with good vibes ... few things go wrong if you're doing good things. You learn to avoid bad people before you run into them."

"I can't live blindfolded," I said.

"For now, you must," Emerson said. "Lucinda ordered me to stop you."

"Can you ...?" I asked.

"Only in bad ways," Emerson said. "I don't want to, but if I don't, she will. Please, I'm trying to help."

"This isn't about magic," I said. "Lucinda is pitting us against each other ... to split us up."

"That may be true," Emerson said.

"So ... what are you going to do about it?"

"What do you suggest?"

"Don't get involved," I said. "This is between Lucinda and me."

"You can't beat her," Emerson said.

"That's never stopped me before," I warned.

We arrived at the bowling alley early. I took Emerson in and rented us shoes, then led him up and down the line, helping him select a ball. He'd never held one before, didn't understand the advantages or disadvantages of light balls versus heavy ones, and he tried many, feeling for the right grip.

"Should I ...?" Emerson asked.

"No," I said. "I will."

"No!" Emerson hissed. *"Lucinda ...!"*

"What harm is there in choosing a bowling ball?" I asked.

"That's not the point," Emerson said, and he grabbed a ball at random. "This is my ball."

"Did you ...?" I asked.

"No," Emerson said. "Who cares? I'm not trying to win ..."

Frowning, we walked up and down the lanes, watching the different styles. Emerson saw some masterful bowlers spin their balls, arcing them down the lane to crash into pins. I pointed out the slow, straight bowlers, who try to catch one of the front pockets. I explained how the pins crash into each other to knock the most down. Emerson thought the spinners bowled better, and I agreed that they did, but pointed out that, like magic, beginners start small.

Bonnie and Lyn showed up. Bonnie's daughter ran off to join her team.

"Julie's staying home with her kids," Lyn said. "Stacy's hosting David's parents; they're driving her crazy."

"She'll probably never see them again," Bonnie said. "They live in Chicago."

"Good thing Stacy never got pregnant," Lyn said.

"Are you ready to bowl?" Bonnie asked Emerson.

"I'll be lucky if I don't drop this on my foot," Emerson hefted his ball.

Bonnie and Lyn brought their own shoes and balls, so they rented a lane and I went and found a ball I liked. We gathered at the lane and Emerson offered to go last.

"Too late," Bonnie said. "I entered your name first; you're up."

I took Emerson's arm, led him through the motions, and showed him how to release the ball, pointing his thumb at the head pin. Then Bonnie argued that I was teaching him wrong, came up and took over ... as if I hadn't been bowling since I was seven.

Emerson bowled for the first time; rolled it straight into the 10 pin.

"Only nine left!" Bonnie laughed.

"Ignore her," Lyn said. "Most newbies toss it right into the gutter."

"It takes a few times," I assured him.

Emerson frowned and tried again. His roll grazed the front pin and knocked down six.

"Seven out of ten; not bad for your first time," I

said.

"The kid in the next lane laughed at me," Emerson said.

"Most kids start when they can barely lift a ball," I pointed out.

"This would be much easier with ... you know," Emerson whispered.

"If you do, I will!" I warned.

Emerson had a terrible game. Bonnie topped 100 by the eighth frame and Lyn and I did by the tenth. Emerson's total was 57.

"It takes practice," Lyn tried to comfort him.

"Four gutter balls ...?" Bonnie sniggered. "Not even a spare ...!"

"Bonnie can't sing," I said, defending Emerson. "Or do basic fractions. Or diagram sentences ...!"

"Penelope spent five years taking piano lessons and can't play Chopsticks," Bonnie snapped.

"Bonnie once dived in a public pool and lost her bottoms," I said.

"Penelope's middle name is Olive," Bonnie said. "She once got nicknamed ...!"

"Bonnie lost her virginity to ...!" I started, slowing my voice to a clear warning.

Bonnie glared, yet relented.

"Glad you girls don't know my past," Emerson said.

"We've been arguing like this all our lives," Julie said. "We're still friends."

"One more game," Lyn said. "You'll get better."

We played again ... and Emerson picked up two spares. We all topped our previous scores, and Emerson felt better.

"I've taught lots to bowl," Lyn started. "If you've

nothing to do while Penelope's in Seattle ...!"

"Emerson won't be around," I cut her off.

"You don't trust us ...!" Lyn complained.

"Joey Masterson ...?" I reminded her.

"We were fifteen ...!" Lyn argued.

"Ben Lawson ...?" Bonnie chimed in.

"He came on to me ...!" Lyn insisted.

"Yea ... an hour after he dropped off Stacy," Bonnie laughed.

"I'll be traveling while Penelope's away," Emerson said. "How about when she gets back ...?"

"You'll miss my daughter going for state!" Bonnie complained.

"I've never been to a gymnastics show ...," Emerson said.

"We'll talk about it," I promised him.

I drove Emerson home listening to him complain how the ball never rolled toward the pins he wanted it to hit. I smiled; eventually he'd be the one sniggering at new bowlers, but no point telling him that now.

Our relationship was maturing. We were moving beyond being new lovers and settling into a permanent, stable couple. Of course, I didn't mention this; Emerson had never experienced this stage of a relationship. I had to ease him into it without frightening him ... or over-encouraging him. I was prepared for a marriage proposal, but he wasn't. He probably thought all problems vanished once you got married; few marriages survive learning that isn't true.

"I have to go to work tomorrow," I said as I made a swift left turn. "We have work to do tonight."

"Work ...?" Emerson asked.

"Tonight has to last me five whole days," I said,

and I started unbuttoning my blouse with my right hand. He stared amazed.

"What are you doing ...?" Emerson asked.

I smiled; it was dark, no one could see, and I was wearing a bra.

"Keeping you from thinking about bowling," I said, and I loosed another button.

"Tease!" Emerson accused as he stared at me.

"Call it a preview," I grinned.

Chapter 56

Alarm clocks are hateful! I awoke, Emerson spooned against me, most of the sheets pushed down. I reached over and slapped the snooze, then collapsed back against him. Yet I couldn't call in sick; Rosanne had my reservations which I'd need first thing tomorrow.

I couldn't stay.

I showered and dressed in record time. Emerson was still asleep, but I bent over and kissed him long and deeply.

"Call me before you leave the house ... or if anyone comes over," I said.

Emerson moaned softly. I ran my fingers across his shoulder.

"Promise ...!" I ordered.

Emerson nodded and made a noise that might've been agreement. His eyes never opened. I kissed his cheek, repaired my lipstick, and locked the door behind me. I was only slightly worried that some local girl might come knocking ... *possibly Nancy or Gwen ...!*

Rosanne was late; I slipped into my office, dropped my things, then hurried to fetch coffee. Docking my laptop starting my screen, and I found two dozen emails from the weekend. I scanned them quickly, hoping none were addressed to me.

"Sorry!" Rosanne said as she appeared at my door, papers in her hand. She reached in and set them on my desk.

"Rough night ...?" I asked.

"I had to drive home, shower, and change ...!" Rosanne whispered, grinning ear to ear.

"Rosanne ...!" I exclaimed. *"Tell me ...!"*

"Can you keep it off the Bismarck Express?" Rosanne asked.

"I'm leaving tomorrow," I said. "Don't you have a boyfriend ...?"

"Not a serious one," Rosanne said. "His name's Cody."

"Cody Johnson ...?" I asked.

"No ... *eeww!"* Rosanne wrinkled her nose. "He's from Fargo, a county judge, here for business with the governor."

"Sounds important," I said.

"He wants to go into politics," Rosanne said. "His position was appointed; to go up, he needs to be elected."

"Is this how a Bismarck girl gets into the White House?" I asked.

"If he can win a few elections, he may try out for Mayor of Fargo," Rosanne said.

"It's a start," I said. "Good luck!"

"I'll tell you more at lunch!" Rosanne smiled and winked.

I grinned and went back to studying the long list of contacts I'd be seeing.

A meeting invite appeared on my screen, and Bessy phoned moments later.

"Penelope Polyglass."

"Pen, its Bessy. I just sent out a meeting invite, but I know you're busy today."

"Am I needed?" I asked.

"It's about cost estimates for Atlanta," Bessy said. "You can miss it if you want."

"I'm reviewing Seattle customers," I said.

"No problem," Bessy said. "Good luck, and have a safe trip!"

"Thanks!"

At lunch, Rosanne rambled on about her new potential boyfriend, from the bar where they'd met on Friday night to staying at her apartment on Saturday night and his motel room on Sunday night. She claimed that he was gorgeous, so I pulled out my phone and googled 'County judge Fargo Cody'. I didn't get a specific link, but I scanned a list of judges for Fargo.

"Um ..., Rosanne ...?" I asked. "Wouldn't a county judge have their own website?"

With a mouthful of club sandwich, Rosanne pulled out her phone and started searching. I hoped she'd find him ... or this was going to be a horrible lunch.

More than an hour later, I went back to the office and made excuses for Rosanne. I said she'd accidentally eaten something she was allergic to and had to visit her doctor. In truth, I'd dropped her off at her car, unable to stop crying, and let her drive home alone.

Her tears reminded me how lucky I was to find Emerson, who seemed to all appearances a potential life-partner. I closed my door and phoned him.

"Hello!" Emerson's voice sounded reassuring.

"How's it going?" I asked.

"Mephistopheles and I are practicing," Emerson

said.

"Stage magic?" I asked.

"Mephistopheles couldn't help me with the other kind," Emerson said.

"You're alone?" I asked.

"Quite," Emerson said. "It's been peaceful."

"When did you get up?"

"Almost two hours ago."

"Eaten ...?"

"English muffins," Emerson said. "Cooked to perfection; I may be the chief chef in the family."

"Family ...?" I asked.

Absolute silence ...!

"Family ... of mankind," Emerson lied.

I smiled.

"I may be able to slip out early," I said. "Bessy excused me from a meeting to prepare for tomorrow, and Rosanne just left."

"I'll be here," Emerson said.

"I'll be home as soon as I can," I said.

"Love you!"

"Love you."

I tried to focus on Seattle clients but my phone rang.

"Penelope Polyglass."

"I know your name," mom's voice said.

"Mom, why are you calling?"

"I heard that your boyfriend was back."

"Yes, he arrived a few days ago."

"And you're leaving tomorrow?"

"I'll be in Seattle for five days."

"A successful husband is more important than a job ...!"

"We've only been dating for two months!"

"Nearly three, and you're not getting any younger!"

"Mom, I'm at work."

"So, you're hiding your boyfriend ...?"

"No ..."

"Good. Then you can bring him to dinner tonight."

"Mom, it's our last night ..."

"See you at 7:00 ...!"

"Mom ...!"

She hung up.

I sighed.

Everyone was trying to control my life!

I gritted my teeth. Mom wanted me married off. Lucinda wanted me dead. Emerson wanted me leashed so I wouldn't do magic ...

I didn't need to be protected!

I closed my eyes. If Lucinda was gunning for me, I'd give her every reason she needed. Better to face an enemy than be hounded forever.

I would not be her obedient slave!

I expanded my senses. I felt for coincidences around me, exactly as I had with cards, pennies, and wine-drops on the mirror. I gave myself over to randomness, the unknown sensations that push us one way or the other. I thought about pure joy.

I opened my eyes.

Visible lines swirled around me, unrestrained by doors and walls. I could see them, like foggy, colored cords, tendons flexing reality. They writhed slowly, living possibilities, surrounding all of us, even animals, all thinking things ... carrying our secret motivations and fears.

Lucinda ...!

I felt her, coiling around me, yet I didn't care. My friend and coworker had been hurt; I wasn't after revenge, but I needed information.

I'd known Rosanne since my first day as a salesperson, sat beside her for two years, and relied upon her for every sales event I'd ever attended. I'd never gotten bumped from a flight or stayed in a fleabag hotel. Part of my promotion was thanks to her.

Rosanne ...!

I found her. I felt her.

She was thinking of him ... Cody!

Her regrets connected me to him, but his timelines were darkly glowing. He was smiling, his triumph complete. He was ultimately proud of himself.

I traced the timelines around him; he was driving ... eastbound. His timelines flowed tightly, in one direction.

He was headed home. He'd phoned someone ... a real judge ... he worked in the judge's office. He'd called to say that he wouldn't be at work today.

He'd missed a day's work to have sex with Rosanne.

He was a junior law clerk.

He'd never been appointed to anything.

I scanned his timelines one by one. All ended in Fargo.

He never intended to come back to Bismarck.

He'd lied to Rosanne, my friend ...! Used her ...! Abused ...!

I mustn't touch a thread. I was just here for information.

Not another David ...!

I let him go and drew back.

Lucinda ...! I felt her!

She knew what I'd done ... and what I hadn't.
Screw Lucinda!

I shook my head. The foggy, colorful strands
vanished like shadows in light. My door was closed. I
was in my office.

Now we'd see what Lucinda would do!

My drive home was frantic. I watched
everywhere, convinced that every car would suddenly
careen toward me. I avoided driving past semi-trucks,
then felt I was being silly. I'd be boarding two planes
tomorrow; a shuttle to Minneapolis and a 747 to Seattle.
If Lucinda wanted to kill me, she'd have her chance.

"Penelope!" Emerson greeted me as I came in. I
set down my things as he came up, showed me the backs
of both of his hands, one high, one low, slowly swung
both to join before my eyes, then suddenly he was
holding a glass of wine.

I took the glass and kissed him.

Some days boyfriends were good to have!

"What's our plan for tonight?" Emerson asked,
grinning wickedly. "Stay in ...?"

"I'd like to," I said. "I should tell you; my mom
wants us to have dinner with her."

"What do you want?" Emerson asked.

"To not have dinner with my mother," I said,
"but she knows you're here and feels left out ..."

"Your family; your choice," Emerson said.

"We can be there at 7:00 ... and hopefully out by
8:00," I said.

At 6:50, we arrived at mom's. She made small
steaks with cheese and shrimp topping, asparagus, and
spiced rice. She invited Emerson inside as an honored
guest, more than family. She was all smiles and
politeness. Her house was spotless.

"So nice of you to come back after your amazing magic show," mom said. "My friend Hilda found your special on her computer. We watched the whole thing."

"My Showtime special ...?" Emerson smiled. "I hope you liked it."

"It was wonderful!" mom effused. "We couldn't guess how you did those tricks."

"Guessing is half the fun," Emerson said. I smiled. This was Emerson in his element, superficial charm oozing out of every pore.

Dinner was delicious; mom's cooking the finest ... although a pale reflection of Lucinda's masterpieces. I felt practically ignored, mom trying to charm Emerson into our family, Emerson trying to charm mom into not asking him to marry me right there. By the time that she dished out ice cream, we'd discussed every unimportant topic in North Dakota.

We returned home smiling.

"What are your plans for tomorrow?" I asked.

"I found an online coupon for a rental car," Emerson said. "The dealer's inside the airport. If you could drop me there when you get on your plane ..."

"My plane leaves at noon, so we'll need to be at the airport by eleven," I said.

"Then I've only got tonight to satisfy your desires until you get back from Seattle," Emerson said.

"You'd best be magnificent," I grinned.

Chapter 57

I hate alarm clocks even when they're set to hours after I usually get up. I didn't want to go ... or abandon Emerson. Yet my plane was leaving soon.

I kissed Emerson, then drug the covers off him. He snarled and groaned. Playfully I pulled him out of bed. I went to start the coffee-maker. He fell back onto the sheets. I forced him up and into the bathroom. Together we showered, still half-asleep; no time to make washing memorable. Then I hurried to dress and dragged him into the kitchen; I didn't know when I'd have time to eat again.

"English muffin ...?" I asked.

We each had one, dripping melted butter and real strawberry jam, and revitalized with coffee. Yet we had no time to enjoy it.

"I'll miss you," I said. "Every minute."

"I'll spend every minute devising a perfect reunion," Emerson said.

I was going to be late; Emerson carried all of his boxes of clothes, I carried my suitcase and reservations, and we had to make a second trip for my computer and mobile display case. We raced to the airport, and

Emerson dropped me at the door with all my things, then went to park. He came back pushing a cart carrying his boxes, met me standing in the security line, and gave me my keys. We kissed good-bye, yet had no time for more; I was in a crowded line and security was watching. Emerson tipped his hat to me, waved, and then he pushed the cart with his boxes toward car rental.

I wondered if I'd live to see him again.

The shuttle to Minneapolis landed without incident, so I boarded the flight to SeaTac a little more calmly. I had a few minutes, so I bought a premade sandwich and ate in the line to board. Then I was in the air, wishing that I'd brought my Kindle, plugged in my ear buds, and watched an action packed movie about superheroes fighting monstrous villains.

Magic was portrayed so differently in Hollywood!

I wondered why Lucinda hadn't punished me ... or killed me.

Rain was falling on Seattle. A line of taxis stood waiting; an hour later, after horrible traffic, I arrived at my hotel, across the street from the Convention Center in downtown Seattle. In twenty minutes, I was unpacked, thirsty, and ready to relax.

The rain wasn't hard but constant. I'd left my coat in my room, so I eyed the hotel bar and walked past it, down a long hall over the street, into the Convention Center. It was busy but not crowded; the main rooms were all on the upper floors, yet they'd be empty today, only workers setting up curtained booths for the convention. The bottom floors had small shops and restaurants, nothing particularly exciting, so I returned to the hotel bar.

I treated myself to a red wine, rich and tart, which slowly calmed my nerves. I hadn't brought my laptop, so I pulled out my phone, opened a browser, and scanned my social media. I was trapped between two loud conversations; one side of the bar sat watching a pre-season football game, Seahawks against Raiders, as excited as if it had been the Superbowl. On the other side, an elderly couple seemed to be having an argument. Upon overhearing 'differing levels of armor and quests', I realized that they were players in Warcraft or some similar game. Both looked over seventy; I tried not to smile, glad that they'd found a mutual interest to keep them active.

"Is this seat taken?" asked a deep voice.

I looked to see a large black man in a crisp suit, touching the back of the barstool beside me.

"No, go ahead," I said.

He sat down and ordered a whiskey sour.

"Here for the convention?" he asked.

"Yes. You?"

"Automated sampling equipment," he said.

"Medical tracking software," I said.

"Are you from here?" he asked. "Seattle ...?"

"No, but this is my third year," I said.

"My second, but my company's been here since the first," he said. "I'm Justin."

"Penelope."

"May I ask ... are you here alone?" Justin asked.

"Alone, but not single," I said.

"Oh, my heart just failed," Justin said. "I saw no ring ..."

"Not yet ...," I said.

"Well, can I at least buy a drink for a friend?" Justin asked.

"Not tonight, but maybe tomorrow," I said. "I've got a lot going on right now."

"Nothing terrible, I hope," Justin said. "I'm in space 134."

"We're almost neighbors," I said. "My booth is 166."

"I'll look for you," Justin said.

"Please do," I said.

After brief conversations about the weather and popular movies, I thanked him for his company, finished my wine, and left. I stopped inside one of the chain restaurants in the Convention Center, got a teriyaki chicken burger and fries, and carried it up to my room. Justin had seemed nice, but I'd feel more comfortable around him tomorrow ... after I saw if he really was working a booth, not some stranger trying to pick up lonely girls.

Besides, I needed to practice magic. *I might need it soon.*

Lucinda had done nothing. I was free to do whatever I wanted; *I was my own queen again!*

Yet I would be more restrained, more careful, before I did anything. I was being controlled, but by myself, which Emerson should have taught me to do from the very beginning.

After eating, I washed my hands, then stood before the window, looking across the north end of Seattle, admiring the Space Needle. The sun was setting, city lights starting to glow. Gray clouds spat a misty rain, barely a drizzle; hard rains were rare here, but low clouds were almost a daily occurrence. Momentarily I wondered if I could cause it to rain harder, yet the image of Mickey Mouse as the Sorcerer's Apprentice made me chuckle. Real magic didn't work like that ... *probably for the best.*

The Sorcerer's Apprentice had attempted magic

he shouldn't ...!

I opened my senses. Thousands of coincidences were occurring right before me, unintended actions, subconscious promptings, and random occurrences. All I needed to do was look past the curtain most humans never peeked behind.

I fell silent, searching for the subtle. I ignored the sensations bombarding me, the soft hum of the air conditioner, the constant din of traffic from the nearby freeway, the plushness of the carpet beneath my feet. I opened myself to feelings seldom felt ... and wondered if I was really feeling external sensations or traipsing through my own subconscious, and projecting whatever I predicted, as Emerson's friends had suggested.

If I did stumble upon what coincidences really were, however miraculous it might be, it would just be a coincidence ... which meant it was unprovable!

The irony made me smile.

Seattle became a miasma of swirling lines, colors bright and dark, every shade surrounding everyone in the city. I stared down at them, master of all.

I could do anything!

My cell phone rang, startling me from my awareness. I flinched, and all the colored lines vanished, cloaking Seattle in a gray, misty drizzle.

Emerson ...!

"Darling!" I answered the phone. "I wasn't expecting ...!"

"Penelope, stop it!" Emerson ordered. "I just bought a plane ticket; I'll be there in the morning."

"What ...?" I asked.

"Lucinda's son called me," Emerson said. "She's in Denver, transferring to a Seattle flight."

"Lucinda ...?" I gasped. *"On a plane ...?"*

"She's coming after you," Emerson said.

"What ...?!?"

"I warned you!" Emerson said.

"You're flying out here ...?" I asked.

"I hope to get there before she does," Emerson said.

"Denver's closer!" I said.

"It depends on what time her flight leaves," Emerson said. "I'll be there shortly after 9:00 AM."

"My convention starts at 9:00," I said.

"Go to work," Emerson said. "Leave Lucinda to me."

"You said she's more powerful ...!" I said.

"I won't let her hurt you!" Emerson said.

"But ...!"

"Leave her to me!" Emerson said.

"You ...!"

"I have to go," Emerson said. "I can't miss my flight! See you tomorrow!"

Emerson hung up.

I stood there, holding my phone.

Lucinda was coming fast ... on her way ... to kill me!

Chapter 58

After a troubled sleep, I crawled out of bed when the alarm went off, yet I'd decided not to do the convention ... not today. Trapped in my booth, I'd be easy to find. It might be safer there, surrounded by vendors and clients, yet Lucinda would know where I was, when I got off, and be waiting for me. *I couldn't give her an easy target.*

I dressed and put on a jacket, then glanced out the window. The rain had stopped, which I was glad for; easier to travel without getting soaked. Lucinda would assume I'd be stationary; I had to keep moving. If I could make her chase me, then I'd know where she was, not the reverse.

I left all my gear, stuffing my wallet into my coat pocket and leaving even my purse behind. I needed speed, the one thing I had that Lucinda couldn't match. I was at least forty years younger than she was, and could walk faster ... run, if I had to.

I peeked through my door with the chain still linked, saw the hallway empty, then carefully locked the door behind me. I knew Emerson could still get in, as he had in Hawaii and Atlanta, yet I suspected his legerdemain skills more than real magic opened locks.

Lucinda didn't have those, so I ...!

My cell phone was still plugged in beside the alarm clock!

I hurried back to my room. I'd forgotten my cell phone ... an unlikely coincidence!

Lucinda again ...!

Locking my door again, I took the elevator down and dialed Emerson from the lobby. It went straight to voicemail; *he was on a plane.*

"Emerson, Lucinda's already started. Call me right away!"

I hung up and headed down the hall. I waved my vendor pass and walked into the convention, past vendors carrying boxes and wheeling handcarts. Everyone was setting up, and if Lucinda was watching, I wanted her to think I was here. Yet I walked down two aisles, found my assigned booth with a badly-scratched table and two folding chairs, and then headed for the express elevator.

I exited into the lobby, street-level, and walked to the north doors. I needed coffee, but didn't want it here ... I needed to be elsewhere as quickly as possible. Besides, Seattle was the home of Starbucks and boasted coffee on every corner.

I walked close beside the buildings, as far from the moving cars as I could, and looked in every direction before entering crosswalks, even at one-way streets. The thin crowd walking early morning sidewalks looked troublesome yet ordinary, most with bleary, sleepy eyes blindly following rat-trails to or from work. Within three blocks, I found a Starbucks and slipped inside for a hot grande.

Sipping to fulfill my caffeine addiction, almost

burning my tongue, I hurried back out. I didn't want to stay anywhere nor move in a predictable pattern. I also needed to avoid walking about randomly; Lucinda could control random occurrences. Letting instincts lead me would send me where she wanted; I had a better idea.

Pike's Place Market wasn't far, only about five more blocks. I'd have preferred the Seattle Center, which was much more open and would let me see anything coming, yet Pike's Place Market was twisted and confusing to those not used to it. I loved it. Every time I'd come to Seattle, I'd gone there for drinks and touristy shopping.

Streets were too open; Lucinda could ride by in a cab without me seeing her. I hurried, almost skipping in my rush.

The big red sign 'Public Market' appeared above its many shops, and I hurried under it. It wasn't open; trucks were unloading, vendors carrying wares, everyone busy, preparing for the day. I slid into a wide opening, turned left, and headed into an interior section of mostly enclosed shops. On the next level down stood an espresso cart, opened early to serve the vendors, and numerous chairs sat before the few round tables. I chose a small table and set my back against a wall; if Lucinda found me, she'd be clearly visible, and I'd have exits in three directions.

I tried to relax. Emerson would be off his plane soon, but any cab from SeaTac to downtown would take over an hour during commutes; I'd be lucky if he arrived within two hours. Lucinda was probably already here ... and she could be anywhere.

A young security guard paused and looked at me. "We're not open yet," the guard said.

"I'm with the belt merchant," I lied.

He stared at me, glanced at my clothes, then nodded and walked on.

I was glad that he hadn't asked me the name of the merchant. One big attraction of Pike's Place Market were the merchants; small business vendors that rented spaces, like a year-round street fair. They sold t-shirts, carvings, paintings, nuts, flowers, vegetables, and seafood; anything sailors could catch, farmers grow, or artisans make, they sold to pay their daily fee. By noon, Pike's Place Market would be packed, and crowds made hiding easy.

I stayed there as long as I dared, until Pike's Place Market officially opened and my coffee cup was empty. I bought another coffee from the espresso cart, and then moved on.

I headed down a long ramp with stores on both sides, yet realized I'd soon arrive at the south exit; I reversed my course. I reached the main section of market, at street level. Most of the vendors were still setting up, straightening their displays. Several vendors shouted; they'd be doing that all day, especially by the fish market. Shouts were a staple of Pike's Place Market's famous ambiance.

The market covered several blocks, with twists, turns, and alleys between buildings. A single cobblestone road divided most of it, which made me grin; cars had to drive extremely slowly here, and cops were everywhere. The odds of getting hurt by accident were small; thousands of visitors came here every day, and the Market couldn't afford lawsuits.

I headed downstairs. Underground, Pike's Place Market was a labyrinth of shops, stairs, ramps, and exits ... with few dead ends. I hurried through, glancing about; I always got turned around down here, yet I couldn't afford to now. I hoped to familiarize myself with its halls before Lucinda appeared. Then I consciously reversed my course, past the wide wooden stairway going down, found different steps leading up, and found myself back on street level. After peering carefully at the cars inching past, I crossed the street and entered the other side.

This east side was more uniform, less easy to get turned around in, yet I wanted to be sure I knew every route. I went north and found the alley between buildings, which ran at least two blocks, mostly restaurants on each side. I turned back and found more vegetable merchants, the bookstore, and a baker selling hot buns; I bought one for breakfast. Then I crossed back; better to be on the western side of the main street, where I could get lost quickly.

I scanned the cars and saw nothing suspicious; no obvious taxis or Uber drivers. Taking advantage, I strolled through the merchants, eyeing their stylish gifts and novelties. I loved shopping here, when not being hunted by angry magicians; I wasn't sure who'd be madder at me, Lucinda or Emerson.

Early shoppers were few and walking by quickly; by noon this aisle would be too packed to run through.

I reached the north end and turned back. I couldn't walk out into the open. I glanced nervously about, then walked south, glancing at my watch. Emerson would call as soon as he landed, yet I felt impatient. Walking around aimlessly, not knowing where Lucinda hid, was maddening. I didn't dare search for her magically; she probably already knew where I was.

Downstairs was a magic store; Emerson probably knew all their tricks and illusions. They might even recognize him. I walked past it, only glancing inside. I didn't want to enter a shop; most stores only had one exit, and if Lucinda appeared in their doorway, I'd be trapped. I kept going, ended up by the comic book store, and turned toward the head shop.

My phone beeped.

"Here," I said.

"Where ...?" Emerson asked.

"Pike's Place Market," I said.

"Have you seen Lucinda?"

"No."

"She's here somewhere. Her plane landed an hour and a half ago."

"I suspected as much."

Pause ...

"The driver says he knows exactly where you are," Emerson said.

"Let's hope Lucinda doesn't."

"I'm on the way."

"Call when you're close."

A deep exhale of relief; *Emerson was in Seattle! All I had to do was stay alive until he got here.*

I went outside, found a concrete platform overlooking the Puget Sound, with a door on the other end, and wide stairs going up and down. I looked out across the bright water; if I could've managed a boat, I'd be safe from Lucinda ... unless the boat unexpectedly sank.

I ascended steps, peeking around each corner, and reached the street level. Foot traffic was growing; more tourists and shoppers were arriving. As Seattle rains so much, good weather is prized, and regulars flood here in droves. Music was playing; two street performers, a guitar and a violin, jammed for donations.

Lucinda ...!!!

Getting out of a cab ...!!!

I ducked down, where she couldn't see, and took a step back, keeping an eye on her. She walked along the street, beside an outdoor flower merchant working under a tent. Lucinda was craning her neck to peer through the jostling crowd.

I hurried back downstairs. She may be more powerful, yet I could run faster.

No one could outrun coincidences!

I had to stay out of her line of sight ... at least until Emerson arrived.

I bumped into two people, apologized, then kept going. I hurried inside, past the head shop, the magic shop, and across the hall. A long ramp led back to street level, north of where she was. Nearing the top, I slowed and peered over the edge, not rising into view. Yet too many shoppers; I couldn't see Lucinda.

I ducked back down. I couldn't go back or forward. I'd no idea where she was. I could use magic, but she probably already was. She'd know my position if we met on a fate-path.

I had to risk being seen; I ducked low, pushed out into the crowd, and hurriedly walked north, past the vendors. I kept glancing from side to side, yet couldn't look behind. I hoped the crowd would hide me.

If I couldn't slip quickly through this crowd, Lucinda had even less of a chance.

Pushing out onto the sidewalk, past tie-dyed t-shirts and strange street art, I reached the end of the Market. A van was at the stop sign; I hurried through the crosswalk to the eastern side. There I rushed to hide behind the building's edge, peeking around the corner. Cars were stopped, one waiting for a truck to pull out of one of the few parking spots, yet the crowd was moving too fast, too thickly, to see anyone clearly.

I checked my watch; Emerson couldn't have arrived yet. I decided to walk around the block, up the hill to 1st Avenue, and soon passed old style shops. I circled back to Pike Street, the intersection over which the main Market sign displayed. Checking behind me, I peeked around the corner, yet there were too many places where Lucinda could be hiding.

I could cross the street again, but the whole intersection was stopped, Seattleites and visitors walking in all directions, not thickly enough to hide me. I waited until a pair of tall, laughing teenagers ambled past, and I snuck behind, hidden by them. Just past the bookstore was a door down into an inside hallway that ran the length of most of the building; I ducked inside and hurried along it. One hallway turned to the left, past vegetable merchants, and led back to the main cobblestone street, restaurants on both sides.

I stopped at a dirty glass door and peered out at the street as best I could. I liked this spot; I could see a large part of the market clearly, yet couldn't be easily seen. I watched the busy shoppers, surprised to see such a crowd so early on a Wednesday, but Pike's Place Market was like Pioneer Square; one of the original cultural centers of Seattle.

Something awaited behind me ...! I glanced back; couldn't see anything threatening, but I felt an evil presence. I pushed outside onto the sidewalk, certain that she'd found me.

"*Penelope ...!*" Lucinda shouted.

I turned; Lucinda was only ten paces away, standing before the original Starbucks, staring at me.

She'd tricked me ... forced me to reveal myself!

I turned and ran, full out, not caring what visitors thought. I jumped between clumps of bodies, dashed out onto the cobblestones, and turned the corner to cut off her view of me.

Where was Emerson ...?
I didn't dare face her alone!

Uphill I ran, diagonally across the street, into the alley. Signs at its entrance listed the stores and restaurants only accessible through it; I slid past a couple trying to emerge and raced uphill.

Crash!!!

I fell sideways against a wall, splattered by flying dirt, shocked by the loud noise and scream that followed. In the center of the alley lay a huge, broken potted plant, fallen off a balcony above. Every onlooker in the alley stared shocked; its shattered remains had missed me by inches.

It must've weighed thirty pounds ...!
If it had landed upon me ...!

I stared in horror, then turned and fled.

Lucinda was trying to kill me ...!!!

At the end of the alley, I glanced back; no sign of Lucinda. Few women her age ran, but could running save me?

I had to keep as far from her as I could. I didn't know most of the city, so I turned downhill and sprinted back to the main street. I paused to peek around the corner; Lucinda was there, somewhere watching me, yet I had no choice. I ran across the street, pushed through the crowd eyeing the vendor's wares, then hurried down the ramp. Wasting no time, I turned and descended the wide wooden central stair, going even lower.

I stared about, lost. Was I on the lowest level? I couldn't recall, so I rushed in a random direction. This floor was darker and less crowded, yet I soon found myself facing only an elevator. I stared at it; I couldn't afford to risk being trapped in a suspended box that could accidentally plummet. I couldn't risk that any coincidence, however unlikely, was past Lucinda's power.

I rushed in the opposite direction, which branched off into two narrow halls. I took the left fork, rushed past some exotic shops, and pushed outside onto a familiar landing. One side had a concrete stair leading up; I suspected that it led to the street level. The other side led to a skywalk over the main road past the waterside, where docks stretched out over the Puget Sound, upon which ferries sailed.

I stood uncertain, trying to choose my best escape.

Beep!

I jumped, then yanked out my phone.

"Emerson!" I almost screamed.

"Where are you?" Emerson asked.

"Lost ... this place is crazy twisted ...!"

"I'm here, just under the big red sign ...," Emerson said.

"Get out of sight!" I shouted. *"Lucinda ... she tried to drop a planter on me!"*

"She ... didn't ...!" Emerson gasped.

"It fell from the floor above ...!" I said. *"It could've killed me ...!"*

"Magician's Challenge ...!" Emerson said. "I can't believe it ...!"

"Turn south, past the fish-sellers," I said. "Stay out of sight! Head for the dried fruits ... I'll be right there!"

I sprinted up two flights of steps to the main

level, jumping past everyone on the stair. I pushed into the crowd, ducking rather than spying for Lucinda. I wanted to run, but knocking others aside would certainly attract Lucinda's attention. I squeezed past the street musicians, hurried past the fish vendors, and ...!

"Emerson ...!" I shouted, and I threw myself against him.

"Where is she?" Emerson asked.

"No idea," I said. "I dared not use magic to find her ..."

"No, we can't do that," Emerson said. "I've never been here ..."

"It's like a maze ... few right angles," I said. "I thought I could hide here ..."

"Let's go," Emerson said, and we headed back toward the cart where I'd bought my morning espresso. A ramp led upwards to several stores, yet we descended to the left, circling to the lower level.

"This hall slopes to the south end," I said.

"Can we exit there?" Emerson asked.

"Yes."

Emerson pulled me along.

We ran downhill past shops on both sides, saw the exit, and headed toward it. Moments later, we were outside.

"Uh, oh ...!" Emerson said.

I glanced around. We'd emerged at a dead end street overlooking the drop to the waterfront. Around us were old buildings, lines of moving cars, and street people walking in every direction. I leaned against Emerson; we didn't have lots of vagrants in Bismarck. These people looked poor, dirty, and desperate.

As if summoned by a unified call, all the street people suddenly froze at the same moment. Their heads turned and eyes focused on us.

In ragged, rumpled clothing, one holding a flask, another pushing a packed shopping cart, they stared. As one, they stepped toward us, converging from all sides.

"Lucinda ...!" Emerson whispered. *"We can't go this way!"*

We ran back inside, up the sloping hall, veered into an ice cream shop, and found an exit out onto 1st Avenue. We dashed north, away from the street people under Lucinda's control.

"We need to get far away!" Emerson insisted.

"Cross the street!" I shouted. *"Seattle's huge ...!"*

We started to cross in the middle of the block ... and suddenly a car swerved at us. I grabbed Emerson and yanked him back; the car crashed into a steel trashcan, and screeched back onto the road as the fallen can spilled garbage across the sidewalk. Not stopping, the car raced down the street.

"She's trying to kill both of us ...?" Emerson sounded shocked.

"We need to get inside!" I shouted.

"Where ...?"

I led us north, back to the main entrance, away from the street people. Lucinda knew where we were, yet I was determined. We reached the crosswalk, but the lights were against us.

"Wait for it!" I said, and I stared at the cars, wary of one going wild, slamming into us.

A car pulled out in front of a truck ...

Sccrrreeeeeech ... Wham!

Emerson pulled me back, away from the accident.

"She's keeping us here," Emerson said. "Blocking us in."

"One chance!" I said, and I pulled Emerson through a door.

We rushed through an art gallery selling ornate woodwork, finely made, pleasingly polished. We fled out its back door, into the south hallway, not far from the espresso cart. Lucinda must've headed toward the street, but in the crowded market, unable to run, she'd be trapped there. We circled the room with the tables, past the espresso cart, up to the next level, and dashed back into the Market proper.

At a run, we reached the corner where I'd met Emerson, turned right, and ...

Splat ...!

A three pound bull trout smacked me in the face.

The crowd screamed.

"I'm so sorry!" a young man with freckles looked horrified. "It was a bad toss ... too high ...! Are you all right?"

Emerson pulled me up as everyone stared. We ignored them, pushed past, and continued running. My face felt slimed from the wet, thrown fish; I should've expected it. Seattle was famous for its 'flying fish', where its workers threw real fish back and forth for the amusement of the crowd. During every other visit, I'd stopped to watch Chinook, Coho, Lingcod, Dogfish, Flounder, and Sole be hurled back and forth ... only to be purchased by amused spectators.

The fish had slowed us down. Lucinda was close behind us!

I led the way past the concrete stair and turned left, down a circle of belt, wallet, and sewn art vendors. At the far end was another exit; we could cross over the back street to the grassy park, west of Pike's Place

Market.

We stepped outside to find a group of kids throwing crushed potato chips to a bunch of birds, a dozen pigeons and some large seagulls, all fighting to eat as much as they could.

"Hey, you ...!" shouted a police officer, looking at us.

We froze as three police officers suddenly turned to us, hands on their guns. They ran forward; *we couldn't fight them!*

Emerson waved a hand. Suddenly the pigeons and seagulls abandoned their food, flying at the officers. Beak-pecks and flapping wings attacked the cops, and Emerson yanked to pull me away. We ran inside, back into Pike's Place Market, and slipped through the crowd as fast as we could.

"Emerson ...!" Lucinda shouted.

We glanced back to see her on the other side, two rows of vendors between us. Emerson kept running, and I followed.

We slid between two flower merchants and out a narrow door onto the cobblestone street. These cars were moving too slowly to be a threat; we dashed between them.

I pulled Emerson into the vegetable section of the building across the street.

"Where are we going?" I demanded. "We can't escape her!"

"We've got to get away ...!"

"You can't outrun coincidences!"

"What do you want ...?" Emerson shouted. "We can't fight Lucinda ...!"

"We've no choice!" I said. "It's us or her ...!"

"She's more powerful ...!" Emerson said.

"Then fight without magic ...!" I said.

"Hit ... punch my mother ...?" Emerson asked.

"Unless you know a better way ...," I said.

Emerson stopped and stared at me.

"No choice," I said.

We looked back. Lucinda appeared, coming out the thin doorway onto the cobblestone street, looking around for us.

Emerson looked back at her, his jaw set, seeing things I didn't.

I reached out with him. Pike's Place Market burst with colored, translucent lines, glowing in ethereal intensity. Fate-paths swirled around everyone, heart-strings waiting to be plucked. Emerson held out his hands as Lucinda stepped across the cobblestones.

Suddenly people cheered. Everyone jumped to Lucinda, stopping her to shake hands, and introduce themselves. Lucinda looked shocked. A crowd encircled her, blocking her from every direction, tourists and natives alike congratulating her.

"Let's go," Emerson said. "Which way ...?"

"This way," I said, pulling him to the right. "What did you do ...?"

"Amazing coincidence," Emerson said as we ran. "The entire crowd mistook her for Michelle Obama's mother."

We ran outside, past the bookshop, headed for 1st Avenue. The crosswalk said 'Don't Walk' yet we ran across it, reached the far side, and continued to run.

"No ...!" Lucinda cried from a distance behind us.

"She got away ...!" I shouted.

"Wait for it ...!" Emerson said.

Siren wails erupted. Behind us, a cop car flew

past, lights flashing, followed by more lights; several fire trucks roared past, blocking our sight of Pike's Place Market, all but the big red sign. More blaring cop cars followed them, racing along, blocking all foot passage behind us.

We dashed to 2nd Avenue, turned right, and ran out of sight of the Market. Passersby stared as we ran ... and then we stopped. Before us stood a young woman walking six dogs on leashes ... three of the dogs uncomfortably large ... and all started to growl.

All six dogs pulled free from the young girl's grip. We reversed our course and bolted, racing only a few paces before loud barks reached us. I screamed; *we couldn't outrace large dogs!*

"Into traffic ...!" Emerson shouted. *"Only hope ...!"*

Cars screeched as we jumped into traffic, running along the side of the street. The barking dogs ran closer, nipping at our heels. We reached the intersection, glancing behind.

"Look out ...!" I shouted, skidding to a halt.

Emerson looked up just in time to see a huge city bus barrel at him ... unable to stop in time. Tires screeched.

"Emerson ...!" I screamed.

The bus plowed into him, hurling him through the air, to land across the trunk of another car.

Two big dogs slammed into me from behind. I fell, toppled under their weight. Yet they didn't bite.

"Emerson ...!" I shouted, ignoring the dogs.

I crawled on hands and knees. The dogs stood beside me, panting, apparently free of Lucinda's control.

Emerson's twisted, fallen form lay on the asphalt behind the dented car. He wasn't moving. Sobbing, I fell upon him, wanting to hold him, afraid of hurting him worse ...

Blood pooled beneath him.

"911 ...!" someone shouted.

"Don't touch him!" a man's voice reached me. *"Is he conscious ...?"*

I stared ... unsure if Emerson was alive or not.

My Emerson ...!

A crowd gathered. A horrified bus driver was frantically apologizing. Sirens came closer.

I couldn't stop staring at Emerson, unconscious before me, perhaps dying. No coincidence could make him better ...!

Or could it ...?

I reached out, expanded my senses, and looked. Colorful lines appeared, swirling around Emerson ... and through him. Each fate-path was dark, none long. I ignored the shortest, reaching inwards with my mind, plucking the brightest, the longest. I didn't care what they did. I didn't have time to examine them. Whatever kept Emerson alive the longest, I plucked it.

Voices spoke. Hands touched me. I ignored them, seeing only Emerson. I'd no idea, nor cared, what they wanted. I had to focus, to keep his heart beating, his lungs breathing. I seized and gripped those timelines!

I had to keep Emerson alive!

Chapter 59

The ambulance ride was a nightmare. Emerson was rushed through the Emergency doors, and I was directed to the desk. I gave his name, yet knew nothing about his insurance ... assuming that he had any.

I was ordered to sit down and wait.

"That will do, Penelope," spoke a voice inside my mind.

I jerked my head around.

Lucinda ...!

Lucinda stood before me, more threatening than ever.

"It's not over," Lucinda said. "He's still alive ... in surgery. His fate-paths are bright and strong. He'll make it."

I screamed and jumped at her, one hand grabbing her aged throat. Shouts came from all around; hands grabbed me, a doctor and two interns.

"Leave her be!" Lucinda ordered, and the hands released me. "She's in shock. I startled her. Please, give us a moment."

As if in a fog, the doctor and interns turned and walked away, not saying a word.

I stared at her. Tears leaked down her cheeks.

"You saved him," Lucinda said. "I've never seen anyone do that. You were incredible."

"You ...!" I started.

"I never meant to hurt him ... or you," Lucinda said.

"You tried to kill us ...!" I seethed.

"If I'd wanted you dead, that planter would've landed on your head," Lucinda said. "This was never about you. This was always about him."

"About Emerson ...?" I asked.

"I'm older than you think," Lucinda said. "Older than Emerson suspects. I'm not much longer for this world. But one of us ... a trained magician ... has to take my place, fulfill my role ... as protector of our kind ... and, more important, protect mankind from the devastating horrors that knowledge of our powers would grant evil people."

"This ... was a test ...?" I asked.

"Emerson ... he's grown so much from his past," Lucinda said. "He knew what it felt like to be hurt ... and how to harm the innocent. Once he grew up, once he saw that he was doing the hurting, he changed his life. He became my best hope."

"You want Emerson ... to replace you?" I asked.

"I'd hoped that he would," Lucinda said. "I needed to test him, to see how he'd fare in a real Magician's Challenge. Yet he loved me ... he'd never fight against me ... except for someone else ... someone he truly loved."

"Me ...?" I asked.

"Who else could make a man turn against his own mother, even an adopted one?" Lucinda asked.

"You hit him with a bus ...!" I snarled.

528

"The dogs were supposed to chase you back to me," Lucinda said. "He ran out into traffic, too unexpectedly, to avoid me, not the dogs. He changed his fate-path expertly, too suddenly, too unpredictably for me to stop ..."

"You didn't hurt him ... on purpose ...?" I asked.

"I'd never hurt my son," Lucinda said. "He's as dear to me as my own flesh and blood. My other son calls him his magic brother ... he only knows about his stage magic, of course."

"He'll be ...?" I asked.

"He'll be fine," Lucinda said. "He was out of danger the minute that he arrived; Seattle's trauma teams have no equal. He'll be here, in the hospital, for a few days ... then he'll walk out of here ... with both of us."

"Can you see his future?" I asked.

"I haven't taken my eyes off his fate-paths since I felt the bus hit him," Lucinda said.

"You risked his life ... so that he could beat your test ...?" I asked.

"Take this as a lesson, my daughter," Lucinda said. "Even the greatest of us aren't gods. We can't see every outcome, and can't control every happening. Yes, I arranged all this to test him. Unfortunately, Emerson failed."

"What ...?" I demanded.

"I'm not a queen, I'm a caretaker," Lucinda said. "The best of our kind always are. Yet Emerson, for all his gifts, couldn't confront me. A caretaker must be powerful, yet they must at times be ruthless ... their job is to protect mankind ... at all costs. In the end, Emerson couldn't fight me; he couldn't do what he needed to."

"After all this, you're dumping him ...?" I asked.

"Dump my son ...?" Lucinda looked shocked.

"With my dying breath, I'll still profess my love ... for him and all my real and adopted children. Yet, he's too gentle. He's not the caretaker our next generation needs."

Lucinda looked deeply and knowingly into my eyes.

"*N-n-n-no ...!*" I stammered.

"An elderly magician once tried to test her intended replacement," Lucinda smiled. "She used the girl he loved to test him, yet she forgot that all those you include in any test ... arc also tested. Her expected replacement failed the test, but the woman that he loved; she proved herself a true magician."

"*I ... can't ...!*" I whispered.

"You must," Lucinda said. "You have ... power equal to his ... and far more maturity ..."

"I'm not ruthless ...!" I said.

"Not unless you need to be," Lucinda said.

"I-I'm not ready ...," I said.

"I'm not dying tomorrow," Lucinda said. "We've got a lot to discuss ... many stories to be learned. I hope that you'll let me visit again; I'll stay in a hotel ... and not be such a bitch ..."

"Did ... did you arrange ... us ...?" I asked. "Did Emerson choose me ... because of you ...?"

"Certainly not," Lucinda said. "He truly found you ... all by himself. Now, all of your fate-paths are intertwined."

"*Fated ...?*" I asked.

"Fated ... for the next few days," Lucinda said. "No magician has ever sensed a fate-path that lasted beyond five days; that's as far as we can see. All relationships take work; being his first girlfriend, yours will be trying at times. He needs a strong woman."

"I can't lose him," I said.

"We can't lose him," Lucinda assured me. "He owes you his life; your magic, manipulating his healing, was astounding. I've never seen its equal. Personally, I can't wait to dance at your wedding."

I couldn't help it; my arms rose. We hugged.

I had two mothers!

My family had just gotten bigger!

I looked at Lucinda's smiling, aged face disbelieving; *she wanted me to replace her!* She could teach me magic ... more magic than I had ever dreamed of ... far better than Emerson had. Yet, I clearly saw, without magic, that if she had her way, Emerson and I would soon be married, even if I had to force it ... *and I couldn't wait!*

My lessons in magic had only begun!

THE END

All Books by Jay Palmer

The VIKINGS! Trilogy:
DeathQuest
The Mourning Trail
Quest for Valhalla

The EGYPTIANS! Trilogy:
SoulQuest
Song of the Sphinx
Quest for Osiris

Souls of Steam
Jeremy Wrecker, Pirate of Land and Sea
The Grotesquerie Games
The Grotesquerie Gambit
The Magic of Play
The Heart of Play
The Seneschal
Viking Son
Viking Daughter
Dracula – Deathless Desire
Murder at Marleigh Manor
Never Date a Magician

ABOUT THE AUTHOR

Born in Tripler Army Medical Center, Honolulu, Hawaii, Jay Palmer works as a technical writer in the software industry in Seattle, Washington. Jay enjoys parties, reading everything in sight, woodworking, obscure board games, and riding his Kawasaki Vulcan. Jay is a knight in the SCA, frequently attends writer conferences, SciFi Conventions, and he and Karen are both avid ballroom dancers. But most of all, Jay enjoys writing.

JayPalmerBooks.com

Made in the USA
Monee, IL
04 December 2024

70750462R00295